The kiss had not even begun and already it was the most erotic moment Alexander could remember . . .

Anna moved that quarter inch closer that brought their lips together.

But then she was gone. She did not move far, just enough to separate them. "This is a woman's power." She spoke quietly. "A woman can tease and enchant. But it is an illusory power. Men are all too ready to grab and then a woman is left with nothing, her power gone."

"I can assure you," he said, "that no woman of my acquaintance has ever complained of being left with nothing."

She tossed back her head and loosed a full laugh. "If circumstances were different I might take you to my bed. Yes, I think we might have suited very well. But it cannot happen now."

"You, my lady, are a tease."

"I am not a lady, but, yes, I am definitely a tease. Well-known for it, in fact. Rumor has it, though, I am well worth it if caught."

He stepped toward her. "And I have caught you."

Romances by **Lavinia Kent**

TAKEN BY DESIRE
BOUND BY TEMPTATION
A TALENT FOR SIN

Taken by Desire

LAVINIA KENT

AVON
An Imprint of HarperCollins*Publishers*

This is a work of fiction. Names, characters, places, and incidents are products of the author's imagination or are used fictitiously and are not to be construed as real. Any resemblance to actual events, locales, organizations, or persons, living or dead, is entirely coincidental.

AVON BOOKS
An Imprint of HarperCollins*Publishers*
10 East 53rd Street
New York, New York 10022-5299

ISBN 978-0-06-198604-8
www.avonromance.com

First Avon Books paperback printing: December 2010

Printed in the U.S.A.

10 9 8 7 6 5 4 3 2 1

For my parents, Charles and Evelyn.
You gave me the love of reading (and so much more)
that led to it all. And especially to my mother,
who gave me so many pieces of this story.

Taken by Desire

Chapter 1

It couldn't be him. *By all the gods in the Pantheon, please don't let it be him.* Glancing once more down the darkened hall, Anna Steele swore softly to herself, the sound of the words making it no further than her lips.

All she had wanted was to sneak down and slip her note into the letters waiting to be posted. She needed to let Mr. Jackal know she'd send more funds as soon as she returned to London. She'd even chosen a book from the library on her way back to her room to give an explanation for her actions if she was caught roaming the halls in her nightclothes.

All she wanted was a peaceful night.

And now this.

Impulse was not something she gave in to. A great deal of thought went into any deed she performed. Listing the times she had considered carefully before taking action would have required a full day, if not longer.

And now this.

The blasted man hadn't been on the guest list for Lady Smythe-Burke's house party. After all the occasions on which she had avoided him, it seemed preposterous that she should be forced into this situation.

She could not proceed past him without being seen,

and if she tried to retreat he would surely hear her.

She didn't need this now. She had enough to worry about without—

Damnation.

She was not mistaken about who stood there or whose room he stood before, his hand on the door.

Alexander Struthers.

She couldn't see the piercing blue eyes that had always seemed to demand her deepest secrets, but there could be no mistaking that angular, powerful frame. It would have been bad enough if he were arriving, but she'd heard the distinctive click of her half sister Maddie's door easing shut.

She closed her eyes, tried to think—never an easy thing to do when Struthers was near. If she stayed quiet maybe he wouldn't see her. Even if he did, she could smile sweetly and pretend that she had not seen him slip out of Maddie's room. Struthers was always as eager to avoid her as she was him.

Then she heard it.

The sharp tap of boots sounding down the hall behind her.

Lord Milson. Maddie's pompous husband. No one else strode with such military precision.

Struthers's head snapped up as the sound reached him. The dim lighting made it hard to see him clearly, but she could imagine his look of bliss and satisfaction dying quickly. His posture tensed and his face turned toward her, the gesture of a wolf scenting for prey.

He saw her then. She could be no more than a dim shadow to him, but he stiffened in recognition. Then his head tilted further as he realized the footsteps were not hers.

There were only two rooms this far down the hall,

hers and the one Struthers had just left.

She saw the movement of his lips and knew he had sworn with even more eloquence than she.

Lord Milson was a jealous man—and a crack shot. More than one opponent had met him at dawn and not returned.

His footsteps drew closer. They would turn the corner any second and then there would be no choice.

This was the moment. She had to do something.

She didn't even consider before she slipped her robe open and shoved her chemise as low as it would easily go. Seduction—that at least she understood.

The sound of a boot tip grinding in rotation as it turned the corner caused her to launch herself forward, pressing herself into Struthers's firmly muscled chest. He took a step back as her weight hit him fully, pressing him into the door he had just exited. His hands came up, cupping her behind, as he fought to keep them both from falling or crashing through the door.

He was so warm, so hard.

She hadn't recognized how much she missed being touched.

Even before the thought was fully realized Anna rained kisses down upon his throat, frantically trying to remove any mark of the woman who had been there before her. It was not so easy to erase the smell of the distinctive, overly sweet floral perfume and the heady musk of sex. She could only hope nobody else drew this close to him.

The footsteps came to a stop. She waited for a cough or some noise from behind to demonstrate that Lord Milson intended to stop matters.

No sound came.

She slowed her kisses, concentrating on the small

hollow of his throat. Small, delicate kisses. Long, slow kisses. She let her tongue dart out to taste him. Let herself imagine for the briefest of seconds that this was real, that this was where she wanted to be, where she was meant to be. It was far easier than it should have been; her whole body ached with the desire to be closer.

He shivered at the touch of her tongue, but made no other move.

Couldn't the man help at all? Did she have to do everything?

A long, deep sigh escaped her lips as she licked again at the damp flesh of his throat. He tasted of salt and man. She rubbed her cheek against his chest, relishing in the abrasion of hair against skin. She nipped gently. No response.

She shifted, pressing her breasts firmly against him and causing her chemise to slip yet lower—the slightest shrug of her shoulder and her robe slipped down to catch at her hips where Struthers's hands still held her. A deep moan and another nip.

Still no movement or sound from either man—neither Lord Milson, behind, nor Struthers, who seemed to be made of stone.

There was only one thing a smart woman could do—she reached beneath Struthers's robe, slipped her fingers into his breeches, and grabbed him. Oh, she wanted to do it hard and with a little twist, but she restrained herself, a soft wrapping of the fingers, the gentle pull and push. Oh, Struthers was moving now—and far more than she would have expected given his recent bout of activity.

Finally one of his hands slipped up and about her, his thumbs trailing over her nipples. She glanced up and met his gaze. His eyes caught the light and flashed once. It was her turn to shiver. There was no comfort or connection to be found in his glance. His lips tightened. His face was full of some emotion—but what?

Then both his hands moved. He tightened his fingers, almost painfully, into her buttocks and lifted her—his head coming down to catch a taut nipple between his lips, his teeth—his tongue circling, wetting the thin linen of her shift. God, the man knew what he was doing. Her whole body arched, her head falling back, half in unwanted pleasure, half in an attempt to see the man behind—to gauge the response to the show.

Her hair was in her eyes. All she could see were her own dark curls. She tossed her head to the side, trying to get a view. Struthers's hand shifted to restrain her, pulling her tight against his arousal. Small shivers formed deep in her belly, lighting flames that raced through her. No, this was her game. She moved her hand, pinching softly, then more firmly—rubbing until the next moan that escaped was his.

That was all it took. A tight voice sounded from behind. "Really, my dear Madeline, couldn't you at least have made it to the bedroom? Killing him there would be so much more discreet."

Lord Milson. She had almost forgotten him.

She gasped, much louder than was necessary, but she wanted to end this situation quickly—it had suddenly become much too real. She pulled out of Struthers's embrace and spun, resisting the urge to cover her breasts. The dampened fabric of her chemise left nothing to the imagination. Experience had taught her well.

She waited for Struthers to speak, but he remained silent, leaving the game to her.

Her mind grew icy clear. A faint glimmer of moonlight fell between the curtains of the long window and she allowed it to fall, illuminating her face and hair, before turning to hide against Struthers's hard chest. As if finally awakening to what must happen, he wrapped his arms about her, protecting her—or at least appearing to. The tighter he held her, the more danger she felt.

She smothered a cough. The floral perfume she had scented before was even more overpowering, almost smothering her—reminding her fully of the situation.

There was the faintest creak and the door they rested against eased open, forcing Struthers forward, bringing them impossibly close together.

"Gerald, what is going on here? I was expecting you a good hour ago," her sister's sultry voice called from the door. And then the sudden intake of breath—so perfectly executed Anna almost believed it herself. "Mr. Struthers, what are you doing here? And—and—"

It was hard for anyone to see who Anna was now that she was completely encased in Struthers's arms.

It was too late to back down.

Anna lifted her head from its protection and stared straight at Maddie. "I would think it's very obvious what we are doing here. The only mistake is that my door is one further down the hall." Her voice was low and husky, as well trained as that of the most costly courtesan.

She clenched her fingers to hide their quake, the only betrayal of her true emotion.

"Anna, how could you—"

"I'll have you know that this is a respectable house. I cannot believe that—"

"Bloody hell, you're even more of a minx now than you used to be."

All three spoke at once and it was impossible for Anna

to distinguish who had said what—except for that last; that could only have come from him, from Struthers.

She snuggled back against him, shifting her hips, rubbing, pressing—enjoying his squirm as she made full contact.

"I must insist you stop that behavior this moment, Miss Steele. I am absolutely appalled that our hostess, Lady Smythe-Burke—not to mention her nephew, the Duke of Brisbane—would allow such—such things under his roof." Lord Milson spoke with a voice as hard as iron. He stepped toward them, and for the first time Anna was glad of the strong arms holding her tight.

Anna turned her face to Maddie—waiting to see if her half sister would even attempt to save her. Anna might have understood what she'd done—but Maddie could not know what had been in Anna's mind when she threw herself into Struthers's arms.

Maddie turned her head, refusing to meet Anna's gaze. Swallowing a brief flash of disappointment, Anna tried to find the words—words that would disarm this situation. Nothing came. It was not surprising. She would never have started this charade if she had not understood the potential for death and disaster that lurked in this hall.

"Miss Steele," Lord Milson continued, "I will make this known to Lady Smythe-Burke immediately. I am sure our hostess will be most upset with your behavior this night. I will expect your departure before morning."

Anna had expected Milson to reveal at least some relief that it was not his wife he had caught. Rather, there was only this cold, icy anger.

She leaned back, letting her head fall against Struthers. Again, she wished she could pretend this was real, wished she could find comfort. Instead there was only more disappointment. He too said not a word in her defense.

She had saved him from injury—possibly even death or murder; killing someone in a duel was still murder—and he didn't say a word.

Lord Milson stared at the two of them, but his focus was only on Anna, making his own impression of the situation clear. She was the woman. It was her transgression, her sin. "Miss Steele, I trust you do not wish to accompany me to Lady Smythe-Burke. I am sure your time would be much better spent organizing your maid to begin with the packing. I will not have you near my wife. I always knew you were trouble." He gave a little snort and turned to leave, giving not one indication that she had ever sat at his dinner table, that he was married to her sister. They had never gotten along and now she was going to pay.

And so she faced disgrace again. Anna would have snorted herself if it would not have made the situation worse. Her dear friends would still welcome her into their homes. They had all faced scandal and worse. Her actions would matter little to them beyond her foolishness in getting caught. It was a sophisticated world in which she lived, and this adventure would do nothing but cause a few giggles.

Oh, outside her own little world a few more doors would close, but they were doors she had no desire to walk through. Still it stung when each one slammed. She pulled her shoulders back and stepped away from Struthers, pulling out of his arms. With as much dignity as she could manage she bent down and lifted her robe from the floor, drawing it tight about her. She turned from Struthers toward her own room to summon the maid.

She would not let it matter—neither his silence, nor Maddie's. She had expected no better—not from either of them.

Struthers reached out then, caught her shoulder, and for a moment the light from the window lit his features full-on. His eyes focused on her face, first her eyes, and then slowly, as if unwillingly, they dropped to her lips. Her breath caught at the intensity of his stare. Her tongue flicked out to dampen her suddenly dry mouth. The minute gesture seemed to shake him and his glance returned to her. His eyes were very dark, the blue sinking to an inky black despite the shining light. There was a question there—and recognition—and something more—something more she did not understand.

"Stop." Struthers's firmly spoken word was directed at Lord Milson, who was half a dozen steps down the hall, but it caught her too. Struthers turned his head and the shaft of light caught his profile, sending him into silhouette. She drew her breath deep. The word might be aimed at Milson, but his glance still held her. In the shining light of the moon she could see the cool consideration of his gaze—if she had acted on impulse, he did not. "If you are to speak with Lady Smythe-Burke it should be to tell her of our upcoming nuptials. Miss Steele has finally agreed to become my wife. You must forgive me if my joy in her answer allowed my baser passions freer rein than is proper. All fault is mine, not hers."

Milson snorted again, but gestured for Struthers to join him. Struthers released her shoulder without another word and followed him.

She should do something. This was not what she wanted. But all she could do was stare, her tongue caught by the shock of Struthers's words.

As the two men disappeared around the corner she turned to Maddie, hoping for some glimmer of understanding, looking for some sign of comfort, some kindness, if only out of remembrance of their childhood together. Anna said, "You do understand I was only trying to help, don't you?"

What Anna received was displeasure. There was no mistaking the cold glare in Lady Milson's clear blue eyes as she slipped back into her room and gave the door a powerful slam.

Anna was left alone, staring down the hallway.

Chapter 2

It was done.

Struthers resisted the urge to lean against the heavy door as it slid silently closed behind him. He pulled his shoulders back and allowed himself one deep swallow.

He had just told Lady Smythe-Burke, the biggest gossip in all the kingdom, that he intended to marry Anna Steele. The words had flowed with surprising ease as he confronted her and laid out his plans for matrimony. Believable. He had actually sounded believable as he explained his sudden love and passion for Anna. An eavesdropper would have thought he'd planned it for months, not scrambled for words in the two minutes it had taken to walk from Lord and Lady Milson's room to Lady Smythe-Burke's chamber and the additional five it had taken the lady to admit them to her sitting room.

He was going to marry Anna Steele.

He allowed another swallow.

Anna was the last woman he would have chosen to take to wife.

Oh, she was beautiful, with her rich brown hair and deep chocolate eyes, and she moved with the sway and confidence of a woman who knew her own appeal and just how to use it.

A single knowing glance from her could reduce a young man to clay waiting to be formed.

But he was no longer a young man.

At three and thirty he knew better than to allow a woman's gaze to persuade him of anything except that he wished to bed her.

Bed her. He would have been happy to bed Anna—what man wouldn't have been? She was a fantasy of the night.

But not of the morning.

Anna Steele was not a woman for marriage.

Not anymore.

Once, years ago, he'd felt differently, but those years had changed so many things. After his years in India he understood the desire for the exotic and seductive—and how quickly it faded. Now he wanted stability and normality.

So why had he agreed—indeed suggested the match?

The problem was he knew damn well why he'd agreed to marry her, and it was not any fear of scandal or even of meeting Lord Milson across a misty field at dawn.

No, he'd done it for Christian, done it for his long-dead friend, done it because of a promise made in the freezing mountains of Spain. And he'd done it for the girl she had been, for quiet little Annie. He could still see her smiling softly at Christian, her eyes glowing as if he were her whole world. She'd been so sweet then, so young, so innocent.

And he could still see her when he'd given her the news—told her what he'd seen, taken away her hope. He'd watched her change in the seconds he spoke to her, seen her eyes open for the first time with the knowledge that the world was not a kind place. He'd often wondered if he'd told her with better words of her fiancé's death if things might have turned out differently.

Damnation. He'd forgotten about Michael. How could he have forgotten about Christian's younger brother? The boy would need to know about the outcome of this evening.

He rubbed his temple as he strode toward his own room, debating whether to stop by Michael's chamber and tell him everything. No, he was too tired for that, and his thoughts were too full of Anna and his promise to Christian, too long unfulfilled.

He was a man of his word and he could only hope it would not ruin him.

Anna was just settling back into her pillows when the authoritative knock sounded on her door. The temptation was great to stick her head back under the covers and ignore it. This night was bad enough without adding anything more to the mixture. She'd had enough problems before the whole muddle began. Ever since she'd received that letter from her cousin Claire, life had been full of troubles. She started to list them silently in her mind and then stopped. Perhaps that had been the issue to begin with—she was so busy dealing with the problems and fears she already had that—

How could the bloody man have said they were engaged? They'd barely seen each other, much less spoken, in years.

The whole idea was ridiculous. She dreaded having to straighten out the whole mess.

She'd already been engaged twice and that was more than enough.

Writing a plan to extricate herself would be her first priority in the morning—maybe she would even begin now; she certainly wasn't sleeping. Granted, she hadn't been sleeping before, not with all her worries. It was why she had gone to drop her letter with the post.

The knock sounded again. Louder. More demanding.

It had been too much to hope she could go to bed and ignore the entire fiasco.

It was probably that bloody, bloody man. She tried to help him and Maddie and this is how he repaid her. Marriage was not something she planned on—not ever—not anymore. Well, perhaps that was not quite true. There had been moments recently when she'd seen friends with their babies that she'd felt a need well up within—a need to hold her own child, a need to know what that was like, a need to love unconditionally.

And despite all the conventions she had pushed aside there was no way she could have a child outside the bounds of marriage. There were some taboos even she dared not break.

But, and it was a very great *but*, Alexander Struthers was not the man she would have chosen as a husband under any circumstances.

He was too big, too demanding, and too—well, just too everything. The man simply knew no limits, and while that was something to be greatly admired, it would not lead to an easy marriage—not that she had any intention of actually marrying the man.

And then there were the memories. She would never forget the look in his eyes when he told her about Christian's death, never forget what it felt like to have her whole world crumble about her.

The knock sounded again.

It was probably he. Who else would pound loud enough to wake both wings of the house?

Sighing deeply—denying the edge of anticipation—she pulled her feet out from the warmth of the covers and set them on the icy floor. Even the plush of the rug could not keep the deep cold of January from seeping up from below. She shivered as she donned her robe, felt around for her slippers, and trudged toward the door. At least she had not blown out the candle before the pounding had begun.

The key was hard to see in the dim light and it took a moment to twist it properly. The moment she heard the click she expected the door to be thrust open. Instead the handle turned slowly and the door eased open to reveal a beautiful and most properly liveried footman.

Footman?

There was barely a second for her mind to form the question before her hostess, Lady Smythe-Burke, swept in, the skirts of a full white night rail and light gray robe swirling about the older woman.

"You may wait in the hall, John," she addressed the footman before turning to Anna. She held herself perfectly straight. "Did you really do it? Accept Struthers? I've always considered you a woman of such sense—not at all the type to be carried away by a moment's passion. I cannot understand how you can have gotten yourself in such a situation."

Suppressing an inkling of disappointment, Anna smiled wryly. "He did talk to you then? I was hoping he'd make a break for it at the stairs and be halfway back to Town." She turned toward the fire. Picking up the poker, she stirred the coals. A pile of logs lay beside the hearth. Should she add another one? How long would this take?

She'd better add several. She'd been friends with Lady Smythe-Burke for years and could not remember ever having a brief conversation. The lady did like to talk. Anna prepared herself for a long night. Lady

Smythe-Burke had ruled society for years and Anna did need her help.

Lady Smythe-Burke began, "Yes, Lord Milson, that bore, marched him up to the door and didn't leave until Struthers had said his piece."

"I didn't expect it to come to this. It never even occurred to me that this could happen. I know it should have." Anna put down the poker and turned back to Lady Smythe-Burke. "Do you know, I never act on impulse. I made Christian court me for two years before I accepted him. And then I delayed longer before I agreed to wait until after he returned from the army to wed. I wanted to be his wife before he faced Napoleon. It was not easy for me to let him persuade me that it would be better for us both if we waited. I am still not sure he was right. And that's not even mentioning Lord Adam. I considered for well over a week before I ended our engagement and would have debated longer had the wedding not been approaching with speed."

"I could only applaud your actions in regard to Lord Adam Darnell. Not every girl would have had the strength to end an engagement under the circumstances," Lady Smythe-Burke said. "And as for Christian Remington, that boy could have persuaded the bees to give up their honey."

This time Anna's smile was bittersweet. "Yes, Christian could always persuade me of anything. He's the only one who ever could." She stepped to one of the chairs before the flaring logs. "Please do be seated."

Lady Smythe-Burke's face was softer than Anna had ever seen it. Her wrinkles softened with kindness. "We must talk about the current situation. Don't think I don't know how many engagements you've avoided. Why choose Struthers? If you were looking for marriage you'd have ended up with my nephew. Brisbane would have made you a fine husband. I know both your mothers would have smiled in heaven."

The corners of Anna's mouth turned up. "No offense, but His Grace, the Duke of Brisbane, would have made me a perfectly awful husband. And if I'd been interested in marriage he never would have come near. The fact that our mothers were closer than sisters is no basis for marriage. The duke has many a year before he considers setting up a nursery."

"You are correct that your avoidance of marriage was probably of prime attraction to him. Brisbane seems in no hurry to do what he must. The duchy needs a direct heir."

Anna turned her face away. She did not wish to discuss nurseries and babies. "Yes, there is some irony in the thought I have put such effort into avoiding marriage, only to trap myself on a moment's whim. I have avoided Alexander Struthers for years—ever since . . . Oh, that does not matter now. I've never felt comfortable around him. And now this. It is not at all the ending I had planned—or rather not planned. As I've already said, I did not stop to consider the consequences of my actions."

"Marriage is still avoidable," Lady Smythe-Burke stated with some force. "Despite the gossip I am known to be, I can hold my tongue."

"Yes, but Lord Milson will not." Anna tried to suppress the glimmer of hope Lady Smythe-Burke's words had given rise to.

"Still, you are not a young girl. You were only caught kissing—at least I assume that is all that you were doing in the hall. Even if there is some talk of your behavior it will blow over. It is not your first scandal."

"Yes, we were only sharing a kiss—although definitely a far from innocent one."

"I would expect nothing less from you. I do hope it was at least enjoyable." Lady Smythe-Burke's gaze suddenly sharpened. "You have just said you avoided the man for years—you did not suddenly kiss him on impulse. What am I missing here, Anna? I do not like not having a full understanding of the situation. Many women have pursued Struthers since he returned from India—rich and mysterious—but you are not one of them."

"Did you know that my half sister, Madeline, Lady Milson, occupies the room next to mine? We have not been close since my inheritance and then her marriage. I cannot say that we remain affectionate, but there is still a definite bond between us. She has always taken care of our father." There was so much more Anna could say about that, but she held her tongue and stuck to the moment. "I could not let her face disgrace."

"So you did this to save Madeline? I do fear I grow quite confused. I must admit I can imagine Madeline with Struthers more easily than I can imagine you. He always did have a weakness for fashionable blondes—although I've never known him to pursue married ones. I thought it was widows he showed a preference for."

Anna pursed her lips, resisting the urge to rub her temple. "I don't quite understand why I did it. Everything we have mentioned is a piece of it, but I would admit it does not lead to a coherent whole. All I know is that I saw Struthers leaving Maddie's room and I heard Lord Milson behind me. I did not want anyone to be hurt."

They were both silent for a moment. Anna watched Lady Smythe-Burke consider.

"Lord Milson is jealous man," Lady Smythe-Burke said after a while.

"And quite a good shot," Anna added. "I know dueling is illegal, but that has not seemed to stop Lord Milson in the past."

"Struthers is not without ability himself."

"Yes, but I don't think he'd kill a man for defending his wife's honor."

"No matter how misplaced that defense." Lady Smythe-Burke stood and began to prowl across the room. "I do begin to understand the situation."

"I wish I did." Anna gave in and rubbed her fingers along her temple. She had not needed this worry in addition to all the others.

Lady Smythe-Burke stopped and turned back to her. "The key is to treat it as a simple matter and take only a single step at a time. I do believe that first you must talk to Struthers and see if you can imagine yourself wed to him. It does not sound like you know much of the man at all anymore. He is much changed since his return from India. If you cannot imagine marriage to him, I will do what I can to manage Lord Milson. I am not without my own persuasions."

"I am sure you are not." There was really nothing else for Anna to say. She might not understand why Lady Smythe-Burke would help her in such a fashion, but she was not about to refuse.

"Fine. I will arrange a meeting between you and Struthers tomorrow in the library. It will have to be early, before many of my guests have arisen. I can delay Lord Milson from speaking, but I would rather not take any chances. Will Lady Milson prove a problem?"

Anna met Lady Smythe-Burke's gaze dead-on. "I doubt she will be about before midafternoon, but I can handle Maddie."

"Good." Lady Smythe-Burke strode to the door with

purpose. "I would not mind seeing you wed. I do believe it always serves a woman well to be wed, with a family—but only if she can find the right man. If you approach marriage with less than a full-hearted commitment it will not end well."

Anna stared deep into the fire after Lady Smythe-Burke left the room. She was going to have to stand face to face with Struthers and talk to the man. They might even make eye contact. A flush of heat rose up through her as she considered how much more than eye contact would pass between them if she actually married the man.

She fanned lightly at her cheeks.

She should never have added that second log to the fire.

Chapter 3

"What on earth were you thinking?" Anna Steele exclaimed as she sauntered into the room with slow deliberation, drawing his eyes to her gently curved hips.

They were not the words that Struthers had expected to hear. When Lady Smythe-Burke had suggested—well, demanded—this meeting, he had imagined that Anna would express gratitude and then begin a list of demands. Women always had demands and expectations. He wondered how long it would be before she began emptying his pockets. She had never struck him as a woman of sound financial sense. Even her night robe had been of thick velvet, an impractical thing.

Still, this was Anna, and Struthers had never known her to do the expected—not even back when Christian had been alive.

It was hard to think of her as Anna. First she was Annie, the little hoyden that followed Christian and him around those few stolen summers of their youth, and then she'd become Miss Steele, the slender girl with the big eyes who had captured his imagination—and then she'd accepted Christian and he'd forced himself not to think of her at all.

Until he'd brought her the news. Again, he was back

in that moment when he'd forced the news of Christian's death from his lips. One second she was the brightly burning girl of his youth and the next she'd changed.

It was a change that he'd observed in her across many a ballroom. She still flirted and enchanted, but there was always a wall between her and those around her. Even when she was her most seductive, and Anna Steele was known for being seductive, she never revealed the inner thoughts that used to shine in her eyes.

"Are you going to answer me or just stand there? What on earth were you thinking?" She certainly didn't sound seductive now, despite her hip-swaying gait as she marched right up to him. "We need to make some sense of this situation."

Of course she would think that—he already understood the situation. He was trapped. He wasn't sure if she had acted with intent, deliberately manipulated him, but it would make no difference to the outcome. Such tricks would not work on him in the future. Marrying a woman like her had never been his intention, but he would live with the consequences of his own foolish actions in being stupid enough to be caught outside Lady Milson's room.

Anna had stopped a foot away from him and stood glaring up. Her chest rose and fell quickly with emotion and he found his attention drawn to the single pearl of her pendant that lay against her breasts, just above the lace edging of her morning gown. The pearl was huge, nearly the size of a pigeon egg, and it shone in a shimmer of colors. It was not the jewel that held his eye, however. Her skin was so pale and creamy, it glowed in competition with the pearl. His gaze held there, watching the pearl sway across her translucent skin with each intake of breath.

His mouth went dry. Maybe being trapped was not so bad.

"I am beginning to believe you really may be an idiot—something I had never previously suspected." Her tone was dry. "My eyes are up here and I assure you you'll get a better response speaking to them than to my breasts."

"Then why do you wear the pearl?"

"What?"

"Then why do you wear a pendant that hangs just there where a man has no choice but to look?"

"I wear it because I like it and it suits my gown. It is one of the first gifts I bought myself when I came into my fortune." She pulled in a deep breath, drawing his eyes back to the pearl.

"Really, that's why you wear it?" He forced his focus to her eyes now, and he watched her pupils narrow and then grow wide.

She drew in another breath, causing the pearl to dance again. His glance dropped, but only for the briefest of moments. His fingers curled in a desire to touch.

Her lips curved up in an unexpected smile, and for just an instant she was the girl he remembered. "You are of course correct. Men are easily manipulated, and a woman must do all in her power to keep them off their guard. That is what you think, isn't it?"

She toyed with the pearl, letting her fingers play across her skin as if she knew that his imagination would follow. Still smiling, she let the pearl drop and turned with a swirl of her skirts to stare out the window. The sun was fully up now and the last of the morning mists was burning off the fields.

"Most women would not admit to that."

"Most men would never have asked." She looked

back at him over her shoulder, and again he was reminded of the girl she used to be—the girl who would never have put them into this situation.

He considered carefully. "I suppose I am meant to answer that I am not most men and you are certainly not most women."

Her eyes grew more serious, very different from that long-ago girl. "No. You are meant to go back to my original question and tell me what on earth you were thinking by announcing our engagement in that fashion."

"I somehow missed that change in the conversation." Why did she keep harping back to that? It had been her doing, not his.

She turned back to the window. "It has always been the subject of this conversation. Forgive me if I am wrong, but I cannot imagine that you wish to wed me."

"You imagine correctly. It was, after all, your actions that brought us here."

That made her turn fast, her skirts spinning out like a rising hot air balloon. "My actions? How can you say that? All I did was protect you."

"Protect me by shoving your tongue down my throat? I can assure you, Miss Steele, that I needed no such protection."

"Men." The word was a curse the way she pronounced it. "Did you wish to end up dead on a field at dawn? Or perhaps you think you would have killed Milson and then fled to the continent? And what of Madeline? Would you have left her to face the scandal?" She switched from foot to foot, sending shivers up the delicate fabric of her skirts. "And if memory holds correct, there were no tongues involved—at least not in throats."

He ignored that last. He had only done what was

right, what was necessary. "You think it was better that I be forced to save you from scandal? I have lived with gossip and rumor and I can assure you it was not pleasant. Now, however, you make me think that perhaps it would have been better to face drawn pistols at dawn."

They stared at each other, and he was glad she was not holding a pistol.

"Nobody forced you to do anything," she said at last, her lips held tight. "I am sure you are well aware I have faced down many a scandal before. I have not been to Almack's since I cried off my engagement to Lord Adam, and I assure you I have never missed it."

Did she really believe he had not been forced? He took a step toward her. "Crying off your engagement to a buffoon is surely different than being caught with your breasts greeting the world."

She stepped toward him. "Not as different as one would think. Besides, I do not consider Lord Milson 'the world.' And Lord Adam was not a buffoon. I would never have agreed to marry him if he had been."

"We could argue that point."

He expected her to argue, but instead she turned and walked to a high-backed chair. She sat, as proper as any duchess. "I did not come here to argue with you." Her voice was calm, but her restless fingers betrayed her as they lifted to play with the pearl drop, again drawing his gaze. He heard her breath catch. "Or to seduce you." She released the drop and folded her hands primly in her lap.

He found himself believing her. "Then why did you come?"

"I came to decide if marriage between us is even possible. You mentioned that meeting over pistols at dawn might have been a preferable outcome. Do you truly feel that way?" There was no hint of sarcasm in her question. It was a genuine inquiry.

He gave her the respect of considering her question. She truly seemed sincere—had it not been her aim to force his hand to marriage? "No, I have never sought death or thought it a game, and I saw enough killing during the war to know its true cost. If I had wanted death I could certainly have found an honorable one in the mountains of Spain or later in the wilds of India. I had not, however, planned on matrimony at this time in my life. I have returned to England seeking quiet and peace—it does not seem likely you will grant me either."

She pursed her lips slightly, considering. "Then why did you propose?"

"What action did you wish me to take? I long ago learned that life does not always go as I plan. You clearly had something in mind when you flung yourself at me."

"Actually I didn't." She lowered her eyes as she answered, as if afraid of her own answer.

"You didn't?"

"No, I just knew I couldn't let Lord Milson find you with his wife, my sister. I didn't think much beyond that point."

"I see. I had forgotten that Lady Milson was your half sister. Did it never occur to you that perhaps there was nothing to find? That I was only there to deliver a message?"

Her brows drew together. Doubt shadowed her eyes for a moment, but then cleared. "I would like to say I could believe that. I must admit I had not considered it—and your tone is sincere. But now, thinking with some care—no, I understand perfectly well what the situation was. And it would not have mattered anyhow. We both know that in society it is appearances that count, not truth."

"I will not bore you with the truth then." Keeping the irritation from his voice, he came and sat across from her, their knees separated barely an inch. If he slid forward in his chair they would be touching. "Did you know that Michael, Christian's brother, is here?"

Her gaze dropped to that sole inch that separated them. "Yes, of course. I spent an afternoon with him. We talked of— You are trying to distract me. Let us return to the point."

"Which is?"

"Why did you tell Lord Milson we were to be married? Surely there was another way?"

"If there was I could not think of it in that moment. In truth, I don't know why I did it. I promised Christian I would take care of you. But mostly I acted without thought—my actions were much as your own and I have as little understanding of them. I have been in similar situations before and never felt the need to speak those words." He was saying far more than he had ever intended.

"Then why did you this time?" She leaned toward him, her knees drawing closer to his own.

"I have just said I do not know."

She smiled ruefully. "I suppose some deeply hidden part of me longs to hear you say that you were overcome by my beauty and could not resist the chance to have me for your own—not that I know what I would do if that were the case."

Her honesty gave him pause. Why had he proposed? He was not a man to act on impulse and the words had to have come from somewhere; his promise to Christian—and his guilt—only extended so far. He could find no answer. “I do not suppose my reasons matter. What is important is how we proceed from here.”

“I would agree with that.”

“Good. Do you wish me to make the arrangements? Or do you consider that a womanly domain?”

“I think you misunderstand me. I agree that we must decide our future. I am not sure that marriage—to each other—is part of that.” She licked her lips nervously as she spoke. He had never realized how many small traits she had that revealed her inner emotions. Or how many of them made him want to touch her, to trace her lips following the trail of that nervous tongue.

“I don’t see that as being up for debate.”

“I believe that it is.” She spoke firmly, but licked her lips again.

“Lord Milson will have spread the word, and besides, Lady Smythe-Burke knows,” he said. “Our course is set. It would be foolish to pretend otherwise.”

She straightened in her chair, but kept her knees that same fraction of an inch from his. It was as if she pulled power into herself, the momentary nervousness hidden. Smiling slowly, she let her gaze settle firmly on his mouth. She leaned forward; her gown gaped and the pearl danced, drawing his gaze. She was so close he could feel her breath upon his cheek.

“Do you think so?” Her words were soft, almost a caress of language. “Do you really believe that we can make this work—that marriage is better than the alternative?”

He had never thought so before. His breath caught at how quickly she wrapped a spell around him. She smelled of roses—deep, velvet red ones.

“Because I certainly don’t.” She pulled back suddenly. “I believe that for us to marry is to court disaster. Lady

Smythe-Burke made me promise to consider carefully if I could be married to you. I see little evidence that it would work."

He was still lost in her magic and it took a moment for his thoughts to settle. He shifted slightly in his seat. "I don't believe there is much evidence—in either direction."

Any softness that had been in her posture fled. "You have already said that you had no immediate plans for marriage. And I imagine I am not the bride you would have chosen. I have never seen you show any evidence that you cared for my company. If anything you have avoided it."

"It is not I who has done the avoiding. I could tell from the moment after I told you of Christian's death that you found my presence intolerable. I only wished to spare your feelings. And, you must remember, I have been away for several years."

For a moment her mask dropped. He could see she was startled by the honesty of his response. "I did not think you realized. It was certainly never my intention to offend you. I was simply never comfortable near you after that. My thoughts always turned back to that moment."

"I did not say I was offended. I understood. He was my friend too."

"I know." She stood, her skirts brushing over his knees as she moved. "It is silly that I mourn still after all these years. Although I have come to realize I mourn myself as much as Christian. I mourn how simple and hopeful life was." She paused and he thought she was finished, but then she spoke again. "Seeing you makes me remember who I was."

"And you wish you were still that way?" He could

well imagine a woman wishing to be young and innocent again.

She turned to him with a wry smile. "No, actually I don't. I rather like who I am now."

"You do?" He could not help the surprise that echoed in his voice. He would have married the girl she had been without question.

"Don't look so shocked. Yes, I do. I am the woman that I want to be." Her smile turned knowing and she stepped toward him, moving slowly, like a great cat approaching its prey.

She smiled and laid a hand along his cheek. Her palm was warm and soft. "The girl I was would have been a much better wife for you, though. It was the only life she could imagine—or want."

He found himself turning his face into her palm, enjoying the gentle touch. "I did like that girl."

"I know." Her voice said far more than the words, as did the thumb that stroked his cheek.

"You know?"

She dropped her hand and stepped away, pulling herself tall. "Yes, a girl knows when she is watched—and wanted. I did not think of it in that fashion then, but I knew. For all that my own thoughts were only of Christian, I knew."

"I never meant you to."

"As I never meant you to realize that I avoided you. Perhaps we are not good at hiding from each other."

He remembered his own thoughts a moment before about noticing her nervousness. "Yes, I do believe you are right. Surely that would be good in a marriage?"

"I have my doubts about that. It might be most uncomfortable. But that brings us back to the center point of our discussion. Should we wed?"

He had not dared to consider that there was a choice. If there was, surely he should take it. "Do you really believe we have say in the matter?"

"Lady Smythe-Burke has said she will be most accommodating if we decide we do not suit. If she holds firm nobody will believe Lord Milson over her—or at least they will pretend not to. And I can face what scandal there is."

"So you do not think we need to wed—and you do not wish to?" He spoke the words slowly. It was hard to imagine a woman who did not wish to pursue marriage. Since he had arrived back in England he had been constantly pursued.

"I very definitely do not wish to—not under these circumstances—not to avoid scandal and fulfill a promise to a dead man." Her voice caught. "I am quite content with the life I have. If I had wished to wed I would have stayed with Lord Adam all those years ago."

"The buffoon—I always wondered what the real story was there."

"No, I repeat, not a buffoon—and there was no real story. I simply decided I did not choose to wed, and being a woman it was my choice not to. It is one of the very few choices left to women."

He sensed there was far more to the matter than she said. He walked up to her and, watching for her reaction, laid his hand lightly on her shoulder, drawing her glance back to him. "But still a choice that caused a scandal in itself. If there was no story, why did you choose to say you would wed him and then decline?"

She smiled slowly then, so slowly it seemed there was no movement and yet soon her face was filled. "My circumstances changed—the whole world knows that. Tell me, Mr. Struthers, do you not see why a young girl of moderate income but no real prospects might choose to marry a sweet man who could offer her a life of security? But that a slightly older woman with a fortune at her fingers might decide that she didn't need such security? Indeed she might feel that she would now actually lose freedom in marriage rather than gain it."

"I don't see—"

"No, being a man you might not. Most women are tied to the men in their lives; ultimately they survive only at the grace of their protectors. I am no longer such a woman. From the moment I inherited my fortune I have been a far different woman, a woman who can think for herself and make do for herself. I have my own power, the power to take what I want when I want it."

He wasn't sure he believed any of it—oh, he believed she believed it—but the basic idea was senseless. What woman would not want marriage? Not want to have a man care for her needs?

She reached forward and grasped his hand, raising it to her lips and laying a light kiss across the back of it just below the knuckles. It was a completely unexpected gesture and he almost jerked his hand back. Her eyes glinted up at him. She had caught his movement.

He cleared his throat in an obvious effort to gain more time. "I do not see what that has to do with us, with our decision to marry. Our needs are based on scandal versus propriety, not security."

She stepped closer, moved until her breasts rested against his chest, until that alluring scent of roses surrounded him again. He sensed her manipulation and did not care. She slid a hand up his chest, playing with the buttons first of his waistcoat and then of his shirt. When she reached his neck cloth she blew playfully upon the bow and then ran a finger around the upper edge of it, before slipping her finger beneath to caress the bare skin of his neck. She raised herself on tiptoe until her mouth was almost level with his, then dampened her lips. Her eyes focused slowly on his. He felt himself being drawn forward as if a line were tied between them.

He could feel her breath in his mouth, taste the lemon she took in her tea. The kiss had not even begun and already it was the most erotic moment he could remember in years.

"No, I definitely don't see why we shouldn't marry." His voice was so husky that he could hardly understand his own words. It was hard to remember he had entered this room resentful of their coming marriage.

"Ah, you are so wrong. This is everything about why we should not marry." She moved that quarter inch closer that brought their lips together. He expected her to control the kiss, to teach him lessons in passion, to lure him into the magic he knew only she could create. Instead she just let her lips lie against his without moving. He could taste her, feel her; her whole body was his to grasp, but the only contact was the soft press of her lips.

Should he take over? Show her two could play at that game? Was she waiting for him? It was a moment full of possibility, and following his instincts he gave in, moved to wrap an arm about her, to taste her fully, to make her his.

But then she was gone. Her mouth moved in the kiss one might lay upon a baby's brow and she twisted away. She did not move far, just enough to separate them.

"That is a woman's power." She spoke quietly. "A woman can tease and enchant, draw a man into thinking he would do anything for her—and some will. But more often it is an illusory power. Men are all too ready to grab and then a woman is left with nothing, her power gone."

"I can assure you," he said stiffly, "that no woman of my acquaintance has ever complained of being left with nothing."

She tossed back her head and loosed a deep, full laugh. "You take me much too literally, Mr. Struthers. My whole point is that a woman must hold her power—not give it away carelessly. Marriage would be careless."

His fingers itched to close on her, to bring her closer, but she was like a fairy queen, within reach, but untouchable.

She caught the movement of his hand and took it between her own palms, drawing it again to her lips.

She kissed the tip of his thumb. "If circumstances were different I might take you to my bed." She ran the tip of his thumb along her lips, and then drew it in, sucking tight in an unmistakable gesture. "Yes." Her tongue played with the heavy calluses years at sea had left. "I think we might have suited very well, but—" She drew his hand from her with some show of regret. "It cannot happen now."

"You, my lady, are a tease."

"I am not a lady and never will be since I sent poor Lord Adam away, but, yes, I am definitely a tease. Well-known for it, in fact. Rumor has it, though, I am well worth it if caught."

He stepped toward her. "And I have caught you."

She sighed, a soft sound that filled his senses. "No, you have not, and now I fear you never shall. I do not wish to wed a man who thinks of me as something to be caught."

Caught. It had been her word, not his. He turned and walked away from her. He was tired of playing her games, tired of being the mouse to her cat. "Why do you test me if you truly think we should not wed? I do not see the purpose of this display."

She was behind him now, but he heard her turn and walk farther from him, her soft footfalls telling him that she too felt the need for space. "I know you don't. I can't explain it exactly. I merely wanted to show you the only power I would have within our marriage. Right now I am responsible for all my actions, all my decisions. What would I be responsible for if we wed?"

Chapter 4

She could see his bafflement, his lack of understanding. Men never faced this issue. Their lives stayed very much the same after marriage as before. She had spent years debating it. When she agreed to marry Christian it had not been a case of considering all the merits of marriage, but rather of being sure that Christian was the right choice. She knew she loved him with all the joy in her innocent heart, but she'd seen enough bad marriages to know that early love was not always enough.

Her parents had loved each other and she had watched her father disappoint her mother time and time again. Maddie had loved Milson when they wed—or at least claimed to—and look at them now. Her friend Violet had been married several times without any of them being truly good. And Violet seemed very happy now—loving Lord Peter without benefit of marriage.

No, marriage was not designed for women.

"What on earth are you talking about? What would you be responsible for?" Struthers asked. "You'd be responsible for the things women are responsible for in marriage—home and family, hopefully children."

Children. It was too easy to picture a small boy with

Struthers's dark waves of hair, and that grin turning up at one corner. "What if I want more?"

"What more? I was not aware that there was more."

She'd known that. Men never had an idea there was more, never faced the longing for control, the longing to lead lives of their own choosing. "Well, there is. At this moment I control my destiny. I have a privilege that very few women are allowed and almost none who are not widowed. Why should I give it up for marriage? And why are you trying to persuade me? You are not looking for marriage and I clearly am not the wife that you would choose."

"What I want does not matter." He turned to face her as he spoke. His lips were still pursed as if awaiting her kiss.

She wished that she could remain unaffected. The whole purpose of the almost-kiss had been to demonstrate her power—so why did she feel so drawn? Why did she want to stare into those striking blue eyes? She marshaled her forces. "Yes, it does matter. If last night had not happened you would never have even dreamed of asking me."

The light from the window filled his eyes and for the moment he had the strangest expression—as if he would deny her words. His mouth opened and then closed. His head bowed. "No, I would not have. I had not intended to marry yet."

"Then be glad that we have a choice. If you have never even considered the questions that I ask—never even realized that there are questions—then I cannot see that we would ever suit."

"Perhaps you are correct. But I promised Christian that I would care for you and honor demands—"

"Honor be damned." She would not be married

because of a promise to a dead man, not even Christian. "This is our entire lives we are talking about. I will not marry you."

He turned stiffly and looked out the window. "If that is how you wish it."

"It is."

She waited a moment, hoping he would say more, but silence held between them. She ran her tongue over her lips.

Placing her hand on the door, she said, "I'll see you at luncheon."

He did not answer.

He should rejoice. He had escaped the noose—with his honor. The fates still smiled upon him.

He could not forget, however, the way she'd licked her lips in those last seconds before she left the room—not in invitation, but from nerves. There was something she was not saying, something that scared her.

He drew in a deep breath and stared past the well-pruned gardens at the fields beyond. He did not want to marry Anna Steele. He had not wanted her since he was twenty-five years old.

Well, perhaps *want* was the wrong word.

He could not deny the tension that had filled him when she drew close.

She had not smelled like roses when she'd been a girl—then it had been lemons—like the tea she still drank. She'd laughed once when he'd remarked on it and said that she rubbed their juice in her hair to bring out the shine. Such a silly thing to recall.

He sighed and let his head rest against the cool window glass.

Honor might be satisfied, but the rest of him was not.

* * *

"Milson told me what happened—that you and Struthers will marry. I am so relieved—and happy for you, of course." Maddie slipped into the small parlor where Anna had retreated from the rest of the company.

"Relieved?" Anna tried to forgive her sister for not attempting to help her earlier. Their relationship had always been complex and seemed to grow only more so with each added year.

"Yes, I was so scared the situation would turn—difficult." Maddie settled into the chair across from Anna. Her expression was that of a small dog who had just secured a rather large bone and was scared to lose it.

Anna looked straight at her sister. Maddie had been so pretty as a girl, but now Anna could see the signs of strain at the corners of her mouth. "We have decided not to wed. It was a momentary foolishness."

"What?" Maddie sat bolt upright.

"Despite our impulsiveness last night, the clear light of day has revealed that marriage between Struthers and myself would never work."

"What?"

Anna did not repeat her answer. It was clear Maddie had heard her and was just having trouble digesting the information. Anna was not sure why. Maddie knew better than anyone that the situation had not been straightforward.

Maddie sat up straighter. "But you have to marry him."

"I don't have to do anything." Anna stiffened her spine.

"You were caught kissing him in the hall in your nightclothes. Of course you have to marry him. Milson says you do." Maddie's voice echoed with childish petulance and just a trace of irrationality.

It was Anna's turn to smile. "No, really I don't. I am twenty-eight years old. I don't have to do anything. As you say, I was caught kissing him in the hall, not fucking"—she said the word slowly, watching Maddie's reaction, looking for some hint of what had passed between Maddie and Struthers—"him in the dining room. There will be gossip—perhaps even a lot of it—but I am not afraid of talk."

"But—" Maddie was clearly at a loss for words.

"And besides, you of all women should know that last night was not exactly as it appeared."

Maddie blanched slightly at that. "You would not say anything."

"No, I would not." Anna smiled ironically. "And even if I did, who would believe me now? Everyone would think I was trying to deflect blame when I had been truly caught. No, if I said anything it would only make me appear more guilty. My best bet is to stay silent."

"That is true." Maddie stared down at her hands. She stared at them for a long moment and then raised her face back to Anna, her voice definite. "Still, you must marry him. It is the only way."

"What? I don't follow why this should concern you. It will be my scandal, not yours. If anyone does speak of you it will only be to wonder if you have anything else to add. You will be sought out by everyone who wants to know what really happened."

Maddie tightened her lips. "If you don't marry Struthers, Milson will always wonder. He is not a trusting man."

"But surely he will accept what his own eyes saw."

"Not if you do not marry Struthers. Milson will believe Struthers is a rake because he did not marry you under the circumstances and then he will wonder what he was doing outside my door." Maddie spoke with great firmness, but also a touch of desperation. "He is already suspicious."

"I think he will realize it is obvious what Struthers was doing and who he was doing it to."

Maddie rose from the chair and came back to stand beside Anna. "But we both know it is not as obvious as it appeared." She dropped her glance to the floor. "I am expecting. The child is of course Milson's, but I cannot afford to have him wonder. He is not a man who needs cause to wonder. If he has any reason to suspect the child is not his, he will do something. I do not know what, but it will not be pleasant. He might hurt me—or the child—or Struthers. Do not give him reason to worry. You have always been the lucky one. Do this for me. You are my family. You owe me. You know you do."

Anna took a step back. Maddie's reasons seemed senseless to her, but it sounded as if Maddie did believe them. There was very real fright in her eyes when she spoke of her husband's reaction. Picking up a book off the table, Anna stared blindly at the spine.

She had thrown herself into Struthers's arms last night without thought. This time she would consider very carefully.

She knew Maddie had always resented that Anna had left her to care for their father. Anna could not blame her. Caring for their father, watching their father was not an easy job. Anna did owe Maddie for that—would always owe her.

But Anna also knew that Maddie's greater resentment started when Anna inherited from her mother's older brother. Maddie had never felt it was fair that she received nothing, despite the lack of blood relation. It didn't matter to Maddie that she'd never even met the uncle in question, never traveled to America to visit him. No, Maddie only cared that Anna had received something, a great something, that Maddie had not.

Anna placed the book back on the table with great care and turned back to her sister. She surveyed her carefully. Maddie was very pale and not looking at all well. There were circles beneath her eyes and she did not glow with her normal good health. Maddie's fingers clenched and released, a clear sign of nerves.

Still, Maddie fibbed with the best of them. Several times Anna had found herself blamed for actions that were not her own as Maddie stared at the world through those innocent blue eyes. Could Anna risk that this was another of those times?

And why was Maddie so convinced Milson would question the child's paternity if Anna didn't marry Struthers? Was there something Maddie was not telling her?

Before she could ask Maddie for further elaboration, the door swung open and Lady Smythe-Burke strode in. She stared at Maddie and simply said, "Out."

Maddie blinked, but did not move.

Lady Smythe-Burke set a cold glare on Maddie. "Scat, child. You are not needed at present."

Maddie hesitated—she probably was not used to being addressed like a cat—and then fled.

Anna felt a chuckle rising to her lips, but she forced it down. "Don't you ever try that with me."

Lady Smythe-Burke raised a brow, but said nothing. She sailed once across the room and then back again. "You will have to marry that man."

"What?" Anna could not have been more surprised. "I thought that—"

"Brisbane is here."

Anna struggled to keep up. Normally Lady Smythe-Burke was too verbose—now she barely said enough to make sense. "What is His Grace of Brisbane doing here? He never attends house parties, not even his own."

Lady Smythe-Burke collapsed into a chair. She lifted a hand and wiped her brow. "Arthur will not be staying long. He had some matter to settle with his estate manager. I do believe he will hide from my guests."

Anna stared at Lady Smythe-Burke's posture; she had not even been aware the lady's spine could curve. "I fear I am still missing something. Why do I have to marry Struthers—who I have already refused, by the way—because Brisbane is talking to his manager?"

"Brisbane brought news."

Anna waited. Lady Smythe-Burke would not stay silent for long.

"Your cousins—your American cousins—have arrived in London," the lady finally added.

A cold weight curdled in Anna's belly. "I was afraid of that."

"As was I. You did not tell me much about your letter from Claire Townsend," Lady Smythe-Burke said. "But I was adding two and two to get four before your mother was born. Arthur told me part of the story, but I understood the rest—probably far better than he—without being told. Do I need to elaborate?"

"Please," Anna answered. Lady Smythe-Burke would keep talking no matter what she said.

"Your colonial cousins—such a better term than *American*—want your fortune. Oh, don't look at me like that. Of course the Townsends want your money.

Franklin, their father, your mother's younger brother, always resented that he didn't get given as much as his older brother, Charles, and blamed Charles for not sharing the fortune he earned with him. Franklin's sons are just the same. Besides, everybody wants to inherit a fortune, whether it was left to them or not. Your male cousins realize that you are the only thing keeping them from that money—and that you are a young woman who shows no signs of wishing to marry. Correct?"

"Correct."

"It is strange for a woman not to want to marry. It might even be a sign of mental weakness, a sign that a woman was not fit to govern her own affairs."

"But—"

"If such a woman were indeed mentally stable she would ask for help from her kinfolk, would she not? If she did not it might be necessary for those kinfolk to take matters into their own hands. And if this woman further showed signs of having sexual appetites that she still did not look to marriage to satisfy, then she might even be dangerous—corrupting. I daresay it might even be necessary to lock her up—for her own protection."

Anna's fingers were clenched so tight that her nails pierced half moons on her palms. Her cousin Claire had written and expressed worry that her brothers intended to try and have Anna put in an institution, but until this moment—hearing it said aloud—she had refused to believe it. She had worried endlessly—but not truly believed. "You don't think—"

"Of course I don't, but many would not disagree. Your cousin Nathanial Townsend is a solicitor, is he not? A man who knows how to use his words?"

Anna could only nod. She had lived in terror of this moment, of her fears being said aloud.

Lady Smythe-Burke tilted her chin to look straight into Anna's eyes. "Before the events of last night the situation might have been salvageable. Now I fear disaster."

Anna licked her lips. "I don't see why last night should matter. It was really a small thing."

"You know better than that, Anna. There is no small thing when it comes to a woman's reputation."

"You are correct. I do know better. But this truly was nothing, a kiss. You even said so, said that I should not marry Struthers because of a kiss."

"I was wrong—and I do not say that often."

Anna could feel the blood fleeing from her face. "Surely you do not mean a kiss could make me the madwoman of London?"

"A kiss no, but questions of your moral character? Licentious behavior? A seeming lack of control of your actions?" Lady Smythe-Burke's tone grew sterner with each word.

"I did not think . . . it never occurred to me . . ." Anna's voice trailed off. "You even said . . ."

Lady Smythe-Burke's tone softened. "I know what I said. There is no reason a kiss should have mattered, but the fact remains—your colonial cousins will do whatever they need to and use whatever they can. They wish to have you declared insane and locked away in a madhouse. There is no kind way to say it."

"The idea is preposterous." Anna tried to keep her voice from shaking, to keep her deep fear from showing. When her cousins' plans had first become apparent she had made it a point to visit an asylum. She wished she had not. She would never forget the patients who belonged there—and even more frightening, the patients who had not.

"Anna," Lady Smythe-Burke said. "You are one of

the sanest women I know—and that means a lot—but that does not change how the world will see you. You are a wealthy woman, unprotected by a man, who chooses not to marry even when you have received offers from the most eligible of men. Believe me, there are those among the many you refused who would rather believe you demented than to believe there was any flaw within themselves."

Anna knew it was true, had always known, but she bridled at the injustice of it. "I never said there was a flaw with them. I always made it clear that it was my own fickle nature that made me not wish for marriage."

"Exactly."

"Exactly?"

"You yourself have said the fault is with you. Do you not think the Townsends will find these men and turn your own words against you?"

Anna could not suppress the shiver that shook her. Was there any fear greater than being locked up among the deranged when one was perfectly sane? "That was not what I meant. Anybody would realize that."

"Would they? Anna, there are many lords who will look at the breaking of your engagement to Lord Adam and your affairs since then as signs of mental weakness. They will think it impossible that any woman could manage a half a million pounds on her own and not be driven crazy. You know our female minds are delicate and cannot withstand such pressure. If you were sane you would have found a man to help you. Instead you have refused all help and all offers of marriage."

"Rubbish." She spoke with as much force as she could muster.

"Yes, but it will not matter. You have a fortune and your cousins, your *male* cousins, believe it should be theirs. They will stop at nothing. They will claim you have mismanaged your funds, acted irresponsibly—and many will agree with them."

Anna tilted her chin up, licking her lips. "I have had my reasons for how I've used my money, good reasons."

"I know. But you have gone through tens of thousands of pounds, perhaps hundreds of thousands. Can you explain what you have done with it all? And should we talk about Mr. Jackal?"

"How do you know about Mr. Jackal? You cannot know these things. Nobody knows what I am doing." Anna knew she licked at her lips again. She was doing the right thing in supplying funds to Mr. Jackal, but few would believe that—or understand.

Lady Smythe-Burke didn't answer.

Anna closed her eyes and wished she could find an answer to her problems, but all she found was her own fear.

"There really is only one answer, Anna." Lady Smythe-Burke stood and walked over to Anna. She placed her hand on Anna's shoulder.

"There is no choice. Even my influence can only extend so far. You will have to marry that man, marry Struthers. You know as well as I the only way to block your cousins' reach is to place yourself out of their power."

Staring straight ahead, Anna did not acknowledge the words. Her mind churned, looking for another possibility.

"I do wish it was somebody other than Struthers. I even told Brisbane he should marry you. He said it was impossible, that he would help in any other way, but that marriage was impossible. I can't think why—but enough of that. Struthers it must be, I am afraid," Lady

Smythe-Burke commented as she patted Anna again.

That brought Anna around to face her. "What is wrong with Struthers? I thought you said that he was quite pursued, very eligible?"

"Oh, he is. He came back from India extremely well-heeled, and that and his pretty face are enough to move both sweet young things and their mothers."

"Then what is the difficulty?"

"I do not normally like to spread gossip—at least not gossip that I do not know the truth of—but there have been vague rumors, almost unheard in society, that he cheated his partners in order to earn his fortune and that one of them killed himself. Mind you, I do not know the truth. Not yet."

Cheating. It did not seem like the Struthers she had known all those years ago. He had always been scrupulously honest. Could something like that change? India changed many men from what she had been told. "I am sure there is another way. I cannot marry a man I do not know. Perhaps my father—"

"Jeremy Steele never helped anyone in his life. I've known him since he was a child and he has always looked after himself. I am sorry to have to say it, but your father is unreliable. Do you think that has changed?"

Anna wanted to say yes. She wanted to say her father cared for her, that he might even love her. Fathers loved their daughters, didn't they? She wanted to say that of course he would take her side, protect her. The trouble was she could not remember a time when he had. He had not supported her when she broke her engagement, threatening to disown her if she did not marry Lord Adam. When she inherited he told her she should give her cousins the business in return for a steady income—paid to him. He even told her that only a crazy woman would want to manage anything beyond a family. She should come home and care for him—meaning she should take him back to his house in the country where he could drink all day and she could clean up after him.

No, her father would not help her—not even if he was sober enough to do so.

She stiffened her spine. "I will find a way—a way that does not involve marriage. I could lose so much in marriage to Struthers, in marriage to any man."

Lady Smythe-Burke's voice was gentle and she squeezed Anna's shoulder. "I know."

"Struthers does not understand—he wants a gentle young wife."

"You are probably right. He is a man, and men never know what is good for them."

"Struthers might take my fortune. He could leave me powerless."

"Yes, he could."

Anna pulled away and went to stare at the dead embers of the fires. Surely they should have been swept away by now. She filled her lungs with one full breath, released it slowly.

For once, Lady Smythe-Burke said nothing further.

Anna turned back. "You always did leave me to argue with myself. In marrying Struthers I risk it all, but I do not know for sure what the outcome will be. If I do not marry him and my cousins succeed, then the fears that creep at the edge of my nightmares will come to be. There is not much question of what they will do to get the money. If I could have lived with their actions I would have given them a share long ago."

Still, Lady Smythe-Burke said nothing.

Anna smiled then, knowing well that it held a bitter edge. "I have never understood how you can win an argument without saying a word. It is most unfair." She pulled her shoulders back as far as they would go. "Yes, I will marry the man. I will go to Struthers and swallow my pride, tell him that I was wrong, tell him that we must wed."

Lady Smythe-Burke nodded. She had clearly known the outcome before she entered the room.

Still standing stiffly Anna walked to the door. "I will go find him now."

"You can tell him Brisbane will attend to the license. There are some advantages to having a bishop in the family. And Anna . . ."

"Yes?" She stopped, still hoping that there was another answer.

"Struthers will be a lucky man, make sure he appreciates that."

Anna swallowed and nodded back, not trusting her voice.

She could only hope that someday Struthers came to agree.

Chapter 5

"Thank you, Mrs. Struthers," Struthers said as the door clicked shut behind him.

They were not bad words. In many circumstances they would have been acceptable.

This was not one of them.

No, a wedding night was not one of them.

A soft thud echoed from the adjoining chamber.

Anna let her head fall back into the heavy nest of pillows, fighting the tightness in her throat.

She had slept in this room for almost two weeks, since before this whole mess had begun. Lady Smythe-Burke had requested that they stay through the wedding and there had been no refusing. At least Struthers had been moved into the adjoining room rather than being expected to share this one with her. She could not even imagine having to spend the night with him if this wall of cold politeness was all there was between them.

Turning her head, she stared ahead blankly. The single candle still burned on the high marble mantel. The low embers of the fire cast their own soothing light. The heavy odor of the roses that somebody had left on the delicate bedside table mixed with the smell of sweat and bodies. She turned on her side and stared at the roses. They were white. She had never been fond of white roses, but clearly somebody thought they were appropriate for a wedding night.

A wedding night.

Her wedding night.

Thank you, Mrs. Struthers. No, those were not the words—almost the only words spoken—that a bride wanted to hear from her husband on her wedding night.

She wasn't sure what he should have said. Were there right words to say? That was certainly not something that was discussed in the whispered tones ladies used when discussing such matters. Maybe if she'd had a mother to advise her she would have known what to expect—

The thought brought the edge of a quivering smile to her lips. How many women were concerned by the words and not the actions? She'd known exactly what to expect on that front—known exactly how the actions would go. No, that wasn't quite right. It had been much more ordinary than she had expected. She'd dreamed of great passion and—

She'd sensed his anger from the moment he entered, his black robe tight about him. He'd walked to the bed without a word and stared down at her. She tried to smile, but felt only her own resentment. She had every bit as much right to be angry as he. If he'd not been in Maddie's room— No, she would not think about that. She forced the smile to her lips. He did not smile in return, merely pulling back the covers and climbing in beside her.

They lay side by side staring at the ceiling. She kept waiting for words. It was their wedding night. There should be words.

She almost jumped when his hand landed on her breast. He squeezed, his thumb brushing across her nipple. It did not feel bad. It even felt good. He lowered himself on the bed until his face was even with her breasts. His mouth replaced his hand. It felt even better.

One of his hands slipped lower in the bed, finding its way between her legs. It stroked her. Sensations rose and filled her.

She started to press her face against his chest, to let her fingers roam his back beneath the velvet of his robe.

He rolled over, onto her, pushing away the contact. "Are you ready?" They were the first words he had spoken.

"Yes." It felt like more words should come, but none did.

He filled her fully. He was a large man.

His eyes did not meet hers. He held himself above so that all she saw was the fine mat of hair upon his chest.

She felt the tightness grow, sensation peak—and then the rush, the explosion, the end.

He collapsed for just a moment on top of her and then rolled to the side. It could not have been a full minute before he slid his legs to the floor, pulling the robe tight about him once again.

"Thank you, Mrs. Struthers." And then the click of the closing door.

The words cut deep. If she'd been confident of what had passed between them she would have taken the thank-you at face value. As it was, she feared that he had found it, found her, disappointing. Not at all the dream of a girl on her wedding night.

But she was not a girl. She sat back up in bed as that thought flowed through her.

She was a woman, every bit a woman.

Damn. She'd let herself get caught up in the events and allowed herself to become the helpless heroine forced to marry the brooding hero. That was not her or her life.

She slid from the bed, reaching out to grab her robe and pull it about her. Pacing across the room and back, she stopped in the middle of the rug to stare at the heavy wood door he had closed so decisively between them.

Should she go to him now?

He did still desire her. Of that she was sure. She could not mistake the way his eyes dropped from her face and lingered, only to rise again to her lips, before he turned his head away. She could feel that caught breath, that wondering of possibilities. And when they had kissed before, the fire had been there, the flames had leaped between them. In that she was not mistaken.

Desire. He felt it. He wanted her, wanted her as she was now, full and ripe and knowing.

And she? She had only to picture his long, strong fingers or the way his jacket pulled tight across his shoulders to feel warmth grow deep in her belly.

She stared at the door, could almost feel the cold of the handle within her grasp—but what then?

What could she do to make it all different?

She refused to fail again.

When she went to him next he would fall before her with want, understand her for the goddess she was. If there was one thing she knew it was how to make men want. She dropped the robe to the floor and walked back to the bed, naked and proud.

Next time she would be sure the roses were red, deep, almost black velvet.

Struthers shut the door behind him gently. He resisted the urge to slam it and resisted again the desire to lean back against it.

How had he gotten himself into this hellish situation?

It had been barely over a week since the whole farce had begun and here he was—married.

His fingers involuntarily curled into a tight fist. He stared down at them, at the white knuckles and straining tendons. He raised his hand to eye level, glaring at the fury he had let himself show in no other way. He longed to pound upon the wall to release the pent-up emotion that swelled within. He contented himself with one soft slam upon the wall that rattled a picture but did no damage.

Damn her.

He'd believed her when she said she didn't wish marriage, and certainly not to him.

He'd remembered her utter honesty and let himself be persuaded that she told the truth. No, no persuasion had been necessary. He had simply believed her.

And he was no longer a man who believed easily. Betrayal had long fingers, and what had happened in India still held him tight. His partners had betrayed him and it would be years yet until he forgot. It was part of why he had decided to wait to marry. He needed time to heal first.

Damn her. He began to trust again—and this was what happened.

He walked across the room and poured a brandy, a very large one, letting the burn eat down his throat.

When she had searched him out—no, hunted him down—later that afternoon, after refusing him so artfully, it had never occurred to him what she meant to do, that she meant to hold him to his promise—the promise she had already released him from.

He had believed they could make marriage work.

Now he was no longer sure.

Damn her. He didn't understand her tricks, her plans,

but he did not like them. She would learn he was not a man to be manipulated.

Others had tried to manipulate him. He'd been an easy target in his youth—a boy of good family, but no prospects. He'd taken any hand offered to him and shaken it in friendship. It had not taken many years to learn that some hands held knives, sharp ones. In the army men were always jockeying for position—and they thought he'd make a good stepping stool. They had been very wrong.

And in India— The bile still rose in his throat when he thought of India, thought of Tom, thought of Sunita.

He took a deep swallow of his drink.

What to do about Anna and her lies?

He had known that she lied when she spoke of needing to marry for Madeline's sake, when she spoke so prettily of the poor baby that was to come and the fear that Lord Milson would harm it.

He gulped another swallow of brandy, enjoyed again the burn.

He had known she lied before she even opened her mouth—had felt the lack of truth.

She had wanted marriage, marriage to him. It was as simple as that. She had set the trap and he had walked into it.

Was she a cat playing with a mouse—letting it go only to pull it back, again and again?

He was no mouse.

He slammed the glass down on the table, restraining himself just enough not to break it.

Neither was he a puppet, but he had let her play him like one.

Turning back toward the door he took a step forward.

He released his hand, then curled it as if around the handle.

Holding back his anger had already cost him. What had passed between them in her room could barely be called sex. His mother had sometimes whispered of marital intimacy, and even that term seemed too lush for what had just happened.

A week ago when he had first proposed he had at least thought that the bedding would be grand. What man would not want Anna Steele in his bed? He'd certainly woken from enough dreams of her over the years with his body crying for the reality of her touch.

He refused to believe that what had just happened was what he was destined to live with.

He would have her and her seductive passion.

He stepped toward the door, her door. He would confront her, get the nonsense of her lies out of the way, and then perhaps the passion that should be there could honestly take its place.

Taking another step, he paused.

He would let his emotions cool and then he would woo her, wrap her in his web, and force her secrets from her.

He smiled and turned toward his own bed.

Tomorrow would come soon enough.

Anna stared at her father as he reclined back in his well-upholstered chair, unable to believe what he had just said. If it had served any purpose she would have stood and marched from Milson's house without another word.

Unfortunately she knew her father too well to believe it would do any good.

"You probably are crazy," he repeated, lifting his glass and taking a large gulp. "There is no other explanation for your behavior. Married over a week and you don't even let me know until now."

"Maddie knew. Surely she must have told you." Anna glanced at her half sister, looking for help.

"That's not the same and you know it," her father added. "A good daughter would have waited for my approval and would certainly not have avoided me."

"I have not avoided you."

"How long have you been back in London without visiting me to give me your news?"

Anna swallowed the desire to argue; she had put off visiting for almost a week—not eager to see either Milson or her father. Milson, at least, had the grace to have been too busy to attend this meeting. She had fancied he might when she sent the note announcing her planned visit that morning.

Her father continued, "You have always acted irrationally. You would have married Lord Adam if you'd been right-minded. What sort of woman turns down a man because he's upset that she bought a house? Any man would be upset if his wife bought a house without telling him." And another swallow.

"Now, Father." Maddie tried to speak up. "You must understand she was still in shock from Christian's death. It was no wonder that she didn't act rationally."

Anna pulled in a calming breath, looking around Maddie's formal parlor. "I was not his wife. We had not yet married. I spent my own funds to buy a lovely home, a gracious home. Is it unreasonable that I did not wish to live with Lord Adam's mother, three sisters, and I don't know how many cousins? I see nothing irrational in a person spending their own money to buy a home—and it was a sound investment. What I did find irrational was Lord Adam attempting to forbid me to spend my own money even before the wedding—and then going to the broker and trying to cancel the sale when he had no rights."

"Your cousins saw it very differently. Sensible men they are." Draining his glass, her father poured another from the decanter of clear liquid. He pretended it was water, but gin was far more likely.

"My cousins?" Anna forced her shoulders to relax, forced her voice to stay calm.

"Yes, the Townsends, your mother's nephews from America. Haven't seen them for years, but they stopped by a few days ago. A pity I didn't know about your marriage then or we could have commiserated on that as well. They would have understood how wrong it is for a daughter to marry without her father's consent."

Anna paused for a moment, unsure whether she should pursue her cousins' visit or argue about the lack of need for her to ask for his consent—not that there had been time to gain it, given the circumstances.

Her cousins were clearly the higher priority. "And what did you talk to Ernest and Nathanial about? I am surprised that they visited. I had not known you were in contact since Mother's death."

Her father pushed up from his chair, almost without a wobble, and walked to stand in front of her. "I was a bit surprised myself when they called. But once they explained that they'd heard rumors about your behavior and were concerned, I understood."

Anna closed her eyes and held them shut for as long as she could without provoking question. "And what exactly did you tell them?"

"That you had never seemed to have the proper

sensibilities of a daughter. That you shuttled me off here to live with my Maddie"—he smiled at his other daughter—"and Milson without a care in the world. That you never took the most sensible of advice and were headstrong in following your own foolish plans."

Had she really considered, even briefly, coming to her father for help? She remembered how coldly he had treated her after she broke with Lord Adam. She'd had to avoid his company for months for fear of being yet again berated. The only way her father would have stood up for her was if there'd been something in it for him, something large.

She turned to Maddie, seeking some sign of understanding from her sister. "And of course you've already said you also told them about how crazy I was to want my own home, one that I chose and loved, instead of Lord Adam's dark Mayfair town house. Was it really so insane to want a home of my own?"

Maddie looked away. She had looked away for as long as Anna could remember.

This was her family.

Was it any wonder that she had gone to such extremes seeking help, seeking safety?

Her father took another step closer, leaning over her. She could smell the gin now. "What is insane is a woman marrying so quickly without giving her family any notice. I may need to talk to your cousins about it. They had such sensible ideas."

"I think, Father, that you may have missed one of the crucial aspects of my marriage. The only opinion that matters now is my husband's. What my cousins or you think is no longer relevant. Only Struthers has say over me."

"Then where is your husband? Don't you think that

he should be here with you, paying a proper visit to your father?"

If only she knew the answer to that question. They had returned to London the day after the ceremony. She had barely seen him since.

Anna placed the garden shears carefully in the basket and looked about her high-walled garden. It was good to be home. The morning visit to her father had left her in need of fresh air. The garden was nearly dead this time of year, but a few of the branches had been damaged by heavy winds while she'd been away, and she wanted everything perfect when the first leaf buds began to sprout.

Everything perfect. It was only here, in the garden, that she even strove for such a thing. Life had a habit of fooling those who sought perfection and so she had long given up trying. Even here things never went as expected. How many times had she babied one flower only to have another rise in stunning glory?

Accept life as it was. It seemed such a simple sentiment and yet was so hard to practice.

She'd barely seen her husband in a week.

She pulled the shears out and trimmed one more branch.

About to trim another, she stepped back. No, it was fine.

Making her garden perfect would not fix her life.

The visit to her father weighed heavily upon her—but it had convinced her that she had done right to marry Struthers.

Struthers—his name brought him to her mind when she had been determined not to think of him.

Damn him. Struthers ignored her, rather than controlled her. In fact, just yesterday she had delivered the promised funds to Mr. Jackal. It had been such a relief to take care of one more small piece of her plans, her heart and mind rested easier.

She should be glad Struthers ignored her.

Picking up the basket from the cold ground, she turned toward the house. It was a wonderful house, tall and majestic, but with large windows to keep it constantly filled with light. It was the first thing she had bought after inheriting her fortune and she loved every brick of it.

When she'd told Struthers that she wished to remain living in her own home, he'd shrugged as if not caring at all. He'd given the carriage driver her direction and only glanced at the house briefly when they had finally stopped in front of it. He'd helped her down from the carriage with the most courtly of airs and then announced that he'd return to his own home to take care of matters.

And that had been a week ago. She'd seen him only once since, three days ago, and that had been hardly more than a nod across the street while shopping. She'd been so angry at his cavalier attitude that she'd refused to even consider calling upon him.

She swung the basket on her arm and moved toward the conservatory door.

She was spending too much time thinking about the man.

She blew out a long breath, misting the chilled winter air.

If only he'd been her lover, not her husband, then perhaps their relationship would have stood a real chance.

But enough of that for now—it was time to stop thinking and start acting. There were plenty of things she needed to take care of that did not involve the bloody man.

Swinging her basket on her arm she walked up the few stone steps and across the terrace. The doors to the conservatory swung open as if of their own accord. Her staff was even better trained than she'd realized.

"I was wondering if you were ever coming in or if I'd have to leave the warmth of the fire and fetch you." Struthers's voice swept out the doors to greet her.

Had her thoughts conjured the man?

It took her only a moment to recover. Somehow she doubted Struthers was the type to huddle by the fire when there were things to be done, unless— "Oh, did you miss me?"

Chapter 6

Anna sauntered toward him, smiling. "Were you in the library? It really is the coziest room—and the most private. The rugs are so soft and comfortable."

He should have expected it. The quiet, well-behaved creature could not last forever. It was amazing that she'd made it this long. He'd never considered Anna to be a patient woman—he could think of plenty of words to describe her, but *patient* was not one of them. Seductive. Manipulative. Contrary. Lively. Enchanting.

And beautiful. God, yes, she was beautiful. The cold of the garden had filled her cheeks with roses, and her lips looked like sweet berries ready to be tasted. Her pelisse hid her curves from him, but not their magical movement, that beckoning sway that women had used since the beginning of time.

What was he thinking? Ever since she'd been a girl she'd had this effect on him, inspiring thoughts more suited to schoolboy poetry than the brain of a grown man. Her cheeks were pink, her lips red, and her hips moved in a way designed to put only one thought in a man's mind.

And she talked of warm fires and soft rugs.

The lady knew exactly what she was doing.

Well, two could play that game. This time he would

not be the one manipulated. It was time they began to settle things between them, and he meant to demonstrate who would hold the reins. He let his gaze wander over her, starting with the tips of slippers far too delicate for outdoor wear, up the warm blue gauze of her skirts, over the thick red velvet of her pelisse—did she wear it to remind him of the roses she always smelled of?—then up to her face past those lips—he might refuse to think of them as berries, but oh did he want to nibble them—and up to those warm brown eyes. They smiled at him now, the corners tilted up, but he could not mistake the hint of insecurity he saw within them. He could read her so easily, see hidden pieces he'd never realized in any other woman—indeed, in any other person.

He lowered his gaze back to her lips, waited until her tongue darted out to wet them as he knew it would. "Perhaps you'd best come into the library then and we'll find some way to warm you. I'd hate for you to catch a chill." His glance went back to her eyes, waited and watched as she determined what move to make.

"Perhaps you should help me with my pelisse." Her hands rose to the ties, but did not undo them. Rather, her small gesture directed his fingers to follow. He sensed the distraction in her movements, but let her lead. She was a master at this.

He placed his larger hands over hers, letting her feel their warmth and strength, and took the plush ties between his fingers. He tugged slowly, feeling each loop of the bow release. She sighed softly, as if he touched her skin and not the fabric. When the pelisse fell open he eased it from her shoulders and held it before him, stroking the velvet. His gaze, however, was not on the fabric but on the delicate flesh that lay above the blue of her neckline. He let his breath fall against her skin. "It's the color of roses. Did you choose it to match your scent?"

She blinked at the question and he could see her mind work. "No—although I did like that it was a rich, lush color. It's the same reason I like the scent. I enjoy things that fill the senses."

He stepped forward until only a hand span separated them. He lifted the cloak and ran it over the exposed skin of her chest. "And soft, and rich. I suppose that's why you chose the fabric also."

She shivered at the touch, her eyes turning so deep a brown that they shone almost black. "Yes, I do like things that are rich."

Like me. He didn't like himself for the thought. But he'd been very aware how many more women had pursued him after he returned from India, with his pockets filled, than had ever been interested in him as the younger son of a younger son. She had money of her own. He knew that, but what woman didn't want more? He'd certainly never met her.

His hand had dropped back to his side, taking her pelisse with it. Cynicism was not an attractive trait, but one could not always fight against the lessons that life taught. "I'll call your porter to take the cloak and then we should go to the library and talk. I'll call for some tea to warm you." He turned from her and walked toward the hall.

Anna felt as if the breath had been sucked from her. For too brief a moment she'd felt the flicker of awareness between them, known what it was that had drawn her to him from the start. But then he'd frozen and she'd felt as if the temperature of the whole room had dropped ten degrees—or maybe it was just that while he flirted with her the temperature had risen by several degrees.

She forced the corners of her mouth up and followed Struthers into the hall.

And he'd said he would call for tea—it was her house, that should have been her role—only it wasn't her house anymore. It was his.

It was good that he'd pulled away, reminded her of how things really stood between them.

But even as she had the thought her eyes were drawn to his broad shoulders and how tight the fabric of his jacket stretched. Her fingers twitched with the desire to smooth it out and see just how much give there was. She didn't imagine it was much. His valet must help him in the morning.

"Won't you be seated?" Struthers asked as they entered the library, gesturing to the delicate rosewood chair beside the fire.

He was doing it again, acting like he was the host and she the guest. The worst part was she could see that it was not an act on his part. His actions were completely natural.

"Actually that's my chair." Without another word she moved to the large cozy wing chair that sat to the other side of the fire. Sitting, she smiled at him, trying not to look like a child who has stolen the last cookie.

He glared at her and she could read the discomfort on his face as he glanced at the remaining seat. He would probably crush it if he did sit, and she wasn't actually sure he'd fit. His vexation lasted only the briefest flash and then he smiled, perhaps the first genuine smile he'd given since this whole mess began. It was hard to remember when last he'd grinned down at her, his eyes crinkling about the edges. He understood her small victory.

"You will forgive me if I stand. I find I think and speak much better if I can pace a bit," he said.

"Of course." She knew exactly what he meant. Words did flow with ease when one could move about.

He turned from her and solemnity swept down his features. "We must speak about how things stand between us. I find it hard to believe that we haven't spoken about it before now. Ours has been a most uncomfortable way to begin a marriage."

Speak about it! She was a mature woman, but surely he didn't mean they should actually discuss . . .

"Oh, get that look off your face. That's not what I mean at all. That, I have faith we will resolve."

How had he known what she was thinking? But clearly he had. "Then what do you mean?"

"I mean this." He came to stand in front of her, but swung his arm wide. "Our basic living situation. You brought this upon us, but do not seem to have thought beyond our wedding night."

"I am still not sure exactly what you refer to, sir."

"I do believe you could call me Alexander, or Alex, or at the very least Struthers. You have called me by all of those in the past."

"And a couple more names I could mention."

"But you won't—being the good wife that you are—or will be." The hint of a smile had returned to his eyes, but it was far from the one he'd worn previously.

Good wife, was that what she was to become? She had wanted this discussion, been ready to demand it, but now that it was here she did not feel ready. Her idea of a good wife and his were bound to differ. Still, she would try. "No, I won't—Alex." The name felt strange on her lips. The boy she had known was an Alex. This man was not.

"Good. In that case let us begin with the most basic of living situations. You mentioned that you wished to remain living here, in your house. I am thinking that perhaps we should remain separate—for a while, until we are . . . more settled. You have a most curious expression. Whatever are you thinking?"

"Just that your plan sounds workable." It did seem a sensible plan for two people who did not know each other well.

"We are agreed then. I will continue to reside at my house and you at yours—at least for the present. At a later date we may decide to change the arrangement."

"Yes." It was beginning to make sense. Perhaps he only wanted the chance to become better acquainted before the forced intimacy of living together. "Do you have a man who keeps your calendar or do you manage engagements yourself? We should be sure to plan several invitations to accept together."

"My secretary handles most such matters and then seeks my approval."

"My secretary works with me in a similar fashion."

His eyes crinkled. "I'll have my man call your man then."

"My woman, actually."

At that his eyes actually laughed, the corners rising high. "I should have known."

"Yes, you should have."

"And what of our announcement? I have held off placing an announcement in the *Times*, but I know rumors will soon begin to flow."

She licked her lips. "I do believe that it is time, something small and discreet."

His eyes focused on her lips for a moment and she thought she read both amusement and the flicker of desire. It was an odd combination.

His words, however, were simple. "Yes, that is exactly

what I was thinking. The barest of facts—let society wonder, but not too much."

"Exactly." They were in accord.

"And what of funds?" he said.

Or perhaps not. "I am not sure what you mean. Do you require money?"

That took him aback. He actually stepped away, so shocked was he at her question. "I was referring to your allowance. I believe that is how these things are done."

Now it was her turn to be shocked. "An allowance? I believe I was clear in our conversation before we agreed to wed that I would retain control of my own monies and you of yours. Do you wish to change that now?" He'd better not. She refused to consider that she might only have made the whole situation worse by pushing for this marriage—it was everything she had fretted about, dreaded.

"No, that was not my intention. I merely thought you might require some more. Most wives regard it as a right to spend out of their husband's purse." She could hear tension in his voice. Did he actually think she wanted his money? The idea bordered on the ridiculous.

"No, I do believe my own funds should be sufficient." He looked relieved also. Had he been dreading handing over monies to her? He was supposed to be a wealthy man and she thought he would have expected to support a wife. Perhaps he was not as well-off as Lady Smythe-Burke's rumors had it. Or perhaps he was merely stingy—that would not bode well for her plans. She pictured Mr. Jackal and his needs. She would need to tread carefully.

"So we are again in agreement," she said. "But there is one more matter. I am not sure of the exact legalities of my accessing my own funds now that I am wed.

Would you have your secretary let my bank know that I am still allowed full access to my own monies?"

"I'll look in to it. My secretary, Timms, will handle it. Send him your information and I am sure he can arrange adequate funds for you."

"I'll do that then." His words were not as reassuring as she would have wished, but they were much better than they could have been. No matter what agreement they'd had before the ceremony, she was all too aware of how little it would mean if he chose otherwise. She'd even heard of witnessed legal documents being found invalid if the husband refused to honor them.

"Yes, do," he said. "I would not want to worry about you lacking money for your pretty things." He glanced about the room and she could just about see him adding up costs in his head.

She did not like it at all. "I do not think you need to worry about that—Struthers."

"And you shouldn't worry either. Mr. Timms is very good at his job. He is more than capable of caring for your accounts."

"But—" She hesitated, unsure how to tell him she didn't want his man managing her monies. She, in conjunction with her bankers, was more than capable of caring for her fortune. "I am happy with things the way they are."

His brow knit for a moment, his eyes sweeping about the room again. "You have a good manager?"

She considered herself a very good manager. "Yes."

"I'll have Timms contact you about the banks." He turned away as if lacking interest.

She closed her eyes and tried not to chew at her lower lip. Struthers did not care about her fortune—if he had wanted her funds he would have asked about her accounts before now. Still, he had not said he would leave things as they were, only that his man would contact her. That could mean anything.

And the blasted man knew it. He was deliberately not giving her a clear answer, deliberately teasing her.

He turned back to her. She sensed his amusement. He was baiting her—deliberately.

She narrowed her eyes, then let her fingers drop to the pearl pendant.

His eyes followed it like a trained dog retrieving a stick.

He glanced up at her face and then, as if forced, his gaze again fell to her chest.

His lips tensed. He knew her game. They were well matched.

Tit for tat.

The thought brought a grin to her lips.

They would see who would win at this game.

He coughed and her eyes swept up to his face.

His eyes were focused on her mouth again. This time they did not slide lower. "I'd forgotten how your teeth slip over your lower lip when you smile—but only a genuine one. When you are faking or merely being polite your upper lip pulls tight and no teeth are visible."

"I hadn't realized. It's something to work on."

"Please don't." He bent forward and swept a finger over her lower lip. "I always worry that you'll rub the skin raw, but instead it just seems to get plumper and fuller. Perhaps you should write an article for some ladies' periodical."

"I have heard of women biting their lips to make them redder, but plumper—I've never thought about plumper."

"Plumper, fuller is very important."

"Is it now?" She leaned forward, aware that even the relatively high neckline of her gown would gape some at the movement. She focused on his lips, but knew that his eyes had dropped to the hint of skin showing through the lace of her gown, to the pearl. "You must nibble your own lips so that I can see. I want to think about the importance of plumpness." She spoke softly, forcing him to come closer. Her gaze locked on his mouth. "Bite. Let me see what happens."

He opened his lips a fraction of an inch. His teeth were strong and white. She couldn't remember ever looking at a man's teeth, much less thinking they were erotic, but as they slipped over his lip and bit down she felt a tremor begin deep in her stomach. His teeth slid back, leaving his mouth slightly swollen. He looked like he'd been kissed and well kissed. She could understand easily why a man would like the look. It captured her imagination and filled her mind with images of what those lips would look like, taste like after they had been pressed against her own.

She kept her gaze focused as she bent toward him until she could feel his breath against her skin. Her tongue darted out and wet her own lips, which had grown dry. She wasn't sure she was breathing at all.

It was one of those magic moments in life that should be frozen to be taken out later. At this second, in this instant, when the desire was hot between them and thoughts were focused on only one goal, nothing else mattered.

Her eyes slowly moved up his face until they met his clear blue eyes. He was staring at her, her own thoughts reflected in his gaze. This was what had been missing on their wedding night, this connection and understanding, this heat and knowledge.

He moved, or at least he must have moved, because suddenly she felt his skin against her own. His lips were not soft—they were firm and invited her to press closer. She resisted, not wanting to move beyond this moment. The want was there, the desire, but so was the risk of losing more than she had planned. Here, now, though, everything was perfect. The promise of more drew her and she could not resist. She leaned into him, settling the curves of her mouth against his.

The movement of mouths was subtle. Too often a kiss changed in a second, going from delicious to too much in less space than a single breath. This kiss lingered, no tongues, just lips and pressure and movement.

A tap sounded.

Her mind refused.

It turned to a knock.

No. She didn't want to stop. Reality could not intrude.

Another knock.

She drew back, her gaze expressing her regret to Struthers. "Yes," she called.

The door opened slightly. She had not even realized it was closed.

"Your cousins have arrived." Jameson's voice seemed to fill the room.

"My cousins?"

"Yes, ma'am. Your cousins from America, a Mr. Nathanial Townsend and a Mr. Ernest Townsend."

Chapter 7

Anna was afraid. It was the oddest thought considering all that had just happened—the great fun of their seduction game—but as she drew back and straightened Struthers could see it in her. There was nothing he could identify that betrayed her fear. Her eyes did not widen. Her breath did not quicken. Her hands did not clench. But still, she was afraid.

Her hand rose to her lips, brushing lightly over them. He wanted to assure her that they were not swollen, at least not more than her own teeth had caused. He opened his mouth to speak, but stopped as the door swung open and two gentlemen entered. Both were on the portly side, but one was tall and blond while the other had curling dark hair.

Gentlemen. He couldn't quite call them that—their grins were too wide and their clothes too coarse. He wasn't sure if it was his own snobbish opinion or Anna's reaction that made him think so. Her smile also was too wide and clearly forced.

The men glanced at him and then away; clearly they considered him of no importance, no more than one of Anna's passing fancies. They looked back to Anna as she stepped toward them.

"Nathanial, Ernest, what brings you here? And how

is sweet Claire? I was not aware you had left Rhode Island. Is your sister with you?" she said, greeting each cousin in turn.

She was lying. He'd known it days ago when she explained why they needed to marry and he knew it now. She smiled smoothly and her voice was not tight, but he knew she lied. She had known her cousins were in London. Why would she pretend otherwise?

"Ah, Anna, it is good to see you. And, no, alas, Claire chose not to come with us. She is well—as I trust you are?" Nathanial said. He was the smaller, darker of the two.

"And why would I not be well?"

Was her voice a trace too sharp? There was something off about it.

Nathanial answered, "Oh, no real reason, although there have been rumors. I believe Lord Adam Darnell said something when we spoke with him this morning."

"Rumors? I do not know what you mean. And why would you speak to Lord Adam? I did not know you were acquainted."

Yes, her voice was not right.

"We had grown concerned by your lack of contact and sought out somebody who knew you well. He expressed great concern about what he was hearing, about the rumors of your behavior—and at a duke's house party. I am sure the rumors must be mistaken," Nathanial replied. "Such behavior would imply that you were not yourself, that there was something for us to be—be deeply concerned about. And it is not just the one weekend."

"I am sure I don't know what you are talking about." Anna turned from her cousins and walked to the window. She held herself lightly, but he could tell something was wrong, very wrong—why else was she not playing the hostess? Despite her words she knew exactly to what her cousins referred. She turned toward him then. At first he thought she sought reassurance, but as their eyes met, as she looked deep into him, she found something that distressed her further and she turned back to the window.

"I was afraid that might be the case," Ernest spoke. "It is why we have come."

"From Rhode Island? You crossed the ocean because of a rumor you have only just heard?" Bitterness leaked into her words. That was honest, at least.

Her cousins did not answer but walked over to her, one standing on each side as if to block her in. Ernest placed a hand upon her arm, his fingers tight. "We are the only family you have. It is our job to care for you."

Struthers was about to announce his identity, but Anna turned her eyes to him and with the merest flit of her lashes held him silent. She wanted to handle this.

"You forget about my father. And I also—" She started to turn toward Struthers.

Nathanial cut her off, "I am afraid we do not, my dear. We spoke to your father just a few days ago and he seems most unconcerned about you. We are in some doubt as to his suitability as your guardian."

"But he is not my guardian. As I am sure you are both aware, I came of age years ago. Why would he even be consulted? And I am trying to tell you that—"

"But every woman needs some help—it is part of their nature." Nathanial spoke again, not letting her finish. "It is why we have come."

The cousins glanced at each other with just a touch of exaggerated sadness, pressing closer to her.

If this went on he was going to interfere no matter what Anna wanted.

She turned her head, staring from one to the other,

and her lips drew tighter. Finally she jerked her arm from Ernest's grasp and stepped out from between the two. Ernest reached for her again and Struthers moved forward. This was not acceptable.

Anna held up her arms. "Do not touch me. Not now. Not ever. And do not interrupt when I am speaking."

Struthers relaxed his step, letting her manage—for now.

"Now, dear Anna, that, I fear, sounds a trifle unreasonable and I don't think you want that, do you?" Nathanial said.

"Yes, Anna, you wouldn't want anyone to think you were unreasonable, now would you?" Ernest added, moving closer again.

Anna paled at their words, but held strong. Her glance met Struthers and then returned to her cousins. "I hardly find it unreasonable not to wish to be manhandled in my own home. I can't imagine that anyone would find it so." She seemed to grow in height with each word. "And now I am afraid I must ask you to depart. I have appointments this afternoon."

"Does it seem peculiar that our dear Anna asks us to leave after such a short visit when we have not seen each other in such a long time?" Nathanial asked his brother. "We were such close friends as children."

"I must say that—"

"Oh stop it, both of you." Anna cut off the discussion. "There is nothing at all strange in a woman having afternoon appointments."

"That would depend on the appointments, now wouldn't it?" Ernest answered. "Are you seeing a doctor?"

Anna glared back at the question. "No, I am not seeing a doctor."

The cousins glanced at each other again. Nathanial

spoke. "So you're not taking care of yourself? We were so worried about that."

Struthers had had enough. He knew from Anna's glance that she wished him to stay out of it, but enough was enough. "I am quite confident that she is taking adequate care of herself and I do believe it is my opinion that matters."

"And who might you be?" Having taken no notice of him previously, Nathanial was more than ready to remedy that now.

Before Struthers could answer, Anna stepped forward. He could feel her dislike of the situation, but she was not willing to give up control. "Gentlemen, I am afraid I have been most remiss in introductions—although I was trying to tell you. Alexander, let me make you known to my cousins from America, my mother's youngest brother's children, Ernest and Nathanial Townsend. And gentlemen, I am afraid that as you have only so briefly arrived in London you will not have heard my wonderful news. Let me introduce you to my husband, Mr. Alexander Struthers." She sounded almost challenging as she finished.

Two sets of teeth that had opened at her familiar use of his first name slammed shut.

"Husband?"

"You can't have."

"We'll have to see if this is legal."

"Most unexpected."

"You little bitch."

Struthers could not tell which of the cousins had said which words, and the last he heard only asundertone—that soft-spoken whisper so easily denied. His fists curled even so. Nobody used words like that about a woman in hearing and certainly not about Anna. He still didn't know what was going on here, but one thing was very clear. "I believe my wife asked you to leave *our* home. Is there a problem with your hearing?" Struthers stretched to his full height as he spoke the words.

Nathanial glanced at his brother in consultation and then stepped toward the door. "No, no problem at all. We just wanted to be sure that Anna was fine."

"I can assure you that she is." Struthers took another step forward and Ernest followed his brother.

They stood in the doorway for a moment, hesitating—unwilling to leave, but not yet ready to take a stand. "We'll visit again at a more convenient time, dear cousin," Ernest said as they departed.

"That sounded more like a threat than anything else." Struthers turned to Anna as he spoke.

She had returned to her spot near the window, but this time faced into the room. Her back was straight and her hands appeared relaxed, but he could see the rapid pulse of the vein that beat along her neck.

"Are you going to tell me what that was about?"

Anna heard the words as if from a great distance. Her mind was too numbed by the threat her cousins presented. Even now, even married to Struthers, she could sense what they wished to do. She could still feel them pressed against her, crushing her.

And what if Struthers heard the rumors and believed them? Her stomach curdled at the thought. No. He knew her. He knew she was sane.

She heard the soft tread of his shoes upon the carpet and focused her eyes as he stepped toward her. She forced her mind back to his question, trying to find a reasonable answer. Was she going to tell him what it was all about? If only she had more time—

She started to speak, started to tell him everything—and then she pictured her father. She had told him the truth, begged him for his help so many times in the past. How could she trust Struthers when she did not trust her own father?

Oh, she knew that Struthers was not her father, knew that he was a better man, but what of the rumors Lady Smythe-Burke had spoken of? Anna knew far better than to believe rumor, but it would be foolish to trust too quickly; far better to play it safe. There was no good way to tell a man you were rumored to be insane. "As you heard, they are my cousins from America, the sons of my mother's younger brother, Franklin. I haven't seen them since shortly after I inherited my Uncle Charles's fortune. They were not pleased that I and not they received the funds. I do believe they thought that as they were men and I only a poor female, they should have received the vast majority of my uncle's interests. I feel sympathy for them, but no responsibility. My uncle left his estate in the manner that he wished."

Struthers pursed his lips and stared at her across the few feet that remained between them. "Why would your uncle have left it all to you? It does sound strange to overlook the men in favor of a woman."

He didn't believe her explanation. She could see it in his eyes and in that strange tilt of his mouth. She couldn't remember ever having such a sense of someone else's distrust. She had not lied, she had merely chosen which pieces of the truth to release. She had not lied either when she told Struthers she needed to marry him because of Maddie and her husband, rather she had just not told the whole truth. He had known it then and he sensed her reluctance now also. She wasn't sure which was odder, her absolute certainty of what he thought or that she felt he had the same certainty about her.

She pursed her own lips. "My mother had always been her older brother's favorite. I do not know whether it was a case of distance making the heart grow fonder or whether it had always been true. He left his estate to her and the heirs of her body, instead of his younger brother's children. His will was slightly strange in that respect—only his actual blood relations could inherit. I don't know what other type of heir my uncle feared, although perhaps he just wished to keep the funds from my father. My uncle apparently never considered him good enough for my mother. He may have been afraid of what my father would do with such funds. In any case, my mother died a few short weeks after her brother and all the funds came to me. It is not really such a complex story, despite what my cousins may believe."

"Your uncle loved his little sister. It is as simple as that."

"Yes." Please let him believe her.

"There is nothing more? No other reason for this strange visit?"

There really was no more to it than that, Anna thought. It was true there were more layers than that, but it was still the fundamental truth. She could tell him the rest later—when she knew him better. "No, nothing more." Her lips felt dry and tight, as if all the freshness and moisture had leached from them, had leached from her. She flicked her tongue over them.

Struthers's eyes swept over her face as she spoke. He seemed particularly fascinated with her mouth. She could sense his further questions, and yes, damnation, his lack of faith in her answer.

Stepping back, he turned and crossed the room,

heading for the door. "If that is all, then I will leave you to the errands you mentioned."

"Oh." She hadn't meant to say anything, but the sound slipped out.

He hesitated when he heard it, but did not turn back to her. "I had planned to attend the Hendersons' soiree this evening. Did you receive an invitation, or should I have my porter forward you mine?"

"No, I have my own invitation. I had not decided yet if I should attend."

"Well, that's that then. Perhaps I shall see you later."

"Yes, perhaps."

Then he was gone and Anna was left in the room.

Alone.

He didn't know what he was going to do. For a man who always had a plan of action, it was a most odd state. He stared down the front stairs of Anna's house as he waited for his curricle to be brought about.

His wife was lying to him.

He hated it.

He knew that people lied every day, harmless little social lies and larger ones of devious purpose. He wasn't even sure which type of lie she was telling. Her problems with her cousins truly could be as simple as she portrayed. He had no reason to believe otherwise. Why should he doubt her? Because he knew. He didn't know how he knew, but he did. She was not telling the truth—not the whole truth.

It could be the simplest of social cover-ups. Perhaps one of her cousins had tried to kiss her at some point and she'd scorned him, or perhaps there had been some childhood dispute that had never been forgotten—or forgiven.

Or perhaps there was more to the inheritance story than she told. Anna might have played up to her uncle hoping to receive the majority of his estate after his death—only the uncle had not been that old when he died, if Struthers remembered correctly. Anna had spent some time in the Americas when she was younger. He couldn't remember who had told him, but he was sure someone had.

How was he supposed to trust her when the past years had left him with such feelings of betrayal? He had trusted Robert and Thomas and they had tried to rob him of everything. And Sunita, he could not even bear to think about her. No, trust was something that needed to be earned, and Anna was proving he could not trust her.

He had come to her today to find a way for them to move forward—and to get Anna back in his bed—that did not require trust. He was determined that the next time they were together it would be all he had imagined.

But her lies and the mystery presented by her cousins made it impossible to see any forward motion—well, perhaps that was not true. He'd enjoyed their seduction game. This time he would simply apply himself with more purpose.

Women were always vulnerable afterward. He would use that to his own advantage.

The clatter of wheels on flagstones caused him to raise his head as his carriage pulled into the street from the mews.

Anna sank down on the settee after Struthers left the room. Her fingers began to tremble and she folded them in her skirts. She hated this feeling of vulnerability. She pulled a deep breath into her lungs and held it, released it. This was nothing she could not handle.

It had been unexpected to have Nathanial and Ernest arrive today, but she had known they would contact her at some point. It would have been easier if it had been after her marriage were more widely known, but it had been fun to watch their mouths open and close like fish blowing bubbles. If she had not been so nervous she would have enjoyed it immensely.

And she had been very nervous. Her mind had lost its customary edge because of it. She should have handled both her cousins and Struthers better.

Well, that was all spilled milk now. The important thing was to form a new plan—something that would both make her cousins understand how the situation had changed and allow her to manage the fact that she now had a husband.

And her husband—what was she to do about him? It galled her that everything depended on him.

For the first time in years she had no power.

She jerked up as the door swung open again. Had Struthers returned? Despite her fears she looked up hopefully.

The angular female shape that entered was unfortunately distinctly not that of her husband.

"I have learned more of Struthers." Lady Smythe-Burke took a chair without asking.

"You have?" Anna turned toward her.

"Yes, although there are still many questions. Apparently Struthers took all his army pay and with a couple of fellow soldiers, a Mr. Thomas Peterson and a Mr. Robert Morris, invested in a tea plantation. Despite their best efforts things did not go well. There was native unrest and the crops never developed properly."

"So he did not really come back with a fortune?"

"Be patient, child. His partners grew restless and decide that they wished to try another venture—shipping silks. Struthers maintained that the land would produce and that they should hold course. Then disaster struck. A fire swept through their land and they were ruined."

Lady Smythe-Burke settled herself back as if waiting for Anna's opinion.

Anna just sat and waited. There was clearly more to the story.

Lady Smythe-Burke nodded and continued. "Apparently Struthers still held out hope. He was convinced that if they planted one more crop things would turn around. He sold all his belongings and found enough native help to continue."

"I am just not seeing the scandal. What rumors could there possibly be? I gather that everything developed as he planned and that is where he earned his fortune."

"Wrong," Lady Smythe-Burke said with some triumph. "The land failed to grow anything and his partners left, telling him to do what he wanted with the land. They were through."

"So?" Anna could see that Lady Smythe-Burke expected some response.

"It is there that things turn strange. His partners found some additional funds somewhere and finally invested in a cargo of silk. Struthers stayed on his burned-out plantation with only a few natives for company—there were those who claim he had gone native himself—taken a native wife and all."

Anna would have liked to ask more about that, but she didn't want to interrupt Lady Smythe-Burke now that she was finally talking.

"And then two things happened," Lady Smythe-Burke

continued. "First a storm came up and the partners' ship was lost, then rubies were discovered in the hills of the plantation. Struthers had a fortune and his partners lost everything. They tried to claim that they still had a stake in land but Struthers presented papers showing that he had bought them out at pennies on the pound from an inheritance he had received. They cried forgery. They even claimed Struthers had set the first fire to drive them out."

"The first fire?"

"I get ahead of myself. During the worst of the arguing over who owned what a second fire swept through. This time it had clearly been set. All of Struthers's servants—including the native wife—died, along with one of the partners, Mr. Peterson."

Quiet ruled for a moment. Anna's mind churned with the plethora of information. There could be so many different explanations for it all. "What happened then?"

"That's where it gets strange. Struthers gave half the money to Mr. Morris without argument, invested the rest in his uncle's shipping, and came home to England. He has said nothing more about what happened and his partner has also been silent. Nobody knows the truth—and so they can only speculate."

Anna rose and paced. It was hard to know what to make of the story. If Struthers had been innocent of wrongdoing, why had he held quiet? But then she knew how little relation rumor could have to truth. "I am not sure if this helps me."

"I didn't expect that it would, but I thought you had a right to know. Now send for tea and let us get down to important matters."

Important matters—what could be more important that this? "Of course." Anna turned and called for refreshment. She'd rather have sherry than tea, but it was probably too early for that.

Lady Smythe-Burke leaned forward, back ramrod-straight. "Now I don't know why Struthers has not yet placed an announcement in the papers, but he had best do it quickly. Your colonial cousins have begun to spread nasty accusations and they must be stopped immediately."

"The announcement will be there tomorrow. And the accusations are nonsense. There is no evidence to back them up."

"When has that ever changed society's opinion? And even if your cousins cannot now have you committed, gossip can hurt. I cannot imagine you want the world speculating on your mental condition, nor on the plans you have with Mr. Jackal."

Anna closed her eyes and wished this would all go away. "Nathanial and Ernest were here this afternoon. Struthers met them."

"So he knows everything then."

"No, I have not yet decided that I trust him—and after what you have told me . . ."

"It is still best that you tell him. I can understand why you hesitate, but it is better you head off the rumors before he hears them. If you explain to him he will understand. He knows you are not insane or he would not have wed you."

"Are you sure? First I say no and then I say yes. I did not speak to him for years and then I throw myself in his arms. Are you sure he will understand—or that he will not see his own opportunity to take my fortune for his own use?"

"That is your fear speaking."

"Do you really think so? Then why did you share his history with me?"

Lady Smythe-Burke was silent.

"Yes," Anna said. "That is the problem. I am almost sure that he will understand and support me. I almost believe I can trust him. I almost have faith he will send my cousins home. But—and it is a rather large *but*—I am not positive."

Lady Smythe-Burke looked solemn, but spoke reassuringly. "I would not have suggested that you wed him if my confidence had not outweighed my doubts. Even after all I have told you today I think you must have faith, you must trust he will understand."

"But can a man ever understand?" Anna stared down at the rug. "How could he? He has never been powerless. You convinced me I must marry Struthers because it was the only way to save myself from the threat my cousins presented, the only way to be sure I didn't end up locked in an asylum for the rest of my natural years."

"It was." Lady Smythe-Burke spoke with firm confidence.

"Well, I am not sure I am better off now. You want me to tell the man who has complete power over me that my own family thinks I am insane? You wonder that I fear to reveal such a fact? Reveal it to a man I hardly know?"

"Yes. There is not a choice and you know you are better off with Struthers. In your heart you know that."

Lady Smythe-Burke was right. Anna raised her head. "It is only my fear speaking. You are of course correct."

"Of course."

"But do I really need to tell him? Is there any purpose? My cousins will leave now that they know they will gain nothing from me. Rumors will fade fast."

"Even if the rumors fade—and I am not sure they will—are you sure your cousins will give up? They have much to lose—as do you. Do you think they will do the sensible thing and scuttle back home?"

"I do not see what they can do. I may not be happy that Struthers now has power over me, but he does. They can do nothing."

"Would they resort to violence?"

"Violence?" She asked the question although she feared she knew the answer.

"If you were dead, I do believe their problems would be solved."

"But as my husband, Struthers would inherit. Except—I forget my uncle's will. You are correct. Only direct blood relatives of my uncle can inherit. I am the problem."

"You or any child you might have. Your marriage does present them with a quandary."

Anna stood and began to pace again. "I cannot believe they would resort to murder."

"You spoke earlier of not being positive about trusting Struthers; are you positive your cousins would not resort to such extreme measures?"

No, she was not. After the stories she had heard of what happened on a ship transporting slaves, how could she believe they were not capable of violence? Both Nathanial and Ernest had captained such ships and she'd seen the loss rates of their "cargo." She swallowed, hard.

"I will tell Struthers tonight. I am supposed to meet him at the Hendersons' party this evening. I will tell him then."

"See that you do. Now where is that tea?" Lady Smythe-Burke asked.

Chapter 8

She'd lost a little weight. Anna pulled softly at the hanging waist of her new gown. She'd had her last fitting just before leaving Town for Lady Smythe-Burke's house party. The gown had been fine then. She pulled at the waist again. Worry had been affecting her appetite. The gown was supposed to be loose, to flow gently down from just beneath her breasts, flowing softly over waist and hips. She wasn't quite sure there was supposed to be this much flow, however.

The deep purple gauze with heavy black embroidery looked like mourning wear, but the rich iridescent vibrancy of the purple saved it from such a fate. Any widow who stepped out in such a gown would have invited great comment. And the neckline—no, that was definitely not something a widow would have worn.

Well, maybe she needed to make that a *new* widow. Her dear friend Clara, Lady Westington, had been widowed several years and she wore gowns much lower. And Violet Carrington. She'd have considered this gown quite conservative.

But the waist. It just didn't seem to fall quite right. She turned to Sally, her maid. "Should I try a different corset?"

"The quilted one with the rose flocking?" Sally answered.

"Just what I was thinking." She normally wore the heavier corset only when the weather was at its coldest, but the extra padding might make the gown fit just right—and it was important to be just right tonight.

If she was going to tell Struthers the whole story, then she wanted to be sure that she looked her best, that he found her irresistible. She had talked of a woman's power. It was time to demonstrate.

She smiled, slowly, carefully, watching the effect of the upturn of her mouth, how it plumped her cheeks, made her eyes shine. She walked toward the mirror in a slow, easy saunter, measuring the sway of her hip, the extension of her leg.

Yes, she would tell Struthers tonight, but not until . . . not until he was completely enchanted. If he'd been attracted before, after tonight he would be completely bewitched.

She pulled a breath in, watching the swell of her breasts at the lace-covered edge of the bodice. "Sally, fetch me my pearl pendant."

Desire was a game she could win—and the one piece of this whole fiasco she could enjoy.

Struthers saw her as she entered. As she passed through the doors he was aware just how closely he had been watching for her. The violet of her gown shimmered in the candlelight and her dark hair glinted with gold. She stopped abruptly and turned to stare right at him. Although the light should have been too dim to see the color of her eyes, they shone across the room like most precious smoky topazes.

When he wasn't in her presence he forgot just how

beautiful she was. He remembered her features well enough, and that slender figure with all the right curves, but in his memory they were always merely very pretty. It was only when he saw her, saw the life that filled her, the way she moved as if she knew that every man in the room wanted her, the way she smiled as if remembering the joy of a small child—and the way she looked at him, letting him know that she was his—if only for this moment, that he understood her true beauty.

She stepped toward him, making no pretense of having any other target, any other desire. As he watched her saunter forward, all his doubts of the afternoon were forgotten. All that mattered was now. All that mattered was this.

"I am surprised you're here so early." Her voice was low, husky. "I would have thought it a good hour before the gentlemen started to arrive, at least those not forced into escorting their mothers or sisters."

"Or wives," he added, his own voice rough as he realized just how low her gown was. There was a deep frill of black lace that made it look decent, but the material barely covered the tips of her nipples. He was sure he could see a hint of deep pink through the lace. And the pearl pendant. She'd already admitted its purpose. He'd been right about her plans—and she wasn't afraid to let him know it.

As if sensing his thoughts—not that it would be difficult given the trouble he was having raising his glance back to her face—her hand came up and played with the pendant, rubbing it back and forth across her skin.

He swallowed. It was all he could do not to let his fingers trace after hers.

He forced his eyes up to her face.

She was smiling. The full, easy smile of a woman

who knew exactly what a man wanted and was deciding whether to give it to him.

"Not many husbands escort their wives," she said, leaning closer to him. "It's not at all the done thing. It's much more fashionable to arrive separately."

It took a moment for him to connect her words with his previous statement, and then he grinned. "It's not so much the arriving I am concerned with as the departing."

"Ah, I am not precisely sure that it's fashionable to do that with one's spouse either." She leaned slightly back from him, but moved in some mysterious way that his view down her dress was actually enhanced. Her corset was pink, or at least the embroidery was. It would take further examination to determine the full truth.

He reached out and drew her hand to his lips, blowing softly on her fingertips, his breath passing through her gloves. "You've never seemed a woman to do something just because it was fashionable."

"And you know me so well." Her voice was slightly mocking.

"I'd like to know you better." It was his turn to lean nearer to her. He pulled his shoulders back, letting her gauge their broadness.

Her eyes followed the movement. "I wasn't so sure that you liked what you learned the last time."

"Many things grow better with firmer acquaintance." He shifted her hand, his tongue finding the small space between the buttons of her long glove, careful to let no one see.

She shivered. "I had not found firmness to be the problem on our last acquaintance."

"And I can assure you that you would not find it a problem on this acquaintance either. Should I demonstrate?" He slipped his leg between hers, pushing against her skirts.

She stepped back, but her smile grew even wider. "Not here. I do have some standards, despite what you might think."

He pretended to frown. "No seduction on the dance floor?"

"Oh, I definitely would not say that," she said as she twirled away from him. "I am, perhaps, just more subtle than you." With one last smile she ducked into the crush and was gone.

He stood looking after her for a moment, and then his grin returned.

This was definitely a game for two.

She'd forgotten how boring most men could be. Anna kept her eyes glued on Mr. Putty's face and tucked the corners of her mouth up in a careful social smile, not too encouraging, but indicating interest. At least all she had to do was smile and nod. An understanding of men and their ability to talk endlessly about a new carriage was beyond her. Horses she could discuss. She even liked them, admittedly not as much as her Mr. Putty seemed to, but when he'd been talking about his matched set of grays she'd had some genuine interest. Listening to him talk about how much bigger the wheels on his new curricle were than the ones on his old one, and indeed how much larger they were than anybody else's, was definitely something else, however.

She nodded. She smiled. She looked desperately over his shoulder for anybody to rescue her. Where were her friends when she needed them? She knew Clara was still in Norfolk, but surely Violet Carrington should be here somewhere.

It would be good to talk to Violet. Her friend had a lot of experience with men and Anna could definitely use a little help. She was very sure she could seduce Struthers, seduce her husband, but what then? She really wasn't sure what came next.

If only the blasted man would reappear. She scanned the room, looking for that dark wavy hair, those wide shoulders.

Several heads were turned to stare at her. It was impossible to ignore the hush of whispers as she met their glances. She did not wish to speculate what they were whispering about. None of the possibilities were pleasant. She turned away, back to Mr. Putty.

"I went with the polished black. I considered a deep aubergine, so distinctive, but in the end I went with the black. It's always such a classic and with just a hint of gold trim . . ." Mr. Putty droned on and Anna tried to step back slightly to see further around him.

She lifted a hand, rubbed her temple, and peered about.

She definitely hadn't intended to avoid Struthers for the rest of the evening. She'd known men liked to chase and she'd been more than willing to leave him a good trail. Only there were just too many blasted people. If she couldn't see him then he couldn't see her. She would have to find a way to leave bigger bread crumbs.

Struthers leaned against the window alcove of the floor above and looked down upon the dancers. Anna was standing at the side of the floor, talking to some gentleman he did not recognize. Based on her expression she was bored silly. Struthers smiled. He'd have to find some way to entertain her. Of course he'd let her stew a bit more first. It would serve her right for walking away from him.

He needed to talk with her. The marriage announcement had been sent round to the papers and he knew just how important it would be that they appear happy this evening. More gossip would be most unwelcome.

He'd worried when she'd walked away that it would be hard to spot her later in the crowd, but the deep purple of her dress stood out whenever the light happened upon it. He took another sip of his brandy and considered just how long to let her wait.

He didn't know this house well enough to find a private corner, and every nook would probably already be filled anyway. The season hadn't even begun and already there were more people crammed into the house than he could ever remember seeing in such a small space.

And besides, Anna and he needed to be seen. At least at first. Later . . . well, later he had his own plans for winning her secrets from her.

He glanced back down and read the irritation that flitted across Anna's face. She was running out of patience. She glanced down at her glass, took a sip of the pale liquid, grimaced. And then he saw it—the tiniest of shrugs. She was done, finished. She was leaving, and leaving now.

Didn't she realize how important it was that they be seen speaking again, perhaps even dancing?

Even as the thought passed through his mind she leaned over and whispered something to her companion. She rubbed her temple and passed her glass over to him. And then she turned. He was correct.

She was on her way to the door.

He had to hurry.

* * *

If she could only make it to the ladies' retiring room she could take a moment and reform her strategy.

Her husband had to be here, didn't he?

Husband. It was not as frightening as she would have thought.

She might almost be able to get used to it.

Although it was a big *might*. There might be heat between her and Struthers, but she still hardly knew the man—and there were all those things Lady Smythe-Burke had mentioned. She would have to find out the truth of that. It was strange to realize that she knew her husband less well than the other men she had been involved with. Years ago she had known him well, but was he still the same man? That remained to be seen.

Now if she could manage to find the blasted man. Did he really find her so resistible?

She refused to consider the possibility.

Reaching the retiring room, she slipped in. She didn't need to use the accommodations, but she did need the few minutes of peace. She settled down on a stool in the back corner. If Struthers wasn't still at the ball she'd have to decide if she should stay or leave.

"I've heard he's looking for a wife." A slim blonde, whom Anna did not recognize, slipped into the room.

Anna rubbed her head again and slumped down on the stool.

"My mother said the same thing. She's trying to decide if I should set my cap for him. His estates are apparently doing quite well. I gather Lady Westington is helping to introduce him to Town." Another woman, this one dark-haired, followed her companion into the room. They didn't appear to even notice Anna.

It made her feel old. Once, not that long ago, she

would have been the one preening before the mirror, spreading gossip. Now she was very tempted to go home and sleep, not that she could. She fluffed her hair and prepared to leave.

The first woman, really more of a girl, spoke again. "I don't know. They say Masters is Violet Carrington's brother and I've heard rumors about her."

Now that was interesting. She'd never heard about Violet's brother.

Her companion answered, "Yes, but she's engaged to the Marquess of Wimberley's brother now."

"I've heard that, but I haven't heard anything about an actual wedding."

"Speaking of weddings, have you heard anything about Mr. Struthers? I heard my mother whispering that he was caught at an indelicate moment at Lady Smythe-Burke's house party and that wedding bells are sure to follow."

The blonde gave her hair a final finger comb and turned to the door. "I hadn't heard that but I would be surprised. My father considered him as a suitor for me, but despite Struthers's fortune my father found his manner unappealing. I heard him say that Struthers had lived openly with a native woman in India. He even introduced her to his friends. And there were other nasty rumors apparently. Still, I can't believe he'd be headed for marriage. Based on my father's comments I cannot believe Struthers could be forced into anything."

"I don't know. If a woman plays her hand correctly a man can be made to do anything."

Anna smothered a cough.

The blonde turned and stared at her. The girl pursed her lips and clearly wanted to say something. Her companion whispered something in her ear and then they both giggled. Anna thought she heard the words *unreasonable* and *unbalanced*, but couldn't be sure. She kept her demeanor calm.

There was a moment of silence and then the blonde made a polite nod and the two scurried for the door. It clicked behind them and Anna was left alone. There wasn't even a maid in the room to help with torn hems and fallen curls. Perhaps she'd had to run off to take care of an errand or pass on a love note.

She walked to the mirror and stared into it. She remembered her confidence earlier in the evening when she'd felt so sure of her own desirability. That feeling was distinctly lacking now. Now she just felt tired.

Gossip would fade—be they rumors spread by her cousins or the scandal of her marriage.

Her marriage.

She'd been avoiding the very reason she'd come in here—to think about Struthers and what to do.

There wasn't really much choice; she would have to circle the ballroom another time looking for him and then leave if he could not be found. Perhaps tomorrow once the announcement was out people would assume they'd left together. The headache she'd feigned earlier was in the process of becoming all too real. She'd had great plans for tonight, but if the man wasn't going to cooperate there was little she could do.

Glancing in the mirror to check her hair, she pinched her cheeks—she really was looking a trifle pale—and headed out to do battle, or at the very least retreat with grace.

She circled the room once, back straight and eyes carefully aimed just above everyone's heads. There was a great art to not being drawn into conversation.

He wasn't there. She didn't know when he'd left, but

unless he was hiding in some back room drinking port and smoking with the men, he was gone. It was enough to make her scream. She forced herself to deliberately downplay the loss that she felt at his absence. It was only a game, one she'd looked forward to—and she thought he had too—but still only a game.

Tomorrow she would call upon him and put it all to rights.

There she was. He'd just about decided to leave when he saw her on the far side of the dance floor. She looked surprisingly pale, her earlier glow gone. He stepped toward her without thought.

And stopped.

He needed to do this right. He could not appear too eager—not to her and not to those watching.

He pulled back his shoulders and strode in her general direction but not directly toward her.

He would greet her pleasantly, show public interest, and only subtly allow her a hint of his deeper desire.

The plan was sound. Let her cast the lures so she did not realize she was the one being trapped.

Smiling inwardly, he glanced toward her—and stopped again.

Anna was not alone. That pipsqueak of a puppy Lord Adam Darnell was offering her his arm—and damn her, she was taking it.

"Lord Adam." Anna said it as a greeting, but from his smile he took it as more.

"Anna, it has been far too long," he replied, holding out his arm to her.

She hesitated, but there was no way to refuse. "Yes, it has." Placing her hand upon his sleeve, she looked up into his light blue eyes. Had she ever thought she loved those eyes? She did not think so. Now she only knew that she wished he were someplace else. If she couldn't find Struthers she wanted to be home. Her mind spun in the effort to find an excuse to leave.

"Is there someplace we can speak in private?" His tone was carefully flat, but she could see the urgency in his glance.

"I was about to leave."

"It really is most important." His fingers bit into her flesh, letting her know just how serious he was. "I spoke with your cousins."

She had no choice then. Her cousins had mentioned the discussion. "The terrace will be chilly, but therefore vacant."

Chilly would be a vast understatement and she had no desire to be alone with him, even within sight of the glass doors. She hoped he did not take her up on it—maybe it would turn out to be nothing. Maybe he only wanted to speak about how ridiculous her cousins' accusations were, assuming speaking was all he was after. He'd made several provocative comments to her on their last meeting, but she'd thought her refusal had been more than clear.

"That will do nicely." He led her toward the doors.

She let him lead, but was careful to step no more than a few feet onto the terrace and to stay within the shining light of the door. If he wanted more than conversation he was going to be disappointed.

"What do you need to say?" she asked. She would keep this brief, very brief.

Stepping back and forth awkwardly, he glanced first at his feet and then up to her face. "I've heard things, Anna. Things I think you should know."

"Such as?" Her heart beat faster and she had to work to hide her nerves.

"At first I thought it was nothing—just the usual comments made by bored matrons—that you had seemed slightly erratic and not quite yourself. I assumed that it was only idle gossip or perhaps jealousy. But earlier today two gentlemen, Mr. Nathanial and Ernest Townsend, came to see me. They said they were your American cousins and that they had grown concerned with your handling of your affairs. That not all your decisions appeared rational. They made me quite concerned. Anna, is everything all right in your life?" He reached out and grabbed her hand. "Do you need my help?"

"I will be fine." No, everything was not all right in her life; she couldn't remember when it had been less so. That was not the most important point, however. "Why were the Townsends contacting you?"

"We were engaged. They knew I cared about you."

"Yes, but it was years ago. We've only spoken rarely since."

"I told them that and it only made them more concerned. It seemed odd that we should have cared for each other so much and then you called off the wedding and you have hardly spoken to me since." He squeezed her fingers as he spoke.

"You have avoided me as much as I have you since our broken engagement. It was awkward. It does not seem a reason for concern that we did not care to be seen together."

"You think it normal that we could have meant so much to each other and then spoken so rarely since? I would admit to a certain awkwardness in the first months, but in the years since I have never avoided you."

Oh dear, how could she say that she didn't think they'd ever meant that much to each other?

"Don't you have something to say, Anna?" Lord Adam spun her so she faced him fully, placing a hand on each of her arms. "I have worried about you for years—it never did seem right that you should break our engagement so suddenly and with no cause—but I never wanted to cause you further distress. Surely you must know that I still care about you, Anna?"

To her horror he leaned toward her and tried to place a gentle kiss upon her lips; she turned her head so that his lips only brushed her cheek. Her horror only grew when she realized that they were still standing in the light of the door and that several people must have seen him. Pushing hard on his chest she stepped away.

"Lord Adam," she began. "I will always be fond of you, but you must know that I have no such feelings for you. And as for our engagement, my whole life had changed and I found that you were not the husband I needed. There was plenty of reason." He had not forced her to explain her decision when they actually parted company; she could only hope he would not now. Telling him he was a selfish lout who had become more interested in her inherited fortune than in her was surely not the best way to reason with him.

"But, Anna, we could form such a strong relationship—a relationship that was profitable for us both." He reached for her again.

She stepped farther away. Was it better to stay in the light and be seen, or risk further scandal in the shadows? The announcement of her marriage was tomorrow. The shadows must be avoided. "Did my cousins not mention my change in status?"

He pulled himself straight. "I don't know to what you refer."

"I married Mr. Struthers nearly a week ago."

He grabbed her arm, his fingers biting in cruelly. "You lie. I would have heard if such a thing were true. I did hear something about your further misbehavior." His grasp became even tighter. "There has been no announcement, however."

"It will be in the *Times* tomorrow." She was glad that she could say that. Struthers deserved thanks.

Pulling her arms from his hands, she stepped toward the door, praying that Struthers would step through it any moment.

He did not.

She walked through the door to the ballroom, shutting it with a decisive twist of the handle. Let Lord Adam stay by himself in the cold. She heard one titter but ignored it. Lord Adam had not kissed her and she was not going to worry. The important thing was to see if Struthers was there.

A quick look around the room.

No husband.

A slower, more careful glance. She was being watched—and there was that tittering buzz that died whenever she met somebody's gaze. Lady Smythe-Burke was correct, being the center of gossip was not pleasant.

She smoothed a calm expression across her face and kept looking for Struthers.

Still he remained absent from her view.

Well, fine then. She was not going to stay here any longer.

This evening had gone from tense to plain unpleasant.

She had had enough.

She made a quick good-bye to Mrs. Henderson, resisting the urge to ask after Struthers, and called for her carriage. An early night was just what she needed. She'd wake up bright and wide-eyed, ready to face the day.

She stepped through the front door and out onto the stoop.

And then she saw him.

He stood just beyond the light of the gas lamps, cane in hand, hat slightly tilted on his head, leaning against the low stone balustrade.

He nodded as he saw her, and stepped forward into the light. "Could I beg you for a ride? I know you said that it wasn't the done thing for husbands and wives to leave together, but I seem to have misplaced my carriage."

She raised a brow.

The corner of his mouth tugged up. "Well, my groom seems to have taken it home just because I asked him to."

She fought the urge to smile herself. "Most inconsiderate of him."

"Yes. So can I beg that ride?"

Chapter 9

"I do like a man who knows how to beg." Anna's eyes flashed in the lamplight.

Of course she did. Struthers had long ago determined that woman's primary purpose was to make men beg. "Well?" It would be hard to consider that begging.

"Oh, of course you can have a ride. What woman could say no to you?" She walked toward the street, awaiting her carriage.

"You don't seem to have a problem with it."

"Well"—she turned to face him—"I am a trifle peeved by you this evening."

"And why would that be?"

"If the announcement is to appear tomorrow, I did imagine that you would request at least one dance."

"I would confess I had planned to, although dancing is not my forte."

Staring up at him, she silently demanded explanation.

"It sounds trite to say I could not find you in the crowd, but it is the truth," he said. "And then I thought I saw you leaving. I came out to catch you and realized that you had not yet come outside. I decided to await you here rather than return to the crush."

"And waiting for me here was more important than

being seen with me, acknowledging our relationship?" She turned away.

"I did not want to risk missing you. I am a man and I must confess that spending the end of my evening the way I had planned did seem of more import than dancing." He walked up behind her, stopping just a little too close.

The curls of her upswept hair tickled at the bottom of his nose. It seemed strange he'd never realized how tall she was.

She did not move away. Indeed, she leaned back toward him. "Definitely a man. A woman would understand the dance was an important factor in determining the course of the rest of the evening." She turned back, looking over her shoulder. Her smile was flirtatious, but her eyes gave warning that all was not settled.

He tightened his lips to hold back a grin. He considered the outcome of this night very settled. "And I would have risked your saying no had I asked for a dance."

"You just don't seem to notice when I do say no."

"That's because I am waiting for you to change your mind," he said, breathing in the scent of roses that clung to her hair.

It took her a moment, but then she stiffened. She didn't actually draw away, but he could feel the tension in her body.

"A woman is allowed to change her mind," she said.

"Yes—but about marriage? It does seem a little unfair to the poor man." He had not meant to lead the conversation here—he was not a fool.

"The poor man being you?"

He should have seen that one coming. "You know, I may be many things, but not poor. That one, at least, I have been spared."

She turned her head to look up at him over her shoulder. There was a distinct glint in her eyes. "Many things—should I try to guess? Arrogant."

"Guilty."

"Stubborn."

"Guilty again."

"Impatient."

"On occasion."

"Miserly."

"I hardly think so. Perhaps, on occasion, parsimonious."

She laughed softly. "I am sure that explains your interest in giving me an allowance."

"I hardly see how offering a wife an allowance can be seen as being cheap."

Her eyes turned serious. "I can see why you would not think so."

He definitely did not want her serious. Not with the plans he had for the evening. He leaned forward to bring their bodies into contact for the first time. "Do I get a turn? I've got some words in mind."

Her lips turned into a pout. "Not yet. I am not done."

"Go on then."

"How about narcissistic?"

"What? Never."

"Then why do you spend so much time working on your physique? I've known enough men to know the muscles do not come from desk work." As she spoke, her hand slipped behind her back and came to rest along the hard planes of his stomach.

He didn't wish to think about other men, particularly when there seemed a good chance her soft fingers might move lower. "The years I spent in India did not lead to fat. My life there was hard and I still go down to the docks occasionally to oversee the unloading of one of my ships."

Her fingers did not move lower, but they did brush across him in a definite caress. She glanced up at him as if gauging his response. "No opium pipes, then."

"No, that is one vice I definitely do not claim. I cannot say never, but I found everything about it distasteful."

"Something we share, then. And what of other vices? Wine? Women?"

His mouth tensed at her words. There was a lingering question in that he was not ready to answer. Although what would she know about Sunita? Who would have . . . Before he could complete the thought there came the clatter of wheels and her carriage drew up.

He looked at it for a moment, trying to gain control of his unruly body before stepping away from her. Those fingers had moved to quite some effect.

It was a very fine carriage. The high polish on the doors must take constant care—and her cattle—he wasn't sure he'd seen a better matched pair of grays in years. Perhaps he would need to turn miserly if this was how she spent money. He could figure almost to the penny how much she'd spent on the rig and he wasn't sure he considered it wise. The thought cooled his body far more than he had wanted.

He turned to her, carefully keeping his face blank. "May I hand you up?"

She caught something of his change in mood. She hesitated and then very deliberately took the hand that had been caressing his midriff and placed the tips of the fingers on his palm. And then she moved them, letting them trace over the sensitive skin until they reached his wrist.

She leaned toward him and whispered, "I think we

need to stop thinking. It seems to cause us nothing but trouble."

"I don't know what you mean."

"I think you will, if you only consider a moment. I do not wish a replay of our wedding night. I have other ideas in mind."

And then he did understand—and she was right. Their bodies knew what they wanted, understood the chemistry that ran rampant between them, but their minds . . . Minds were much more complicated. They imagined all the problems, all the difficulties—remembered all the anger—rather than simply enjoying what was. Minds reminded him of all the reasons that—

Her breath caressed his cheek. "You're doing it even now, husband. Stop. Just stop. Tomorrow is soon enough for all those nasty thoughts and revelations." As she spoke she pulled her fingers back across his palm until their hands rested against each other. "Help me up. I find myself growing chilly. I do think it is your duty to make sure that I am properly warmed."

He took her arm and, ignoring her expectations, slid his hand up her arm and then down to her waist. His other hand joined it and he lifted her carefully into the carriage, his fingers lingering on her soft curves.

When he released her she did not turn and sit, but rather backed into the carriage, her eyes locked with his. When she lowered herself onto the bench and let her fingers run over the heavy velvet he could almost feel their caress along his thigh. He swallowed, his mouth dry. Her glance dropped to his lips and he could feel her thoughts. Her tongue slipped from between her teeth and played along her lower lip.

He lost the ability to breathe.

And then she patted the bench beside her. The breath

rushed into him and he stepped quickly into the carriage.

He knew her game, but did not care.

Later, it would be his turn.

She moved aside, but not far enough. He sat down, legs brushing.

No, he was no fool.

Could they manage not to think for five minutes? Anna figured that was about how long a good kiss would take—a kiss that would let them know if this was worth pursuing. And if that worked she figured they could go another ten minutes without further thought. And if they managed those ten minutes—well, if they weren't well beyond thought then she'd been a fool all along.

And she had no intention of being a fool.

She knew how this night had to end, with her telling Struthers the truth about her cousins and asking the truth about his past—in the morning when he was unguarded. She would give herself the rest of the night as a break from worry.

With that thought in mind, and swearing to herself that would be the last thought for five minutes, Anna leaned forward and stroked the velvet of the seat beside her, inviting Struthers in.

He responded faster than she had expected, jostling the carriage with his rapid action as the door swung shut behind him. As he settled beside her on the seat she bent toward him, using the slight rocking of the carriage as an excuse to let her hand land on his thigh. His eyes darkened at the gesture, his glance falling to her hand. She squeezed his firm muscles, letting him know that her move had not been accidental. They were both adults and there was no reason for pretense between them.

Not that pretense worked anyway. He seemed to read her like a familiar book. Every time she even stretched the truth he knew. All the more reason not to think.

"Stop that." His deep voice filled the small space of the carriage.

"Stop what?" She blinked up at him.

"I thought that we weren't going to think and I can see the wheels turning."

Damn, he was right. Instead of answering she squeezed his thigh again and leaned toward him until she could feel his breath on her cheeks. She dropped her gaze to his lips, watched as he pulled air in and then released it. Breathing deep, she lifted her eyes to his. The carriage was dim and his eyes looked nearly black. She dropped her glance to his mouth again, letting her own tongue stroke along her lower lip as she thought about doing the same to his. She looked up again. His eyes were locked on her mouth. She parted her lips, breathed deep.

"I love this moment," she whispered.

"I know," he answered, no further explanation necessary.

Three more breaths. Three more up and down glances. Three more seconds of feeling she couldn't wait another moment.

And then together they moved, their lips coming together softly, gently, sweetly.

There was no hurry, no urgency. It was perfect—and yet she felt that each additional second of waiting was agony.

She felt his breath fill her mouth, tasted the brandy that was so much sweeter than the foul lemonade she'd been offered. She hoped he didn't taste that.

"You're thinking again." It was more of a murmur than a sentence as it slipped past his lips.

"I'll try to stop. But you taste so good."

"Hmm," he replied as he pressed his lips more firmly against hers. His tongue eased out, sliding along the crease of her mouth.

She was tempted to open immediately, but resisted for a second, enjoying the sensations he evoked without rushing further ahead.

His hands shifted about her, pulling her onto his lap. She could feel his firmness beneath her buttocks and settled herself more comfortably, enjoying his squirm as she rubbed against him.

"You mentioned wheels turning."

"What?" His word filled her mouth.

"In my head. You said the wheels were turning. The only wheels turning now are the ones beneath us. I feel them through your legs. The vibration tickles me, leaving me unsure if I want less or more."

"Definitely more." His tongue licked over her lips.

This time she opened, giving in with an invitation as old as womankind. He didn't rush in as she'd expected, but rather entered slowly, exploring. The tip of his tongue circled her mouth, slipping into that tender space between teeth and inner lips before making a more direct assault. Her own tongue came to meet his, dancing, tasting, rejoicing.

There was no thought—only pressure, and movement, and wonder.

The kiss grew more intense. The fires grew hotter. His hands moved up from her waist, cupping her breasts.

But still it was about mouths. About how much could be shared without words, without thought.

She opened the eyes she had not even realized she'd closed and stared up at him.

His eyes were closed, his brows knit together. She

could see that for him too the world did not exist beyond mouth and tongue, taste and sensation.

And then his eyes opened, met hers—and thought began again.

She could see understanding form in the deep pupils, sense the moment he realized where he was, who she was.

Their mouths separated in a breath—it was almost a physical thing pulling apart between them.

He kept looking at her, staring at her.

"I planned that for five minutes. How long do you think it took?" she asked, unable to lower her gaze from his.

"I don't know." And then further thought kicked in. "You planned this?"

She smiled. "Well, you did too. Don't even bother to deny it. I've known encounters to happen spontaneously. This was not one of them. You have already implied you were not waiting for my carriage by chance."

He leaned against the cushioned back of the bench, but did not take his hands from about her. "I needed a ride."

"I do believe that your house is the opposite direction from mine and only a block or so away from the Hendersons'. And if you have not noticed we are not heading to it now. I daresay we would not even have begun our kiss in the time it would have taken to reach it."

"My dear Mrs. Struthers, did you just assume I was coming home with you? Awfully forward of you."

"I made no assumptions. That is what the five minutes was about. I figured we would kiss for five minutes and then decide how to proceed," she replied.

"And what decision have you reached?"

"I left the option for an additional ten minutes of testing. I must admit that the kiss was more than satisfactory, but we do seem to have this dreadful habit of being distracted by thought. I can't remember it ever being an issue before. Do you suppose it is because we are married?"

His brow tensed as he considered. "No, I don't think that is it. While I can't deny that my thoughts frequently involve our marriage they do not often start out that way."

"I fear you are right. It is a most perplexing problem. Do you think that is why our wedding night was so bad?" She slammed her lips shut even as the question escaped. One thing a woman learned quickly was that you never cast question on a man's performance in the bedroom—no matter what the truth of the situation. "I don't mean bad—I mean—well—if there were any problems I am sure that they were because of me—and it certainly wasn't bad—it just wasn't—" She stopped and pulled in a deep breath. "I am only making this worse."

"Yes, you are." He did not seem angered. In fact, a large grin had spread across his face and he seemed more relaxed than he had at any point since entering the carriage. "And I am afraid that I must agree about our wedding night. I would not go as far as *bad*, but could we settle on surprisingly mundane?"

"That is apt. I mean, everything did work."

He laughed. He actually laughed. "I never thought to imagine the day that somebody would console me by saying everything did work."

"Well, it is better when it all works."

"I wouldn't know—have you had such an experience—one where it didn't?"

That silenced her. What could a woman say to that? She certainly wasn't about to tell stories, and whatever she said, either she or someone else was going to come out badly. She liked to think it was their fault—she'd certainly never had any complaints. "I didn't say that."

He laughed again. "No, you didn't, and I'll take pity on you and let the specific subject drop. I do think, however, that the broader subject does require further pursuit." His glance dropped back to her lips. She resisted raising her hand to see if they were swollen. They certainly felt that way.

"Do you think so? I do rather agree. As I said, I had planned another ten minutes after the first five."

"I wouldn't want to ruin your plans." He leaned forward and placed another soft kiss upon her lips.

The kiss grew between them as it had before, starting gently and rapidly becoming more. His hands were on her bodice, in her bodice, thumbs pressing, moving—but—

"You're keeping track of time." He whispered the words against her cheek.

"I don't have a watch."

"Still . . ."

"Fine. Yes. I am aware that we have about two minutes until we reach my house and I must decide whether to tell the coachman to wander for a while."

"And?" He somehow managed to nibble on the corner of her mouth as he spoke.

"I don't think so."

That got him to sit upright. "You don't?"

"This doesn't seem to be working."

"It doesn't?"

"Well, it's not exactly not working, but clearly a coach with built-in time limits is not the place for this."

"True." He leaned forward and nibbled again, his hands rising to her breasts.

She batted them away. "Stop. I do need to think."

"Why?" His hands moved again and a small sigh escaped her.

"Because I am good at this. I tend to be good at most things."

"You don't hear me complaining," he murmured.

She hit his hands this time. "Yes, but you're not swept away by passion either."

His hands dropped. He shifted beneath her, letting her feel his erection. "I don't know. I do believe I am feeling quite passionate."

"But not swept away."

He paused. "No, not swept away."

"Then I am not doing something right."

"I don't think I'd agree." He moved against her.

"Would you stop that? Listen. I have decided to invite you in—although given that it's now your house too, I don't suppose it's really much of an invitation, but does it help if you know it's going to happen? Tonight?"

He leaned back against the seat. "I suppose the only price is that I have to listen and partake in this discussion."

"You are such a man—never able to think beyond—"

"It. I believe you just called it *it*."

"Sex, lovemaking, riding the two-backed beast, swiving, diddling—I am sure that I missed many but I am capable of using all the words. I can even call it a good fuck. Only . . ."

He sighed. "Only?"

"Only I don't know what to call it between us yet. On our wedding night the only term that came to mind was *marital relations*."

"Fitting."

"And now—well, now I am just not sure. We have

moments when it seems it will surpass all my words and then sometimes it just seems like sex."

"If I am a man," and he swiveled his hips to demonstrate, "then you are very definitely a woman. There are some things that don't need to be thought out and certainly don't need to be discussed."

"How can we ever know if—"

"Why do we need to know?" She could hear the exasperation in his voice. "Some things don't need names."

It was her turn to sigh. "That is the problem. I'd be perfectly content if I were so swept away that—"

The wheels of the carriage ground to a halt.

Struthers rapidly began to straighten his hair and reached to help with her bodice, pulling the fabric up over her pink corset.

She pushed his hands away, gently this time, before taking over the task herself. "My coachman would never think to knock or open the door without my giving him some type of signal that it was an acceptable time."

"Then why the worry about time?" he asked, pulling the loops of his cravat tight.

"Well, it may be that my groom and coachman would sit atop the carriage all night and never raise an eyebrow, but at some point the neighbors would wonder. As a slightly scandalous single woman I do try to avoid having the neighbors become too occupied in my affairs. The appearance of a quiet existence is always best."

"I can understand that." She could tell he didn't really, but was refusing to let his bother show as he glanced over at her. "You look fine." He rapped on the top the carriage once. "However, you are now a respectable married woman and are allowed more freedom."

A shiver passed down her spine and the faces of her

cousins flashed into her mind. She'd wait a bit more time before risking any further public censure. Still . . . "Do you mean that you don't care if I am scandalous? That I can have my coach stand idle for hours while I occupy it with strange men?"

"Only if you consider me strange. And don't give me that look. You know perfectly well what I meant. And now, wife, I do believe that I have had enough teasing for this evening—teasing of any variety."

The door swung open and she let him help her down, twisting to let her breasts brush against his arm. "Are you sure? I rather thought you liked to be teased."

His face turned toward her, his eyes darting down to her bosom. "Just be aware there's a punishment for teases."

"As long as I get my turn too."

"I believe that can be arranged."

They entered the main hall of her home. A wide staircase hugged the wall in front of them and then curved along the back wall opening onto the upper chambers.

He stopped and glanced up the stairs. "Do you realize I've never seen your bedchamber?"

"Nor your own?"

"My own?"

"I mean here. The first thing my servants did upon hearing the news of our wedding was to prepare you a room. We do want to keep up appearances if I am to be this proper married woman that you spoke of."

He took a step up the stairs, holding out his hand. "Then perhaps you had better show me."

Chapter 10

She was right, Struthers thought. He was a man, and as a man he had one clear goal. Get her clothes off. Get her into bed. He didn't care in the slightest whether it was her bed or his, although he rather fancied seeing her in her own surroundings. All this talk of thought and what to call what they did was irrelevant—at least until after they'd done it. It. Now she had him thinking that way. And thinking too much.

"Get your dress off," he almost growled, trying hard to suppress the strength of his feelings.

There would be time to think and plan when this was done.

She shut the door with a definite click after shaking her head at somebody in the hallway—probably her maid. "I rather thought that you'd wish to help with that."

"Normally I would, but in this instance I think it is better to just move things along."

"So you wish me to rush—not linger?" She eased the edge of the bodice down a fraction until the pink edge of her corset showed. Her pearl pendant drew his gaze to the perfect spot. He thought there might even be a hint of nipple.

He ran his tongue over his lips, wetting them.

He knew he was giving her the power, opening himself up to her spells. He should fight back but in this moment all he could do was follow her lead.

She sauntered toward him slowly, letting her fingers play along the lace edge. She did not push it any lower, rather she came up to him and spun slowly until her back was to him. She turned her neck, emphasizing its long lines, until she could glance up at him. "I do need your help. I dismissed my maid. Despite my reputation I've never liked having a watcher. I trust you don't mind?"

"If that was your maid I noticed with the sturdy figure and several chins, I can't say that I mind at all," he said, although his mind was much more occupied with creamy shoulders and that delightful spot right at the base of her neck. Woman loved it when you caressed them there—and he must admit to being rather fond of the activity himself. He wondered if he could get her unlaced before she'd even realized he'd begun. Perhaps he'd even get that damn pink corset down along with the dress. He leaned forward and blew softly on the back of her neck, intent on finding out.

"Oh, I love that," she exclaimed, letting her head fall forward.

The bloody minx probably had planned the move knowing exactly what she wanted—not that he actually had a problem with that. He licked her where only his breath had touched her, delighting in her shivers. His lips followed his tongue, pressing softly against the delicate skin, and then he nipped, not hard but hard enough to leave his mark.

She jerked slightly, but then relaxed against him, putty in his hands. Although having her pressed against him did make it rather difficult to finish the laces. Still, he was a man and more than up to the task. He ran kisses up and down the sides of her neck as his fingers continued their task.

She sighed and turned her neck further, inviting his lips to meet her own. It was an invitation he was more than ready to accept. He changed position, bringing his mouth down on hers, not tenderly this time, but commanding, taking, claiming. She was his. His wife.

He froze momentarily at the thought. Damn.

As if sensing his distraction she shifted her hips against him, emptying his mind of all but desire.

He pressed back, settling himself firmly between the cleft in her buttocks. He slid his hands down her body, letting her dress follow.

She stepped forward, but before he could protest she shimmied slightly, letting her gown and corset slip to the floor. She turned as she moved back toward him, stepping over her fallen clothing. This time when she pressed against him he found himself flattened against soft, warm, feminine belly, only inches from home. It was his turn to sigh, although in truth it was more of a moan.

Her hands made rapid progress on his collar as she tossed his neck cloth aside.

Then her lips laid a brief kiss at the indent of his throat before beginning a slow journey of light nips and tastes along his collarbone. His hands found their way to her hips, pressing her even closer. God, she felt good. He couldn't remember anything ever feeling as good as her warm body tight against him.

Her fingers moved down his shirtfront, buttons slipping open beneath them while her lips continued their distraction. He was reminded of his own successful plan to have her gown unlaced before she even noticed. She was evidently of the same mind. He chuckled at the thought.

She pulled her upper body back and stared up at him. His fingers dug into her hips, holding her tight.

Her lips pursed. "You laughed."

"It was a good laugh. I was just thinking how similar we are in many ways."

"Thinking again. I thought we had decided to stop that."

He tried to hold his face serious. "It is hard."

"Yes, it is." She moved her hips against him, leaving some doubt of what she spoke.

He slid his hands around her buttocks so he could lift her slightly, settling her just where he wanted her. Only the thin linen of her chemise lay between them. "I do want you, though."

She pressed up even higher. "I don't doubt that."

"No. I mean I really want you, like I can't remember ever wanting another woman. Even when my thoughts distract me, the wanting is there."

Her lips tightened again and then relaxed. She bit on the lower one as she considered and he couldn't resist bending forward to lick at the small indent that she left.

She lifted herself on her toes, and then lowered herself slightly, pressing against the hands that cupped her behind. The motion tore a moan from him.

It was her turn to laugh, low and deep in her throat. "And I want you too. Strange, isn't it, to want something so badly and not quite be able to reach for it without other thoughts prevailing?"

Her tongue darted out and licked along her lower lip. His gaze followed it, his mind filled with the knowledge of just how that lip felt. He longed to taste it again. His gaze flitted back up to her eyes and stopped. She knew exactly what she was doing.

He lowered his glance back to her lips while tracing

his tongue along his own mouth, mimicking her action. He looked back to her eyes again and then down to her lips. He could feel the gentle intake of her breath every time his eyes moved.

Anticipation.

It was a word full of power and wonder.

A scant few moments before he'd been intent on nothing but getting her clothes off and her flat on the bed. Now he wondered. Perhaps a little slowness was required. He wasn't sure that even the actuality of completing the act could compete with the sheer pleasure of the anticipation.

That was an odd thought. He couldn't remember ever not just wanting to get on with it.

Gads, he was thinking again.

He glanced up at her eyes and saw her bemusement.

She dropped her glance to his lips—and then lower. "I'd complain about you thinking again, but it's getting old. And"—she wiggled her hips against him—"it doesn't seem to actually be hindering matters."

He chuckled again, and giving her buttocks a good squeeze he lifted her off the floor and carried her to sit on the edge of her bed. He stepped back and stared at her. Her hair was still up in her elegant coiffure, but her lips were red and swollen, her eyes large and black—and, well, she was clad only in the sheerest of chemises. Even in the dim light of the candle he could see the darkened tips of her breasts and the shadow between her legs. The chemise hung off one shoulder and his fingers itched to push it further. "Lie back. I want to see how you look here, in your own world."

"I've never been one for taking orders," she said even as she complied with his command.

"I am your husband."

"All the more reason not to begin as I do not intend to go on." She settled comfortably back into the richly embroidered brocade of her coverlet. The pillows lay covered in crisp white linen, highlighting the darkness of her curls, but the actual bedclothes were covered in heavy blue and crimson thread and her body gleamed against it. He was reminded of sketches he'd seen of a painting by Goya of a well-coiffed nude woman lying back among pillows. Anna was still loosely covered, but the painting had been filled with a mysterious glory, and Anna had that same strength.

For a moment all he could do was stare. A small smile flitted across her mouth and he knew she understood her power.

She'd have to understand that this worked both ways. He shrugged his shoulders and her eyes dropped to his chest. He'd spent years working in the hot sun and he knew the muscles of his shoulders had turned more than one lady's eye.

Her eyes widened for a moment and her smile grew. She pushed up on one arm so that the translucent fabric of her chemise fell even farther, barely clinging to the tip of one breast.

He swallowed and tugged loose the buttons of his trousers.

She smiled wider. "I think you'd better take your shoes off first. I've always thought a man trapped with his trousers about his ankles was one of the oddest sights."

He shrugged. "It was much easier on our wedding night when I only had a robe." Backing over to a chair, he sat and dispensed with shoes and stockings.

"I am not sure easier is better. I can't remember taking

the time to look at you on our wedding night and I must admit that I quite enjoy the sight."

He kicked his shoes aside and leaned back in the chair. "Back to the wedding night. I must admit that I did look at you—what man wouldn't—but I can't say I savored the experience properly. I don't think I was in the mood to savor anything."

Anna stretched, her hands pulling far above her head, and with the movement her nipple pulled clear of the fabric.

His mouth went dry.

"And what are you in the mood to savor?" she said.

All he could do was stare at the dusky pink tip. He knew exactly what he wanted to savor, to taste, to relish.

He should resist—work harder to cast his own web about her.

"Are you looking at this?" Her arms came down and her hands cupped the breast, holding it out. One thumb brushed over the nipple and he jerked as if she had stroked him—and gave in completely.

She brushed the nipple again and he saw a light shiver cross her. She pushed the fabric down tight over the other nipple. He swallowed as he imagined the feel of the fabric, imagined the roughness of even the finest weave. He leaned further back in his chair, trying to find a more comfortable position.

"You don't look happy." She wet her lips. "I'd offer to come over there and make you more comfortable, but I do think I'd rather have you come over here." She stretched again; the second breast popped free.

It wasn't going to be the only thing popping if he wasn't careful. He stood and, following her invitation, stepped forward, finally managing to finish unbuttoning his trousers as he neared the bed. He sent them sliding to the floor with a casual twist of his hips.

No, she definitely had not looked at him properly on their wedding night. He truly was magnificent. Somehow in her mind he'd still been the boy she'd known, and she'd failed to appreciate just how much he'd changed from the time years ago when she'd spied on him swimming naked with Christian. He'd been beautiful then, but in the way of a young horse or an almost-grown pup—fluid grace over muscles that had not yet caught up to the frame they covered.

But now—it was hard to even think of words to describe his perfection. He had the outlines of some of the Greek statues she'd admired in galleries and collectors' homes, but there was no way to compare this living, breathing man to hard stone, to compare the warm bronzed skin that covered him with pallid cold marble. Her eyes dropped lower. There was definitely no comparison between that and the small, delicate members that tended to endow even the most powerful of statues.

That could be a statue by itself.

"You're staring." Struthers's voice forced her eyes back to his face. "I don't mind being stared at. I often rather like it. But for once I seem to be having a hard time reading your expression."

There were so many possible answers to that. "You tempt me to make a comment about hard times, but that is much too obvious. And if I say I am experiencing awe it will go to your head, and you've already admitted to your arrogance. I could say I was amused or make a humorous but slightly derogatory comment, but neither of us would find it believable. I guess I'll just say I was thinking that I had trouble with words."

He smiled in a way that demonstrated the very arrogance of which she'd just spoken. Men were very proud of their toys—and she had to admit he had reason for his pride.

He took another step forward, stopping only at the edge of the bed. "You are very beautiful yourself."

She wanted to deny his comment. A good figure and a strong face were not enough for beauty, but as his eyes swept over her, lingering in one spot before rushing on to the next, she felt beautiful, more beautiful than ever before. She shifted back in the bed and moved to a sitting position. She allowed one knee to fall to the side, opening her legs slightly. His eyes followed the move with amazing speed, even though her chemise still covered everything. His eyes seemed frozen to the spot. She let her other knee fall and used a hand to inch the fabric of the chemise up her legs slightly.

His breathing grew heavy.

Trying to remember that she had a purpose in all of this—it was not strictly for her pleasure—she stretched a leg, wiggling her toes toward him. "What else do I need to do to get you up on the bed? Do I need to issue a formal invite?"

Once her words were spoken it was amazing how quickly he moved. One second he was standing there looking at her and the next he was kneeling between her legs staring down at her. She wasn't sure she'd actually seen him move.

He sat back on his feet, bringing his head level with her own as she rested against the pillows.

There was a moment of awkwardness as each tried to decide what to do next.

"I think you should finish taking your clothes off," he said after a moment.

"What?" She didn't know why she asked. It did seem the logical next step. It was simply hard to comprehend anything when he watched her like that, as if she were the most delectable thing he could imagine. She grew warm beneath his gaze.

"You do look beautiful in the chemise," he said as his eyes continued to move over her. "There is much to be recommended in the slightly veiled look. But now. Right now. I want you naked."

That was certainly direct, certainly masterful. Temptation to find some smart rejoinder filled her, but it was not as great as the temptation to do as he said, to watch the ever-increasing desire in his stare.

She pushed herself upright, to full sitting position, bringing them eye to eye. She smiled to herself as his eyes dropped to her naked breasts when they came close to touching his chest. Now came the difficult part. She was seated on her chemise and she either had to lift her hips and wiggle it up or else push it down to her waist and then shimmy it past her hips and then—well, he was seated between her legs, which meant that she was likely to be trapped in as ridiculous a pose as he had almost been with his trousers about his ankles. Neither option held any allure. This was not supposed to be so difficult.

"You'll have to help," she murmured.

"Do you want me to rip it?"

"Do you desperately need to prove your manhood? If not, I rather like this particular chemise. The linen is worn to that perfect point of softness."

"Which would make it easy to rip."

"Do you want me to kick you?" Her eyes moved to make it very clear where she would kick.

He lost his grin. "What would you like me to do?"

"If you can push my chemise up past my hips as I lift them, then you can just pull it over my head."

Of course it wasn't that simple. First, there was the feeling of his hot fingers pushing the thin fabric up her legs—she almost fell back into the pillows from the sensation. Second, there was the look on his face as he pushed the fabric past the apex of her thighs and she lifted her hips. She'd never seen the particular visual attraction of that part of her anatomy, but he clearly did. His mouth actually fell open for a moment, and his expression as he closed it, the way his tongue ran across his lips, causing them to glisten, made her insides quiver. Even without her strange understanding of his thoughts she would have known exactly what he wanted. Third, and this was all going to kill her with pleasure if she wasn't careful, he pushed the fabric up over the tips of her breast, grinding it ever so carefully into them. His thumbs followed behind, flicking over the turgid peaks, and then his mouth—she hadn't known his mouth was necessary in the removing of her chemise, but—ohh—ohh—she certainly wasn't going to tell him that.

He pulled back a moment and stared at her. "We were wrong."

"Wrong?"

"Wrong. It's a very good thing when you think. I can feel you doing it, and I like the way your thoughts work."

Before she could reply he'd yanked the chemise up, past her shoulders, past her face, and—and tangled it about her arms, her wrists. He smiled then and in one move pulled her back until she fell flat across the pillows, his hand holding her arms tight above her head.

"On the other hand," he whispered, as he brought his lips down on hers, "I like it when you don't think too."

He shifted a bit, bringing his other hand down to her hips. And then he was in her, filling her.

She would have gasped with the suddenness of it, but her mouth was too busy with his.

He pulled his head back for a moment, grinning with ultimate male satisfaction. "I was afraid we'd never get to it with all the talking, so I thought I'd just move things along a bit."

She made an incoherent sound and raised her lips, looking for his. She was not going to interrupt this by talking any further. He was right about that. Talking was fine, but there were some moments when—

Goodness, he hadn't moved like that on their wedding night.

Or like that.

She shifted, moving her hips beneath him, helping to set the right pace for them both.

Chapter 11

Her hands were still tight above her head and she pulled at them insistently. She wanted to feel him, touch him.

He held strong for a moment, and then released her using his free hand to brace himself up, improving his position even more.

Drat, her hands were still wrapped in her chemise and it was more than she could do to pull them free. Instead she slipped them over his head so that she was in effect tied to him. It did allow her, however, to run her fingers over the satiny strength of his shoulders. Her nails dug into him as he used the leverage of his freed arm to push even higher into her. His other hand dug into her behind, moving her just where he wanted.

Clasping all her inner muscles along him, she twisted to show that she was not so ready to give up control.

They struggled for a moment—each winning victories from the other.

Then there was no thought, only bodies. Salt. Sweat. Musk. Satin skin. The abrasion of hair. The glory of ever-tightening muscles. The wait. The anticipation. The almost there. The tiniest movement that caused them to jerk and moan.

He pulled his head back suddenly, rising above her to stare down, his hips becoming still.

She opened her eyes and stared up, knowing exactly what he thought, what he felt.

And then he moved again, still holding her eyes, making this more intimate than she could ever remember.

His hips lifted and fell, hers rising to meet him.

The sensations overwhelmed her. She felt the climb, the reach, the need to find that release.

She held on, resisted, saw the same feelings reflected on his face—and gave in, soared, felt him come apart above her.

He fell on her in a heap, boneless. Struthers knew it was not good form to crush your partner in the aftermath, but he was powerless to move. He'd never worked so hard to hold back. He still could see her face in that final moment as they both struggled to come last.

He wasn't actually sure who'd won.

He smiled and buried his face in her curls.

"That was wonderful, but I am afraid I do need to breathe." Anna's voice tickled along the hairs of his chest.

He rolled to the side, separating them. She had cupids painted on the underside of her bed's canopy, fat, happy, ridiculous ones.

"They're horrible, aren't they?" She pushed herself up on one elbow. "I couldn't resist them."

"They look like they should be in a bordello."

"I don't know if I should be flattered or insulted. They are all draped, however, if you notice. I didn't need to look at their little willies when I was trying to sleep."

He stared at one particularly obese one. "Is that what you call it—a willy?" He glanced down at himself. "I am not sure I like that."

She smiled at him, knowingly, and then pushed herself up further so she could stare down at him, her eyes following his own gaze. "No, I don't think I'd call it a willy." She glanced up at the canopy. "They would have willies." She glanced back down. "That is— Do you really want me to give it a name, a title?"

He shifted, uncomfortable with her scrutiny. "No, I don't believe that's necessary."

"Are you sure? We could just go with the standards, cock, prick, mighty manhood." She smiled as she said the last. "And I can also just say penis and call it what it is."

"I said it's not necessary." He hoped it didn't sound too much like he was speaking through gritted teeth.

She grinned. She knew exactly what he was feeling. "I've also known of men to give their manly parts Christian names. I could just say Eugene, Claude, or Melvin. I kind of like Melvin." She glanced down at him again.

He was going to swear to only refer to it as his penis from now on. It might sound clumsy, but clumsy was rapidly becoming better than any of the alternatives. "No."

She looked back at his face, her eyes laughing. "I am sorry. I fear I am punishing you for downplaying the importance of using the correct term, *sex*."

"We've moved from marital relations to sex, have we?"

"A good lusty bout, although I do fear that is still not correct." She looked very serious, but the laughter was still in her eyes.

"Do you want me to offer some terms?" He tried to look like he too wanted to be serious.

"That will not be necessary. My vocabulary is quite extensive."

"Then perhaps I can help in another way." He reached up to her and caught her lower lip with his thumb, stroking across it. "Perhaps a little more—experience to help you decide on a term."

She sucked his thumb into her mouth. He needed no other answer.

She stared up at her putti, her dear sweet cupids. They always made her smile, if not laugh. She thought Struthers saw the humor of them, but it was hard to be sure. He clearly had not been earnest in his disdain for the dear little things, but determining humor was proving far more difficult. Did he appreciate that she appreciated them, or did he truly appreciate them for themselves? It was difficult to know.

She rolled over and stared down at his sleeping form. She wanted to run her hands over his well-defined shoulders. Touching him was rapidly becoming one of her great pleasures in life. One night and she was already thinking of him in terms of her life. That was not a good sign. Although given that he was her husband it might not be so bad either.

And she had not told him the full story or asked about his past—despite the hours they had spent whispering to each other. She could try to excuse it because she had given herself the one magic night and—well, there had never been an after sex, just an in between—and then he had fallen asleep, but she knew the real reason. The perfection of the moment had wrapped about her, making the risk of ruin too great.

It would, however, be so much easier now if the words had already been said. Why was she so scared? She knew he would never believe her insane no matter what the rumors. He was not like her father, a man capable of twisting everything to his own advantage.

Perhaps she was as frightened by Struthers's answers

as her own. Did she want to know if he had been dishonest or treacherous? Could she risk finding he had loved another woman? No, she had no wish to consider any of that, not as she lay so warm and snug at his side.

She allowed herself to lightly pet his hair, careful to put no weight behind the gesture. She did not want him to wake now. They'd woken each other enough times throughout the long night and now, as the first traces of dawn lit the sky, she just wanted to relish the quiet of having him here. It had been years since she'd enjoyed the lingering satisfaction of waking with a man she wanted in her bed—a man she wanted to be there as opposed to wanted in the more usual fashion. Although the two did tend to go together. The problem with morning was that so often one did not want those things that had seemed more important than life itself the night before.

Thankfully this was not one of those mornings. She could think of nothing more pleasurable than to be lying here, in the quiet, beside Struthers as he slumbered away.

Only—"You're not sleeping. You're thinking again," she said. She struggled to smile as she realized the moment had come.

Her secrets needed to be released—and now.

He rolled over slowly. He was not smiling. "I was just considering the fact I do not have a clean shirt. I really must return home." He rose to sitting, the sheet falling back from his chest.

She opened her mouth and closed it again. She should have told him last night when he'd been warm and agreeable. Telling this hard-faced man her fears was unimaginable—and it was impossible to imagine his sharing the secrets of his soul with her.

Her dreams of waking happy next to a man who she wanted to be there were dying fast. It distinctly ruined the feeling when the man you were just thinking you wanted gave every sign of not wanting you. Did he regret the night before? She almost asked. She'd know if he lied.

She held herself back. Regret was not what he felt. Staring at his turned face she tried to determine what it was he felt.

Was there anything she could say to him? Anything that would change this sudden chill?

His back was stiff and he swung his feet to the floor without his usual grace. "I will manage without my valet this morning, but for future reference can your porter or some other member of your household tie a decent knot?" He held up his mangled neck cloth.

At least he implied that there would be another morning. "I really don't know. I would imagine that something passable could be managed. I don't know what your standard is."

"I am no dandy, but I like something neat. And do you mean that you are unsure if your staff can tie a knot or are you just unsure of the quality? It will make a difference."

That, at least, she understood. It would have been easier if he'd asked the question directly, asked if she had lovers spend the night—although she certainly sympathized with his not asking. Was he jealous? The possibility warmed her, but looking at his stiff face made it seem unlikely.

Still, it made all possibility of speaking to him of her cousins vanish. "I do not know what skill my servants have with knots and neckwear. I told you last night that as a single woman I must watch my reputation. I have never invited a lover here for a tryst. I cannot say they have never been in my house, because given the workings of society it would have appeared most odd if they avoided calling on me. But my house has always been for me, my sanctuary—mine alone. I have never brought a man here to spend the night."

"Never?"

"Don't look so disbelieving. Never. My father has on occasion spent a few days, but I do not know who ties his cravats or indeed that anyone did. They always look rumpled and he may very well tie them himself."

"We are of course only speaking of what has happened in the home."

She did not bother to answer the implied question. There were some things that just should not be spoken of. She wished his tone did not imply such negativity. He had seemed to accept her past before. But what of him . . . "And when I am at your home, I assume one of the maids can lace me, and I equally assume that you do not have anyone on your staff who has skill with a lady's hair. However, we both know that is not the real question. Have other women—not family—ever regularly spent the night at your house? What type of reaction may I expect from the staff?"

He turned and looked at her. "Like you, I do not know the exact skill of my servants in attending to a woman's needs. I would guess that you are right about lacings and hair. Also like you, I have never . . . entertained at home. Is there more?"

"Not that I would expect you to answer."

He nodded, pressing his lips tight, clearly understanding she was setting the rules on what she would not answer. He finished buttoning his shirt and wrapped the neck cloth loosely about it. "I must be going then. Do you have plans for this evening?"

Did he mean evening or night? She would assume

both. "I had planned on attending a musical evening at the Joneses'. I am hoping that it ends early. I only attend because I am godmother to one of their younger girls."

"I do not think I will be attending that. Perhaps later you might stop by Lady Carrington's. I understand she is putting on an informal evening at home."

"I did not realize you knew Violet." Had he slept with her? Anna had not considered that possibility. She did not want to think of him with one of her friends—not that she wanted to think of him with any other woman. She felt her own spurt of jealousy.

"I became acquainted with her shortly before she announced her engagement to Lord Peter. We flirted some, rode in the park, and drank too much tea, then she made her feelings for Lord Peter clear. Despite her lack of taste in men I still find her entertaining." He was telling her the truth.

Anna drew in a deep breath, surprised at the relief she felt. "Violet is always fun. I would be delighted to visit with her. Will you need a ride home? Is your coachman in the habit of mislaying your carriage?"

There was a distinct glint in his eyes, a hint of the man he had been the night before. "Yes. I do think I'll need a ride."

He'd needed to get out of there. Struthers stared at the near-empty street. In less than an hour it would begin to bustle, but at present night's quiet still clung to the shadows. He'd forgotten he didn't have his carriage even as they'd joked about her giving him another ride this evening. He swung his cane in a slow circle and walked down the path to the street. This was far from the first morning he'd walked home at dawn.

He tapped the walking stick along the pavement as

he went. Discomfort followed him and he did not like it. He'd awoken in plenty of beds with the desire to leave full upon him, but he couldn't ever remember the desire being based on feeling too comfortable.

It had felt right waking and knowing Anna was watching him, her and those ridiculous fat baby angels. What type of woman had fat babies with bows and arrows painted above her bed? And their devilish expressions—as if they knew his very thoughts. It was utterly tasteless and unimaginable—and it made him smile. They were so silly as to be wonderful. He understood exactly why she had them there, not that he would ever have dreamed of such a thing. A man had to have some standards.

He was avoiding the main point. He swung the cane waist-high and let it fall back to the ground. He hadn't awoken wanting to leave—which had made him flee. He hated to admit to such cowardliness, but it was the truth. He had fled rather than admit that he wanted to be there, that he enjoyed her and their light conversation far too much.

And he hadn't even asked her again about her cousins and the full story there. He had come to her ready to spin his web and instead—instead he'd been drawn into hers.

He drew a full breath, swinging the stick again.

It was just the sex. He was a man. She was a warm, willing woman.

It was just the sex.

He wouldn't think about how many times they'd fallen on each other over the course of the night, or consider that he'd never before combined the need to stay with the desire for a morning tumble.

It was just the sex. Definitely just the sex—he needed it to be.

The wall rose high at the corner, blocking all view

of the street beyond. Tapping his stick along the bricks, he wondered if there was a garden inside, someplace private, a sanctuary. Such a place would have been most welcome as he tried to piece together his scattered thoughts and desires.

He heard the sound of wheels as he turned the corner, understood the speed from the sound—but as the hack took the corner too tight, cutting off all hope of escape, he could only think that he should have stayed in Anna's wide bed—as he'd truly wanted.

Chapter 12

Anna lay back against the chaise, a damp towel over her eyes. Her head was pounding and she had no one to blame but herself. Each burst of pain reminded her of the truth.

The night had been wonderful—the morning less so.

The truth remained unspoken.

The light from the window shone in her eyes and she pulled the towel lower. This would not do. She would tell Struthers tonight. There would be no more excuses. It was time to release the knot of anxiety that was her constant companion.

Once they talked they could really begin their marriage.

So why was she waiting? Even as the thought flitted through her head, she sat up, letting the towel fall.

She would go to him now. There was no reason to wait.

Her gown needed to be changed and she would have Sally put her hair up. This morning she had just pulled her hair back in a loose knot. If she was going to see Struthers she needed something a little more elaborate, more alluring. A soft curl at her cheek. The slight disarray would remind him of her hair spread across his pillow the night before.

The tightness at her temples relaxed as she contemplated visiting him.

He was not an unreasonable man. He would understand. Her worries were silly.

And then—her mood lifted further—they could begin this marriage as it should have been begun. Everything that she did now with purpose she could do just because she wanted to.

She paused at the thought. Was she fooling herself? It was hard to imagine starting a life with the man who had left her bed that morning. It was impossible to imagine trusting him.

But the man of this morning was not the man of the night before, not the man she was beginning to know—and he was miles away from the serious boy of her past.

Something had upset him this morning, made him behave that way. Something had set him off.

She didn't know what, but she would find out. Finding things out had always been one of her skills.

Skirts twirling, she walked to the door, ready to call for Sally.

Before her hand could reach for the handle, there was a rap on the door, and then it opened inward before she could answer. She stepped back as it swung toward her.

"I can't believe you didn't tell me. Married more than a week and this"—a newspaper fluttered—"is the first I hear of it." Lady Violet Carrington strode into the room.

All Anna could do was stare at the newspaper. The announcement. She had forgotten all about the announcement.

"I didn't tell anyone." It wasn't much of an answer, but it was all she had. "I wrote to Clara but who knows when it will reach her—although I hear she may be back in Town. I wanted to tell you in person."

Walking to a chair, Violet sat down without asking. Her gown was the freshest of spring greens and very modestly cut. There was nothing modest about the body beneath it, however. Anna had never understood how her friend could always look ready for seduction no matter how she dressed.

Violet nodded, but answered, "I did not realize I was *anyone*. But that is not really the purpose of my call—or at least only a part of it. Last night I heard various rumors about you. First, I heard a couple of old birds wondering if you'd a few bats flying about your attic. They seemed to think you'd been allowed too much freedom for too long and that now you were doing unmentionable things in the halls at house parties. It was nonsense of course, but there was a distinctly unpleasant taste to their words. Just as I was getting concerned, Lady Dander arrived from the Hendersons' and the whole room filled with murmurings of you and Lord Adam Darnell. Speculation that the two of you had reunited after all these years flowed around the room when I stopped at the Heckels' late last night. I disregarded it—I do know you. But then I opened the paper with my chocolate this morning and saw the announcement. You and Struthers. A week ago. What on earth have you been doing with yourself, Anna?"

"They were talking about me and Lord Adam?" Anna sputtered, ignoring the other rumor. "I cannot believe it. It was not even really a kiss—his lips only brushed my cheek. There was nothing to say."

"You know better than that, Anna. With women such as us, society will always find something to say. And if nothing happened, why did you kiss him at all—and on a lonely terrace?"

"He tried to kiss me. I did all I could to avoid his

attentions. As for the terrace, Lord Adam told me he needed to speak to me privately. It was such a crush at the Hendersons' that I could think of nowhere else to go."

"You should have been smarter. I know that you know better. Never be alone with a man, unless you want to be."

"I do know better. I intentionally stayed near the door and in the light of the ballroom. I did not realize that he would still try to kiss me and that we would be seen. I thought I was doing the safe thing. I have known Lord Adam for years. He has rarely shown any interest in me since I cried off."

Violet said nothing, but stared straight at her.

"You are right," Anna added. "He did make an improper suggestion a few months ago, but I disregarded it. Many men, thinking only of my reputation, make such suggestions. I do not put much weight on them."

Violet still remained silent.

Anna considered. "That is why I stayed in the light. I wanted to discourage such behavior. It never occurred to me he would risk public opinion. Lord Adam has always been much more concerned than I with what people think."

"Then he must have had some purpose. You should think on that. And what does Struthers say?" Violet asked.

"I did not tell him. I thought there was no need. It really was nothing. The brush of lips on a cheek."

"Then why not tell him?"

"I had other thoughts on my mind? I do not believe I was trying to hide it from him. Truly."

Violet sighed. "Men are difficult, but in my own experience truth is the only way. Things tend to grow way out proportion if you are not careful. But speaking of men, where is your delightful husband? I did consider him once, you know. He does have quite a way about him."

Anna sat down across from Violet and tried to decide where to begin, how much to say. Violet's words about truth had only magnified Anna's own beliefs and her feeling that she had put off telling Struthers for too long already. She would give herself a moment to choose the right words. "He is not here."

"I can see that, but where is he? Not still asleep, surely? Have you worn the poor man out?"

A slow rise of heat spread up Anna's face. He should have been tired out, but still he'd left at the first sign of dawn. "No. He left early."

"Left early? Isn't that just like a man." Violet settled back comfortably. "He must know that you'll be over-run with callers today wanting to offer their congratulations, get a sight of the happy couple—and of course see if they can detect any sign that you did kiss Lord Adam last night and that all is not well between you and Struthers. Society does so love a couple that can't stay happy for even a week."

"I am sure he had important matters to attend to and that he will return as soon as is possible."

"Do you really think that or do you just wish it?" Violet leaned forward and her face grew serious. "I may tease you about not telling me, but I am concerned. It is unlike you to marry a man in such a rush. I was unaware you even knew Struthers. I am very aware that you are avoiding telling me the whole story."

It was Anna's turn to lean back and stare at the ceiling, giving up all pretense of ladylike demeanor. "I've actually known him for far longer than I've known you. He was a school friend of my first fiancé. I was hardly out of short skirts the first time I met him."

"But I have never seen you together and Struthers never once mentioned you—and I know the man quite well."

Anna felt her gut tighten—she was definitely jealous. "Not too well, I hope."

"Sit up and look at me. No, not too well. If I had not been involved with Peter things might have been different, but definitely not too well. I am, however, glad to hear that note in your voice. You do care about the man."

That caught Anna by surprise. "Yes, I suppose I do. Perhaps I always have. It is really too soon to be sure. I sometimes think that I am truly beginning to care, but in truth I know so little of the man he has become. It would be imprudent to care too much before I know more."

"And does he care about you?"

Anna straightened up and looked squarely at Violet. "I don't know. How does one know? How did you know with Peter? You had always sworn never to marry again."

"I wish I had some secret to share with you. It was never an issue with Peter. He loved me from the beginning, as he would be the first to tell you. Peter is the rare man who has never doubted his feelings and has no shame in them. I was the one who took time to come around." It was impossible to miss the satisfaction in Violet's voice.

It was hard not to be jealous—not of Peter, but of Violet's utter contentment and satisfaction. Anna doubted that she would ever have that.

Violet's face softened with sympathy. "Struthers is not like that, then? I did not imagine he would be, but that is part of his attraction, that air of mystery."

Air of mystery? Anna had never perceived that. It was something to consider. Was the mask he presented to the rest of the world different from the face he showed to her? "I am not sure. He holds his feeling and thoughts very close to his chest. It does not matter—we are married now."

"Which should make it matter more. You do wish a happy marriage, do you not? If you had been ready to settle for a typical society marriage you would have had a husband years ago."

How much should she tell Violet? "We did not have a choice."

"You're not—? No, I know better. And besides, there has not been time. So why?"

"We had an indiscreet moment and were caught."

Violet scrunched her lips. "No, I don't think so. You don't need to tell me if you do not wish to, but you would not marry for anything less than a full scandal. And I am not sure Struthers would offer even then."

"You are wrong. Struthers announced our engagement almost before our lips had parted. It is such a long complicated story. I am trying to figure out how to explain it to you. It involves so much more than Struthers and myself, but I can assure you that in the end it was I who forced him, who held him to his proposal."

"I do want to hear the whole story, but I have never known Struthers to be forced into something he did not wish. Perhaps you have your answer right there. If he did not care for you he would never have taken that step. I know the man has no fear of scandal himself. He would not be upset to never appear in society again. He married you because he wanted to."

"He married you because he wanted to."

Those were the first words Struthers heard as he entered the room. The temptation to turn and leave before being seen filled him. Gritting his teeth, he stepped into sight, carefully keeping his cheek turned to the right.

"What other reason could there be?" He stated it as a question, but one that clearly desired no answer. "Violet, it is so good to see you. I was not expecting the pleasure until this evening." He made a slight bow in her direction, ignoring the ache at the small of his back and along his left knee.

Violet turned to him with a womanly grace that had once drawn him. "I could not wait so long to offer my felicitations. I was just chiding your wife for not letting me know before I saw the announcement in the paper. Two of my dear friends wed and neither thinks to tell me. Shame on you both."

"It was wrong of us." His tone was that of a chided schoolboy, but he kept his stance tall—it was easier than bending given his pain.

"I suppose I must forgive you then." Violet rose to her feet. "And also make my good-byes. I would love to stay and watch the two of you together—but that will have to wait until this evening. If I do not leave now I am sure other guests will arrive and then I will be forced to linger longer—not that I object to being forced to linger with you, but Peter will begin pulling out his hair if I leave him to deal with tonight's gathering on his own. And I do so like his hair."

Anna stood and gave Violet a brief hug of farewell. "We will talk more later. There is still much I must tell you," she said.

He had never realized how close the women were. He was not sure he liked it. Just what was Anna planning to tell Violet? Some things should remain private.

Violet and Anna were similar in many ways—strength, beauty, an ability to disregard society, the knowledge of how to smile at a man, of how to walk across a room like a queen—and they both excelled at saying no. He wished he had noticed the similarity earlier—it might have made him pause before . . .

He married you because he wanted to.

There was more truth to the statement than he wanted to admit even to himself. No matter what the outside threat or societal pressure, he would not have married Anna if he truly had not wanted to—and he should not have wanted to. He had never thought to marry a woman with a past—not even Sunita. It was not something he wanted to think about—particularly given what he was here to say.

He waited until the door clicked shut behind Violet and turned to face her fully. "What were you doing kissing Lord Adam Darnell, that buffoon, on the terrace at the Hendersons' last night? I spent half the evening looking for you and you were out on the terrace kissing another man!"

The smile that had played on the corner of Anna's mouth faded. "Who told you that? And what happened to your face? Are you all right?" She moved toward him.

"We will talk about me later. For the present, I notice you do not deny your involvement with Lord Adam." He strode across the room until he stood right before her. "And does it matter who told me? I was actually informed by several helpful friends. It made for a most pleasant afternoon."

Anna gulped in a great breath. "I did not kiss him." What had happened to her husband? There was a deep bruise forming along one cheek and he was not moving with his customary ease. Had he been in a fight? With Lord Adam? She wanted to reach out and stroke his cheek, but sensed her caress would not be welcome.

"Surely you can do better than that." He stepped back slightly. "You were seen."

"I did not kiss him. He tried to kiss me and I turned my head." She wanted to bring up his injuries again, but he gave her no chance.

"Then why were you on the terrace with him—alone?"

If she said that Lord Adam had wanted a private word with her Struthers would want to know why—this did not seem like the moment to tell him.

Only perhaps it was. She must make him see that he had no argument with Lord Adam.

"Nothing to say." Struthers's chest was rising and falling rapidly beneath the blue damask of his waistcoat.

Her eyes fastened on the pearl buttons. She could not even imagine meeting his clear blue eyes. She should have told him the truth before now.

"Why didn't you just marry him? I don't understand the entire pretense with me if you really wanted him—or doesn't he want you anymore? Being thrown over once was enough—now he has less honorable intentions."

Struthers's words stung. Did he really think so little of her? At least he had held back from saying that he should have realized she had no honor to guard—even if he had apparently already fought for it. She raised her glance to his cautiously, needing to know what he was thinking.

Anger filled him. It took her aback how much fury she saw there.

"Are you with child?" His question caught her off guard.

Was that why they had fought? "No—or at least I do not think so. I cannot be sure after last night." She tried to let her honesty show. He seemed to know when she dissembled. Surely he should know when she told the truth.

His chest filled, and emptied. Filled, and emptied. "If I choose to believe that then why did you force me to this marriage?"

"I told you—Maddie and her child."

"And what else?"

The question hung between them.

Yes, there was a truly bad time to tell him—and this was it.

He stood, towering above, eyes blazing, waiting for an answer. An answer he was not inclined to believe.

If she told him now he would not believe her. That certainty filled her. It was too simple a story to seem possible in the face of this anger.

But if she did not answer then he would never believe her. It all seemed so impossible. That also was a certainty.

She turned from him, scared that he would grab her and hold her back. He did not.

She walked to the mantel and stared at the small collection of pottery figurines that stood there. They had been her mother's, silly ugly things of no actual value, but still endlessly precious. She picked up the statue of a fat cat licking a paw. "I need to tell you a story," she began.

He crossed the room behind her. She did not hear him or see him, but she knew. The air felt like it parted around him, leaving her nothing to breathe.

"A story," he said. "Does this seem like the time for stories?"

"If I am going to do this you must let me do this my way."

"I don't have to do anything. You are my wife."

His words sent shivers through her. The absolute belief with which he spoke could not be mistaken. He'd had a fight with Lord Adam without even asking her opinion. That showed how highly he regarded her. The figure of the cat blurred as her eyes filled with water. She batted her lashes, trying to keep back the tears. She never cried, aside from funerals and weddings. The only blessing was that he could not see. She refused to give in. Now if only she could hold her voice steady. "Nonetheless, if you want to know I will tell it my way."

She felt his breath on the back of her neck, hot, heavy, angry. For a moment she thought he would refuse to listen—although given that she was trying to give him what he wanted it seemed a foolish thing. Thinking he was foolish was so much easier than considering the actuality of the man behind her.

Placing the cat back on the mantel, she turned. He was too close, but she managed to step aside and move to her favorite chair before the fire. Her fingers trembled as she sat and she hid them in her skirts. "I was six years old the first time I met my uncle. It was a brief visit, but unforgettable. He was like no one I had ever met, big and brash with a laugh that filled not only the room, but the house. My mother was so happy while he around."

Was there going to be a point to this? Struthers's whole side ached from where the hack had scraped against him. If it hadn't been for a recessed doorway in the wall he'd have experienced even greater injury. The bloody driver hadn't even stopped; if anything he'd whipped the horses faster. And then to go on to his club, after changing his torn clothing, and to be confronted with his wife's betrayal. He tried to concentrate on Anna's words but all he could see was that popinjay Lord Adam kissing her, touching her, caressing her.

He'd known she'd been engaged before, known she wasn't a virgin—far from it, but to be confronted with the knowledge that she'd allowed Lord Adam liberties on the terrace during a party—while married to *him*—that was a step too far. It was more than jealousy. He would not be a cuckold. He wanted to swear—loud and long.

After last night he'd begun to hold out some hope that this mess of a marriage could work. He'd actually planned on returning to sit at her side like a doting swain while she received callers—a task he hated. But then Dander had cornered him and with only the best intentions—that was a laugh—told him of the rumors of Anna and Lord Adam Darnell. And it wasn't only rumor, the people who were reported to have seen her were not the normal herd of gossipmongers. No, Anna had to be spotted by the best and most reliable of society.

He was a fool—and a perhaps even a cuckold.

"Are you even listening to me?" Her voice was quiet as she spoke.

He turned and fixed her with an icy stare. "No, I don't believe I am."

"Then do you wish me to continue? I am only answering the questions that you asked."

"You know, at this moment I believe I don't care."

She flushed and her hands dropped back to her lap. Her fingers twisted in the sprigged muslin of her skirts. Was that dull dress really what she was wearing to receive callers? He'd have thought better of her.

And then she straightened. He could almost see the fire rekindle in her eyes. The tension did not leave her fingers, but it changed. Her hands moved to grip the wooden arms of her chair, the knuckles showing white. "Then I shall not be bothered. It will be a long time before I try to answer your questions again or ask my own. You are a boor."

She stood then, a young queen, brave and unafraid.

No, that was not accurate. He could see her nerves, the tightness of her fingers, the flick of her tongue over dry lips.

He thought she would walk away, but she stood firm. "You act as if you can tell when I lie. Can you not also tell when I speak the truth?"

That stopped him. "I don't know."

Her breasts rose as she drew in a sharp breath. The pearl was absent from her neck today, not dangling, taunting him. "Do I seem like I am lying?" She looked him dead in the eye. "Nothing happened with Lord Adam. That is what this is all about, is it not? I did not want him all those years ago and I do not want him now. If I had wanted him he would have been mine long ago—in whatever fashion I wished. And"—her voice rose—"if I had wanted him I would not have chosen a well-lit terrace as a meeting spot. I told you last night. I have never dreamed of being watched. Now tell me, do I lie?"

He did not think she did. It was so much harder to be sure than it was with a lie. He had utter confidence he knew when she twisted the truth, but this was different. Did lack of evidence provide proof? "And with me—at Lady Smythe-Burke's party? You did not mind being watched then—in fact you set it up."

Her shoulders drooped and he could see her work to pull them back. "Will our lives always come back to that? It was different and you know it. If I have to explain it all to you again then we are clearly already lost."

Would they never get past what had happened at Lady Smythe-Burke's party? Could he ever be sure that he had not been tricked? Would he ever understand his own motivation? "I do not know."

"That seems to be your answer—indeed it is both of our answers. I do not know why I saved you from Lord Milson and you do not know why you announced our engagement. Are we back at the beginning?"

"And you will not say why you held me to that engagement after first releasing me from it—and do not say Maddie."

She laughed bitterly at that. "She was part of it. And if you had bothered to listen just now I was trying to tell you the rest of it. A mistake I will not make again. You are clearly much more interested in whether I kissed a man I barely even like. So interested that you fought with him without even talking to me first."

He clenched his lips tight. He knew she spoke reason, but he was not feeling reasonable. "I do not know what you are talking about. I have never fought with Lord Adam. And you talk of honesty. Claim that I should know you are not lying. Do you believe me when I tell you nothing happened with Lady Milson? Yes, I was in her room, but not for the assumed reason. Do you believe I did not have sex with your half sister and then announce that I was to marry you?"

Chapter 13

She wanted to know more about his injuries—how had he gotten them if not from Lord Adam? But his question hung in the air, filling it as surely as a smoking fire.

Did she believe him?

Reason told her not to. Men lied. They lied all the time. She did not even truly consider it a lie to be less than honest about sexual partners. It was just good manners. Some things should not be discussed—were no one's business—and the only answer was to bend the truth.

Did she believe him?

Did he have any reason to lie? She could not think of one—beyond manners—but what other explanation could there be?

"Why were you in Maddie's room then?" she asked.

He did not answer. His mouth stayed shut tight, small lines marking the corners.

"You do not want to explain," she stated. "You want me to trust you. And yet you do not trust me."

"You have not told me the whole truth."

"I tried. You would not listen. And how is that worse than not saying anything?"

Again he did not answer, but just stared at her, steadily.

The tension that had throbbed through her head

returned. She longed to lay a cool cloth upon it, but would not show such weakness before him.

Did she believe him?

The problem was she did. When she thought of Maddie she did not experience the twinge of pain that she did when she pictured him and Violet—although she did believe Violet that nothing had happened between them. She could not picture Maddie and Struthers together. Her sister did not seem challenging enough for him. He was a man who was not happy without challenge.

She drew in the deepest breath she could, filling her lungs until they were ready to explode. "Yes, I do believe you. If you tell me you did not have relations with Maddie I will believe you."

"I have already said I did not."

Something inside her relaxed at his words. It was not something big, hardly noticeable at all, but she knew it was important. "Now tell me, do you believe me about Lord Adam?"

He would never be sure if the rap at the door that sounded as she finished her question was a blessing or a curse. He knew there was more to say—but equally knew that more thought might be desired on exactly how to phrase his beliefs.

"Yes," he called, not waiting for Anna. He saw her eyes narrow at his presumption. She would have to grow used to it. It was his house now, as she had already remarked.

The door opened with care and her porter looked in. "Mrs. Struthers, you have several callers at the door wishing to express their felicitations on your marriage. The Henrys, Mrs. Williams—"

"You may send them in," Struthers answered, again without waiting for Anna to reply.

The porter backed away, leaving the door open a tad.

"That was badly done," Anna said.

He turned to her. "Why? It is my house."

Her eyes flashed, but her voice was surprisingly level. "Yes, it is. And I am your wife. It is too late to debate those points, but is this really how you wish me to appear before visitors? And today of all days? If you had given me a moment I would have excused myself first and then let Jameson show them in. I would have repaired my appearance and then returned."

"Do you believe I wish to entertain our guests for hours on my own?" His tone was sharper than he had meant. He was not over his anger about the incident with Lord Adam, and his bruised knee was throbbing painfully. But she was correct. He should have allowed her time to change. Her simple dress and loosely knotted hair might raise question on this occasion. He hated being wrong—which did not improve his temper.

"Is that what you are used to, women who take hours to dress? I must admit it might do you good. However, my maid is a wonder. I doubt you would have waited ten minutes."

He did not have time to answer before the visitors began to filter in. He knew several of the gentlemen and a couple of the ladies. Anna obviously knew them all, and liked most of them. He could see in her eyes which greetings were genuine.

"I was so happy to read the news, Mrs. Struthers," said Mrs. Henry, moving to the front of the pack. "I have always thought you needed the steadying influence of a family."

Struthers expected Anna to take affront at the comment, despite the genuine warmth which with it was offered. Instead she surprised him. She grasped Mrs.

Henry's hand and smiled as she thanked Mrs. Henry for the sentiment.

Mrs. Williams stepped forward next and swept Anna up and down in single glance. It was apparent from the pinch of her mouth that she found Anna's appearance wanting. "Yes, it was good to read the news and—so unexpected. I didn't believe you'd ever marry." She stared at Anna as she spoke, making it clear that in her opinion Anna lacked what it took to attract a man.

Struthers found himself wanting to step forward to explain to Mrs. Williams just how mistaken she was. His feet were actually moving when Anna took Mrs. Williams's hand and held it to her breast.

"I understand why you would feel that way," she said, her voice warm, but her glance icy. "It must be so hard to believe I could accept another man after turning down your sweet son. Has he found someone else to bestow his affections upon?" Somehow her glance exactly matched Mrs. Williams's, making it clear that she found any prospect of the son finding a wife as unlikely as Mrs. Williams had found her marriage.

Mrs. Williams stepped away from Anna. "No, I am afraid he is still unattached. It's a pity he doesn't have a fortune like yours to help him."

Did the old cow think that money was Anna's only attraction? He started forward again.

"You do know my husband, do you not, Mrs. Williams?" Anna turned and took Struthers's arm as he moved toward her. "I can assure you he was in no need of my fortune. Indeed, I don't think it even entered his mind when he proposed."

"That I can assure you it did not," he said, nodding to Mrs. Williams. "When I decided to marry my dear Anna, money never even entered my thoughts."

Mrs. Williams's eyes narrowed. "What a unique man you must be, Mr. Struthers. So different from Anna's other suitors—and so understanding."

She was talking about Lord Adam and last night. Her meaning was clear to all. There was a slight shifting of feet as their visitors awaited his response. He gritted his teeth and waited for inspiration. Even the thought of Lord Adam touching Anna fueled fires within him. He wasn't sure if he cared whether she'd been a willing participant. No man kissed his wife.

He shifted and winced as his thigh screamed in pain. He hadn't realized he'd pulled it. He could only wish he had injured himself by pummeling Lord Adam as Anna had believed.

He forced the tension out of his jaw. "Why yes, I am. I know my Anna well. She would never do anything to disappoint me."

Anna squeezed his arm hard to let him know exactly how she felt about that sentiment.

"I am glad you have such faith." Mrs. Williams's tone clearly said it was misguided.

"Have you injured yourself?" Mrs. Henry asked, noticing his wince and trying to redirect the conversation.

He pulled in a breath and looked at Anna; the question was clear in her eyes. "Yes, I am afraid I had a bit of an accident this morning—an out-of-control hack. I am afraid I was a bit distracted and didn't see it in time."

He watched Anna consider—and decide that he was telling the truth, but not the whole truth.

"You are lucky you were not killed. The streets really are becoming too crowded. There should be some type of regulation. A woman just isn't safe," Mrs. Williams was happy to start a new topic as long as she could speak at length.

Anna continued to watch him, trying to judge how badly he had been injured and whether he had been in actual danger. He felt his earlier anger ease under her tender and caring gaze.

The greetings went on in a blur after that. Visitors came and went. Anna seemed to know half of London and they all seemed to want to come and gawk at the new couple. And the tea—didn't anybody realize that situations such as this called for brandy, not tea and biscuits?

Finally he could take it no more. Anna might be in her element—he was not—and all he really wanted was a soak in a hot tub.

He stood with only slight difficulty. "I must be off. Again, my thanks to all for your warm regards. It is indeed a joyous occasion." He turned to Anna, ignoring her worried, searching look. "I will see you this evening at Lady Carrington's." He felt the gasp at that. His relationship with Violet had not been discreet—for all that nothing had ever happened. He raised a brow at Anna, making it clear he knew exactly what he had done. Let her try to settle those whispers.

That evil, evil man. Anna almost tossed the brush at her vanity. She knew damn well he'd made that comment as revenge for the whispers about the previous evening. If society was going to whisper about whether she had a lover then they could wonder about him as well. She'd have liked to have been able to get mad for Violet's sake, but she knew her friend would only laugh. Lord Peter too.

Damn Struthers. She'd actually enjoyed the first couple of hours with their callers. It had been delightful to pass poking comments back and forth to him with no one else the wiser. Well, Mrs. Henry had seemed to understand, but she always did. Anna had never been sure whether it was the truth or merely an air she knew well how to adopt.

The only problem had been her worry. The bruise on his face had darkened as she watched and it was impossible for her to miss the difficulty with which he moved. Why hadn't he told her about his accident? She would have refused all callers and sent him to bed after a hot bath and fresh tisane to drink.

She could only hope that he'd done exactly that once he headed home.

Headed home leaving her to the likes of Mrs. Williams.

Evil man. He'd known exactly what he was doing.

And he had never said if he believed her about Lord Adam. He had been about to, or at least about to say something, when Jameson had interrupted.

She picked up the brush and yanked it through her hair, too impatient to wait for Sally to return from fetching the dress she wanted.

He had been about to say he believed her, hadn't he?

"Is this the one you wanted, ma'am?" Sally reentered the room. "I thought you had intended to attend the Joneses' musicale."

Sally didn't even need to say that she found the dress inappropriate. It was not Anna's normal choice of attire for an evening in society, and particularly not one where her goddaughter would be present. The gown was so deep a blue as to almost be black. But, like her purple gown of the previous night, it had a shimmer and iridescence about it that glowed with color and life. It made her skin look dusted with pearls.

That was not why she had ordered it, however. No, it was the back that had lured her. It swooped low in a curve that left one wondering if she could wear anything at all under it. When she danced, a man's hands might brush her bare skin—Struthers's hands might brush her bare skin. She rather planned that they would.

Tonight.

Tonight would be what last night had been, what this morning should have been.

She'd take the chance to kiss each of his wounds—inspect them with great care and closeness. Maybe she'd give him a kiss for each piece of what had happened he told her.

The clock ticked in an endless countdown.

It was so much easier to think of the end of the night instead of the beginning.

Tonight she would tell him the whole truth—they just had to get through the soiree first. The longer she waited, the larger the worry grew.

If only Struthers had said he believed her about Adam.

There was a large space between what she believed he'd meant and what he'd said.

A large space she might disappear into if she were wrong.

She picked up the skirt of the dress, wondering at what a mastery of construction it was, layers and layers of silk that appeared as one. "Yes, Sally. I'll wear this one. I will wear the green paisley shawl at the Joneses'. The dress is perfectly acceptable from the front."

Sally snorted, but did not bother with a verbal reply.

Anna rubbed the skirt again. What Sally didn't understand was that she needed every weapon she could avail herself of. If Struthers spent the evening distracted, thinking about what she wore under the dress, he would not be wondering about other things—things like Lord Adam and what had happened with her cousins.

There she was—and alone.

Struthers breathed a sigh of relief. He had not wanted

to think what he would do if she showed up with Lord Adam. The glimmers of imagination had not been pleasant. He did trust her, he was slightly shocked to realize. It was his own judgment that he questioned.

He had never doubted himself before and he did not like it.

The blasted woman had his mind spinning in circles.

She was beautiful, though. The midnight gown she wore followed her body to perfection, showcasing her high breasts and slender waist. Her neck glowed bare. The pearl was absent. He hoped no message was contained in that.

He felt much better after his long soak and some evil-smelling liniment supplied by his valet. And despite their earlier arguments he had no doubt where he wished this evening to end up, where he planned for it to end.

She was his wife.

She saw him. He could feel her gaze as if it were a physical thing. She focused on his bruised cheek, noted that it was already fading. She gave a quick nod. Her eyes twinkled as their gazes met, and then she turned—oh so slowly—letting the emerald shawl drop from her shoulders. Her eyes still held his, and it took a moment for him to realize what she had revealed.

Her dress didn't have a back.

No, that was not true. It ended only inches beneath the base of her shoulder blades, but what inches they were—smooth, creamy inches. Inches that showed not a hint of chemise or corset. Inches that drew him closer, made him want to feel and touch—and explore.

Did she have anything on beneath that gown? Anything at all? He didn't see how she could.

His eyes flashed back to her face. She knew exactly what he was thinking. In fact, he had not a doubt that she had planned his very thoughts. She was pulling on the lead strings—again.

She bowed her chin in acknowledgment and then turned to Violet, pulling the shawl back up to cover herself. But it was too late for him. He knew what was hidden and could hardly wait to uncover it again.

He forced himself to look away from her, all too afraid what secrets she was about to share with Violet. The two of them together were a dangerous combination.

He couldn't resist turning back to see if she'd lower her shawl again. Anna caught his glance and raised a knowing brow, before leaning forward to whisper something to Violet. Violet turned to look at him, giving a subtle wave.

A weak will had never been his problem. Even with Violet, probably the most seductive woman he had ever known, he had remained himself, able to turn away when her games grew too costly. Anna's allure held him in a different way, refusing to let him maneuver as he wanted.

Disgruntled, he headed to the card room in search of a large glass of brandy. Last night would not be repeated. He'd not lose track of his wife, but he'd get some reinforcement first, because the one consolation in this whole mess was that he had the feeling his wife had exactly the same problem dismissing him from her mind.

It was then that he saw the man. Nathanial Townsend stood leaning against the wall, on the other side of the room. The man met his glance and gestured toward the card room. Struthers nodded and followed him out.

Her heart dropped to her feet and then fell through the floor. Anna could actually feel the pain of its descent. What was Nathanial doing here? She knew Violet wouldn't have invited him. Her hands clenched tight at her side as she watched him meet Struthers's glance, and then the two men headed off in the same direction. Measuring the space between them with her eyes, she calculated. No, she couldn't get between them in time.

She turned back to Violet.

"They're headed to the library," Violet said. "That is one of your cousins, I take it. I can assure you, I did not invite him."

"The library will mean brandy, cards, and men. There will be no women. I cannot follow."

"Can you not? When have you ever been bound by such rules? From what you have just told me, you had better talk to your husband—and fast."

Anna considered. "No, I do not know what I would say in a roomful of men. Even with just the two of them together it would be difficult." She glanced from the two men to the doorway of the library. Perhaps she should beg Struthers to come with her, explain to him in private.

No, there was no way she could get to him in time without causing a scene.

And a scene would only make Struthers think her secret was bigger than it was. It wasn't as if she had lied. Damn, it really wasn't that important. Why hadn't she just told him last night? Now he would remember that she hadn't told him about Lord Adam's kiss and this would grow out of proportion.

Maddie approached her from across the room and Anna turned, pretending not to see her. She was not ready to handle her sister at the moment. She glanced back at the library. All she could do now was wait—and worry.

Chapter 14

Struthers turned and faced Townsend as he entered the crowded library. Clouds of cigar smoke permeated the room, emphasizing how little privacy they would have. He stepped to the drinks tray and refilled his brandy. "I was surprised to see you here."

Townsend answered honestly, "It's not hard to get invited along. I heard of your past relationship with Lady Carrington and hoped you would be here."

Struthers arched a brow.

"I wanted a chance to make my apologies," Townsend answered. "I am afraid both my brother and I were overcome by the shock of hearing of your sudden nuptials. I am afraid we spoke without thought."

Struthers rather thought that the rudeness had begun well before the marriage announcement and had been addressed to Anna more than to him. "I see" was his only reply.

"Good, good. I'd hate to get off on the wrong foot with a new relation."

"Was there more you wished to say?"

Townsend fetched himself a drink, taking a large gulp of the strong brew. "I hadn't planned on doing more than welcoming you to the family." He turned back to Struthers. "And what did you do to your face? It looks quite painful."

"It's not bad—merely a bruise."

"I am glad you were not badly hurt."

Now that was a lie. Struthers didn't need the extra sense he had with Anna to see through such a blatant falsehood. Townsend would have been very glad to see him injured.

Despite his comments, the man would not have found it easy to get invited along to Violet's party. She kept a very exclusive guest list—only those persons she actually liked—and Struthers had a hard time imagining who among them would have invited the American. He gestured to the well-populated card table. "Do you play?"

"I'm a shipper. I know my way around a deck of cards, but find my gambling instincts are satisfied by my business. You?"

"Some games. I prefer skill to luck."

"Don't we all." Townsend took another swig.

Struthers glanced at the table. No, there were plenty who cared for luck, who sought the chance for the unexpected, undeserved payoff. He nodded and put down his half-full glass. "If that's all, I'll return to the ballroom. I rather fancy a dance with my wife." And her backless dress.

"There is one more thing—almost an afterthought," Townsend said, putting his own empty glass beside Struthers's.

"Yes?" Here it was. He had known it would be coming.

Townsend glanced about the room. "Is there someplace we could have more privacy?"

"About an afterthought?"

"About your wife."

He had been right. The story contained far more details than Anna had provided. He thought of Anna and Lord Adam—she had chosen the terrace for privacy. He glanced out the window. A light rain had begun to fall. It was still tempting. He rather fancied making Townsend stand in the drizzle, but that would mean he'd be wet also. He didn't mind, but Anna might. He did still intend to get that dance—regardless of the outcome of this meeting. "There is a small study, Lady Carrington uses it to keep accounts."

"Does she manage the household herself then? I would not have imagined that from all I've heard." Townsend walked to the door.

"The household and several large estates," Struthers added.

"It is a pity she has not found a husband then." Townsend stopped and turned to him. "That is rather what I wanted to talk to you about in regards to Anna."

He called her Anna. Struthers tightened his lips. Childhood friends or not, relations or not, he did not like it. "I rather supposed it might." He allowed a hint of temper to slip into his tone.

"Is she giving you problems already, then?" Townsend clearly had missed the hint. "Show me where this study is and I'll tell you what I know."

Struthers preceded him through the room and led him further from the crowd. He had a lingering impulse to fetch Anna, to let her be part of this. It was only an impulse. If Anna had been fully honest with him this would not be necessary.

The door to the study swung open with ease. He was relieved Violet had not locked it. "Here we are."

Townsend strode into the room and turned to face him. "Your wife is a woman."

That was the big revelation. Struthers had to fight not to laugh. "Yes, I do believe that she is."

"That is not what I meant." Townsend paced across the room, searching for words. "She has been managing large amounts of money and refusing help."

That did not surprise Struthers. "And you think she should have asked you?"

"I am family, but if not me, somebody. Her judgment has not been good."

"No?"

"Just take a look at her funds. It is shocking how much they have diminished."

Struthers paused and considered. "And you know this because?"

"We have several business interests in common."

Ah, this might be getting somewhere. "I thought your Uncle Charles left everything to Anna. Did she mislead me?"

"Not exactly." Townsend's voice rang with bitterness. "It is more that my uncle and my father had several joint ventures together. Anna might have inherited my uncle's share but there were certain stipulations."

"Such as?"

Townsend hesitated, and Struthers had the feeling he had said more than he meant. "Nothing important, just some safeguards to be sure it was kept in the family," Townsend said at last.

Struthers longed to pursue the topic, but like any good hunter knew there was a point to let the prey head back to you. "And you say Anna has been foolish?"

"Yes."

That was simple, but said so little. "How so?"

"Little things. She never reinvests her capital," Townsend replied.

That was not such a little thing. Struthers thought of her overly fine carriage and horses, and jewels—that pearl must cost enough to feed a family for a year. "Tell me more."

"There is not much more to say."

Again, that could not be true. Townsend would not have brought him here if that were all there was. "Then I'll go find my wife for that dance."

"There is still one more thing."

Of course there was—there always was.

Townsend swallowed, hard. "Anna has been trying to sell her share of the shipping interests. They're not as great as they were a decade ago—our uncle moved much of his money into textile mills—but they are still substantial, and profitable."

"Why is she trying to sell them then?" Something was not ringing true.

"Why do women do anything? She probably wants a new wardrobe and thinks this is the best way to get it." Townsend looked away.

"I thought she had plenty of money in the bank. I keep hearing about her fortune."

That caught Townsend off guard. "You have not taken over management of her accounts?"

"My secretary is looking into the matter."

Townsend blinked, then blinked again. "You don't know about Anna's fortune?" He sounded disbelieving.

"I know she has one—or is rumored to. I must admit it was not on my mind when we decided to marry."

Townsend seemed speechless.

"Is that all?"

"Yes, but don't let her try to sell her interests. It would not be advisable." There was a slightly threatening note to the last, but Struthers disregarded it. He must be mistaken. A man did not move from speechless to threatening with that speed.

"I'll say farewell then and find my wife."

"Do that. And I do hope you have better luck tomorrow. I'd hate for you to have another mishap. The roadways can be so dangerous." Nathanial turned and left the room.

Had he said he'd been hurt along the street? He didn't think so, but he must have. Or perhaps somebody else had mentioned it. There was probably gossip from their visitors that morning. The vague edge of threat wafted up again, but he ignored it. He wanted to find his wife.

Anna's big secret was that she had mismanaged her monies. He could understand why she had hidden it from him. She had probably been too embarrassed to accept the allowance he offered her. He would have to speak to Timms about it. It would be necessary to be sure she didn't overspend in the future, but he could certainly provide her with more than adequate funds.

He left the room with only one intention.

It was time to claim his dance.

Where was her husband? Well, she knew where he was. The question was—how long could a conversation take? Nathanial might have a lot to say, but he had never been verbose. Where was Struthers?

Anna's heart was still located several feet beneath her and with each beat it felt as if it were hitting against solid rock.

Where was he? And what was Nathanial saying? Did he have a new plan? A new way to ruin her?

She walked across the room toward the door leading to the library. She would not go in, but perhaps she could sneak a look. Maybe they were just playing cards.

Just because they had entered together did not mean that they were actually together. A card game was not an agreeable place for discussion—private or otherwise.

It had prevented her from interrupting. Surely it would prevent them talking.

Only they weren't there.

She peered around Lord Summerton's shoulders. It was hard to be sure, but she thought she'd notice Struthers, and his dark curls, if he were there. Her cousin was harder, more ordinary-looking, but she saw no sign of them anywhere.

Did that mean . . . ? Even as the thought formed she saw Struthers coming from Violet's study. She backed away quickly, not wanting to be seen. He didn't look unhappy or angry. Perhaps her worries had been groundless. Perhaps he had not talked to her cousin.

Attaching herself to a group just inside the door to the ballroom, she listened to their congratulations, made polite conversation back, and waited.

He strode in, looking about. Saw her. Smiled.

No, he was not angry.

Her shoulders relaxed. She turned her head to glance at him over her shoulder, acknowledged the knowing gleam in his eyes, let her shawl drop a fraction of an inch, saw his eyes follow the movement, and let the shawl slip a couple of inches more.

He headed right for her, not even making a polite pretense that he had any other goal in mind.

She turned as he arrived. She would not pretend either.

"Struthers," she said.

"Wife," he answered.

She made quick introductions to those she stood with, nodding and answering them all, but all she could think about was his fingers on her back. His hand had slipped under the shawl and with light feathering movements he stroked her. It was difficult not to moan. It felt so good.

He leaned his head toward her and whispered. "I just spoke with your cousin—Nathanial."

"I saw." There was no reason to pretend otherwise.

"He tells me you've been a very bad girl."

She gasped in a breath, covering it with a cough as the others turned to glance at her.

"I'd better get you some refreshment, Anna," Struthers said, taking her arm. "Some lemonade, perhaps?"

She followed without protest, although she did whisper back, "No lemonade."

"Then a dance." He slipped the hand that had trailed down her back to her waist and pulled her to the floor just as a waltz began.

"Did you plan that?"

"What?"

"The waltz. It began as if you timed it."

"I would like to take credit, but really I cannot. Luck shone on me. I was just telling your cousin that I did not like luck, but at this moment I would confess to being very pleased with it." He pulled her closer, still within the bounds of propriety, but only just.

As he turned her she saw Nathanial standing along the far wall. His eyes were focused on them and his expression was not kind. She pulled her stomach muscles tight to fight the nerves that filled her. "You said Nathanial had spoken of me."

"Yes."

"Did he tell you everything?"

"More than you ever have." Some of the pleasure left his voice as he spoke.

"I did want to tell you, but it never seemed the right

time." She gazed over Struthers's shoulder, not meeting his eyes. "Actually I did tell you yesterday, but you did not listen."

"It would have been much easier if you had simply been honest from the start."

"Yes," she answered.

At least he did not seem angry. Nor did he look at her as if he now questioned her sanity. It would be a great stretch to say he was pleased, but he did seem to accept the situation.

He slid his fingers beneath the shawl, slipping them under the top of her dress. "I will have my man Timms look into the situation more on the morrow. I trust that is acceptable to you."

"Does he have some legal training?" She didn't see how his secretary could help with her cousins' attempts to persuade the world that she was insane. And if Struthers was behind her, there was nothing they could do. Nothing legal, at least.

She still needed to tell Struthers about Lady Smythe-Burke's concerns that her cousins might aim to do one of them physical harm. It seemed unlikely at this moment. She peeked over at Nathanial. He glared back at her. He hadn't even had the courage to talk to her directly. The edge of satisfaction in his smile gave her pause.

"No. No formal training. But Timms is amazingly capable." His fingers delved deeper beneath her dress, feeling for some hint of a chemise or corset.

She caught herself just before she purred aloud with contentment. Thoughts of her cousins could wait. "What did you say?"

"I said Timms is very capable."

"I am sure that he is." She was losing track of her own thoughts. His fingers worked magic and she was giddy with the relief that Struthers knew the truth and was not outraged.

They turned and she saw Nathanial still watching her.

He was a threat. She would be foolish to pretend otherwise, no matter how relief filled her. She didn't understand what he had hoped to gain by telling Struthers that he thought she was crazy. Perhaps he had not thought it through himself. Nathanial had always been sly, but quick to act without thought.

"Do you have anything on beneath this dress?" Struthers's fingers were halfway down her back and she knew they had encountered no obstacle.

"That's my secret." She leaned back so that she could look up at him. His eyes were dark with desire and she felt the joy of power surge through her.

He leaned forward, his lips brushing against her ear. "I don't think we should have any more secrets between us."

He nipped her softly, his lips hidden by her hair.

She laughed. The man always gave as good as he got.

His thumb pressed along her spine in an upward motion. Sometimes he gave better.

A gasp in the crowd drew their attention. Struthers's hand continued to stroke as they turned.

Maddie stood across the room, her face gone pale. She threw up a hand and slid to the floor in a dramatic swoon.

"Do you need to go to her?" Struthers's fingers were slipping deeper beneath the edge of her dress.

"Maddie can faint with the best of them. The only time I've seen her really faint she just collapsed to the floor in a heap. She probably just found out that her dressmaker is moving to a less fashionable address. If we slip out now nobody will ever know we were here when it happened."

Struthers's breath blew against her neck. "If you're sure."

Anna rolled over with a sleepy stretch. Her whole being ached and she loved it. Struthers's body pressed warm against her. It was hard to believe that she'd ever had doubts about him. The man was a wonder.

Oh, there were still details to be worked out, but nothing insurmountable. The more she observed him, the surer she became that there must be an explanation for Lady Smythe-Burke's stories. And he'd made some comments about interfering with her finances but so far had made no move. She stretched again, careful not to move enough to wake him.

Watching him sleep was fast becoming one of her favorite pastimes.

He stirred in his sleep and threw an arm back, reaching for her. She snuggled against him obligingly. Temptation to wake him, to enchant him again, played through her mind, but she restrained herself. Just being cuddled against his warm strength was more than she had ever hoped for.

She should be wary of the morrow when they would need to discuss her cousins' exact words and any possible actions they might take, but now, just now, she was going to revel in the comfort of this moment.

Struthers pulled the pillow over his eyes as the first light of dawn crept into the room. Last night had been a time of magic and wonder, but now the duties of the day threatened. He rolled over and peered at his sleeping wife.

She had been all he could wish for last night, but now it was a new day.

He traced a finger over the delicate curve of her shoulders. Batting at his fingers as if he were an errant fly, she burrowed deeper into the covers. She did not wish for morning either.

He pushed himself up to sitting, leaning back against the multitude of pillows. He turned his head and stared at the cupids above him. They laughed down at him, full of their inner secrets.

Secrets.

Did he know hers now?

Anna might spend too much money on foolish things—he was sure that she did. He had, however, seen no evidence that she was familiar with debt. It was possible that her funds had been so mismanaged as to bring her close to ruin, to necessitate the sale of all her remaining assets, but it seemed unlikely. He had never heard anything but that she was an heiress, and society always knew when funds were lacking. It might choose to overlook the lack, but it knew.

He remembered well his early days, before India, when his family's good name had been enough to assure their place at any table, but their funds had been such that they always found themselves near the foot. Even as a young man he'd frequently been invited to attend dinners when an extra man was needed—and one often was—but he was never chosen to escort the young, the innocent, the marriageable. A poor man could be a fine escort for dinner. He was not expected to become part of the family.

The same was undoubtedly true for a woman. A beautiful one would be a pleasant addition to most any party—particularly one old enough not to provide competition for the family's daughters. Only a rich or titled one would be desired as wife for the sons. And Anna had been desired. If he'd faced fortune hunters after his return from India, she had been pursued by even more.

She stirred in her sleep, drawing the covers tight about her.

No, she was still rich. How rich was yet to be determined, but his wife was not lacking in funds.

Her cousins were wrong about that.

They might not be wrong that her funds were mismanaged. He had heard no mention of a manager and she had mentioned that her secretary was a woman, surely not the best to meet with her bank managers. He would have to get Timms on to it quickly, today even.

Lifting his arms above his head, he stretched, feeling the relief in his sleep-laden muscles. He turned on his side and ran a hand lightly over her mussed curls. Did he want to wake her? And if so, for what purpose?

Did he confront her with her cousins' accusations or did he let it lie, let Timms figure it all out?

It was not really a question. He'd never been a man to let others solve his problems. He was more inclined to solve theirs. Hence his current mess.

He stroked his hands deep into her hair, massaging her scalp. She opened her large brown eyes and stared up at him, licking her lower lip.

Yes, he'd confront the situation—in a few minutes.

Chapter 15

She needed to talk to him. When she awakened this morning that thought had been firm in her mind—but the man was most distracting. She arched her back, letting small aches relax. Life felt good. Ruining it with words seemed such a shame.

Still, she had put this off for too long. She might feel great relief after the previous evening, but there were still many things that needed to be dealt with.

She pulled the covers up over her still-tender breasts and turned to look at her husband.

He was thinking about clean shirts. Such a thought should not have been so immediately apparent, but she had no doubt.

The man's thoughts were filled with starch and neck cloths.

Not the most flattering thing at this moment.

She considered lowering the sheet again, arching her back. Even after all they'd just done, she was confident that she could pull his thoughts away from neckwear.

Only . . .

Only that was just a delaying tactic.

What she really wanted was for him to turn and look at her and see her—not her body, but her—to look at her and want to talk, to discuss what her cousins had said, to discuss his own past, and to decide where they should go from here.

Struthers swung his feet to the floor and stretched—the play of sinewy muscles across his back was momentarily diverting. She forced her eyes away and stared up at her putti. Their happy smiles only irritated her.

"I'll need to return home for fresh linen," he said.

"Yes." What else was there to say?

"Perhaps I should have some sent over. I do not like this sense of rushing in the morning."

"That would be fine."

"You are most agreeable this morning."

"Why would I not be?" Her very pleasantness was a delay. It was so hard to talk to the back of his head. It was time to take charge.

"I must admit I feel quite agreeable this morn also." He turned and looked at her over his shoulder, borrowing her own technique. Nobody could smile like that without intent.

"We need to talk." There, that was more like her, direct and to the point.

"What do you call what we are doing? I believe I hear words and sentence structure—an exchange of questions and answers."

That was hardly worth replying to. His expression had turned devilish. The man knew exactly what she meant.

She pursed her lips like an old woman spying a girl with too much ankle showing.

"You look exactly like my Aunt Mildred."

She added a glare.

"Fine. I know what you mean, and yes, we do need to talk. I merely was hoping to put it off until I had a clean shirt. I will feel at distinct disadvantage if I am wrinkled and smell of yesterday."

"I doubt you ever feel at a disadvantage."

That earned her an honest grin. "True, but I would still prefer not to do this half dressed. Perhaps you could call on me after luncheon? You have not yet seen my house."

"Trying to put me at the disadvantage by claiming the territory?"

"No, it is growing late and I merely thought that you might be overcome with visitors again seeking to wish us well."

"Hmm, you could be right. I do not fancy trying to hold our discussion in the midst of a crowd or putting it off another day. We do seem able to avoid the subject we must talk about."

"I do not see it as avoidance. Merely that at times the world delays us." His eyes dropped below her face.

She tugged the sheet back up. "I do see your point. We could talk now, before guests are likely to arrive."

"I would not wish to risk the interruption and I have business matters to attend to this morning. Things which cannot be put off."

Coming in behind his business matters. She was not sure she liked that, although from what she had seen of the world it was often the way for a wife.

She rose from the bed, leaving the covers behind. She walked away from him, toward the mirror, careful to keep her eyes only on herself. She stretched up on her toes, lifting her arms toward the ceiling. Could there be a better possible position for a woman? She knew his eyes were on her, both on the curve of her buttocks and on the small of her back, but also on the reflection in the mirror, upraised breasts and drawn-in stomach. Her eyes held steady on her own face, on the skin still chafed from his morning beard and eyes still dark with sleep.

She waited, counted to ten, and then turned slowly from the waist, arching her back to best advantage. "I'll come by at two. I am sure I can think of ways to occupy myself until then."

She walked naked to her dressing room, shutting the door behind her without even a click.

Blasted, blasted woman. Struthers didn't know how often he'd had the thought over the last weeks. He couldn't remember ever being so constantly aggravated. At least not since those summers when Anna had been just a girl. She'd been constantly aggravating then too. Every time she looked at Christian he'd felt a slow burn of anger. Would she ever look at him that way, with that look of adoration and completion?

The woman he had married did not seek completion from any man.

He pulled on his stockings with a hard yank, then his pants and shirt. Slipping on his jacket without the help of a valet presented some trouble, but nothing he could not overcome. The limp rag of his neck cloth—he remembered Anna pleating it between her fingers—was another story. He shoved it into his pocket.

She had not liked knowing that his business came before her. Although given how she'd chosen to show her ire, he was glad that she had not known his business was all about her. He needed to discuss her accounts with Timms before he discussed them with her. The man would have been investigating her from the moment he heard of the marriage. Further instruction might be required, but he was confident of Timms's abilities. One of the key points any businessman learned if he planned to succeed was to enter all negotiations prepared.

Putting his lips together he whistled happily as he left the room and headed down the stairs. Just let her listen to that. He would have her know he was not off-put in any way by her display. If anything, he looked forward to their later encounter. The volume of his ditty increased.

Anna put down her slice of toast. Breakfast was often her favorite meal of the day. The food brought comfort and security. The choices varied little from day to day and that was just how she liked it, toast and coddled eggs—sometimes boiled—thick slabs of bacon from one of her farms, shining raspberry jam that filled her mouth with the sweetness of late summer even on the coldest of mornings. Who could want for more? And coffee! The cup steamed before her, frothy from the rich, fresh cream she'd just poured into it. The scent alone was enough to improve the worst of days.

And today was far from being the worst of days. It might not yet qualify as the best, but she held out hope. As she'd walked away from Struthers that morning she'd felt her own power for the first time since their marriage.

She was still herself.

The thought comforted her.

Pulling in a deep breath, until her ribs were tight against her corset, she straightened her back and then chomped another bite of toast, this one heaped with jam. In the days since her wedding she'd allowed herself to forget how strong she was. No matter what happened, only she could determine her choices.

Which brought her to Mr. Jackal. It was time to give him an even greater contribution, one of truly momentous proportions. It was tempting to give him enough that she'd be free forever—if such a thing were possible. She'd been held back by fear of her cousins for too long now.

It was time to act.

She wondered if anybody could understand why she did what she did. Most people truly would consider her mad for giving away hundreds of thousands of pounds. But they could never understand the guilt that filled her each time she considered how those funds had been earned. She'd heard William Wilberforce speak once and had never been the same since. She did not fool herself that she truly understood what the slave trade was like despite the efforts she made to speak with those who'd sailed on her ships. The descriptions had left her cold with horror. She had never sailed on one herself and could only be glad of it. But she did know right from wrong, and how her fortune had been earned was wrong.

And so Mr. Jackal had entered her life. She'd never met a man so determined to do good. He inspired confidence, and nothing she had managed to discover had given her any cause for worry. He would take her fortune over time and turn it into orphanages and homes for destitute women. He found ways to help the needy she would never have thought of in a million years.

Only what would Struthers think? Could he possibly understand her purpose?

It seemed unlikely. There was a vast difference between thinking slavery was wrong and thinking there was reason to give away half a million pounds.

Once it was done, though, he would have a hard time undoing it.

She placed her lips together and tried to imitate

Struthers's whistled ditty of that morning. Nothing more than a bubbly hum escaped, followed by a low laugh. Butter, crumbs, and whistling did not combine well.

She reached for the napkin and wiped her lips hard. If he could whistle so could she.

She was still rubbing at her mouth when the door burst open.

"I am surprised to find you alone, cousin dear." Ernest stepped into the room, followed by a scowling Jameson, with Nathanial bringing up the rear.

"I am so sorry, ma'am. I did ask them to wait while I announced them," the porter began.

"It's all right, Jameson," Anna replied. "I know some things cannot be helped. You may be excused now—but leave the door open."

Jameson left and her cousins lined up across the table from her, shoulder to shoulder.

"She's worth what?" Struthers hoped he was not actually shouting.

"So far I've accounted for well over half a million pounds in her financial accounts. That does not include her remaining shipping interests, several textile factories she appears heavily invested in, and various agricultural holdings. There may be some other bits and pieces of miscellany, but that is the gist of it."

"A half-million pounds." Struthers sat back in his chair. He was a rich man, a very rich man, but he could barely imagine this.

"Well over. It could be closer to a million when everything is valued."

"What was her uncle thinking? Why would he leave so much money to a girl?"

"I could not say, sir," Timms answered with utmost correctness.

"There is something more. I see it in your face. Out with it."

"It was not cash when she inherited it. Your wife has sold off most of her holdings and deposited the monies at the Barons and Company Bank. The only nonagricultural properties she has left are some shipping and textile interests that are owned jointly with her cousins, a Mr. Nathanial Townsend and a Mr. Ernest Townsend. She has made attempts to sell them, but the properties are set up in such a fashion that she can only sell them to one of the other owners. To the best of my knowledge neither of the Townsends have the wherewithal at present to buy her out."

"She sold property. It seems a reckless thing to do. And what is this bank? I am not familiar with it."

"I am surprised. Its senior partner is Lady Brattle."

"Surely you mean the earl himself, Lord Brattle."

"No, she exercises her rights personally. In fact, her husband has received a royal license to add the name Barons to his surname."

Struthers leaned his head against the back of the chair. "And I suppose Lady Brattle manages the bank well. Anna would of course bank someplace run by a woman. She does champion the cause, if in a rather quiet fashion."

Timms swallowed, and Struthers could see that he was having a hard time imagining Anna doing anything quietly. And he hadn't even met her personally. He grinned ruefully at his secretary. "I suppose that Anna's funds are also managed by a woman?"

"Actually, sir, I believe she manages them herself."

That did not surprise him. "I don't find that hard to believe."

Timms walked over to the desk and shuffled some papers, his jerking fingers betraying a certain nervousness. "Other than the initial sale of her assets I find nothing questionable in the actual management of the funds."

Struthers leaned forward. "What are you not saying?"

Timms cleared his throat. "It's just that there are frequent very large—almost insane—withdrawals that seem to just disappear. I inquired at the bank and she takes the money in cash. It is not their business to ask what she does with it. I cannot say if it is mismanaged or not without more information."

"And?"

"And unless she is stuffing it into a mattress it seems to just cease to be. I can find no trace."

Closing his eyes, Struthers rubbed his temples. Nothing was ever simple with Anna. "And what do you believe is happening with the money?"

"At first I believed that there was some form of embezzlement. That, all signs to the contrary, your wife was not noticing that tens of thousands of pounds were slipping away. However, once I realized that she was withdrawing the funds herself, I could come to only two possible answers." Timms clamped his lips shut.

"Which are?"

For a moment Struthers was not sure the man would answer. Then, in a sudden breath, out it poured. "Could your wife have a gambling problem? I've known of men to lose fortunes, even larger than this, on the turn of a card or the speed of a horse."

Struthers stared up at the ceiling, considering. "You mentioned two possibilities."

"Blackmail. Perhaps she is being forced to turn the money over to someone. I have heard rumors of her wildness, of her past. Perhaps somebody knows something that she is paying to have kept silent."

That caught Struthers. It seemed all too possible that her cousins could work such a scheme. Would she pay them, though? She'd seemed so defiant before them, and yet there had been that air of fear as well. Why then would Nathanial Townsend be hinting at possible mismanagement of Anna's monies? That made no sense. Could she have another secret? "Has she withdrawn any money since our marriage?"

"No, although she withdrew a quite sizable amount several weeks earlier. I would imagine just before leaving for Lady Smythe-Burke's house party. The only activity since then has been some bills from her modiste."

"Is it possible that she is using the money to pay for dresses and furnishings? She does have lavish taste."

"I would not imagine so. The amounts are extreme. Also, there are regular bills from the modiste, the jeweler, and various dry goods emporiums."

"Tell the bank that they are not to release any more funds without my consent."

Timms turned red and looked down at the pile of papers. "Actually I've already done that—or as good as. I let the bank know of your marriage and have directed that any calls for payment should be directed here. They cannot allow your wife access to her accounts—now your accounts—without your permission."

Chapter 16

"We have come to ask that you desist in your efforts to sell your share of the shipping company," Nathanial began.

Anna stared across the table at her cousins, aghast. What made them think they could disturb her breakfast? They had never been so bold before, and if anything they had less power now. "I believe that it is common knowledge that I cannot sell except to one of you—or perhaps your sister, Claire. And we all know that none of you have the monies for such a purchase."

Nathanial squared his jaw and glared at her. Ernest remained outwardly calm, but she knew him too well to believe in appearances.

"Will you not invite us to sit, cousin?" Ernest spoke, his gaze cold upon her.

She wanted to say no. It was what she should do, but the manners her mother had taught her won out. She nodded toward the chairs across from her. "Would you like plates also?"

"No, we do not have time for that," Ernest added before she could call for a footman. He leaned back in his chair and surveyed the room as if he owned it. "Yes, cousin. I am very aware of the details of our uncle's will. I am also aware that you have hired a solicitor to try and find a loophole to get around that. It is not wise."

How did he know that? "You know why I don't wish to be involved in the business, why I sold everything else that I could."

"Yes." He said the word as if it were a curse. "And I am very aware that our uncle would never have left you all of his estate if he had known."

"Are you sure? I always thought that might be why he did." Anna met his gaze full-on.

"Yes, I am sure. He may have had an argument with our father"—Ernest glanced at his brother—"about changing the cargo we carried, some silly notion of following the changing laws instead of the profits, but he would never have countenanced selling off the business altogether."

"Changing cargoes. You do not speak of cargoes, you speak of people." Anna could hear her voice rising. "The laws have changed for a reason. Slavery is not only wrong, it is immoral. And the way you treat your 'cargo' is even worse than that."

Ernest placed his hands on the table and pushed himself up so that he was high over her. "You seem happy to enjoy the profits of such immorality." He waved his hand about the well-appointed room. "It was not your father's family that paid for all of this."

Anna's glance dropped to the hands curled in her lap. He spoke nothing but the truth. She loved nice things, adored them even. The joy in a new dress or suite of jewels was intense. Reasoning that not all of her uncle's money had come from the slave trade, that some of his profits were honest, only justified so much. She was not as good a person as she wished. Still—she raised her face and stared straight up at Ernest. "You are right."

"I know," Ernest replied. "And I would suggest you

think on both that and how you like your current life. It would be truly awful if something were to happen that ruined it. I would hate for you to experience tragedy. Your husband's accident was such a close call. I wish I could say I was sorry, but he has not been at all agreeable."

Her glance jerked back up. Nathanial smirked with quiet satisfaction.

"And Lord Milson—so sad."

"What about Lord Milson?"

"Oh, have you not heard? The poor man has been shot. His wife, your sister, fainted when she heard."

Anna looked with longing at the settee. It would be wonderful to lie back and let the maids bring a cool cloth for her head. Between her cousins' visit and her own visit to Maddie and Lord Milson, her head was pounding.

Maddie had been pale and barely responsive during the visit. She said almost nothing and spent the time twisting her hands in her lap and glancing anxiously to the stairs leading to Milson's chamber above. "He may yet recover," she had repeated over and over.

Their father had filled in a few more gaps. "The damn fool was in a duel. They were barely countenanced in my day, but not only can Milson not seem to stay out of them, but he has to take a bullet in the lung. He'll be dead before dawn." Her father had refilled his glass of gin then and only rambled. Anna had been unable to determine why Maddie had not been informed of the duel until evening. Surely it must have taken place at dawn.

She'd considered staying, but Maddie had been clear that she was not needed—or wanted.

Until Milson either recovered—or not—there was little she could do.

There was guilt that she had not comforted her sister

at Violet's soiree. Clearly she had been too quick to judge. Remorse ate at her that she had not bothered to find the cause of Maddie's great swoon. Her half sister was truly worried today—that had not been playacting.

And there was further guilt—was this all her fault?

Her cousins had implied some involvement in their casual mention of both Struthers's accident and Milson's shooting. The accident seemed possible, but the duel? She had heard of men being set up and Milson was normally such a fast shot. She would have to find out more.

She walked to her desk and began to jot down notes.

The clocked chimed in the hall.

It was time to visit Mr. Jackal again. She always felt better afterward, cleansed. The guilt she felt from the source of her fortune eased—and today she had so much more she needed ease from.

But first a visit to the bank was called for. She glanced down at her gown again, this time with a more practical mindset. It was perfect for the visit to Barons, and afterward, with a plain wool cloak over it, it would be more than suitable for her ventures into less savory neighborhoods of the city.

And then Anna would visit Lady Smythe-Burke. She was sure to know about Milson. Anna glanced down at her notes again.

She only hoped she wouldn't be late for her appointment with Struthers. The one thing that could completely turn this day around would be finally getting things right with him.

Soft yellow light fell through the thin lace drapes that covered the windows of his parlor. Struthers didn't think he'd ever noticed either the drapes or the delicious light they let through. They must have been hanging when he bought the house after returning from India, but he couldn't remember.

He wondered what Anna would think of the room. In most respects—drapes included—it was a typical English parlor. His mother would have been comfortable here—as would Sunita. But he'd added bits and pieces of the treasures he'd returned from his travels with—a table inlaid with mother-of-pearl, candlesticks encrusted with semiprecious stones, and the fabrics; nobody did silks and colors the way they did in India. He'd resisted trying to replicate the true feeling of the country. He found nothing more ridiculous than the current fashion for designing rooms after foreign locales—and India held too many memories. Still, he fancied he'd brought something of the exotic, of the mysterious, into his home. Something he hoped Anna would like.

Half a million pounds.

And it was all his.

How it would gall her if she knew he'd even had the thought. He understood well now her desire to keep him from her accounts. Did she think he would not find out? No, he rather believed she thought he had known all along.

Half a million pounds.

Why had some man not abducted her and forced her to the altar years ago? Not that Anna could be forced into anything.

So why had she married him? She'd been forced into that.

He hadn't realized it at first, but now the certainty grew within him.

Something, and not Maddie's baby, had pushed her toward him. He glanced at the clock on the mantel. She would be here any time and then he would have his answers. And then . . . well, he could only fantasize about the *and thens*. He let his gaze fall upon the rich crimson of the rug before the fire. He could only imagine how Anna's skin would gleam against it.

Almost as if she sensed his thoughts, he heard a pounding upon the outer door and then her voice.

A voice that did not sound happy. Not at all.

"I cannot believe you." Anna pushed through the double doors and into the room without waiting for the porter. If everything she owned was his, then, damnation, everything he owned, including the house, was hers. "You say that I can talk to your man about my accounts and then with no further leave from me you deny me access to my monies. Mine, not yours."

"You know as well as I that is not true. In the sight of the law they are now mine." Struthers stood as she entered the room. His voice was flat and calm.

It made her want to scream even louder. The blasted man continually interfered with her plans. She certainly hadn't been able to visit Mr. Jackal with empty pockets, and she wasn't going to visit Lady Smythe-Burke in the mood she was in. The lady was too astute. Forcing a deep breath into her lungs, Anna strove for calm. "That is only a technicality and you know it."

"I know no such thing. I only know what is."

She crossed her arms across her chest and wished that her eyes could shoot bolts of fire at him. Betrayal burned deep within her breast.

And foolishness. That was perhaps the worst of all this. She had trusted him. Oh, she been wary and suspicious, but never had she believed he would do this, never believed that he would act as her father had tried so many times.

To add to her ire, Struthers turned from her and walked over to pour himself a drink. Did he actually think she was bad enough that he required a midafternoon brandy? Well, she probably was. She'd heard the expression *blood boiling*, but never before had she felt its truth. It was a wonder that the skin on her body did not bubble and blister from the heat she felt growing within her.

After taking a large sip from the glass, Struthers turned back to her. "Tell me what money you need and I'll be glad to give you the funds."

"I told you I did not want an allowance."

"I do not understand your problem." He took another sip, portraying outward calm, but she saw how his fingers wrapped tight about the glass.

"I want access to my accounts."

"I am offering you any funds you may need." A vein in his neck pulsed.

No, he was not as calm as he wanted her to believe. He understood very well what the problem was. So why the pretense? "That is not the point. They are my accounts, left to me by my uncle. You have no right to them."

"I believe that we are back to where we began. As you know, I have every right to them. That is what you find so difficult, is it not? That I do have the right." He took a large swallow and then placed the glass on the table, walking toward her.

"Legal right, perhaps, but you know we agreed that you would leave my fortune alone." She would not back down before him.

He walked forward until only inches separated them. "I agreed to no such thing."

She started to answer, but he continued, "I do not believe I even implied it. I was clear that I would look into matters and then decide."

"And your decision is that you will take it all. Leave me no control." She was working hard not to sputter.

He placed a hand upon her shoulder, very softly. "Actually I have made no decision."

"Then why do I not have access to my funds? I need money."

His fingers tightened. "Tell me what you need the money for and I will give it to you."

She pulled back, almost yanking herself away, turning from him. "It does not concern you."

"That is where you are wrong."

"What does it matter how I spend my money?"

"What have you done with over a hundred thousand pounds in the last year? Money that has just vanished without a trace? You walk into Barons Bank and leave with your pockets full, and the funds are never seen again. What are you doing with it?"

"I like expensive things?"

"So if I went to your home, went through your belongings, I would find a fortune of goods that you paid for with cash rather than having bills sent? It seems an odd practice."

She shut her lips tight. She had no answer for him. None that would seem reasonable, at least. It was her money. He had no moral right to it. A knot was growing deep within her belly. This was all she had feared. It was worse than all her imaginings.

No, it was not worse. It was not as bad as what her cousins had planned—what they might still plan.

Should she try to explain Mr. Jackal? Would Struthers even listen, much less understand?

"Do you gamble?" he asked.

"What? No," she answered before she could think.

"I thought not."

Curses formed on her lips. Gambling would have explained it all and been almost acceptable. He would undoubtedly question her habits, but among their class it would not have been an impossible amount to lose—if one could afford it. And she certainly could.

"Blackmail, then?"

Struthers watched her face pale at his words. That was it, then. Somebody knew something about her, something bad. A thousand possibilities played through his mind. A married lover? A hidden child? Murder? Theft? Most of the ideas were ridiculous. But one kept repeating. Had she had a child? It would certainly not be unheard of in a woman her age. How would he feel about it?

"No, I am not paying off anybody." She spoke calmly and with complete believability.

He wanted to trust her. His instincts said to trust her, but for once he trusted his mind over his gut. If it was not blackmail, then what other possibility was there? "Then where is the money going?"

Her lips pressed together so tight they lost their color.

He tried again. "Just tell me, Anna. What could be so bad?"

Her eyes widened and for a moment he thought she would tell him. Emotions played across her face. She wanted to tell him. That was perhaps the hardest thing; he could see her desire to trust him. But then, just as he thought she would, she turned her back on him again and walked to stare out the window.

"It is my business, not yours," she said. "As it is my money, not yours. Why do you believe you should have a right to it? Why should signing a single piece of paper take away everything that is mine?"

"It is just the way it is. And it was not just a piece of paper, it was promises before God."

"And you believe that?" Her voice rang with disbelief.

"Actually, yes, I do." He walked over and stood behind her. Placing a hand on each shoulder he rubbed gently, trying to ease the tension that was visible in the tight lines of her neck.

"And do you believe that God would want you to have control over all my belongings?" The cords of her neck did not loosen at all.

"He did create man. And woman."

Her head sagged forward. "That is just silly. He created the sexes for reproduction, not property rights."

He did not want to argue. Why could she not understand that she could trust him? He would take care of her, solve her problems, protect her. Whatever was wrong he would do his utmost to fix it. She had married him for a reason, she just needed to tell him what it was. "Why did you marry me?"

That brought her head up. She turned to look at him over her shoulder, but without the playfulness of other occasions. "I thought my cousins told you. Isn't that how you found out about the money?"

"Timms, my secretary, told me about the money. He made inquiries at the banks after our marriage. He also informed me of the extent of your fortune—and where it came from. I honestly had no idea."

"No idea." She sighed. "And now that you know you want it all."

"Not particularly."

"Why should I believe you? I've heard about what happened in India." She turned fully and stepped toward him. "That you are supposed to have swindled your partners to gain a fortune. Why should I think this is any different?"

How did she know about India? Nobody knew the truth of the situation and he had always intended to keep it that way. "My past is not the point. I do not need your fortune. I just don't want to see it wasted or put to bad purpose."

"I am not wasting it—and I don't see why your past is not relevant. You are always questioning mine."

He ignored the last part of her statement. "Then tell me what you are using the money for."

Her chest rose and fell in a great sigh. She was going to let his past lie—for now. "Why don't you tell me what my cousin told you? I believe I may be under some misconception of what you discussed and if I understand what you know then I can at least perhaps satisfy some of your curiosity."

She was evading the subject, and he knew that she knew he knew. They were both avoiding what they did not wish to discuss. He stared down at her serious face, eyes dark, skin pale, lips slightly pressed together. She was not going to say more about the money. They could talk this conversation in circles and she would not speak. She was so stubborn.

He wanted to put his hands on her shoulders and shake her.

He wanted to clasp her to him and reassure her that he would take care of everything.

Instead he brushed a curl off her cheek, then turned away. He chose a chair and sat, leaving her to make up her own mind. "Your cousin Nathanial Townsend told me that you had been managing your own accounts."

She moved toward him, wary. "Yes, that is true. But you know that."

"I did not know it when he told me; however, I was not surprised."

Her lips smiled slightly at that; her eyes did not. "I do not see the issue."

"There is none, but Townsend also told me you had been mismanaging your assets. He assumed it was because you were a woman."

"As do you." The hint of a smile left her.

"As do I. Although I admit that Timms expressed some admiration for your management, with a few exceptions."

She took another step forward. "Such as?"

"He is unsure why you sold almost everything you inherited. It did not seem a wise choice."

Another step. "Perhaps it was not. Nonetheless, it is what I wanted. I found I did not care for my uncle's business interests, and as I had no interest in managing them myself, it seemed prudent to sell them and take the capital."

He stared down at the floor. "I can understand your desire to distance yourself from the slave trade. It has never been an admirable business."

"No, it has not."

"And of course having sold everything you felt the need to invest with a woman?"

The tiny smile returned. "Have you met Lady Brattle? I assure you that you will not find many people more capable—of either sex."

"If you say so." Agreement was easy when there was no meaning behind it.

"You are humoring me." She turned and stepped away. "Is there more my cousins said?"

He tapped a finger upon his knee. "They said that you never reinvest your profits and that you are trying to sell assets that your uncle's will prevents you from disposing of. They advised most firmly against your doing that. I would have felt threatened if the whole idea had not been so ridiculous."

She paled. "Did they say more than that? Talk about your accident."

Touching the rapidly fading bruise on his face, he said, "Nathanial did mention it. Why do you ask?"

"Is it possible it was not an accident?"

What was she suggesting? "I would have said not—but why do you ask?"

"It is complicated."

"Then tell me. That is what I have been trying to get you to do for days now."

Dithering for a moment, she finally came and sat, although she chose the chair farthest from him. Her hands played with her skirts, folding them like a pleat. Tilting her chin up, she licked her lips, a sure betrayal of nerves. Her eyes flickered with indecision. "And if I tell you all you will release my funds and give me control over that which is mine?"

"If I deem your reasoning sound."

She jerked up from the seat and began to pace back and forth. "If you deem my reasoning sound. And why do you get to decide? I think I'd rather live on the streets than allow you control over me." Her voice rose with each word.

He would have to be careful or she might become hysterical. "Calm yourself. That statement is deranged."

If she had paled before she lost all color now. When she spoke it was almost a whisper. "I guess that is your answer. If I do not act as you see fit, then I am insane."

Chapter 17

Anna knew that her every word only gave him more reason to question her rationality. He undoubtedly considered her a hysterical woman, and the world knew there was not a great step between that and insanity. If only her day had not been so impossible she could have held on to her temper.

He had called her deranged—she believed he had not meant it seriously, but it stung at all her fears.

She swallowed hard, fighting the quiet terror that had begun to grow within her. There must be something she could say to Struthers, something that would make him understand the whole situation. "Do you truly think that?"

"Think what?" He looked troubled.

"That I am insane."

Now he just looked confused. "I did not say that."

"But do you think it?"

"No." It sounded as if the word had been forced out of him. "Unreasonable—yes; unfathomable, irrational—yes. Insane—no. I just believe you are a woman." He sounded almost as if he attempted a joke. His eyes narrowed and he examined her face with care. "You do not look well."

"I must admit I have a headache. It's been a most unbelievable day." Confessing to the ailment was hard, but in the last second her temples had resumed their pounding. "My cousins came to visit this morning. It was not pleasant."

"I would imagine it was not."

"They mentioned both your accident and Lord Milson's shooting."

"My acci— Did you say Lord Milson's shooting? Who did he shoot?"

Anna rubbed her brow. "Milson was shot—in a duel. He is injured and it is unclear if he will live. I called upon Maddie when my cousins left. She is in a state of numbness and my father had downed several glasses of gin before I arrived. It was impossible to get a straight answer from either of them."

"And then you found out you did not have access to your accounts." It was a statement, not a question. "It is no wonder that you have a headache."

"Undoubtedly you will take it as another sign of feminine weakness."

He was about to reply lightly—she could see it in the way his mouth shaped—then he stopped. "No, I think it actually takes strength for you to admit that now."

They were quiet for a minute, each waiting for the other to lead the conversation. Anna still wished to argue about control of her money, but she could tell that nothing would be resolved at this moment, far better to wait and plan how to persuade him.

She did not know what kept Struthers from comment. She could see his temple tense with thought, but he didn't say anything.

Before the silence could be resolved a light rap sounded at the door, and Struthers's porter entered. "I have a note for you, Mrs. Struthers." He held out a silver tray with sealed note.

Anna took it and opened it quickly. Her hands trembled as she dropped it back on the tray. "I must go. Maddie needs me. She does not say why, but I worry that Milson may be worse."

"I will get my coat and come with you." Struthers took a step to the door.

Anna held up her hand. "No, until I know what has happened I would rather be alone. I will send for you if needed."

Struthers sat for a long time staring at the rich reds in the rug before the fire. He truly didn't know what to make of his wife.

The sentiment irritated him immensely.

Knowing how to react had always been second nature to him. Put him in a situation, any situation, and he could see the path to follow. Except with Anna.

She hadn't wanted him to come with her. She was upset and she hadn't wanted him.

He kicked at the tassels of the rug with his foot, ruining the perfect line his maids had prepared. Damn her. He could see the meaning of every expression of her face and it helped him not at all.

He stood and strode to the window and back again. She had not been happy that he had taken over her affairs—but then he had known she would not be.

And what was the talk of her cousins and his accident? The threat had been clear in Nathanial's voice the night before and he had dismissed it. Now he was not so sure.

There was more going on here than he knew—or than his wife would tell him.

He walked to the door and called down the hall for Timms.

"Have you found any new evidence of mismanagement of my wife's accounts?" he demanded.

Timms looked up from the book he was carrying. It had been only a few hours, his expression said. Did Struthers expect miracles?

"No" was the man's only reply.

"I want you to go over everything again—twice. And look for any reference to her cousins—the Townsends."

"May I ask why?"

"You mentioned blackmail this morning—they seem the most likely of suspects. Do you have any more information?"

"No. No more than this morning."

Struthers considered for a moment. "Approve any requests for money my wife submits—but find out what they are for."

"Yes, sir." Timms did not sound at all happy.

"Be sure that we have someone follow my wife or whoever comes to withdraw the funds. I want to know where every penny that she spends goes. Do you understand me?"

"Yes, sir." This time the reply was much more enthusiastic. This task Timms could clearly understand.

Struthers watched as Timms returned to his office. "And Timms," he called out. "Set an investigator on the cousins. There is something that is not right."

Anna opened her eyes. Light shone through the slim parting of the drapes of her bedroom. Morning or evening? She rather thought early evening. It lacked the rosy warmth of morning. She had slept only a few hours then. More than she liked, but less than she feared. The rest had done its job. Her mind felt clear, able to once again attack the problems that faced her.

First, the easier issue—Maddie, their father, and Lord Milson. Not that it was an easy problem. Milson was dying; there could be no doubt about that. What she could deal with—or hopefully, if Struthers was reasonable, what she could deal with—was the number of creditors who had suddenly appeared at Maddie's door demanding payment.

Milson, it appeared, was in a very bad way financially. Maddie did not know the details, indeed had known nothing of the situation until the creditors appeared, but it did not look good. Anna, with Maddie's hand-wringing encouragement, had looked over Milson's desk, and what she found had left her cold. Gambling vowels filled many drawers, the IOUs cast haphazardly about. Anna had found no evidence that there was much in the way of funds to cover the debts. She would have to speak with Milson's secretary of course, but in the meantime payment would come from her own pockets.

Her own secretary would need to gather a complete list of what was owed.

Assuming of course that Struthers would allow her to cover the debts. She hated not having control of her own life. Damn him.

And that was her second problem—not insurmountable, she thought, but a great deal more trouble than it should have been. The blasted man had seemed so reasonable.

She pulled in a deep breath—she had been as unreasonable. It was perhaps understandable that he didn't wish her to waste her fortune on he knew not what.

She could force herself to examine the situation from his point of view and try to understand his actions, but it was not easy. He started with the widely held societal view that women were not as capable as men, and she actually expected that they were more so. It was women who kept the world moving while men went off and played their games of business and finance. Struthers would never believe that.

Aggravating man. So incapable of understanding just how powerful women were, how much they were capable of.

How could she make him understand about Mr. Jackal when he had so little faith in her and her judgment?

She hated being forced to ask for what she needed, being so helpless. Helpless. Her husband controlled everything.

Or did he?

An idea began to form.

She remembered their discussion when they'd first talked of marriage, when she had explained the power that women held.

It was time to remind him, of that and more.

The man was surrounded by strong women and didn't even know it. Maybe she could show him.

Unfortunately, even if she could manage Struthers, the problem of her cousins remained. She wasn't sure what to do about them—if indeed there was anything to do about them. Were they a threat or was it all words?

Were her cousins capable of committing physical harm or even murder? One never liked to believe that people one knew were capable of such actions, but as she replayed the details of their childhoods she was unsure. It was all too easy to remember the petty cruelties and selfishness they had displayed as boys and young men. It seemed a great step from shooting cats to murder—but it made her doubt them.

She would have to find out the truth before she could proceed.

First thing in the morning she would visit Lady Smythe-Burke, as she had planned earlier, and find out all the details of Milson's duel. Lady Smythe-Burke might have some knowledge of her cousins' recent activities. It might also be wise to see about hiring a Runner to investigate.

Standing up, she walked to the window and pulled the drapes open wide. The sun was still above the rooftops, but only barely. Soon dusk would fall and the sky would be awash in reds and golds. Sunset continued to be one of her favorite moments of the day—or was it night? Perhaps that was what she loved, the endless possibility of being caught between.

She considered her plans again. They just might work. It would not be easy to change Struthers's mind about her, but perhaps it would open his eyes a little—let him see what women could manage.

She had forgotten who she was. It was time to remember.

He was in a foul mood. Struthers admitted it freely. After the last two mornings of waking next to his warm, willing wife, he did not like waking alone. And even more he did not enjoy waking after the amount of brandy he had consumed the night before. His brains felt fogged and his belly was not quite sure in which part of his body it wished to settle.

Nonetheless, he had things to do. He must check with Timms and see what more had been discovered about Anna. Had she tried again to retrieve her funds? He would not put it past her, with or without his permission.

Had she truly been too tired to see him last night after her visit with Maddie, or had her avoidance been a form of punishment? She would withhold her favors as long as he withheld her funds?

That didn't sound like Anna. She was too straightforward for that. No, she would try persuasion, not punishment.

The next time they were together it would be here, in his bed.

He glanced up at the plain canopy of his bed. He even missed her baby angels.

There were more unpleasant matters to deal with before he could woo his wife. He had business of his own—with the Townsends.

That edge of a threat had been eating at him for a day—and that was without the hints Anna had given him. He was good at reading people and their hint had not been idle. The Townsends wanted something and they intended to get it.

He would make it very clear that he stood in their way—and that no carriage accident was going to stop him.

He rolled over onto his side, hoping the change in position would help to settle his stomach. It did not. Misery was evidently his companion for the day. He could blame nobody but himself. His anger and frustration had driven him to join a crowd of young bucks gambling and drinking the night away in one of the worst hells around. He could remember trying to go round for round with Michael. Christian's younger brother was eager to enjoy every second of his youth.

Unfortunately, Struthers knew he was no longer that young, and now it was time to pay for his folly.

Stiffening his shoulders, he got out of bed and strode to the window, casting the curtains wide. It was still early. After all his years of living at sea he no longer had the ability to sleep the morning away. He looked out across the rooftops toward Anna's house. He could not see it, but he could imagine her still warm and sleepy, snuggled beneath her angels. He doubted she ever rose much before noon—although she'd always been up when he'd visited.

He called for his valet and requested a draught for his head. Wondering if this was how Anna had felt the previous afternoon, he splashed water on his face and waited for his valet to return. A close shave and meticulous wardrobe would be necessary for the visit to the Townsends. Strength was in the details.

There was a scratch on the door and then it opened quietly.

He took the drink and downed it in a swallow.

Then he noticed the note that also sat on the tray.

He couldn't remember ever noticing Anna's handwriting, but he knew without a single question that it was hers. He picked it up, turning the thick cream stationery in his hand. Elegant, costly, but not overstated. Very much his wife.

He broke the wax with his thumb and opened the fold. There was only a single sentence.

Do you like to play?

There was no signature, but he knew that she was not trying to be mysterious. Rather she expected him to know it was from her—as he had. He rubbed his fingers over the words. *Play?* What did she mean? And had she forgiven him, or was this some game? Well, obviously it was a game, but what did she mean by it?

He caught his valet's curious look and wiped the beginnings of a grin from his face. He gestured to the warm shaving water and sat.

Between Anna and the visit to the Townsends it was going to be a most interesting day—perhaps not miserable after all.

Would he be curious enough to answer? Anna knew that Struthers was not one to forgive easily—not that she had done anything that needed forgiving—but he was a man and undoubtedly saw the situation differently.

Had she forgiven him?

She rather thought she understood him, understood his reasoning.

But forgive him?

No, she had not, did not.

He was wrong. He had wronged her. No matter the law, she knew they'd had an agreement between them that her funds were to remain hers. They had never discussed that her funds were hers only as long as she didn't waste them.

No, her money was her own.

She stood and walked from her desk to stare blankly at the books upon the shelf.

She had never before hated being a woman. Not even her cousins and the threat of insanity they offered had made her feel like this.

She had known this was what marriage was, but had never believed it would actually trap her.

Damn him. She wanted to throw one of the books across the room and through the window, wanted to demonstrate that she still had power in her world.

But that would be insane. She ran her fingers over the spines of the books on the shelf. Wanton destruction was not the answer. She knew very well what it was she wished to destroy—Struthers's view of how the world worked.

And she would use the one tool he had left her, the one tool women always had.

If only he would reply.

As if in answer to her thoughts, there was a light tap on the door and Jameson entered at her call. "There is a note, ma'am, from Mr. Struthers."

Holding her fingers steady so as not to betray her nerves even to herself, Anna ripped open the note.

Play what?

He had not signed it. She pursed her lips in satisfaction. He was playing already, whether he knew it or not.

She took a small package carefully wrapped in tissue from her desk drawer and quickly jotted a note to accompany it. She did not have all the details in place yet, but she certainly knew how to set the lure.

It was not the first step she had planned, but it had come to her that some things were far better demonstrated than told.

She could only hope he would understand.

Jameson took the package from her and quietly left the room, leaving the door open a good two feet.

It was time to see Lady Smythe-Burke. Anna glanced at the clock—late enough to be proper, early enough that there were unlikely to be other visitors.

Perfect.

She cleared the top of her desk, carefully locking the drawers.

First she would visit Lady Smythe-Burke and then call on Maddie and their father. That visit she did not look forward to. Perhaps she should visit Struthers and his secretary, Timms, first and be sure she could secure the necessary funds—no, she was just avoiding unpleasantness and hoping to see Struthers.

She was just about to leave when Jameson knocked at

the door again and entered. "You have a caller, ma'am. Lady Smythe-Burke."

Now that was convenient—almost too much so.

Without waiting for Jameson to retrieve her, Lady Smythe-Burke sailed into the room. "Greetings, Anna."

Anna gave Jameson a small shrug of acceptance and nodded that he could leave. "Lady Smythe-Burke, it is a pleasure. And you must tell me how you do that."

That caught Lady Smythe-Burke by surprise. "Do what?"

"March into room without waiting to be called and still seem like it's the most proper thing in the world. It should be the worst of manners and yet you make it seem the utmost of propriety."

"I've always loved that you never just overlook things. You should be much too direct for a woman of your tender age, but somehow you do not offend."

"And I take it that is my answer also."

Lady Smythe-Burke merely looked back, giving the appearance of an accepting smile although Anna would have sworn not a muscle on her face moved.

"Your nephew, the Duke of Brisbane, can do that also—answer a question with a look the viewer is never quite sure is there."

"And who do you think taught him? I can assure you it was not his father. But, yes, that was my answer. It is all attitude. If you act like something is completely natural, then so will others. I think you know that already. Although I must admit that age helps also. These days if anything I am merely seen as eccentric." Lady Smythe-Burke's glance settled on the comfy seat before the fire and Anna invited her to sit, moving to join her.

"Should I send for tea?" Anna asked.

"We both might wish something a little more potent," Lady Smythe-Burke replied.

"At this hour?"

"I imagine you have heard that Lord Milson has been shot and is not expected to live."

Anna stiffened and then settled back in her chair. "Yes, I heard yesterday. Maddie is distraught. I was actually going to come and talk to you about the details. Maddie is beyond answering questions and my father—well, you know my father. I know that Milson was injured in a duel, but little more."

"It is not surprising that it was a duel, but the circumstances are not quite what one would expect. I do not know all the details—yes, I know that is surprising—but there was some talk of cheating. It is unclear from which side. There may also have been some talk of his wife's delicate condition—that is less clear. What I do know is that Lord Milson was ruined. There is hardly a penny to his name—less, I expect."

"So I learned last night. It was the one thing Maddie was coherent about—my need to pay her bills," Anna answered.

"I cannot say I am surprised. Given what you have already done for her, and she for you, it could only be expected that she would ask for more."

"She is my family."

"It would be very easy to offer her everything in the face of her loss."

"There is only a limited amount I can do at present. Struthers has taken over my accounts. He has offered me an allowance."

Lady Smythe-Burke betrayed no emotion, but her voice was sharp. "Isn't that generous of him."

"I thought we had an agreement that he would leave my money alone."

"There were all those rumors about India and what he did to secure his fortune. Is it surprising that he wants your fortune?"

"You told me to marry the man."

"And I still maintain it was the best solution given your options."

"I will have to confront him about his past—and come clean about my own, and my plans. Then at least I will know how to proceed."

"It is the only way. Now tell me, is there more news of your cousins?"

"I was going to ask if you had heard anything. They have mentioned both a minor accident Struthers had and Milson's shooting. They were very careful in their words, implying threat without actually taking credit for causing the problems. I do not know what to make of it. I could believe they hired somebody to run Struthers down on the street, but how do you cause a duel?"

Lady Smythe-Burke pressed her hands together and considered. "It is not as difficult as one might think. You find somebody who is a good shot and get him to provoke Milson. An accusation of cheating or comments that Milson was not the father of Maddie's child would do it. Although I am not sure how your cousins would have met Mr. James—the man who shot Milson. And James has already fled to the continent, so there will be no asking him."

"It seems more likely to me that they are merely taking advantage of a situation that already exists, implying threat when in truth they had nothing to do with it."

"That is certainly possible."

Anna rose from her chair and went to fiddle with the porcelain figurines on the mantel. "It is hard not knowing for sure—if I knew, then I could take action. I have asked my secretary to hire a Runner to look into the matter."

"That is sensible. I wish I had more information for you. I will certainly keep my ears open for any rumors about the Townsends."

"Thank you."

"Now we have strayed from the subject of your husband—what are you going to do about the man?"

"Let me send for that tea, with perhaps some sherry on the side." Anna leaned forward, inviting intimacy. "I need to ask your advice."

Chapter 18

"There, I've found it." It had been years since her father had responded with such joy. He entered the room waving a sheaf of papers about. Her father's joy was particularly surprising because he'd stormed from the room half an hour ago. Both Maddie and her father had been far from enthusiastic when she had told them she could not pay off the creditors instantly. She'd explained briefly, without detail, about Struthers and her temporary inability to access her funds. Her father had called her "ten times a fool" and proceeded to rant that Struthers had no such right.

"I'll be out in the streets," Maddie proclaimed, and then sank into a chair, tears running down her cheeks. Anna couldn't recall her shedding any actual tears for Milson, who still lingered abovestairs.

Her father had let loose a stream of curses she didn't want to repeat even in her mind and walked away—she'd rather thought he'd gone off to drink. But here he was waving about a bunch of papers and looking like he'd won the lottery.

"Your betrothal to Lord Adam was never broken. You can't be married to Struthers," he cried.

She resisted the urge to laugh. The idea was preposterous. Silly. Ridiculous.

And yet—

It would not be the first time that the farcical had held true. She remained quiet, waiting—not wanting to risk her father losing his train of thought.

"I signed contracts with Lord Adam's father."

"I have never heard of such a thing. Lord Adam asked and I said yes. You and his father were not involved." That had to be true, it had to.

"We did not sign them then. It was after you inherited. I went to his father—said I wanted to protect you and your property. I was to be given a certain portion upon the marriage to set aside for you should anything happen."

"I cannot believe even you would do a thing like that without at least informing me."

"I did not wish to disturb you with things you did not need to know." Her father waved the papers in the air again. "We are saved."

If her father had hidden it from her he had done it for himself, not for her. "And why do you mention this now? I am married to Struthers." Even with all her doubts about Struthers she knew he was a better choice than Lord Adam.

"Are you sure?"

"Yes, I am rather—I can see that I might owe Lord Adam some legal recompense, or perhaps I owe it to his father. I can assure you I would have taken care of it at the time had I known of the contract's existence. Still, the world has changed; a betrothal is not the same as a marriage."

"You are right that the world has changed. However, you did consummate your vows—whether they happened or not."

If she had felt sick before, now she truly felt nauseous.

Her father did not lie. It had been only once, and she had tried to forget it for years, but it had happened. "That is still not the same as marriage. And how do you know?"

"Lord Adam told me—and I believe I could find many that would disagree with you. A betrothal contract. A consummated pledge. I do not think that society has changed as much as you believe."

"Society may not have, but the law has." She pulled her stomach muscles in tight, trying to settle herself. "And why would Lord Adam tell you?"

"He was trying to persuade me that you must honor your pledge. Unfortunately you had quit speaking to me at the time so I could not mention the contract."

She did remember that. Her father had been impossible in the face of her broken engagement and she had refused to see him or answer his letters. "It matters not. I am married to Struthers. There was no actual wedding with Lord Adam—no lines, no parish register, no witness—no wedding."

Her father looked perplexed for a moment. For whatever reason he had thought she would welcome his news. "I'll have to think about that. It would be so much more convenient if you had married Lord Adam."

Yes, bigamy would have been so much more convenient. She held her tongue; sometimes there was no reasoning with her father.

The clock chimed on the mantel.

She was late to meet Struthers. It made a poor start to her game.

Where was Anna? He'd been unsure of her motives. What man wouldn't have been? She'd been angry enough to pull hair when she left him yesterday, and today the flirtatious notes. She was planning something. The only question was what. He'd given up his meeting with the Townsends to be here.

He slipped a hand into his pocket and caressed the soft leather of the glove he'd placed in it. Soft crimson leather. It was so very Anna, simply cut, unmistakably feminine, and yet extremely classic. Why had she sent it? A single glove—what did it mean?

Pulling out the note, he read it again.

What fun would it be if I told?

That was all the note said. It had been accompanied by the single glove well wrapped in tissue, with a sliver of paper tucked in its palm. An unfamiliar direction was on the paper along with simple instructions—*Dress simply, old shoes, and be prepared to drive. 2:00.*

It was now two-fifteen and there was nobody here. He felt a fool as he sat in his curricle and waited. Was she coming? Was anybody coming?

Fingering the glove again, he considered. Her not coming was possible. Something could have come up. Or perhaps she had never meant to come.

Even as he rejected the thought he saw her hurrying down the street. A plain dark cloak was wrapped tight about her, but even if she'd had the hood up he would have recognized that distinctive walk.

She lifted her face, saw him, and smiled. It was a guarded smile, but still definitely a smile.

"I wasn't sure you'd wait—if you came at all," she said, pulling level with the curricle.

Swinging down to hand her up, he replied, "I wasn't sure either—that you were coming."

Her skirts filled the seat as she settled beside him. "I was with Maddie. For all she doesn't seem pleased to see me, I feel a responsibility to visit and wait with her. Milson still lives."

"I am glad. I know that his passing will not be easy on her."

Her face stilled at his comment and it was hard to tell what she thought beyond a slight grimace of displeasure—and was that insecurity? It seemed unlike her, but he rather thought it was. "I will need to speak to you about that later. It appears that Milson may have been in debt. I must supply some funds while his matters are straightened out. It will also be necessary to supply money for my father's care."

He noticed that she carefully did not ask him to release the funds, acting more like it was fact that she would supply the money for her family. "I have already instructed Timms to release monies as you need them—he will require to know what they are for."

Her lips pursed, but she said nothing. Instead she reached into her reticule and pulled out another slip of paper. She handed it to him.

"This is quite a drive, well over an hour—maybe two."

"Yes, I know just where it is. I will give you more exact direction when we are close," she responded, looking straight ahead.

The imposing brick building rose before them. Even seeing it from a distance made Anna shudder. Objectively the building was quite unremarkable. Even the presence of several boarded windows and several windows with bars locked over them did not deter much from its relative normality.

Still, she shuddered. Even the first time that she'd seen it, before she'd walked through its great doors, it had made her shiver and flinch. It was not the gently rolling park that surrounded it, or even the high stone wall with only the solitary entrance to the road that had frightened her. The high-peaked roof, the ivy climbing one side, the sound of birds in the trees—there was nothing startling about any of it.

But there was something, something that made the viewer beware.

Could despair be seen?

"What is this place?" Struthers asked as he steered through the open cast-iron gate. He looked around with curiosity, but also, she believed, a certain wariness.

"This is Sherberry. There's a small plaque near the door, but otherwise they leave it unmarked."

"Sherberry?" he questioned, then a pause. "You don't mean the asylum, do you? The home for the deranged and insane?"

She stared at the great wood doors, beautiful—but oh so thick and heavy. "Yes. You called me insane. I wanted you to see what it really meant—and what the results of such an accusation should be." Only with great effort did she hold her voice level.

"This seems like rather a large step to take. I can assure you that I meant nothing by the comment—and would have understood if you had explained."

There was still so much more to tell him—after they had been through the building she would explain about her cousins. "I would admit it is not what I had planned as the first step of our game. I did have something significantly more entertaining in mind. I do think you need to see this, though."

"Are they expecting us?"

"No, but they are used to well-to-do visitors coming to gawk. I can assure you we will be most welcome for the price of a few shillings."

"You seem to know the place well."

"I had my reasons to visit. I know it is not the normal thing for a woman of my station, but it was important. I have also sent gift baskets for the inmates from time to time."

They pulled up in front of the entrance and Struthers turned and stared at her. He was clearly questioning her motivation. She did not say anything, but waited for him to hand her down.

They walked up stairs to the great door and Struthers knocked upon it. It felt like the sound echoed within her chest. Anna turned and watched the groom walking the horses down the drive. She wanted to follow him and leave this place. There was a reason she had sent baskets of food and small items rather than returning herself.

A tall, slightly gaunt man dressed in neat black opened the door and allowed the entrance. It was a matter of moments to explain what they wanted and slip a few shillings to the man. He led them down a dark hall to a locked door at the end. "The attendants should keep the worst of them from you, and the very worst are of course restrained. I do recommend, however, that you do not try talking to patients as they may be riled."

He unlocked the door and they stepped through.

The first thing to hit was the smell. Dank and dark, it swirled about them as they peered into the dimly lit room. It was different from the smell of sewers or of filth, but it contained elements of both. Sometimes it would visit her while she slept, turning her dreams to nightmares.

Slipping her hand into Struthers's arm she led him forward. A cluster of men sat at a table near the door staring blankly at one another. Another black-clad attendant reminiscent of a soldier stood nearby. Two of the patients were in restraints, leather cuffs holding their arms tight against their bodies. One had a fierce burn across his forehead. "They brand them sometimes, high on the head, to help bring them to their senses. I have not had the courage to ask if it ever works," she whispered to Struthers.

They passed several small antechambers bare of all but cots. Several had shut doors, and loud screams and rants came from within. She inched closer to Struthers.

An attendant approached. "Is there something in particular I can help you with? Something you want to see?" His words were simple, but his tone implied much.

"I'd like to see the women's wing." Anna spoke firmly, but knew she was squeezing Struthers's arm hard.

"You sure? It's not bath day and we don't have any pretty ones at present." He glanced at Struthers. "Visitors always like bath day best. How about the spinning room? There are a couple scheduled for treatment. There's nothing like watching their faces as the chair picks up speed. We're not supposed to let visitors in, but you look like good people." The attendant's fingers moved, requesting payment.

Anna slipped another shilling into her palm and handed it over. "The women's wing will be fine. We are not looking for anything special."

The attendant eyed them. Struthers stayed silent as he had since they entered, but his hand slipped about her waist. The amount of protection and safety contained in those warm fingers surprised her. She leaned back into his chest.

Shrugging his shoulders, the attendant led them across the room and through a second locked door. This room was hardly more than a long corridor with a high fogged window at one end.

Only a couple of patients even looked up as they

entered. On the far side of the room a woman suddenly began to thrash around, screaming obscenities. Another attendant quickly grabbed her and hustled her into one of the adjunct rooms. The door slammed shut and one shrill scream echoed. Then silence. The attendant exited. The patient did not.

Anna forced herself to walk toward a table of seated women. Only one looked up as she approached.

"Hello," Anna said gently.

Nobody answered. The woman who had looked up glanced nervously at the attendants.

"Did you get the basket I sent?" Anna addressed the one woman she recognized from her previous visit, a hunched, pale blonde. The woman just stared at her hands and did not answer.

"I sent books like you asked. Did you get them?"

Again no answer. Then the woman lifted her hands and placed them flat on the table, or as flat as she could. Her fingers were bruised, the knuckles swollen, several fingers bent at wrong angles as if broken. Anna could almost feel the rod coming down hard upon her own hands. She tucked her fingers more tightly into the strength of Struthers's arm.

After a moment, the woman lifted her face and stared straight at Anna. Her eyes brimmed with despair and hopelessness. She turned her hands over. There was a single deep burn across one palm. "Women do not read. It is bad for the mind, promotes hysteria. I wish only to think dutiful thoughts." Her eyes dropped back to the table.

Anna started to answer, but stopped. There was nothing she could say that would bring comfort. The last time she had been here, only a few scant months ago, Mrs. Jones—the woman's name slipped into her mind—had still held out hope. She had told her story to Anna and asked if Anna could send some books to fill the day. Anna had complied, her conscience salved by the simple gesture. Now guilt plagued her. Had she caused the brutal beating of Mrs. Jones's hands?

She turned to Struthers. "I am ready to leave."

He nodded. "Will you tell me why we are here? I can assure you that I will never doubt your sanity again—or make any comment which makes light of such places." He glanced around, the distaste for the place clear on his face.

"We will talk on the drive home. Now I just want to be gone." She glanced back at the table, not at Mrs. Jones, but at the other women. The ones with blank eyes, not even despair left to show who they had once been.

He waited for her to speak. It had been half an hour and still she stayed quiet. He had never been to such a place before and hoped never to be again. He'd seen more horrible sights in life, but none had been so blanketed in tragedy. Even in the worst of war there was hope for survival. That had been lacking there.

Why had she brought him there? He glanced sideways at her. Debated whether to speak.

She met his gaze. "Do you remember before we were wed we spoke of the powerlessness of women?"

"Yes." How was that relevant?

"The woman with the broken hands—her name is Mrs. Jones—she is at the core of what I said."

"I do not understand."

"She objected to her husband spending more money on his mistress than his children. This is her reward."

"I am still not sure that I follow."

"She spoke against her husband and he declared her insane and had her brought to Sherberry. I wish you could have seen her the last time I was here. Now she looks almost as if she belongs, then she did not. I do not know what happened to her—and I do not want to know. What is important is that she represents the reality of a woman's power in the world. We belong to our husbands and they can do with us what they wish—short of blatant murder."

"I can't believe—"

"Do not pretend to be so naïve. You know it as well as I."

He pulled the horses to a stop so he could turn to her fully. "Yes, I do know that it is true. And I know that bad things happen. I do not see what that has to do with us."

She pulled in a deep breath. Even with her heavy cloak wrapped around her he could see the rise and fall of her breasts. "You can take all my money—just because you are my husband—and you wonder at the relevance."

"So this is about your money?"

Her breasts rose and fell again. He shifted in the seat. He had not thought about his desire for her, his want for her, since they had pulled onto Sherberry's grounds. Now with a few deep breaths he was reminded all too well.

Her eyes flashed as she caught his gaze dropping. "No, it is not about my money."

He looked into her eyes again. "What then?"

"You have asked again and again about my cousins and their hold over me. This is it."

He blinked. "What?"

"They threatened to have me declared insane."

"I don't see how . . ."

She held his gaze steadily. "It would have been far easier than you think. I am almost thirty and unmarried despite being asked multiple times. I control a fortune—or at least I did—and have never asked for a man's help. I—I have had several lovers and while I have been discreet, it is not unknown. If you combine these factors it is clear that I cannot be in my right mind. Our public display in the hall would have been the last straw."

"Your father?"

"Is more concerned with who pays the bills than my welfare. I daresay my cousins could bribe him and he is resentful that I have not followed his guidance."

So much suddenly made sense—all those moments he had sensed quiet fear in her. She had been terrified that she would end in a place like Sherberry—or perhaps someplace even worse. Feeling her discomfort, he turned back to the road and gave the reins a jerk. The horses started forward. "Are you scared that I would do such a thing?"

"I cannot deny I have given it thought—but no, not really."

"Good." The thought of Anna in such a place disquieted him so greatly that he pushed the thought away, hard. "I assure you I deal with my problems much more directly."

"Do you?"

"What does that mean?"

"I have heard many rumors about India—that does not sound so direct."

He jerked the reins again, stopping. "That is no one's concern but mine."

"There is talk of another wife."

"I did not marry Sunita." He knew that she could hear his regret.

"I would like you to tell me the whole story. I am your wife now. Does not that give me a right?" She laid a hand upon his arm.

The warmth of her fingers leaked through his jacket, inviting and demanding.

"I do not know," he answered.

Her thumb stroked up his arm.

He turned and looked down at her. She was licking her lips. He felt a desire to kiss her nerves away and forced his gaze back to the road. "I will think on it. That is the best I can do."

She had not wanted him to spend the night. He'd thought their glances and quiet conversation had meant something, but when he'd pulled up in front of her house Anna descended and said she would see him on the morrow.

There had been a slight smile and indication that he could expect another message from her, but she'd been clear that she did not wish his company, did not wish for him.

He could have insisted, but after the day they had spent even the thought was distasteful.

And so he was heading home alone.

Damn. The woman knew how to punish him.

Only he didn't think she meant it as punishment.

She truly wanted to be alone. He would actually have preferred if it was punishment. Anger would have been easier to deal with than whatever it was he felt.

He pulled up in front of his house and waited for the groom to take the curricle back to the mews.

Before he'd even made it down the front stairs he saw the man. Michael Remington stood across the street, staring at his home. Relief marked Michael's face when Struthers turned and walked toward him.

Michael hurried across the street to Struthers. "I must talk to you."

"I will certainly not prevent you from doing so," Struthers replied. "Surely you could have waited inside. I am sure my porter would have granted you entrance."

"I wanted air," Michael said. "Milson is dead."

"You mean shot, wounded."

"No, he died an hour ago." Michael shuddered visibly.

"Why do you care? You did not kill him—or have anything to do with his death."

Michael did not answer.

"Can you in any way be implicated in his death?" Struthers asked.

"No, damn it, I wasn't there. I was out with friends. I hadn't even seen the man in well over a week."

"And Lady Milson, had you seen her?"

Michael paled at the words. "No—but you have the core of the matter. I have not seen Maddie since Lady Smythe-Burke's party, but—but it is said that Milson was in the duel because doubts were cast on his paternity of his wife's child. What if somebody knows of my relationship with Maddie?"

"I had not heard that rumor. I thought he was accused of cheating?"

"No, it was that he was a cuckold."

"Are you worried that there will be talk you were involved in the shooting?"

"No, a good crowd saw him shot and can say who did it. Mr. James made derogatory comments about Maddie and Milson's virility. Milson challenged him immediately. Milson was a good shot. He winged James, but James shot him straight in the chest. Milson did not have a chance."

"No, he would not have. And you say he is dead?"

"Yes."

Anna would not have the night alone that she had requested. "And what of Lady Milson?"

"What of her?"

"You do realize you will need to stay away from her until all has settled down—give her a decent time to mourn."

Michael turned his head away. "That will not be a problem. She made it clear that she was through with me after your conversation."

"Good, then why are you concerned that you are the cause of the gossip that she was unfaithful—although I can assure you that she has been many times."

Michael paled further. "I am not naïve."

"Then you should be aware that James probably was just provoking Milson for his own reason. There are enough rumors that he did not need to know anything specific."

"But why would he—"

"That is not your concern. You should keep as far away from the whole affair as is possible. Even if you were not involved rumor is unpleasant." Struthers wished he could just send Michael away, but the boy was young and since his father's death had not had a male figure to advise him. It was such a shame that Christian had died before taking over the estates. It was a wonder this boy had not lost it all, something Struthers was determined to keep true. Christian's family had always accepted him when he'd been a rough boy and he was determined to return the favor.

"If you say so."

"I do. Now does anyone besides me know of your involvement with Lady Milson?"

"A couple of friends—but they will not say anything."

"Make sure they don't. Lord Milson's death changes things. You want no connection between yourself and the new widow. I would advise you take a trip, get out of London for a while."

"Why? I don't see what purpose that would serve."

"It will keep you away from Lady Milson."

"I told you—Maddie is done with me."

"You might find things have changed." Struthers placed a hand on the boy's shoulder. "She might do nothing, but you say the woman has just found herself made penniless and has a child on the way. She might find you and your holdings a nice catch."

Michael paled by several shades. "I never thought—"

"You said that nothing had actually happened between you until Lady Smythe-Burke's house party. Is that true?"

"Yes, what reason would I have to lie?"

Struthers could think of several, but he did not feel the need to burden Michael with them. The boy's very confusion indicated that he spoke the truth. "It does not matter. What does matter is that Lady Milson began to talk about the child then. If that is true then the child cannot be yours. It is undoubtedly her husband's as she has claimed. I think you have nothing to worry about, nothing to feel guilty about—but stay away from Lady Milson."

Color flooded back into Michael's face. "I will head to my estates. No doubt they need tending." The boy nodded and was off.

Chapter 19

Anna looked about her office, the high book-filled shelves, the neat row of pens and ink, the thick unmarked blotter, the dark wood desk, its drawers filled with neat piles of correspondence and her accounts. This room was the heart of her home. It represented all that she liked about herself.

Well, maybe not quite all—she was coming to be rather fond of the power to draw her husband like a moth to flame. She'd never quite appreciated just how wonderful a woman's power could be. Oh, she'd enjoyed demonstrating it in the past, but she'd never really enjoyed it the way she was now.

She glanced down at the note she was in the process of writing, the next step in their game. Her lips curled up at the corners. She could only trust Struthers would find this step much more enjoyable than the last.

A large, indelicate yawn escaped her, making her glad she was alone with no need of feminine pretext. Last night had been awful once she'd heard of Milson's death and hurried over. Maddie had wailed and wailed, repeating over and over that she had nothing now and would be out on the streets with her baby. Anna had stroked her back and comforted her, telling her that of course she would take care of Maddie and her child.

Maddie had not appeared to hear her. Finally in the early hours of the morning Maddie had drifted off to sleep and Anna had been able to return home.

Their father had been notable only in his absence.

Stretching, Anna glanced down at her note to Struthers. She refused to let Milson's death govern her life. When Maddie called for her she would come—but until then she was determined that her life be her own.

She pulled another tissue-wrapped package from the drawer and slipped her note into it.

This task was much more enjoyable than the last. She could only hope that Struthers felt the same.

St. Andrew's Rectory. 11:00. So here he was. Where was she?

Was she going to keep him waiting every time?

And why the second red glove? What was he supposed to do with a pair of ladies' gloves?

He'd been considering that for a good ten minutes. He rubbed his hands together, trying to warm them. He had his own gloves in his pocket, but had not bothered to don them.

He'd been surprised when the note arrived this morning. She must know about Milson, so why was she still playing games? Unless their game was that important to her. The thought brought a faint smile with it.

"Mr. Struthers, I did not expect to find you here."

He turned at the sound of the voice.

Violet—Lady Carrington—was hurrying up the street. "Have you come for the meeting?" she asked.

He almost asked what meeting, but restrained himself. He must remember that Violet and Anna were good friends. If she was here it must be related to Anna's note. "Why, yes. It is a pleasant surprise to find you here."

"I am surprised Anna didn't mention it. I've been trying to get her more directly involved for quite a while. She should know that starting something and running it are entirely different things."

So his wife wasn't going to be here. He should have known a church rectory was an unlikely place for her—although it was for Violet as well. And just what was it that Anna had started?

Violet took his arm and gestured for him to precede her up the steps. "I am surprised you didn't go in. I am frightfully late and Lady Pereson always starts a few minutes early. Ah, well, come along."

With a swish of her skirts Violet headed up the stairs. He almost laughed. She held his arm. He was supposed to lead. How very like Anna she was. Well, it was time to see what fate and his wife had in store for him.

Women's Community Fund.

I went. I listened. I donated.

Anna folded Struthers's reply and placed it on her desk.

She was tempted to reply, *With whose funds? Mine or yours?*—but she did not. It would spoil the fun of the game, and perhaps the lesson, if she did. Besides, she was confident that he had used his own money. It was simply the type of man he was.

She'd spent the day working on her accounts and waiting for Maddie to send for her. It had been an extremely productive afternoon and she felt more herself than she had in weeks. The clock chimed and she glanced over at it. She'd have to leave for Maddie's soon, summoned or not. Her absence would be remarked on and she had no desire to court any more gossip.

But for now—she glanced down at Struthers's note.

What had he thought when he'd walked into a room full of women planning how to invest the funds they'd collected in ways that were both profitable and created opportunities for other women? When she'd first helped Mr. Jackal set up the organization to help women with slight funds invest in markets they could not afford alone, it had seemed a small thing. Then they'd purchased a shipment of China silk that had tripled their investment. It was amazing how a room full of practical-minded women could understand just what would sell in nine months' time.

Struthers had used the word *donated*. She wondered how he would feel when he realized it was a sound investment—that a group of grocers' wives could choose investments more soundly than anyone else she knew.

Jameson tapped on the door and entered carrying correspondence on a silver tray. From across the room Anna could pick out her sister's stationery. It was time to go. She nodded politely at Jameson and waited until he'd left the room to release a great sigh.

She glanced at the clock again. She could afford a few more minutes.

Pulling another package out of the desk she considered. Was it too soon for another note, another step in her plan? No. It was not.

Struthers leaned back and stared down at his desk. The previous afternoon he'd received a pair of silk stockings clocked with roses—red ones that almost matched the gloves. Was she planning to send him an entire wardrobe? Was she going to strip herself naked sending him gifts?

Even as he had the thought he knew the answer. Yes, she was. That was the purpose, the reward, the win.

One naked, willing wife in return for, what? Following her directions?

He glanced at the next sheet. *How willing are you*? Enclosed also was the direction to Barons Bank and an appointment time for today. Did Anna really expect him to have her funds released because he'd seen a bunch of women working to invest money and had been persuaded to add some of his own?

Granted, there was much he would do to have Anna naked in his bed, in his home—a feat he still had not managed. And he was beginning to think he'd release her funds to her anyway. Would it hurt to do it on her command? He would naturally have to be clear that it was the course he had chosen before all this nonsense had begun.

It was only stubbornness that kept him from doing as she wished. He rather liked the idea of her gratitude if he released her funds. He was not so sure that he wanted her to believe she had in any way influenced that decision.

And—he did wonder about her plans. It might be enjoyable, very enjoyable, to see just how far she was willing to go.

He went to his desk and jotted down a note to Timms. Should he write one to Anna or just show up for his appointment at the bank? A reply, yes, definitely he should reply. He took up his pen again and jotted it down, along with further instructions for Timms. Two could play at this game now that he understood the rules.

He was whistling as he grabbed his hat, cane, and gloves and headed toward the front door without waiting for the porter. Stopping, he stepped back to his desk and grabbed the red gloves, slipping them into his pocket and then turning once again to the door. He'd spend the rest of the morning at his club, complete his errand at Barons Bank, and have a quiet dinner back at the club; a nice early evening—unless his wife was ready to join him.

She was probably busy with Lady Milson. He'd have to add a condolence visit to his list. He'd go before visiting the bank—save the fun for after.

She'd spent five hours sitting with Maddie and her other callers last night and another four this morning. Anna's eyes felt like they hadn't closed in a week. She held her head perfectly upright and willed her lids to stay open. Between Milson's death, wondering what her cousins would do next, and the game with Struthers, she had lain awake most of the night. At least thinking about Struthers had not been unpleasant—but neither had it been restful.

This morning she'd been fine, but now as midafternoon approached, all she could think of was sleep.

Gads, that was nonsense. All she could think of was Struthers.

Thoughts of him filled her even in this black-draped chamber. She glanced about Maddie's parlor at the old biddies who'd come to "condole" Maddie. There was no way to think of them except as biddies—or perhaps crows—this black-clad crowd of older women who seemed to arrive whenever the news was bad.

They'd looked askance at her and her deep blue gown. When exactly did they think she'd had time to get a black one? Not that she was sure she was going to. She'd never gotten along with Milson and didn't wish to pretend to feelings she didn't have—and Maddie was barely tolerating her presence.

She didn't know why her half sister had taken such a sudden dislike to her, but it was there in her every movement. Maddie did not want Anna there. Some of it clearly had to do with Anna's failure to pay all of Milson's debts instantly.

She'd been to the bank to arrange the funds, but she wanted a far better understanding of exactly what was owed before she took any further steps. She'd brought enough to cover Maddie's day-to-day expenses, but Maddie clearly wanted and expected more—not that Maddie hadn't grabbed the proffered money from Anna's fingers readily enough. Once Maddie had it in hand, though, she was ready for Anna to leave.

The worst was that Anna had missed Struthers's call on Maddie because of her visit to the bank. It seemed ironic that while she was at the bank with Lady Brattle, Struthers was with Maddie, and now that she was with Maddie . . .

Had Struthers visited Lady Brattle at the bank yet? It was still an hour until the appointment she had made, but she grew impatient.

She looked at the biddies again. Could they look at her any more coldly if she left? There were no strict standards of protocol for a half brother-in-law.

And she needed another gift to go with the next package. She knew just where and what she was going to send him.

One of the old biddies coughed and sent her a glare, and Anna realized she was smiling. She forced her face back into a flat look of grief.

The biddy would probably shoot fire from her eyes if she knew what Anna was really thinking—what she intended to do as soon as she left.

"Please be seated," Lady Brattle said as she led him into her office. She gestured to the chair on the opposite side of the large wooden desk. The top stretched smooth between them, completely clear.

"I imagine you know why I am here." He saw no need for pretense.

"Yes, your wife mentioned you might be interested in starting an additional account with us."

He stopped a minute, the reply he had been about to give suddenly irrelevant. "Don't you mean to discuss my wife's accounts and allowing her access to them?"

Lady Brattle placed her hands flat on the desk in front of her. "My understanding is that as of your wedding they became your accounts. How you choose to handle them is completely your own business. Barons Bank does of course hope that you will leave the monies here, but we really have no say in the matter. Miss Steele—forgive me, Mrs. Struthers—knows how this works. We have corresponded on the subject many times over the past few years. She would never do anything as improper as to suggest that I talk to you about such a matter."

"Then why am I here?"

Impatience was written across Lady Brattle's face as she answered, "I do believe I just said that I had been told you had interest in setting up an additional account. I was given to understand that you had some nervousness at putting your funds in a bank with a woman as one of the principals. Was I misinformed? I do assure you that I have other ways to spend my afternoon."

Struthers leaned back in his chair. Anna's game differed from what he had expected. Still, he was not averse to seeing where this went. If nothing else it would assure him that Anna had invested wisely, although he had to admit he had few remaining doubts. "Why don't you tell me how you would advise me to place my funds?" he asked, leaning in toward Lady Brattle.

* * *

It was the most beautiful chemise Anna had ever bought. It was hard to resist the urge to slip her fingers into the package to feel the fine cotton. Rose petals could not be softer or gentler on the skin. It was an incredible luxury to have an undergarment made out of fabric that would normally be saved for a summer gown, but Anna could only imagine Struthers's face when he saw her robed in the translucent fabric, every curve revealed, every shadow hinting at further delights. The garment was deceptively sweet and innocent, but once she put it on . . . Even she had been shocked when she had seen what an effect her body had on the soft white cotton.

She began to hum as she slipped from her modiste's storefront and scanned the street for her carriage. It was a glorious day that could only grow finer. She was not going to think of Maddie or Milson's debts or her cousins. She would think only of her husband and the plans she had.

She nodded at an acquaintance and stepped back into the shade of the building. There was her carriage, far down the street. Her driver must have moved to make way for another vehicle to pass.

She raised her arm to wave. Suddenly she was jostled, pulled back, hard fingers biting into her arm. She turned, trying to shake free, when she felt the cold bite of the blade against her throat.

Chapter 20

She'd been robbed. Anna collapsed into a chair and stared into the fire. She'd been robbed.

In full daylight on a busy street.

She put her hand to her throat. The cold feeling of the knife pressing against it remained.

There was no mark. Only a few bruises on her upper arm remained to demonstrate what had happened. Without their reminder she might not have believed it was real.

There were things she should do, people she should let know, but her mind refused to cooperate.

Pulling in a deep breath, she tried to relax the muscles in her neck, to release the tightness in her shoulders. It was all so unbelievable.

For a moment she'd thought it was the end, that her cousins had decided to take that final step.

She'd seen Struthers's face in her mind, wished she'd had the chance to resolve things between them, the chance to find out all that their marriage could be.

Then her reticule had been grabbed, the straps broken—and the knife was gone. The man was gone.

Her coach had pulled up, the driver unaware that anything had happened. She'd gotten in without a word, her mind blank.

At least the man had not grabbed her package, her next reward for Struthers. Pressing a hand to her head, she admitted the absurdity of the thought.

And now here she was—at home safe—and still not doing anything.

She should tell her husband. She should tell the authorities. She should— She wasn't even sure what she should do. Nothing like this had ever happened to her before.

There was a package on her desk. A wrapped bundle. Papers, perhaps?

Had her husband sent her something?

She reached out to open it, and stopped. Her fingers were shaking. She flexed them open and closed and open again, until they began to obey.

Pulling her penknife from the drawer, she carefully slit the cord—and stopped.

It was not from her husband.

There was no note, but only her cousins could have sent this—this thing.

Her eyes skimmed down the document as shock turned to anger.

It was a contract agreeing to pay her cousins to take over her remaining shipping interests. The gall of the men. It was not enough that they demand she give them her share of the company, no, she had to pay them to take it.

And the timing.

Could it possibly be coincidence that this arrived immediately after her attack? It seemed most unlikely.

Sitting with iron control, she forced herself not to fidget, only to think. She was a woman. She was used to operating without being under anyone's control. It had been the purpose behind her game with Struthers—to begin to teach about the power women didn't have and the power that they did—behind the scenes.

She tapped her pen on the desk again and considered. She began a careful list of pluses and minuses—and another of possibilities. She might have more choices than her cousins thought.

If only she dared.

She refused to be a helpless woman.

But she also didn't wish to be a dead one.

How much risk was there? How far would her cousins go?

Setting aside the package, she grabbed her pen and wrote quickly to her husband, both setting him another task and asking him to meet her at the Wimberleys' ball tonight.

The marquess had always thrown a wonderful party, one of the best of the season. If her cousins held true to form they would be unable to resist.

There would be safety in confronting them in the midst of a crowd, safety in telling them just what she intended.

And with Struthers there she'd have security. She wanted her husband's support, needed her husband's support—with him there she would have the courage to do what needed to be done.

She called for her maid and went to dress.

The ballroom glowed like her mother's jewelry box in candlelight. The swirl of bright gowns filled the room with wonder. It was far from the first such affair Anna had attended. It might actually be far from the hundredth, but still she was struck by the magic of it all as she entered the room. The Marquess of Wimberley had always thrown a magnificent party, but on this occasion he had outdone himself.

Yes, it was a magical evening—a true crush, but

somehow without the actual sense of being pressed against.

The only difficulty was that she felt as if she were outside it all looking in, a child with her nose pressed against the bakery window. People laughed, couples flirted, and everyone smiled—everyone except her. Oh, from the outside she probably had her lips curled up, an appropriate expression of pleasure upon her face, but Anna knew that the sense of enjoyment went no deeper than her skin.

Inside she was a mass of nerves—the shock of the robbery still with her. Were her cousins here? When would Struthers arrive?

"Anna, I am so glad to see you."

Anna turned, startled, to see her friend Clara, Lady Westington, coming toward her. Damn. She would love to talk to Clara—but not now.

Clara continued, "I feared that handsome husband of yours would sweep you off to the continent for a wedding trip."

Anna pulled in a deep breath and chose her answer with care. She might have written her friend about the wedding, but this was not the moment to share the details of her marriage. "No, Struthers decided it was best to stay in Town for the season."

Clara eyed her carefully and then asked, "Are you well?"

Anna could feel the probing in the simple question. A part of her longed to share all with her old friend; for now, however, until she decided what to do, discretion was the better answer. "Yes, I am well. And you?"

Clara wrinkled her lips. Clearly she wanted more detail, but all she asked was "And Struthers, he is well also?"

"Yes." Anna found herself unable to say more, hoping that Clara would let the subject drop. She wanted to be searching for her husband, not talking of him.

Clara was not so obliging. "I was surprised to hear of your nuptials. I did not even know that you were acquainted with the man. I played cards with him on several occasions and he seemed an—an unusual choice as a spouse."

She hadn't even known Clara knew her husband. Granted, it was not surprising—Clara had always moved with a wild crowd and it was only to be expected that she would have become acquainted with Struthers. Anna had known that Struthers liked to gamble, if not to excess. She worked to smile at her friend, ignoring the kernel of jealousy that caught at her chest. "You mean you charmed him into throwing in his last penny?"

"No, not at all." Clara laughed. "I never played a game requiring deep pockets with him. His play was far too serious for me."

Clara clearly knew Struthers far better than Anna liked. She forced a light response. "Struthers does take his games seriously. All of them."

"You still have not mentioned how you met."

"We became reacquainted at Brisbane's house party. We had known each other years ago." She could only hope Clara would not inquire further. It was not the story for a crowded ballroom.

"I haven't spoken to Brisbane for months," Clara replied. "His aunt still writes frequently."

"Does she fit as many words into her correspondence as her conversation?" Finally a chance to change the subject. It was far easier to discuss Lady Smythe-Burke or even Brisbane than her absent husband.

Clara lifted a brow and gave her a clear look. "You

know Lady Smythe-Burke. What do you think?"

"Mrs. Struthers. Lady Westington. It is so good to see you both in Town." Lady Howe joined the conversation, her husband in tow. "I was not aware that you had arrived so early for the season. Although I did of course see the announcement of your marriage in the paper, Anna. It was so bad of you not to have a formal wedding. It's a shame you were in such a hurry." It was impossible to miss the way Lady Howe's eyes dropped to Anna's stomach as she spoke.

It was almost enough to make Anna exclaim that she was not pregnant. She pressed her lips tightly closed and counted to ten before giving a polite reply. She had to get out of there.

She glanced over at Clara to see if she had caught the implication, but her friend's eyes were searching the room. Anna could not see for whom she was searching. Still—

"You must excuse me," Anna said. "I see Lady Wimberley, and as I arrived late I did not have a chance to greet her." She hurried off before anyone could notice that Marguerite was nowhere in sight. She would need to make a point of hunting her down later—although Marguerite was sure to ask more questions and Anna really did not have the energy to answer another question.

She was just about to step into an alcove to hide for a moment when she heard the dreaded voice behind her.

"It is good to see you, cousin. I was afraid you had taken ill—or perhaps suffered an accident as we have not heard from you in over a day," Nathanial said.

Anna stopped and turned, wishing she could grow six inches taller and tower above the man. What did he know about the robbery? "I do not remember Rhode Island being so different. Surely it takes more than a day without contact to assume someone has been overtaken by the plague?"

"Ah, but we've been expecting an answer to our generous proposal."

Anna held back all the words she wanted to say. She had only had the contract a few hours and already her cousins were pressing for an answer. Why were they in such a hurry? If only Struthers was here. She always felt safer when he was around.

Why had he not responded to her note?

Playing for time, she said. "Is that what you call it, a generous proposal?"

"What else?"

"Why not call it what it is—blackmail."

"I don't know what you are talking about?"

"Then why do you mention my accident? I assume you are referring to the robbery this afternoon? You should have had your man kill me. That is the only way you will get what you want."

Nathanial's eyes flickered. "I can only repeat. I do not know what you are talking about."

She was glad she had come. Her cousin was nervous. He might swagger and sound firm, but there was something he was not sure about. She only wished she knew how to find out what.

"Just as you know nothing of Struthers's accident, or Milson's duel? If you are going to threaten me—do it straight. I am not one for games." *At least not games of this nature.*

Where was her husband? She did not wish full confrontation until he was beside her, supporting her.

Nathanial pulled himself up to full height. "All I will say is that we expect those forms and soon or you may not like the consequences."

A part of her wanted to give in, to take the easy road. But she did not like his threats to her—or to Struthers. They gave her renewed strength. "You will just have to wait. You may believe you hold all the power, but I am not a fool. I am aware of all that you would lose by playing your card. You might be rid of me—but the estate might be tied up for years in court. I think you need things resolved slightly sooner than that. I have heard that your finances are not all that you would wish." She let the words hang.

Nathanial's lips drew together tightly until they were only a crooked line across his face. "Do not wait too long, little cousin. Do not wait too long."

Struthers stared down the long, dark street leading to the wharf. He was more familiar with the area than he would have ever admitted in society. He strode forward toward the tavern that was his target. His eyes moved from side to side in the pattern familiar to any who regularly walked these streets. There was the need for constant wariness.

And that was without the Townsends' threat. He did not discount the hints that Anna had sent his way. It was possible he took them more seriously than she.

He moved to the center of the street as he approached several dark alleys, swinging his cane in wide circles. Whistling a ditty that marked him as no stranger, a sailor's song with bawdy lyrics, he approached the tavern and swung open the door.

He nodded to a couple of sailors from one of his own ships, big brawny men, men who would not shirk a good fight.

They were not his target. He glanced about the bar quickly, a searching look that was careful to intrude on no one's business. There were many here who would not welcome scrutiny, and he knew better than to look too closely.

There, in the corner, was the man he sought, the investigator he'd hired to find out about the Townsends. He approached and sat down, signaling for two pints.

"You sent a message that you had information."

The man took the pint and took a hefty swallow. "Not me exactly." He nodded to two worn-looking sailors leaning on the bar. "They used to sail on one of the Townsends' ships. Left after the last journey. I would suggest you listen to what they have to say."

Chapter 21

Anna stared down at the document on her desk. She didn't know why she hesitated. Once it was done she'd be able to breathe again, to prepare for the life she wanted. The knot of anxiety in her belly might finally unravel.

The threat from her cousins was becoming unbearable. She did not even want to think what would happen if she did not stop them. But would this do it?

Struthers had not come to the ball—and he had not showed up for the meeting she had arranged with Lady Smythe-Burke as the next step of the game. She wondered how he would have reacted to being closed in a room with Lady Smythe-Burke and her cronies helping to decide the fate of England for the next year. She rather imagined that it would have taken only minutes for him to realize the power of this group of older women, plotting how to advise their husbands and sons. It would have been eye-opening for him.

Only he hadn't come—either to the ball or to Lady Smythe-Burke's.

She felt very alone.

Touching her neck, she felt the bite of the knife again.

If she signed she would be done.

She picked up the pen to sign with a decisive flourish.

If she was going to do this she would have no regrets. She had debated enough, plotted enough, spent enough time thinking—she could find no good choice in this mess.

This was the best move she could make.

Nathanial and Ernest would not like it—but that would only be a plus.

Shaking her head in an attempt to clear her thoughts of the circles they were trapped in, she placed the pen beside the paper and stepped away from the desk. She needed a good walk to clear her head, to decide if her idea was really possible.

Before she could even call for her cloak Maddie came through the door in rush.

She stared at Anna for a moment, her face filled with emotion. "Have you heard my child is Struthers's—not my husband's?"

Anna could only stare at her sister, her jaw hanging open. She knew what Maddie had just said, but the words did not begin to make sense. "Can you repeat that?"

"Oh, how can you not be listening to me? It is one of the most horrible moments of my life and you are distracted," Maddie said as she almost dove across the room onto the settee.

Anna felt the desire to roll her eyes, but suppressed it. Maddie had just lost her husband, and surely that was reason enough for such melodramatic behavior. Still, Anna could not shake the feeling that it was mostly a show for her benefit. Maddie had not seemed particularly fond of Milson for years and Anna had never been able to blame her.

"The rumor is spread all across London. I don't know who said anything—unless you did—but everyone is talking about Lady Smythe-Burke's house party and me and Struthers." Maddie laid a hand across her eyes as if to block out the light.

Anna snapped her mouth shut. She'd been afraid that was what Maddie had said. "I don't see how that can be the case. How could you have let him marry me if he'd—he'd fathered your babe? It is impossible."

"I didn't say he was the father—just that the rumor is everywhere. I think Milson's younger brother is responsible for spreading it—but I don't know how he found out." Maddie peeked out from beneath her arm as if to gauge Anna's response. The odor of a distinctive, overly sweet floral perfume wafted across the room.

Anna knew that perfume. She remembered Struthers reeking of it as she'd thrown herself into his arms. He'd been slipping out of Maddie's room covered in her scent. "So is Struthers the father?"

Maddie moved her arm over her eyes again and said nothing.

"Is this why you were so displeased with me yesterday?" Anna tried a change of subject. "Did you think I had said something about the house party?"

"Yes, it is the only thing that made sense. I am still not sure that you didn't. There is nobody else who knows."

"Somebody clearly knows something. Is there other reason to believe that the child is not Milson's?"

"The baby is legally Milson's and I see no reason to say otherwise."

That was a far more reasoned response than she had expected from Maddie. "So you will not tell me if my husband could be the father? I cannot believe that you would have not stopped me from marrying him if you thought the baby could be his."

"If that had been the circumstance, I believe I would have felt that you didn't want to know your sister—even if only half a one—was having your husband's baby. It was necessary that you marry Struthers."

That was undoubtedly true, but it still felt wrong to Anna—if not downright disgusting. She wasn't sure she would have married Struthers if she'd known, not even with all her problems. Besides, it was probably even truer that Maddie had been very content to let her lord husband believe he was having a child, hopefully a son. With Milson dead the whole picture changed.

Anna's stomach began to sour. "What do you want from me? If you do decide to claim Struthers is the father—and I notice you do not deny it either—is it not Struthers you should be talking to?"

Maddie pushed herself up to sitting. There was moisture on her face, but her eyes were far from red-rimmed. Anna could not forget how easily Maddie had always been able to make herself cry as a child when she wanted something—or how easily she had lied. What was her sister's true purpose?

Maddie sniffed. "I thought it would be easier to talk to you. If my child is a boy it may not be an issue, but if it is a daughter—" She covered her face very prettily with her hands and let her words hang.

Anna was glad Maddie had covered her eyes as she shut her own and tried to hold her emotions in—not the fury she had expected, but rather a mind spinning at dizzying speed as she tried to grasp all that this meant.

With a voice full of all the careful calm she could find, she said, "Legally it is still your husband's, even if he is dead."

Maddie's shoulders stiffened. "Yes, but only a son will inherit. If it is a daughter then we will be out on the streets. Milson's brother has never cared for me—hence my belief that he is behind the rumors."

Holding back a tart reply was difficult. Maddie's infidelities had long been speculated on and there was undoubtedly reason for rumor—whether or not Struthers was involved. "Why don't you just tell me the truth about the baby then."

"Oh," Maddie wailed. "I thought you'd be more sympathetic. You are a woman and must surely understand my pain. My husband newly dead, my heart breaking, and now I find myself in this situation. I was sure you would want to help me, as I've helped you—and Father—all these years. You know that I have creditors at the door. I will rest so much easier once they are paid."

And there it was, the emotional threat. Maddie wanted what she always did—money.

If Maddie's heart had really been broken, maybe she shouldn't have been carrying on with other men before Lord Milson's death. Anna was unsure if any of the sentiment was true—well, Maddie probably was heartbroken by the lack of money. "I have said I will pay them, but you must be patient. I must verify who is owed what or I will be paying them twice or more. And I do have sympathy. It cannot be easy to lose a husband. I am surprised you are out at all and not taken to your bed."

"That will come soon enough." Maddie sniffed again. "Once society's busybodies have their way I'll be forced to stay home—with Father—or only attend the most boring of functions, and nobody will call on me after the first visit. And even when it's over I'll always be the extra woman. People will only invite me when they need to fill a chair or have the young girls chaperoned and they'll never invite me if there are eligible men that they think might be more interested in me than in their daughters." Maddie sank down into the cushions and began to cry what Anna suspected were genuine tears.

Anna felt her emotions soften. What Maddie said was very true. There would be no going back to being a fun-loving young woman for Maddie. Being a widow would not be easy for her—and a widow without many funds even less so.

"It is all your fault, you know," Maddie began again, before Anna could formulate more words to say. "If you had just left well enough alone then Struthers would still be free and he would marry me. It's not as if you love the man or anything."

Love the man. The words caught Anna's attention, halting all other thought. No, she did not love the man—that was preposterous—but she had become fond of him. She could not even imagine him married to Maddie. He deserved far better than that. "If I had left well enough alone, as you phrase it, then Struthers would have killed your husband and if the situation"—she glanced at Maddie's still-flat stomach—"had necessitated marriage you would have been forced to live abroad for the rest of your lives. I do not believe that is what you would have wanted either. And if by some chance Lord Milson had killed Struthers, then you would still be possibly lying about your child and facing poverty."

"If Milson had killed Struthers—I hadn't even thought of that." Maddie's tone implied this might not have been such a bad outcome. Then her head jerked up. "Poverty—you will never let it come to that. What of Father? What of my baby?"

Anna wished Maddie would make up her mind. Did she believe that Anna would pay her bills or not? Or was the question merely how much? "You are of course correct. I have paid Father's bills, and I have said I will pay Milson's bills—just give me time."

"I still need some more gowns. I will need more black."

"You could dye some of your present dresses." Yes, the question was how much. "Surely that would work and be much less costly. You know that by the time you put mourning aside most of what you now own will be out of fashion." Anna knew it was not the answer that Maddie wanted, but surely her sister could see beyond clothes. There were so many other obstacles about to come her way.

"Then everybody will think that I am poor. And Father will need new things also. Or perhaps he should come live with you and Struthers? I am sure he would be happier away from my grief." This time it was more of a moan than a sniff—one that sounded very genuine.

"It is not that I am unwilling to help you with more funds, but I still do not have full control of my money," Anna said quickly. "You are my family and I want to do right by you, but a new wardrobe does not seem the place to start."

"Perhaps I should have gone to Struthers. I am sure he would not be so mean."

Anna was not so sure about that. She knew that Struthers would do everything necessary to help a child that might be his, but she was not sure that he would think new dresses fell into that category. And he did not understand the debt she owed Maddie for caring for their father all these years. "You still have not explained why you did not go to him immediately—why you came to me first."

Sitting straight up, Maddie faced her dead-on. While her face was still wet, she gave up much of her pretense of grief. "I thought you would be kinder, more generous. As we say, you are family and I thought you would do all you could to help me—and more. You know that you have always been the lucky one, receiving far more than you are entitled to. This seemed like a chance for you to make it fair. I was not expecting much, a few new dresses, for you to make sure that I can stay in the house, and perhaps a small annual income. All things of which I know you are capable."

Not expecting much. It sounded like a great deal to Anna. "And why would I do this?"

"Why, because I am your sister—our father's daughter." Maddie's eyes narrowed. "And because you truly don't want me to tell Struthers about the child, do you?"

"Surely Struthers will realize if the child might be his?" Anna replied.

"Maybe yes. Maybe no. Men often do not see what they do not wish to. What matters is that with my husband gone I will need money—and a lot of it. I do not see why you should not provide it as you have in the past."

And that was the heart of it. Anna got up and paced across the room. Everybody wanted his share. It didn't matter that the money had been left solely to her, everybody wanted some of it. Her cousins were not entitled to any of it and yet they were all willing to do anything to get it. She found herself surprised that Maddie had not tried a touch of blackmail and guilt earlier.

Was that a lesson of life? Did everyone always think he deserved more than he got?

Everyone except Struthers. Anna sank into a chair, far from Maddie, as this thought struck. He might think he should control her money, make sure she was not acting improperly with it, but she had never sensed it was because he wanted it for himself. She sensed he regarded it as more a job than a treat—a job he had to do, but still a job.

Perhaps that was why she believed that he could not have betrayed his partners in India.

She glanced at the clock on the mantel.

She straightened her spine and turned to Maddie. "I will think on what you have said."

"But—"

"Things have changed since my marriage and I have yet to understand it all. Now go home and have a dress dyed black for the next few days—I will talk to Struthers about allowing me further funds. I will send my modiste to supply you with a new gown. I do understand you may need some cheering. I am sure that you will continue to have plenty of callers coming to offer you their comfort."

Maddie nodded reluctantly.

With her sister gone Anna could think again.

The possibility that Struthers was the father of Maddie's baby added an unhappy wrinkle to her affairs.

She looked again at her cousins' package.

Turning, she called for her pelisse. She would take that walk after all.

Chapter 22

"I am sorry, Mr. Struthers. She is not at home."

"Is she not home or is she not receiving? Remember that this is my house now and that you are now my servant."

Jameson paled at the question and Struthers felt an unreasonable bully. He should just have walked into the parlor and waited for Anna to appear. The words were mean and petty—and unnecessary. Anna's servants already clearly understood his position. Anna might not have liked the power their marriage gave him over her and what was hers, but she had never denied it. He respected that about her.

It was just that his night had been so long—if informative. There was still much to be learned before he could make his move or even discuss it with his wife, but he wanted to see her. He knew she would be displeased that he had not attended either Lady Smythe-Burke's tea or the Wimberleys' ball. He had not received the messages—or the chemise of fine, translucent cotton—until this morning.

His mind filled with the image of Anna in the garment. That reward would be worst almost any cost.

"I am afraid she is truly not here," Jameson replied

after a moment. "She left about half an hour ago with no explanation."

"That seems odd."

"Actually it is not. Mrs. Struthers frequently takes herself off without notice. She is never gone for long."

"So she should be back soon?"

"Most probably. You can wait in the parlor or her study if you care to. I'd be happy to provide you with tea." Jameson's voice indicated that he would also be pleased to provide Struthers with something stronger.

"That would be fine." Struthers stepped toward the parlor.

"Although . . ." Jameson hesitated, as if trying to decide whether to say something. "She did ask Cook for a bag of bread before she left. She only does that when she is going to the park to feed the ducks. She often sits on a bench at the near end of the pond for a while."

"I'll head to the park then." Struthers picked up his walking stick and stepped toward the door. He turned his head back. "And thank you."

The park's ducks surrounded her like a shield against the world. Being in the midst of a quacking cacophony was exactly what she wanted. She threw the last handful of stale bread and then settled on her bench, content to let her winged protectors circle around her, bills down, seeking every last morsel.

The largest white drake pushed the others aside without a care as he searched out the biggest pieces. He'd have to be careful or somebody would think he looked fat enough for the pot, not that she could imagine anybody hunting park ducks. He quacked warning to a small brown duck that had gotten too close and then turned and stared at her, a triumphant grin on his face as he lifted his head to let a particularly large piece slide down his throat.

Could a duck grin?

This one certainly had.

Then they were gone, the last crumb devoured. Her protectors were fickle things. They stayed as long as crust remained and slid back to the water as one when the last morsel was gone. She'd seen it before, but still felt alone as the last duck gave a single quack and glided off across the pond.

She felt bereft for a single second and then began to laugh. Society was so like the ducks, swarming for any crumb of gossip and then paddling away fast in search of more plentiful bounty. It was good to remember that whatever the outcome of her current problems, it would pass.

And then she looked up.

He was standing there—barely ten yards away—staring.

His eyes seemed to burn through her.

The sun was behind him and it should have been impossible to see his features, but those eyes caught her, forcing the laugh from her lips.

"Don't stop," he said, stepping toward her. "I haven't seen you laugh like that in years. It's good to know you still can."

"You must have seen me laugh."

He moved even closer. "Yes, I've seen you laugh, but never like that, just for your own amusement. It's always been the polite laugh across a drawing room, or that low husky one designed to draw a man closer. It's been forever since I saw you laugh solely for yourself."

"Oh." She was shocked at his perception. She'd accepted the uncanny ability he had to read her face, but this went a step beyond that, hinted at something far deeper. She stood, brushing a few stray flecks of bread from her skirt. "What are you doing here? It does not seem like your normal territory."

"I should create some story, but the truth is Jameson indicated you might be here."

"He knew?"

"I think the bag of bread gave you away."

She looked down at her hands, unsure what to say next. There was so much between them, and yet this innocent moment did not seem like the place to open it all up. And she was still unsure why he had not appeared the night before.

As if sensing her hesitation, Struthers held out his arm. "I am sorry I did not attend the Wimberleys' last night. I did not get your message until this morning. And I am even more sorry not to have attended Lady Smythe-Burke's. I do hope you do not require me to return my—my present. Now would you like to stroll? Or do you care to sit further?" He gestured back to the bench.

She took his arm and without further comment they began to walk.

Now that he was here he didn't know what to say. She'd been so beautiful, but so alone, sitting there surrounded by the ducks. Struthers had seen worry in her face, but also joy—and that laugh. He wanted to see that laugh again.

And he did not want to discuss last night, not yet.

In fact, everything he could think of saying would take away from the pleasure of the afternoon.

"It's a beautiful day," he began.

"Yes, it is. You can feel change in the air. I can almost

believe that I will awaken tomorrow and suddenly the weather will be too hot."

"Yes. I know what you mean."

They were silent again.

He was intensely aware of her as they walked along, of her fingers wrapped about his arm—he thought he could feel their warmth even through the thick wool of his coat—of the soft sound of her breath, of the sun glinting on her hair turning the brown to gold, and of her eyes. They did not look at him, indeed they stared straight ahead, fixed on the path, but he could feel the uncertainty in them, knew that she struggled just as he.

She stopped, not suddenly but with subtle yet unmistakable clues. She turned and faced him straight on. "Thank you."

He paused, puzzled. "For what?"

She stared at him, her eyes calm and clear. "For allowing me almost free access to my funds. I know there is still much to be discussed, but it is a relief to know I can pay Maddie and my father's bills. I will need more than I had at first expected, but I understand from Timms that I need only to apply to him when I need more."

He had expected gratitude, but her quiet words shook him. This was not flirtation and fun—these were words from her heart. "I have actually decided to tell the banks that you may access you accounts whenever you wish—with no need to notify me or Timms."

"Why?"

He should have known she would not just be content. "I hate to admit that your game has affected me. I hope that in truth I would have realized on my own. Seeing the women in Sherberry did make me stop and think. And when you said your cousins were trying to do the same to you—I realized that it was a matter of small steps between my thinking I had the right to decide what to do with your funds and my deciding I had the right to do whatever I wanted to you. I have seen no evidence that you are irrational or that you are mismanaging your funds. In time, I hope you will tell me where the missing money is going—but for now I will wait."

She waited a second to see if he would continue, and then replied, "It is hard to explain how much it means. I could give you a light, easy answer, but that would not be to either of our advantage. I only realized after you had taken my rights how important they were to me. Oh, I knew that I felt I should be in control of all of my monies, but it wasn't until I lost them that I realized they were actually part of my identity. It makes me feel very shallow in many ways, but I am not actually sure it is. We all need some way to think of ourselves—our position, our relation to our family, a profession. Who we are is words—and *heiress* has become a large part of me. I cannot explain what your allowing me freedom means—and that does not even mention what it means that you trust me. Perhaps that is another part of my self-definition."

The words made sense. He had never thought of himself in that way, but he examined the different ways he had thought of himself over the years and the importance of those definitive words. Son. Nephew. Student. Property owner. Trader. Englishman. And now husband. "You are now a wife—my wife. And hopefully soon a mother."

She stopped for a moment as if something had startled her, but then recovered.

She reached out to lay a hand on his cheek. The smooth leather of her glove was a thin layer between their skin. "I know, and I do not discount that, but it is new and

I am unused to it—and—and I think I need more than that. Perhaps when—if—I become a mother that will be enough. But I want to be more than a wife. I want to be a person, and a person is more than one word."

"You are beautiful—does not that count?"

"Would you want to be known strictly for your appearance? For something you had no control over? I've known many women who take great pleasure in their sense of fashion, who put hours into choosing gowns and slippers and making sure that their fans match their hairpieces, but to be quite frank, I have never cared for such affectations. I do not discount those for whom such things are important. I must admit to loving a beautiful gown and I can go into raptures over a pretty piece of fabric, but I do not see making those choices as a life. They are the fun that comes after the work."

He was struck again by her beauty. It was something so indefinable. She had always been pretty; smooth skin and strong features granted that. But always he had seen more in her. Fashionable beauties might be more striking, their coloring more dramatic, but they lacked the vitality that filled her, that sense of being more present in any given moment than anyone else in the room. He could have gone on about her eyes, her lips—so full and inviting—and the creamy skin that always invited his touch, but he knew it was none of these things that actually drew him. No, it was all of her—some mysterious way that all the pieces combined to be more than the total.

She had been a wonder as a girl. She was even better as a woman.

"Did you just snort?" Her question caught him off guard.

"Did I?"

"Yes, you did," she answered. "And I would take offense, but the pause between my own words and the sound was long enough that I may delude myself that they were unrelated."

"No delusion is necessary. I was merely amused at how fanciful my own thoughts had become."

"You have never struck me as a fanciful man."

"Hence the snort."

"So what were you thinking about that brought such amusement?"

He certainly was not going to tell her that. "It would bore you. I am more interested in your statement about seeking fulfillment beyond fashion. I am trying to reconcile the things I know about you. You have a fortune and clearly have enjoyed spending it on the best of the best, but I must admit that despite some extraordinary purchases—your horses border on the unbelievable—you do not seem extravagant."

She did not seem extravagant. She would take that as a great compliment. It had been impossible to miss Struthers's tendency to frugality and so she sensed he meant even more by the statement than most men would have.

"You snorted this time," he said.

"I was just thinking that we are complementary opposites. I love lush and beautiful things and fight to restrain myself on many occasions. I have no desire to be wasteful. I've worn every item in my closet at least twice."

"Ah, is that the standard of not being wasteful?"

"I am afraid it is. Society does demand a lot from a woman like me. If I am seen in something too many times it draws comment. I would actually prefer it was different. I have some gowns I love and can't bear to get rid of but there is no longer a single place I can wear them. They are too fancy for anything at home, and any occasion to which they are suited demands something new—or at a minimum new trimmings. It really is a great difficulty. You may not believe it, but I would be quite happy with fewer things—although all of beyond the best quality."

He laughed. "Is that where you see us as complementary—we both like to have the best?"

She wrinkled her nose. "You did choose to marry me."

His mouth opened, then closed. She knew what he had been about to say. *I was not aware I was given a choice in the matter.* It was more of an automatic response than one deeply felt—and even so she saw him catch it and hold it. Knowing what somebody was thinking when he said not a word was the oddest thing.

She glanced quickly about the park, her eyes darting quickly, looking for any observer. There was no one else in sight. Leaning forward, she kissed him softly on the lips. "Thank you."

"For what?"

"For not saying what you thought. And you always did have a choice, all you had to do was say no." This time the kiss was not gentle. She ran her tongue along the seam of his lips. "And you certainly didn't say no."

His hands came up and grasped her waist, pulling her tight against him. "No, I didn't say no. You are certainly right about that." With his hands on her waist he lifted her and moved her behind a tree, shielding them both from the path. Pressing her back against the tree, he lowered his mouth again on hers.

They were quiet for a moment; nothing mattered beyond lips and breath and heat.

"I've missed you," he breathed against her when they both pulled back to fill their lungs.

"It has only been a few nights."

"I know." He rested his forehead against her, closing his eyes.

"It does seem like longer . . ." She pressed her lips against his cheek. Closing her own eyes, she rested against him, face to face. There was so much she should be saying, but circumstance held her quiet. This was not the place—and not yet the time, but soon, soon she would need to tell him all.

She pressed another kiss against his cheek. Understanding her own motivation seemed beyond her. Normally at this moment there would have been nothing but passion flowing through her, but now there was so much more, the desire to comfort, to understand, to cherish and to be cherished.

Did she cherish? Cherish was awfully close to love.

She had already decided that she liked him—hard as that still was to accept.

Was she—even just to herself—ready to take that next step? Could she love him?

And what of Maddie and her child? Was she ready to forgive that? Was there anything to forgive? Maddie had not said the child was his.

Anna filled her lungs with air and let it out slowly. Could she love him?

The thought was frightening. Love brought responsibility and a lack of freedom. Could she stay the woman she was and love a man like Struthers? Love Struthers?

Instead of admitting the answer she knew was there, she turned her head until their lips met yet again. Her tongue darted out and licked his tight lower lip. It softened almost instantly and his eyes slowly opened.

They stared deeply as their mouths moved. The sensations that his lips wrought filled her from her toes to the crown of her curls, although his mouth never moved from hers. She moaned softly, feeling that her knees might give out.

He tightened his fingers even deeper into her waist, supporting her as if he sensed her weakness.

"God, I want you." It was his turn to moan.

He pressed her harder against the tree as one of his hands moved up over her bodice, slipping under her pelisse. His fingers sought entrance at the neckline, but the dress was too high and fitted. Anna moved her own hand up to help. Her nipples were pressing tight against the thin linen of her chemise, and all she could think of was granting them release—well, that and his lips. The pressure of the kiss continued to fill her, both satisfying her and leaving her wanting more.

She pressed herself against his palm, moving back and forth in small jerks that only increased her wants. There was the sound of a small tear as his fingers sought to satisfy them both. She forced herself back, trying not to pant.

"We have to stop this," she said.

"Why?" His breath was heavy against her cheek, her neck—his lips began a downward path.

She grabbed his hair and yanked. "Look where we are."

His head came up. His glazed eyes slowly cleared. "I'd forgotten."

"I had too. I am not sure how one forgets that one is pressed against a cold, damp tree or that a screaming brigade of children could come crashing by at any moment, but I had."

He shifted in such a way that his lower body pressed

against her own and she could feel how hard he fought for control, and how great the struggle was. She curled her fingers into fists before she could reach down and examine that proof.

He reached out and cupped her chin in his hand, directing her glance into his. "I think my house is closer."

Her mind quickly calculated. "I am sure it is."

He stepped back and surveyed her. "I think you'll pass. You will to need draw your pelisse tighter. I am afraid that your dress is rather the worse for wear."

Glancing down, she could only agree. The rip he had caused might be small, but its location was rather noticeable. "My maid will have no trouble guessing how I did that."

He raised a brow that clearly said, *So?*

A giggle rose and tickled at the back of her throat. It was true. She cared not an iota.

It was the matter of a moment to pull everything back into decent order and to reach over and take his arm. They began to stroll down the park's paths toward the gate nearest his house. The cold nipped at her cheeks, forcing clear—and unpleasant—thoughts into her mind.

Her steps slowed. "I think we need to talk."

Chapter 23

Did women always say those words? Struthers didn't think it was deliberate, but it was amazing how often they would heat a man up and then say those words guaranteed to shrivel him within his trousers. *We need to talk.*

The worst was that he did not disagree—however, it did not need to be now.

He stared straight ahead and stepped forward firmly, pulling her along. "Later."

"I think what I need to say should be said first."

At least she did not say *we.* A man could listen with half an ear while his mind moved on to more pleasurable pursuits. Perhaps he could even begin those pursuits while she talked. Women did seem to be able to concentrate on something else while participating in love play. He'd known them to talk about the details of invitation lists in the midst of everything. He'd never heard of a man thinking of anything but the obvious—not that he'd ever discussed the matter with his friends, but still, a man heard things.

Her feet dug to a stop, and she yanked on his arm. The gesture should have seemed petulant, but that was clearly not her intent. "You are not listening to me."

There was not much he could say to that. She was right.

Anna continued, "I must tell you that a man bent on seduction should at least pretend to listen."

Hadn't he just been thinking that—well, his mind had been further along than seduction, but the concept was the same. He nodded attentively and they began to walk again.

Her gaze turned serious. "I did mean that we need to talk. There is something I must discuss with you before things can proceed between us."

She was finally going to tell him her secrets and he found he didn't care. The thought was almost enough to stop him where he stood. He did not care. First he was going to release her money without knowing the details of how she planned to care for it, and now he was prepared to overlook whatever else it was she'd been avoiding telling him. He would have liked to think—illogical as it was—that he was simply swept away by passion, but it was far more than that. It was she.

He trusted her.

He liked her.

He found himself unable to doubt her.

He . . .

His mind refused to contemplate the final sentence. He did not believe in love. It was a myth used to excuse lust and to give the emotionally needy hope for the future. He had never felt the desire to excuse his lusts, and as for being emotionally needy—the thought made him laugh.

He must have actually made a sound because she turned her face toward him in question.

"We're here," he said, hoping she would keep silent.

She knew that he wanted to let the subject drop—not that he even knew what the subject was. Normally she would have pursued his snort, wanted to know what thought had caused that strange expression, but now she had more important things on her mind. She had allowed herself to be distracted by their kiss, but she needed answers before they could proceed.

Was he the father of Maddie's baby? And if so, where did they go from here?

And there was the worry over the situation with her cousins. She needed to tell Struthers of the robbery and that bloody contract sitting on her desk. What would he think of her solution? Even when she wasn't thinking about that it always sat there in the back of her mind like a tack in the bottom of a shoe. It didn't always hurt enough to force her to action, but the ache was always there, never leaving her free and comfortable.

Except when Struthers kissed her. That had left her neither free nor comfortable, but she certainly had not been thinking about the tack.

"Now you are not listening to me." Struthers's voice echoed as they entered his house.

"I hadn't realized you were speaking."

He raised his brow again, but this time his expression was far different. It was tit for tat. It was *I knew it.* It was *I am so amused by you.* The only thing he said was "I know."

"So what were you saying?" She smiled at him ruefully.

"I don't know if I should tell you." He tossed his hat aside. "I was just saying that I thought talk could wait until dinner and that we could find other ways to fill the afternoon." Again his brow rose and again it said something different. How did the man do that?

"I wish that we could, but I fear that if we do not talk now then we never will."

* * *

Struthers wanted to deny the truth of that, but instead all he could do was nod. There had been so many conversations between them left unfinished. He wanted to tell her that what she had to say did not matter, that he could forgive her anything, but the words stuck. He might be willing to forgive her, whatever the offense, but he did want to know.

Anna nodded to his porter and asked for tea to be set up in the parlor.

She turned to him. "Between waiting for the tea and the large front windows, I am hoping that we really will talk and not be distracted by other matters." Her glance ran over him, letting him know exactly where her mind was wandering.

He let his own gaze follow suit. She'd removed her outerwear when they entered and the small rip at her neckline was visible. He focused on it and the creamy skin it almost covered.

Her hand came up and covered the tear. "That was really quite bad of you. If I were home I would change immediately, but that would have taken time and I do want to get to this. Give me your cravat pin."

The pin was one he'd had for years. Its simple design bespoke quality and expense, plain thick gold with a single cabochon ruby at the top. His father had given it to him and he'd rarely worn another. Yet he did not even question as he pulled it loose from his neck cloth. "Only if you let me fasten it."

"You do like to play with danger." She smiled and stepped closer.

He'd never been so aware of the heat of another person. He could sense every bit of her as she stepped closer. If he closed his eyes he knew he'd be just as aware.

He thought he'd be able to feel her walking through a crowd of strangers.

His fingers trembled slightly as he took the pin and worked the fabric of her dress together. The tight fit of the wool forced him to pull the fabric tight and even with the high neckline he could see her breasts swell beneath his touch. He swallowed, unable to lift his eyes back to her face.

The lightest of scratches on the door had him fastening the pin hurriedly with some irritation and stepping away. A young maid entered carrying a heavy tray. He couldn't remember ever seeing the girl before, and judging by her wide-eyed look she had not been in his employ long.

Anna stepped forward to direct the maid toward a table. The tray wobbled slightly as the girl lowered it to the tabletop and Anna placed a hand on the edge to steady it. The girl looked up, frightened, but Anna only smiled. "I've never seen such a wonderful tea. I think Cook must have emptied the kitchen for us."

The maid nodded, her eyes grown even wider.

"That looks beautiful," Anna continued as she helped arrange the dishes on the tray. "Why don't you leave the rest to me? I do love playing at the domestic arts." She patted the girl's hand and watched with a careful smile until she'd left the room. She turned back to him with the grin still upon her face. "You do like your tea extra sweet, do you not? It seems to be the way with strong men. They either take their tea with several scoops of sugar or black. I wonder why that is?"

"You're rambling," he said.

"I know. I want to be sure that the maid does not return. She seems like she'll work out well once she gets over her nerves. Do you know her name? I do like to address the staff by name. I think it makes everything run smoother. Perhaps it's because we had so little staff when I was a girl. I never can get over calling all the staff by the same names. When I want someone, I want a particular someone. Lady Smythe-Burke calls all the footmen John and they always seem to know exactly whom she means. When I try that I just end up confusing the whole house. It must be something you are born to."

"I don't know the maid's name, but I will find out. I believe she's Polly's sister, up from the country. I like that you ramble and I like that you care about the maids and about helping the household run smoothly." He took a step toward her. "What I don't like is how far away from me you are."

"Then come and take your cup and I'll fix you a plate of nibbles. I was serious that your cook has fixed an extraordinary tea. I want to try a bite of everything, even if I end up looking like a whale."

"I've seen whales and I can see no comparison. You are trying to keep my hands busy with plates and cups, aren't you?"

Her eyes danced. "You do know me well." She grew serious. "Take that seat over there, before the fire. I will sit here on the settee. Then we can talk and not be distracted by other matters."

"I think I would have to put my head in a burlap sack coated with cow excrement in order not to be distracted when I am in a room with you. And even then I would remember how your skin felt as I slipped the pin through the fabric of your dress."

"The scent of cow excrement—I had not realized I was so distracting." She grinned again but it did not reach her eyes. "Now sit. We must talk."

He sat. "I love it when you are bossy."

She paused at his comment and he thought she was about to make a reply. Instead her mouth shut tight for a second, then her tongue darted out to dampen her lips, and when she began to speak he was sure it was not her original thought. "Tell me about Maddie."

He could only stare at her. The cup of tea rested in her hand, just above her knees, and her back was as straight as any chaperone's. Only her eyes—and those lips—betrayed her nervousness.

He blinked. He'd thought she was going to reveal her secrets—what was this about? "You want to discuss Lady Milson?"

"Yes, tell me about her."

"I don't know what you could possibly expect me to say. You know her far, far better than I. She is your sister."

"Only my half sister. And perhaps I do know her better in some senses of the word, but I have never been caught leaving her bedroom in the late hours of the night."

"So that is what this is about." Not again. Would she never grow bored of the subject and just let it be? It was not his secret. It was Michael's and he could not say anything.

"In part. Now tell me all about you and Maddie—things have changed with her husband dead."

He was beginning to feel aggravated. It was one thing to have his seduction interrupted to learn Anna's secrets. It was another thing to listen to her suspicions about himself and Maddie. It wasn't something he could talk about anyway. Michael was entitled to his secrets. Hopefully the whole matter would resolve itself now anyway. With Milson dead and Michael beyond her reach, he imagined that Maddie would soon start searching for a new protector—an unmarried one. "I really don't care to talk about that now."

"But . . ." She leaned toward him.

"Later." He placed his tea on the table untasted and rose, walking to her, his eyes focused on her face. "I've decided that you have it wrong. We keep delaying our conversation not because we are avoiding it but because other matters are more important." He trailed his fingers across her cheek.

Pulling her head back, she stared up at him, her resolve strong. "No, we need to discuss this now."

He caught her hair and pulled her back toward him, laying a nibbling kiss along one cheek. "Are you sure it can't wait until later? I promise to listen."

"I never believe men's promises. "

"I always knew you were a wise woman, but I am not any man. Look at me and tell me that I do not tell the truth."

She raised her glance to his, staring deep into his eyes. He could feel her try and penetrate his thoughts and knew she was lost.

She shouldn't be doing this. How many times could they try to speak and not accomplish it? There was so much between them and the words were necessary. She needed to ask about Maddie and then finally tell him the full truth about her cousins and the threat they presented. She had not even told him of the robbery attempt. And until they were honest with each other there could be no more between them than this—the physical.

His lips brushed along her cheek again, dropping lower to her jawline. She'd never realized how sensitive that spot was. He nipped just below her ear and she squirmed. Perhaps the physical was enough for the moment.

She turned her head until her lips met his, tasting, caressing. "We shouldn't do this here, if we do it at all—the windows."

He pulled back and glanced out the window at the street. "I do see what you mean. But I doubt anyone will come near enough to see in."

"Your servants." She was struggling to stay rational. It was bad enough that she was giving in at all—the last thing that she wished was to court more gossip.

"My servants are as well trained as yours and will not enter unless called. And while it might be possible to see us from the window—only possible, mind you—it would not be possible if we were lower, say on the rug."

Her glance followed his to the thick carpet before the fire. "I've never been fond of rugs. I always find they abrade my skin."

"I'll be on the bottom."

"That I'd like to see. I don't think you ever let yourself not be on top—of anything." She pushed against his chest, forcing him back. "I would rather see your bedroom. Don't you think you'd like to show it to me?"

His eyes narrowed and then relaxed. He had won.

"If that is what you would like. I must confess I've had a hankering to see you there. Still, you should be aware that I will require you to get naked and then you will need to redress and I cannot swear to my maids' proficiency nor provide you with a new gown."

Her mind was cooling rapidly from the heat of passion, letting reality intrude. Could she do this without talking to him about Maddie?

Yes. The decision took less time than the beat of a bumblebee's wing. Everything would change once they talked. She would take her moment and enjoy it.

She walked a few feet from him toward the door, then turned her head, looking at him over her shoulder. "Do bring a plate. That tea truly is too delectable to leave and I do believe I may be quite hungry in a bit."

Struthers stopped and piled a plate high with tasty bites before following her out of the room.

Chapter 24

He ought to feel he had won. Struthers was getting what he had wanted. Anna had not put up more than a token protest. But somehow she always managed to turn things topsy-turvy so that he felt she was the one leading the way—which she was doing very literally at the moment. She'd never been to his bedroom, yet she strolled down the hallway like a queen. Although he didn't think queens moved their hips in such a fashion. The gentle sway, back and forth and back and forth, drew his eyes and held them. He knew it had to be deliberate—he was sure she had not walked in such a manner in the park—but it was so completely natural, an extension of her very being, that it was impossible to imagine her not always walking like that.

She paused before the dark wood of his door—how did she know which room was his?—and turned back toward him, looking over her shoulder, in that way that was so much a part of her. She smiled slowly, letting her mouth curve up from one cheek to the other. "Should I let you go first? Do you have any secrets you need to hide?" she asked, her eyes moving down his body.

He came up behind her and, placing the plate of tidbits on a table, set a hand on each of her hips, lowering his lips to the nape of her neck. He nibbled at the smooth skin. It might be his favorite spot on her. Well, that was not true—but it was definitely a favorite. When she turned her head to stare back at him, her eyes twinkling with knowledge, he always wanted to taste her there, to bury his face against her neck and smell the faint musk of her skin and the rich rose of her perfume.

He bit just hard enough to make her gasp, then pulled back. "You are doing such a wonderful job of leading, I think I'll let you continue." He gestured toward the door handle.

She gave the knob a decisive twist and stepped through. Her glance was still back toward him and he waited as she turned her head toward the room.

"It's not at all what I expected," she said as she stepped in.

Grabbing the plate, he followed.

He looked at the room, imagining it through her eyes. Most of the furniture followed traditional lines, but as with downstairs this room carried an air of the Orient, delicate inlaid tables, ornate brass lamps, the faint scent of incense—and the bed.

Anna stepped to it and laid her hand on the rich, bright silks that covered it. "I've never seen anything like this. I am surprised that balls are not filled with gowns made of this material. I feel like I am trapped in the dragon's cave in some fairy story and all I can do is admire his treasure." She lifted a piece of the coverlet. "Or maybe I am trapped inside a glass bottle surrounded by rainbows. I can't think of anywhere else that such colors could exist."

"The Indian women use the cloth for their dresses, or saris, as they call them. I had a friend whose bed was covered in such a way and despite never having an interest in fabrics—other than in shipping them and trading them—I knew I wanted such a coverlet for myself."

"Do you have more of them?"

"Thinking of yourself now, are you? Do you fancy covering your own bed with them?" As he asked the question he found he no longer liked the thought of her having her own bed—much less her own house. He wanted her here in his.

She gave him that uptilted glance over her shoulder. "Actually I was thinking of a dress—something that would be the envy of all who saw it. Or . . ." Her eyes grew sultry. "Perhaps something just for us. Some of the pieces are so sheer I can imagine the firelight must shine right through them."

A picture grew in his mind—as she had no doubt intended—of Anna dressed only in a wrap of sheer red and gold silk, standing before the fire. He'd seen her naked, but the picture his mind drew was even more enticing.

"I thought you'd like that." Her laugh was low and easy. "Do you have any scarves? Here, in your bedroom?"

Now he was lost. "I think there are some in the chest against the wall."

She sauntered over to the chest and opened it, surveying the wealth of silk and fabric within. "And you don't lock it? You are a trusting man." She leaned forward and drew out a couple of blue strips shot through with gold. "I begin to understand why it is so unfashionable to be in trade. I do declare all the lordlings are scared of their ladies flocking to any man who could provide such fancies." She flicked her wrists and the scarves unfurled, flowing like banners from her hands.

Reaching out to grab the end, he pulled her toward him. "So you want to play, do you?"

"I do believe I do. I don't think either of us plays enough."

He quickly wrapped the scarf tight about her wrist. "Is this what you had in mind?" He'd never played at bondage with a woman of his class, but somehow he didn't think she'd mind.

Her lower lip pressed out, tempting him to lower his mouth and kiss it. "Actually no, that is not what I had in mind."

She lifted her arm and the silk slowly unwound.

He stared as the fabric snaked about her arm. They were both fully dressed and yet he could not remember ever being more aroused. "What, then?"

She moved her arm with more grace than a harem dancer, the silk following. "I was thinking of a blindfold. If we double the silk it should be substantial enough."

Now that had possibilities. "You want me to blindfold you?"

She wrinkled her nose in a way that should have been cute, but just made him want to nip it. "Actually I was thinking I would blindfold you."

"Me?"

"I don't think you give up control nearly often enough." She lifted her hand with that magical grace and ran her fingers across his cheek, then stroked back through his hair, the silk trailing behind, running across his eyes. "I think I'd like to enchant you this evening."

"You always enchant me." He moved to push the fabric away.

She stayed his hand. "Have you ever been blindfolded before?"

"No."

She laughed, low and husky, her voice surrounding

him. "I knew you would say that. I really think you should give it a try."

"And if I don't want to?" This was not going at all as he had imagined. He would admit that he heard nuances in her voice he had never noticed, but he wanted to see her face, to understand her pleasure.

Her fingers reached and pushed the swatch of blue lower until he could see. "We won't do anything that you don't like. I've never enjoyed games that did not bring both parties pleasure."

There was relief in that. He had never imagined that she played in those circles, but the reassurance was pleasant. "But it would bring you pleasure if I did—allow you to blindfold me, that is?"

"Only if you enjoyed it too."

He had to smile at that. "I think you could do anything to me and I would enjoy it. As long as you are here and touching me I will be happy."

She nodded and gestured to the chair that sat before his writing desk. "Move that to the center of the room and sit."

He did as she said, finding unexpected pleasure in obedience.

She stood uncertainly, as if surprised by his ready acquiescence. Her fingers played over the silk still caught about her wrist. Then she walked slowly behind him, coming so close that her breasts rested against the back of his head.

He let his head fall back, enjoying her sweet softness.

"No, none of that. Lift your head back up." Her voice was gentle, but commanding.

He swallowed deeply and did as she requested. He could still feel her but only in the most tantalizing of manners—he knew she was there, could sense her every movement, feel her like a breeze moving his hair—and yet it was all phantom. She blew lightly at the crown of his head, and shivers raced down his spine.

Then the silk came down. She lowered it a fraction of an inch by a fraction of an inch, gradually cutting off his sight. Even doubled the fabric was thin enough that he could see light through it, but that was all.

With a single pull she yanked it tight, tying it behind his head. "Can you see anything?"

"I could tell you where the window is, but that is all."

She moved behind him, only a half step to the left, but he could feel how the air swayed about her. She ran a finger down one of his cheeks, lightly, caressingly. He turned his face toward it.

"Don't move," she whispered against his ear, disturbing his hair.

Her hands moved down his neck, lingering at the turn of his jawbone.

The short stubble of his beard tickled her fingertips. Anna ran her hands over the hard edge of his jaw again, trying to decide how to proceed. She'd never done this before. She'd always been much more of a follower than a leader when it came to intimate matters.

She bent and blew against his ear again, watching a tremor run through him. She blew again.

This was fun, heady even.

Her hands progressed down his neck. She wrapped them as close to all the way around as she could manage, her thumbs not quite touching. She didn't squeeze, but just held them there. There was a joy in the power she held, even if she realized that it would be a matter of seconds for him to reverse their positions.

He didn't move as she held him, although she could feel the increase in his pulse. She bent forward, cradling his head between her breasts. His pulse grew even more rapid.

"That's for being good," she whispered.

He made no reply, but his Adam's apple bobbed beneath her fingers. She ran a finger across it, wondering for a second at the normally unremarked difference between man and woman. It differentiated them so clearly, but never before had she taken the time to experience the difference, to revel in the masculinity of a man's neck apart from the well-developed tendons that marked its sides.

Leaning over him she buried her face in his hair, breathing in the scent of sandalwood and musk, and just the faintest trace of hardy sweat. Her whole body responded to that one breath, becoming even more alive.

She slipped her hands lower, to the collar of his shirt, tangling her fingers in his neck cloth. One quick jerk and it fell loose. "Should I bind you as well?" she asked, drawing the linen up along his cheek. The thought held little appeal, but it was fun to say the words. She ran the cloth back down his arm and dangled it so it just touched his hands and wrists. "No, I don't think so."

The cloth dropped to the floor.

Her fingers moved to the top button of the shirt, playing a moment before releasing it. Then she released another, and another, until she could fit her whole hand inside his shirt. His skin was so hot and that rapid pulse seemed to fill him, beating against her palm wherever she put it. Feeling her way, she placed her hand directly over his heart until the beat began to fill her also. She closed her eyes and tried to imagine what he must feel, blinded except for touch, the touch of skin.

* * *

Could touch be seen? Struthers found himself pondering this question even as his mind emptied of everything except the feeling of Anna's palm above his heart. Although his eyes were covered he could picture her small, pale hand against the darker skin of his chest. It was almost impossible to remain still as her thumb began to move in small circles. How could one tiny movement set his whole body on fire? She was stroking only a few small inches of skin, but each touch radiated outward as his blindness focused his attention on that small patch of flesh.

Her fingers moved back to his buttons. "I want to see you." Her breath brushed against him.

Clasping the arms of the chair tight, he fought to stay still as he felt her move about his body. She came to stand before him and used a knee to push his legs open so she could step between them. Until this moment he had not realized that he knew the feel of her knees, the round bone and soft thigh above, but as she pushed against him he knew exactly which part of her touched him. He let out a long, soft sigh.

She freed the last of his buttons and pulled his shirt wide. "I love your chest. How does a city man stay so dark? I've seen men working in the fields whose arms are that color, but never a proper city gentleman. Hands sometimes—I've known men who don't wear gloves to ride, but then I always wonder what their arms look like. It would be odd to have dark hands and pale arms."

"Are you going to keep talking of other men—now?"

She laughed, low and easy, the vibration filling the air. "I do like you blind. If you could have seen my expression you would have known how hard it was for me to keep a straight face. You are fun to tease."

He felt a light tickling along his jaw. He turned his head, trying to figure it out. "What are you doing?"

"Why, teasing you some more, of course. Don't you like it?"

Was it a feather? "You're rubbing your hair against me."

"Yes and you like it." She pressed one rounded thigh forward until it pressed directly between his legs. "Yes, you definitely like it."

"I never said that I did not."

"Lift your arms. I want your shirt completely off."

He raised his arms and enjoyed the feeling of her moving about him, all warm, rose-scented woman. As she reached around his back to free him completely she leaned almost over him, smothering his face with bosom. It would have been a wonderful way to die.

He felt her breath against the side of his face again. "You still haven't told me how you got so brown," she said. "I know the color only goes to your waist or I'd really wonder. You can't have been swimming in this weather."

"No, although that is a good guess. I do love the water. Will you give me a reward if I tell you?"

"And what would you like for a reward?" She rubbed her leg against him, feeling his full arousal. "Did you have something particular in mind?"

"You take off this blasted blindfold."

"Now why would I do that when we are both having so much fun? I think you'd be disappointed if I did."

"I want to see you."

"You've seen me already. It's not as if it's our first time, nor indeed our second or third. I can assure you that nothing has changed. Round behind. Waist that needs little corseting—thank heavens. Adequate breasts. Pleasant face."

"I seem to remember it differently. If that is how you believe you look I may have to give you some descriptions."

"Hmm," she hummed against his neck as she leaned forward, letting her breasts rest against his chest for a moment. "I might like that, but I think you will have to describe how I feel rather than how I look."

"You'll have to strip down, then, unless you want me to describe the texture of your dress's fabric." He lifted a hand and brushed against her. "Wool, I believe. Of very good, but not the finest quality—and I do find that surprising."

"It's from a farm I own on the Scottish border. We're working on improving the quality of the sheep, but we are not quite there yet."

"I don't think I want to talk about improving the quality of the sheep at this moment. And I am learning—your voice tells me that on this occasion you are not teasing."

She snorted. "No, I am not. I fear I do take my properties rather seriously—those I did not sell."

He reached out and gathered her near, glad that he seemed to have found all the best parts. "Are you trying to distract me with talk again? I must admit we seem to be back to thinking rather than—rather than, well . . . I am still searching for the word that will satisfy you."

"You do a fine job of satisfying me." Her hand reached down between them and gave a featherlight stroke to his erection.

God, the lightest of touches and he was ready to fall at her feet and beg for more. He tried to grasp her more tightly, but she wiggled out of his touch and stepped away. He started to rise to follow.

"Don't do that. I am getting your reward ready," she said. "Now are you going to tell me where you walk around outside without your shirt?"

"I want a taste of my reward first." He held out his hand.

"A taste? I don't think so." He heard the rustle of fabric and then she stepped toward him. "Not a taste, but a touch, perhaps."

He felt her small fingers wrap about his hand, lifting it—and then there was the fullness of her breast. There were some things he could recognize perfectly, sight or no sight.

How had she managed her laces? The thought was gone before it even formed. He rasped his finger across her nipple, gratified by her small murmur of pleasure.

"Now tell me." Her voice was still full of command, but it had developed a distinctly husky quality.

He stroked the nipple again, listened for her response. "It's quite simple, actually. I occasionally travel to the docks and help unload the ships. In all but the coldest weather, carrying cargo can raise a good sweat and shirts tend to be discarded. It's not very gentlemanly, I know. But I've never managed to break the habit. My body feels so much better when it is frequently engaged in vigorous activity, and I find simply riding hard is not enough. I tried boxing, but I fear I am not a bloodthirsty soul—unless driven to it." Even as he spoke the words he had a sudden image of Nathanial Townsend's face. He didn't imagine it would take much for the man to drive him to it.

Her voice whispered softly against his ear. "You are the one thinking now. It certainly is a problem for us. I should, I am sure, be highly insulted that you are so distracted as you grasp my breast, but . . ." She leaned forward and trailed her fingers across his cock again. "I can tell that you are not unaffected."

"No, I am not." He just about swallowed the words as her stroke turned into a grasp. "I can promise that if you keep doing that I will not be distracted at all."

"Hmm, but what would be the fun in continuing to do the same thing?"

"I've never minded repetition." He stroked her nipple again. "I don't care how many times you make that whimpering noise. I'll enjoy it each time."

"I do not whimper." He could hear her teeth clench as she spoke.

"I'd ask what you call this sound, then." His fingers teased her again. "But we'd just end up in another discussion of what to call things, and I am not yet sure that I understand the purpose."

"I could argue about that last, but you are right, this is not the time."

"Then why don't we let things progress?"

She was supposed to be in charge. What had gone wrong? It might have been taking off her dress. It had been much easier to feel in control when he was half naked and she was fully clothed. With the situation reversed, he still half dressed and she now naked, things changed. He couldn't even see her and he made her vulnerable.

And the talking—she would never understand why the closer they got, the more intimate they became, the more words seemed to flow. She was hotter for him than she had ever been for a man, and yet each time she touched him her mouth seemed to spew irrelevant drivel. Well, not truly irrelevant, nor drivel, but definitely not needed at this moment.

An idea slowly began to form in her mind. They never seemed to talk about the things they needed to. While conversation was definitely not normally stilted between them, it also never seemed to flow with ease—except at these moments. Did she dare?

What didn't she dare?

She drew her shoulders back and straightened her spine. She could do this.

Struthers reached out for the breast he had lost hold of when she straightened. She pushed his hand away and moved to stand behind him again. She placed a hand on either side of his neck and began a deep massage. He moaned in pleasure rather than passion, his head falling back to cushion itself against her breasts.

"I think I could die happy at this moment," he said.

"Oh, but then you would miss out on so much." Her hands moved down to his chest, massaging continually. She bent forward until they were cheek to cheek. "Don't think, just feel."

He didn't answer, but leaned his cheek into hers.

She trailed her hands about his body as she came before him again. She would have liked him naked, but she sensed that things would progress much too quickly from that point on. She walked her fingers up his chest and then cupped them behind his head, drawing him toward her. Bending forward, she laid her lips against his in a sweet kiss. Her position was awkward, but she was not yet ready for greater contact. For this moment she wanted his whole world to be her lips and hands.

She removed her mouth from his and ran a finger across his lower lip. "You have such a beautiful mouth."

He sucked her finger in and she let him, moving it back and forth. Then she pulled it back slowly and replaced it with her mouth. This time the kiss was deeper.

She parted her lips and he needed no further invitation. His tongue dove into her mouth, caressing and feeling its way.

She wished that he would become lost in feeling, but now felt herself in danger. Her own tongue moved to meet his, inviting him into a game that could have no winner—and no loser.

His arm reached up to grab her waist, but she placed a hand on each of his shoulders and pushed back, holding them where they were. This was her game and she would play it how she wished.

She deepened the kiss, driving them further into desire. It was all she could do to keep herself from pressing forward, moving toward that final merge, but she knew what she wanted, and time and planning were required—although how she was supposed to plan when his teeth were doing that she didn't know. Only she did. She grabbed his lower lip between her teeth and pulled back slightly, not enough to cause pain, but enough to send prickles shooting through him. His body jerked, indicating her success.

She let her hands loose then, giving them leave to move from his shoulders. They caressed his back again, before moving forward to play over the muscles of his chest. She could have just stroked him for hours, but her own wants pushed her forward, not allowing for too long a delay.

It was a heady mix, fighting her own desire while driving his on.

Her hands slipped lower, feeling the hard planes of his belly. Did the man have any fat? Anywhere? As her fingers began to play about the waist of his pants she felt his whole body tense. It only drove her further. Her fingers delved and pulled back, worked at buttons and then moved on without releasing them.

"Are you trying to kill me?" he groaned.

She leaned forward and kissed him again, laughing against his mouth. "Now wouldn't that make me the wealthy widow? I hadn't even considered the possibility. Widows can have so much more fun than wives or single ladies. Didn't you indicate you had a *tendre* for Violet Carrington? She certainly had fun."

She let her hands play lower, just brushing at the crown of his arousal, and his reply was barely in English. "Jealous, are you?"

"Do I need to be?" She squeezed him delicately.

"No."

"Was that a word or a grunt? Or was that word—oh yes, a whimper. Was that a whimper?"

"Call it whatever you want. I don't care. Just don't stop."

Of course that made her pull back. "It's my turn to set the pace of play."

He started to reach for her and she stepped away.

"Come back," he said.

"Oh dear, that sounds a bit like an order, and I think we've already established that I am not very good at taking them."

"Please."

"That's better. Put your hands back on the arms of the chair."

He did as she directed and she came to stand before him, lining her knees up with his so they touched. She pursed her lips, considering. "Ah, so many possibilities."

"Just do something. Touch me."

"Giving orders again, are you?" She wiggled back a

half inch. "Move your legs together. That's good. I am glad to see one of us can obey."

"Don't push me—and I don't think of it as taking an order as much as working toward reward."

"That I can understand." She moved until she was straddling his lap and then sat, rubbing her behind along his legs, easing her own aches.

He started to say something, then stopped, his hands reaching out to grab her buttocks as he pulled her closer.

"Not going to ask permission, are you?" she said, circling her hips just enough to make him moan. His head fell back.

"I've learned that asking sometimes gets you a no. It's a careful thing, when to talk and when not to."

She moved again and he stopped talking.

His arousal was firm against the most sensitive parts of her body and she slowed her movements, deliberately driving them both crazy. She pushed and pressed, softened and drew tight. Her own head was back now as she strained to control herself. She wanted him in her so badly, but held off. In another moment it would be time.

She drew her thighs together, squeezing him between them.

His head snapped up. "Take off the damn blindfold. If we're going to do it this way, I want to see you, see your pleasure."

"In a moment. I want to uncover other things first." She placed her feet flat on the floor, lifting herself so that her hands could fit between them, making quick work of his buttons. Her hand slipped inside, freeing him from his undergarments. He was so hot and velvet. It was all she could do not to sink down on him, to use him to bring herself to that so-desired peak.

Instead she positioned him carefully, just at her

entrance, neither in nor out. Still keeping her feet pressed against the floor, she slipped her hands free and moved them up to the blindfold.

They both stilled, caught in a single perfect second of time, knowing that movement would bring ecstasy, but also an ending. Here, now, there was only endless possibility.

She wished she could have held on to that moment, but reality would not allow it.

Gripping the scarf tight, she tensed once, then lowered herself smoothly, taking him deep. Her eyes closed with the pleasure of it—and then a thought came, unexpected, unwanted, but there. It might be manipulative. He might take long to forgive her, but a sudden certainty filled her that if she didn't know now, she would never be sure.

She yanked the ends of the scarf, freeing the silk so it dropped from his eyes, revealing his face to her.

In that same instant she squeezed tight with every inner muscle she had, causing a deep moan from him.

This was the moment—her chance to be sure. Her lungs pounding with the effort of control, she looked deep into his eyes, still blinking from the sudden light, and asked, "Is this what it was like with Maddie, when you planted your child within her?"

Chapter 25

"What?" His mind asked the question even as his body fought to ignore all but her tight sheath. Was she really asking about Maddie now? God, she was. He could see it in her eyes as easily as he could see the desire that burned there.

Anger built within him, even now, that she could trust him so little, manipulate him so well. "Damn it, I never slept with Maddie—that was Michael. I've barely been alone with her." The words left his mouth before he could consider. They were truth, but he would have told her anything at that moment—and he resented her for it.

He stopped moving, punishing her, punishing them both.

He saw a variety of tensions build upon her face.

Then he laughed, letting it rumble free from his chest in one deep gasp. There really was no other woman like her. "God Almighty, Anna, only you would do that now. Talk about ruining a moment. What on earth were you thinking?"

"I don't know that I was thinking, only that I had to know."

"And you couldn't just trust me?" He began to move again, slowly.

"I did, but I was scared of being a fool." Her voice was soft, vulnerable.

He stared down at her, seeing into her, understanding the intimacy of the moment. He moved faster. Then there was only one thing that mattered, one thing that must be completed. He was through with games. The time was now. He grabbed her hips tight, his fingers digging into the soft flesh, and began to move her.

"You never slept with her—but I saw you that night—that night at Lady Smythe-Burke's party—you smelled of her perfume."

Would she not just shut up and wait? Did she really expect further conversation now? He closed his eyes and emptied his mind of all but the physical. Nothing existed except the weight of her on his legs, and the tight warmth of her about him—and her breasts; they bobbed against his chest with ever-increasing speed.

Instead of answering he buried his face in the wonderful hollow beneath her neck, breathing in her scent—refusing to acknowledge that anything existed besides the here and now.

She didn't ask again. It was not important now. She had been foolish to doubt. What was between them was stronger than any question. Her hands gripped his shoulders, nails digging in. She was panting hard, her body moving without his direction. She'd braced her feet on a cross brace of the chair and was using it for leverage in ways he'd never dreamed possible.

Her thighs squeezed him tight as she rose up, then loosened as she lowered. He pushed his own feet against the floor, moving to meet her halfway. He grabbed her face and held it, staring into her eyes, waiting to see that moment when she was as lost as he.

She was already there. Her eyes focused on his,

looking just as deeply, but he could see the glaze also, watch as her muscles tightened and her mouth gaped. And then the joy and relaxation. Her whole being jerked, once, twice, then was still.

He let her collapse against him, moving more slowly within her as he sought his own satisfaction. He'd never gone slower at the end, and it took great restraint. But then it was upon him. He grasped her tight, melding her body with his as his hips spasmed up and all dissolved in dark and color.

God save the king. It wasn't much of a thought, but it was all that filled her mind. The man was an act of God. She couldn't ever remember it being like that. Oh, the physical had been spectacular—perhaps the best ever—but it had been the look on his face as she came that had thrown her over. Her joy really had been his. She'd known men who always made sure their partners finished first, but it had almost seemed like simple good manners. With Struthers it had been so much more. He'd needed her to come, taken his own satisfaction in it. It seemed ridiculous to think that he'd have been content to stop at that point, but she could not help the niggling feeling that he would have been. His utter gentleness as she'd melted against him had only grown that seed of thought. Even after her question he had made it about her. Oh, she might have a bruise or two from his final moment, but that had so clearly been beyond his control.

She couldn't resist her own secret smile at the thought. She loved that she could do that to him, send him spinning so far from his normal control.

They lay together now on the hardwood floor of his chamber. There was a thick rug only a few feet away but the thought of moving that far was exhausting. They'd slithered off the chair and Anna wasn't sure they would ever move again.

"I meant it when I said I'd never slept with Maddie." Struthers's voice was faint but unmistakable.

"I am sorry, but I suddenly needed to be sure, to never have even an inkling of doubt wander through my mind. I did see you leave her room—and the smell of sex was distinct."

"And yet you do believe me." He said it as flat fact.

She turned her head and stared deep into his dark eyes. "Yes, I do. I don't know why, but I do."

"What made you distrustful now?"

"Maddie came to me—she said there were rumors swirling about that her baby was not Milson's and that your name had been mentioned—someone knows about what happened at the house party."

"I do not see how anyone could—but even so it is only rumor."

"We had— But . . . I don't know. Maddie refused to say that you were not the father. She never mentioned Michael. I think she wanted to leave all options open for her to decide what is in her best interest."

Struthers rolled on his back and stared at the ceiling. "I had not meant to tell you about Michael. He was a foolish boy, seduced by beauty. I only wanted to protect him from being no more than a plaything. I was in the room to be sure that he had left and to warn Lady Milson away from him. I knew her husband was coming soon and I wanted to be sure she did not seek to play a more dangerous game. I should have realized that I was leaving myself open to being caught."

"So Michael could be the father." That would complicate things. There was no good way they could marry while Maddie was in mourning. That would only lead to more scandal—particularly with the baby on the way. No, they would have to let the baby remain Milson's and then later Michael and Maddie could marry. He could never claim the child, but he could raise it. And support it. If Milson's affairs were as described, then Michael could take responsibility for Maddie's expenses now—albeit quietly. Christian had had a decent estate and Michael would have inherited all of that.

Struthers coughed. "I can see the wheels turning in your mind and the plans you are laying. I hate to ruin your scheme, but Michael is not the father. He says—and I believe him—that that night was the first with Lady Milson. The timing would not work for him to be the father."

"Some other man?"

"It is possible, and you are right that she doesn't want to block any possible path she might choose to tread in the future."

"She was quite clear in not being willing to state anything definitely—about you or any other man."

"I expect that she was mostly hoping that you would cover her needs to keep her away from me or that if you were unwilling then perhaps she would turn to me and press me to help her out in return for her silence about Michael."

"She is not such a bad person." She spoke quietly, trying to convince herself as much as him.

"Just a desperate one."

"Desperation can cause us all to do things we otherwise would not." She remembered agreeing to marry Lord Adam. That had been desperation. She'd known she would die if she spent another day under her father's roof.

"Yes." He rolled on his side and stared at her. "That

was most unfair of you. I would have answered your questions if you had just asked."

"You have already admitted you would not have told me about Michael. I understand why—and I do respect your reasons, but you would not have told me if I had asked you in a different manner."

"Still . . ." His voice trailed off.

"And I was not truly trying to manipulate you—well, at least not entirely. It merely occurred to me that only during sex did we seem capable of truly open conversation. I merely sought to put that to my advantage."

"Oh you did, did you?" He pushed to his knees and then to his feet.

My, he was a tall man, and so beautifully put together. If she'd been a painter she would have wanted to capture him from this angle, looking up his long legs, past the manly bits, and that chest—oh yes—that would deserve a little extra consideration.

He held a hand down to her and pulled her up. She came off balance as she rose and ended cradled against his hard body.

"You're much smaller than I always think," he said. "When you are dressed and full of emotion you possess such force that it fills a room."

"I think I'll take that as a compliment and not a remark that I am little and scrawny."

His hands slid up her waist and settled on her breasts. "No, definitely not scrawny. I might even be moved to say that you were rather perfect."

She leaned toward him but his hands were moving lower again. Starting to protest, she was shocked when he locked his hand about her waist and suddenly lifted her in the air, tossing her high onto the bed.

Before she could gain back her breath he was beside

her, then over her, a thigh locked on either side of hers. "I believe we just had your turn. Now this is my turn."

"What?" She didn't know what else there was to say.

"Raise your hands over your head and keep them there."

Again she could think nothing but "What?"

"Do as I say." There was play in his voice, but it would have been impossible to ignore the degree of seriousness also.

She did as he commanded, finding a strange thrill in being obedient. If she had never before taken command as she had earlier, neither had she ever been so quick to follow direction.

"Stretch more. I love when your breasts are spread before me like the most fantastic of delicacies, displayed only for my enjoyment."

Some part of her wanted to protest that, but the look in his eyes and the tone of his words had her squirming. Stretching higher, she tried to imagine herself as he saw her. Her mind could not begin to form a picture that would account for the look in his eyes. He looked like he wanted to eat her, all of her.

He sat back on his heels, leaving just enough weight on her pelvis to hold her captive. He wet one of his fingers with his tongue and then drew it around her nipple like a painter with a brush.

She squirmed, desperately wanting to be free, but still obeying his command.

When he leaned forward and blew against her damp flesh it was almost too much. Her arms began of their own accord to reach for him, to draw him closer, to turn teasing to satisfaction.

He allowed more weight to settle against her and used his eyes to draw a direct line from her eyes to her hands.

Once again she stretched them up and tight.

"Such good behavior deserves a reward. You were most generous with me, what could I possibly offer you? No, don't tell me—this is mine to figure out."

He lowered his hands until they covered her breasts, then tightened the fingers slowly, squeezing and then releasing—all the while being sure to move the rough skin of his palms against her most sensitive peaks.

Her head began to twist from side to side as she sought relief from his most pleasurable torment.

"Do you want me to kiss you?" he asked. "No, don't speak. A nod is enough. We can save our words for later."

She stared up at him, nodding slightly, completely in his power. Her arms were still stretched above her head and she kept them there, delighting in her torment. Moments before, she had rejoiced in power, and now she relished her own passivity—there was a certain relief in giving over command for just a few moments.

He was staring back down at her, his fingers and hands moving relentlessly over her breasts, but his eyes stayed fastened on her face as if her every response were more precious to him than the lush curves of her body.

She parted her lips beneath his stare and he lowered his head toward her slowly, oh so slowly. He paused just before their lips touched. His breath filled her mouth and she blew it back to him. His lips quivered as he inhaled and then touched—the petal of a flower brushing her lips, so soft it was. But that was only for a second, then his mouth settled hard, his tongue sweeping in to dance.

She could kiss this man forever—each time was like the first, and yet filled with the comfort of feeling they'd been doing this for years.

She gasped as his lips moved lower, nipping the point of her chin, weaving delicate trails down the cords of her neck. He passed over her breasts quickly—barely the flick of a tongue over each peak—before moving lower. He seemed determined to trace each rib with lips and tongue.

Her breasts cried for his lips, but then his hands returned, comforting and taunting at the same moment.

It took all her effort now to keep her hands high. They wanted to be tangled in his hair, massaging the muscles of his back—scratching, feeling—moving. That last was the truth. She wanted to move, to squirm, to urge him faster. But instead she bit tight on her lower lip, holding in the desire that grew within her.

He edged his weight lower, sliding down her thighs to her knees. She gasped as his tongue circled her navel and then slid even further down. He blew softly as he reached her curls, causing them, and then the rest of her, to shiver.

His body lifted then. She should have felt free, but still she was his captive, helpless as he spread her legs and stared.

It was broad daylight.

The thought suddenly filled her mind.

She was as exposed as any woman could be and the room was filled with sunlight.

He smiled and his face was as bright as any light. "You are thinking again. I thought we had managed to pass that."

"And I thought we had decided not to talk." She was becoming even more aroused—if that were possible. How did this man's every word affect her more even than his touch?

"No, we just postponed conversation. I could give

you a thousand words now about how beautiful you are. Your skin glistens in the sun as if dusted by pearls. Your lips are so full and lush from my kisses that I want to bite them hard and taste their sweetness. And your breasts"—he lifted his hands from them and stared—"are so perfect there are no words."

And she'd thought he was arousing when they discussed thought.

He placed a hand on each of her knees and spread her legs farther, looking down as if at some glorious piece of art. "I love women's bodies. The roundness. The curves. The tender skin. And the secrets. The simple perfection of nook and fold." He leaned forward and blew softly on her most sensitive spot. "And this. How did God ever think of this? To hide such a secret in such a simple spot—so easy and difficult to find all at once."

She could be still no longer. The look in his eyes, the feel of his breath, all conspired against her. Her hips rose off the bed, seeking his touch. He blew again. And then his head lowered.

He found the spot like an arrow aimed at a target. There was no play, no pretense, just lips and tongue and—

Explosion. The world broke apart before she could draw another breath.

That had been fast. He'd meant to draw it out longer, to play with her as long as possible, but she was so uncontrollably hot, so—so overpowering. How could he win and lose in the same turn? His own body was aching for release and he shifted, drawing himself away from her warm skin. God, he'd meant every word he'd said. She was the most amazing thing he'd ever seen. He didn't know why she was so different, but she was. She called to him on so many levels that no woman had ever touched before.

Closing his eyes, he sought control, both emotional and physical. He was close to saying words he'd never said before, words he was not ready to say. And there was still so much he needed to know.

He opened his eyes again and perused her, seeking to see what it was that made her so different. He'd seen it all those years ago when she'd been Christian's, and now that she was his it was still there and just as indefinable.

Her eyes were half closed, her face turned from his. She breathed fast, but softly, trying to recover from her climax. Her breasts rose and fell, causing the sunlight to dance across her skin. His body clenched, reminding him of his own need for release. He sat back on his heels and moved her knees, granting himself free access. Then he moved, rising above her until the head of his penis rested just where it wanted to be.

Her face turned toward him, her eyes opening fully, and she smiled—the smile of a woman who knows just what she wants. "I knew once would not be enough for you. It certainly wasn't for me—I am not even sure twice will be."

Of her own accord she spread her legs even further, edging lower on the bed until he pressed tight against her entrance.

He laughed, low in his chest. "I'd actually forgotten that we'd finished once only a few moments ago. My body is so eager for you that it feels like days, if not weeks."

He thrust forward then, beginning the age-old rhythm.

Still he watched her, listened to her breath, gauged

her reaction. He had to do this right, just as she had.

He counted forward, backward, recited Latin proverbs, did everything he could to deny his own body's cry for release. This was about her. He watched, waited.

Her breathing sped, he could feel her body begin to shift, the muscles to tighten.

He pulled back, filled his lungs with air, and stared straight into her eyes. "Where is your money going?"

He hadn't. Her mind could not believe even as her body pressed forward, urging. He did not move.

"I am giving it away," she gasped. "I am setting up charities and trying to make sure it all goes for good."

He sank into her again, pulled back, waited a moment, and buried himself deep. Then he stopped again, his gaze holding her steady. "Why?"

She squirmed, her body on fire. If she clenched tight she would win. His brow was covered in sweat and she could see how tenuous his hold was. It had taken her all to gasp her question at him, and she could sense that his control was just as slim. A single squeeze and—"I cannot feel right with a fortune made from the slave trade, with money earned from the misery of others."

His face blanked at that. For a moment she thought he would pull back, roll off her. She would not have blamed him if he did.

"Do you mean to give it all away?" His lips had narrowed so they almost disappeared.

"I don't know—probably—at least most of it."

He did pull back, but only to bury himself again. And again. And again.

Any passion that had disappeared with their words grew and multiplied.

There was something else there, as well.

Her body burned at his touch, her whole being centered on that core of nerves that pulsed and tightened, drawing her along her course. But her mind—her mind ran free, soaring with passion as it never had before. She had told him all and he was still here. Still with her. Oh, he was so with her.

She didn't know what would happen after—he could be a man and turn against her, his pleasure taken. But here, now, he was hers and she loved him.

Her mind didn't even pause at the thought.

She loved him.

The thought filled her even as her body rose to a crescendo. She loved him. She loved him. Her body clenched and spasmed as release came. She loved him. A scream tore from her lips. His name.

She loved him.

Her body fell back even as he collapsed above her, his weight pressing her to the sheets.

She closed her eyes—let the sleep of aftermath fill her.

She loved him.

It would be a long time before she'd let him know, though.

She intended to give away half a million pounds. Thought returned slowly as Struthers fought his way back to consciousness, fought his body's cry for sleep.

Half a million pounds to charity.

It was such an absurd thought that he could hardly even think it.

Her cousins had reason to think her insane, anybody would think her deranged.

Wonderfully, delightfully crazy.

Not that he would ever say that to her.

He remembered the madhouse, remembered her fear.

How brave she had been to proceed against such threat.

He was so proud of her.

He lay back on the pillows, trying to decide if he should wake her. They did need to talk. He should have listened to her earlier, before they— But perhaps that was nonsense. Something about the lovemaking had introduced both an intimacy and an honesty to the equation. He did not know why—but then he did not need to know. All that mattered was that he trusted her.

He still wasn't quite sure he understood her reasoning, but he did trust her.

If she felt the need to do this then it was what she should do.

He didn't need to understand—although he hoped she would explain.

He closed his eyes. Postcoital sleep did not normally last long. He would let her have her rest and then when they were both ready they would get out all the details.

Wrapping an arm about her, he pulled her close. It was so good to simply hold her.

Anna was surrounded by warmth. Her memory could not recall a time when she had felt so secure. Slowly she opened her eyes. At first she thought she'd slept long and that darkness had begun to fall. A moment later, as the fuzz of sleep cleared, she realized that Struthers's arm was thrown across her brow, sheltering her from the light. The desire to stretch filled her, but she did not wish to move, did not wish to wake him.

Then she heard it. A pounding from below. The door, perhaps? It must have woken her. She had always been a light sleeper.

Yes, it was definitely the door.

If she strained she could hear the slow masculine

steps of the porter walking toward the door, and then the creak of it opening, and then—

Maddie?

Was that Maddie's voice? Damnation, it was.

She pushed Struthers's arm away, feeling him stir and wake at the action. A dozen curses sounded through her mind as she slid from the bed and began to look for her stockings and undergarments frantically.

"We are married, you know." Struthers's voice sounded from behind. "Even if that is the sound of callers—as I gather you fear—there is nothing wrong with your being here."

She glanced at him over her shoulder. "Men. You never understand. There is a difference between not being wrong and being acceptable. Husbands and wives do not do this—not in the middle of the afternoon."

"Do not what, make love?"

Her head jerked up at that. Had he just called it lovemaking? He had avoided the term before—as had she. But now it did seem to fit. Oh bother, though, there was no time for that. "It's not just callers below. It's Maddie. I don't want her to catch me like this, but neither do I wish her to leave. I think we need to resolve things with her."

"We do at that." He sprang from the bed and reached for his trousers, pulling them on in a single movement.

Why did men have it so easy? Ignoring his lack of undergarments, Anna got busy with her own. If she appeared without her corset Maddie would have no doubt what had just happened, not that she wouldn't guess anyway. "What will your servants tell her?"

Struthers stopped. "I don't actually know. They've never been confronted with this situation before." Then he grinned. "I imagine they will get used to it in the future, however."

She opened her mouth and then closed it. She couldn't actually disagree. Pulling her dress over her head, she presented her back to him as she tried to shake wrinkles out of the skirt. She might have managed to get out of her dress on her own, but lacing it back up was another story.

Struthers's hands made rapid work up her back and then he quickly finished his own clothes as she found her slippers.

"You look fine," he said, glancing over her. His tone didn't sound confident and she deliberately did not glance in the mirror. She could only imagine her hair and puffy lips—and the cravat pin still holding tight the rip.

Just as Struthers pulled on his second shoe there was the lightest of scratches at the door. He answered and was quickly informed that Lady Milson awaited him downstairs.

"Should we go?" They spoke at the same time, but neither one smiled as they headed for the door.

Chapter 26

"I can't believe you sent my Michael away. And don't deny you did it. Nobody else would have come between our true love." The words had barely left Maddie's mouth before Anna followed Struthers into the parlor. Maddie could only stare goggle-eyed as Anna strolled serenely to a chair and sat.

"So are you saying the baby might be your Michael's now and not my husband's?" She waited to see how Maddie's story would change. Her sister had always been a master at finding a new turn to take.

Maddie's glance moved rapidly from one of them to the other and it was almost impossible to gauge her thoughts. It was clear, however, that she was not pleased to see Anna. "I thought you would be at your own home" was all she said.

Anna answered, "I expect you did. I do believe that I may move in here, however."

"I was actually thinking I might move in with you," Struthers added. "I do believe your home is more comfortable, Anna."

Anna did actually agree, but rather thought that perhaps his mammoth bed should make the journey with him. Still— She turned back to Maddie. "You have not answered the question. Is the baby Struthers's?"

Maddie stared straight at him for a moment. The desire to lie was evident on her face. Anna could see her measuring Struthers and his reaction. Finally she spat, "No. It is not."

Struthers opened his mouth, but Anna headed him off. "And I believe Michael has said that given the timing it could not be his, but we will get back to that in a moment. First, tell me, did you ever sleep with my husband, have sex with him?"

Maddie's glance again flew between them, a rabbit caught between two hounds. Anna knew she would have lied if she dared. Anna didn't know why Maddie so wanted to hurt her, but it was there in her expression. Finally Maddie's gaze locked on Struthers. "No, I did not. He has never been to my taste."

"Ditto," he replied, in stylish Italian.

Maddie's lips stretched into a thin line.

"Why did you imply that Struthers might be the baby's father?" Anna asked. This was at the heart of it all for her. She had done all she could to protect her sister and did not understand Maddie's ire.

Maddie stood again, beginning to pace around the room. Her stiffness of carriage made her discomfort clear, and Anna wondered if even she knew why she had acted as she had.

At last Maddie paused before the window and turned to them, her blond hair filled with afternoon light. "I am desperate. Do you know what it is like to have creditors pounding at your door—all with bills that you cannot pay without help? I cannot even leave my home without sneaking through the servants' entrance. You should have brought the funds to pay them. And then to hear the rumors about me and Struthers—to know that Milson's brother is ready to push me out if he can. Nobody could have told him but one of you." Her voice quivered with what Anna took to be true emotion, but then she steadied herself. "That said, all that matters is what we do now. Or perhaps I should say what you do now."

"I am afraid I don't understand," Anna answered, her mind still caught by the glimmer of fear she had seen in Maddie's eyes.

Struthers moved to a spot near her chair, his hand resting on her shoulder in protection.

Maddie sounded like a child on the brink of a tantrum. "I will not be left penniless—not after all I have done. My son will have more than his father's title. You owe me for all the years I have watched Father and the rumors you have helped spread. If you didn't want me to suggest that Struthers might be the father then you should not have done that."

"I did nothing. I had no desire to have my husband brought into this mess and I am sure neither did he." Anna did not have it in her to ask what Maddie would do if the child was a daughter. "Is Milson the father? Tell me so we can work this out."

"Given the timing—yes." Maddie continued to stare at her. She clearly was not happy to be forced to say it.

"Do you know the full extent of his debt?" Struthers spoke up, stepping between Anna and Maddie's stare.

"No, it is all unsettled yet. I did not even know he was no longer wealthy until the afternoon after he was shot when creditors suddenly began to appear in droves." Maddie's voice broke as she spoke, revealing that this was the heart of it all.

Anna felt her sister's vulnerability, remembered back to the time after Christian's death when she had felt helpless, alone in the world without choice. Her vulnerability had led her to Lord Adam. How could she blame Maddie if her choices had been no better?

"It isn't fair." Maddie's voice picked up a whine. "I am prettier than you and I've always done everything I was asked to. Father said I should marry Lord Milson and I did. It wasn't my fault that I never got with child until now or that Milson always suspected me of cheating on him. I don't think I ever would have if he hadn't constantly accused me of it. He had three duels with men I'd barely spoken to. Is it a wonder that I finally gave in and took a lover?"

"Some might have thought that with a husband prone to shooting at lovers it might have been wiser not to take one." Struthers sounded very cynical.

"The men always knew what Milson was like. They loved me in spite of it."

Anna could only wonder if it was not the other way—that the men liked the idea of pretending bravery by pursing the wife of a man known for jealousy, if they hadn't liked what it did to their reputations.

She closed her eyes and prayed for strength. Maddie was correct that the world had not always treated her fairly, but when did it treat anyone fairly? It had certainly not been fair when Christian died or when Anna's cousins threatened to have her committed. Maddie had never been known for strength and fortitude. Perhaps that was where the injustice truly lay. Anna opened her eyes again. "So what do you want? I am assuming you did not come here for a social chat?"

"Money. It is as simple as that—and more than is required to simply pay Milson's creditors." She stepped toward Struthers.

Anna stepped between them. "But I would give you

money anyway. I do not need threats to care for you and your child."

Maddie moved back at that. "It is so easy for you to say. So easy even for you to do, to play Lady Generous. I want enough that I need never feel like this again."

Anna could understand that. Money was nice. It brought comfort and security, gave a woman power, but it had never been her own motivation. "So how much do you want, exactly?"

"I don't think you owe her anything—except for your father." Struthers spoke very softly.

"It is my choice though?" Anna kept her voice flat.

"Of course—I will not change what I have told you." Struthers turned from Maddie and faced Anna.

"Oh, stop it. The two of you make me ill." Maddie flounced toward the door. "I will be at the Gadsworths' ball tomorrow night. I want my money without delay." She paused and spoke only to Struthers. "And don't think to deny me. If you do, I will make you both sorry, very sorry."

And then she was gone.

Anna could only stare at the still-open door.

"I am glad we discussed that before she arrived," Struthers said. "I would have hated to have you doubt me."

"I am not sure I could anymore." Anna rubbed at her temple. What had happened to her sister? Was she really that desperate? "I will need to think, to plan what action to take. Do you realize we have not even eaten?"

"Shall I ring for something?"

"Will your cook be preparing a proper meal, a real dinner?"

"I would imagine so."

"Then I will go upstairs and—I was going to say I

would go and change into a clean dress, but I have nothing here," Anna said. She glanced down at the rip in her bodice. "I'd even forgotten that I'd torn this. I am surprised Maddie didn't say something. It is unlike her not to have taken the chance to mention it."

"It is really not that noticeable." He turned and stared at her. He wanted to ask something, but what?

She'd hoped he'd say she should move her things here or that he'd again express willingness to return to her abode. Was that what his glance said? Should she say something? "I must go home and get something fresh to wear."

"But you will return?"

"Yes, we have much to talk about."

"I will have my cook prepare a proper meal then." He walked toward her, stopped and stared down at her.

It was hard to resist rubbing her nose to see if there was a smudge on it, so intent was his stare.

"Do you like a good roast beef?" he asked. "I always have a roast on Thursdays and I am not sure I want to miss it."

"Roast beef on Thursdays. And you act like I am overly spoiled."

The corners of his mouth turned up. "It was hard to get a good piece of beef in India. I've been rather indulgent with myself since returning. I don't mind spending money, I just don't like wasting it."

Her stomach tightened at that. They had still not discussed Mr. Jackal and her giving away her fortune. What did Struthers think of that? Did he regard it a waste?

It was time. Struthers watched Anna cut into her roast. She cut the daintiest of pieces and then glanced at him as she brought it to her mouth. Her eyes glinted with mischief as she formed her lips into a perfect O and wrapped them about the fork, pulling it back with utmost slowness.

"You really should not do that if you intend for us to talk," he said.

"Do what?" she said, moving to cut another piece.

"You know exactly to what I refer. And don't you dare reach for that asparagus."

Her eyes flashed with innocence, but her mouth—there was nothing innocent about that mouth.

"Stop it, Anna. You are always the one saying that we need to talk. Well, now I am ready. I know that you believe we are more honest when we—"

"Are you blushing? Can you really not say the words? I thought we were long past that."

"It is simply different across a dinner table. I've never had a discussion of an intimate nature across a dinner table."

She smiled, wide and full. "I cannot say that I have either—but I would not be surprised if there are many in our future." She forked a piece of asparagus.

He shifted in his chair as she brought the whole thing to her lips—her tongue caressing the tip.

"Are you trying to avoid discussing the fact that you plan to give away your fortune?"

She placed the asparagus back on her plate. "No—or at least not really. I would admit it is hard to know where to start."

"The beginning is always good."

"And you, will you start at the beginning?"

"I am not quite sure to what you refer."

"Yes, you are. I want to know about India. If our marriage is to be a success you cannot leave me wondering."

"You doubt me?" He pulled up straight in his chair.

"I said wonder, not doubt." She leaned toward him. "No, even without knowing a single fact I do not believe you betrayed your partners or burned your own fields. I would confess to being less sure about the native woman—but that is your business. You have not asked about my past lovers and you have believed me that nothing happened with Lord Adam and the kiss. As for the rest, what happened with your partners, that I think you should tell me. People will always comment—and I would like to know the truth. I believe you will tell me the truth."

It was hard to keep his eyes on her face; when she'd leaned forward her dress had revealed much and she was wearing that damn pearl pendant. He was forced to remind himself what he had just told her—they needed to talk. "You do not need to convince me. I had decided to tell you everything."

"You had?"

He let his eyes drop for an instant. "Yes, I had."

"Then I suppose I had better start. I had intended to tell you soon anyway. I was just not sure how."

"You did not think you could trust me? I made it clear at Sherberry that I would never say you were insane."

He watched Anna swallow. She looked more nervous than he had ever seen her. "Yes, you are right, I could have trusted you with it. But that has not been the situation for long. Do not forget you prevented me from accessing my own money. How was I supposed to tell you that I was setting up orphanages and starting schools, providing loans to the destitute, working to get prostitutes off the street? I even have a fund that is trying to help former slaves set up lives for themselves."

"I am surprised you're not just buying them freedom by the dozen."

He knew he sounded slightly sarcastic, but her answer was calm. "I am trying to figure out how that can be done. It doesn't serve any purpose to buy a man's freedom if there is no place for him to go and live. I do not have all the answers. I merely begin to try and address a problem."

"A problem? Your fortune?"

That brought a faint smile to her lips. "Yes, my fortune. I do not rest easy knowing where my wealth came from."

"Do you truly mean to give it all away?" He could understand the concept, but not the reality. How could anyone give away close to half a million pounds? Were there enough charities in all of England, in all the world, to make use of such a sum?

"No." She spoke very softly, but took a large gulp of wine.

"No?"

"No. I am afraid I am neither that noble nor that stupid. I have no desire to be destitute. As you have remarked on, I do like nice things. I had originally planned on trying to give it all away, but that has proved impractical. I made a decision that some of the money must have been earned through legitimate means and that therefore it is not necessary to give it all away. I realize I may simply be justifying my own wants, but I also realized—even before my cousins began their plan—that I would be seen as unbalanced if I left myself impoverished. Living well was actually the safest thing I could do."

"That is rather convenient."

"I know. I have debated and planned and debated more trying to decide if it was just my own selfish wants that had me so convinced. What doubts I had fled when my cousins began their plans. No court in the land would have found me sane if I had tried to dispose of it all. No, after some conversation with Mr. Jackal I decided that the best plan was to continue as I had. I could always leave it all to worthy causes in my will."

"Who is this Mr. Jackal?"

"Have I not said? Mr. Jackal is the manager of my charitable commitments. He makes practical what I only dream about."

"I will want to meet this Mr. Jackal, see who my wife does allow to tell her how to spend her money." He said the words with a gentle tone so that she would not take offense. He grew more serious and added, "But what of your children if you give it all away in your will?"

She blushed, and most delightfully so. "I had never planned to have any. It was part of why I did not wish to marry."

"It is luck that you married a wealthy man then, isn't it? One who is more than capable of providing for his family."

"That seems like a good point to switch the conversation. Tell me of your wealth and how you came by it."

Chapter 27

Anna watched as Struthers closed his eyes at her question. His forehead tensed, the small furrow between his brows deepening. Then he opened them and stared right at her.

"Why don't you tell me what you've heard. Then I can fill in the blanks and correct any misapprehensions. It is in reality a simple story."

That was fair. Anna quickly recounted everything that Lady Smythe-Burke had told her—leaving it very clear that she was not sure what to believe. Her words slowed when she discussed the native wife. His lips tensed whenever she mentioned the woman.

"Her name was Sunita."

"What?"

"The woman to whom you refer. Her name was Sunita. If nothing else she should have a name."

"I am sorry that she died. She did die, didn't she?"

"Yes."

"If you do not wish to say more about her, I do understand. I said she was your business and I meant it. I am curious, but I can live with curiosity."

"The rest of what you have heard is largely true—as far as the actual facts go. Tom and Robert and I were as big a pack of young fools as you can imagine. The war was not yet over, but we had seen enough and were free. We all had some money—both from pay that had never been spent and from our families. We were determined to make our fortunes—and innocents that we were, we chose India."

"Why do you say that as if you were fools? Many fortunes come from India."

"I say it because we were. India is a land of possibility, but only if you know what you are doing or have connections. We had neither. My uncle had some business interest there, but I did not want his help. Instead we pooled all our funds and bought a piece of land from the first man who promised we'd be rich."

"That never ends well."

"No, and it did not for us. We were lucky there was even an actual piece of land. I learned later of young men who spent everything and then found out that they had just bought a piece of a royal hunting preserve or that the town their land was near was not on any map. Swindlers always know where to find an easy target."

"But you did actually own land?"

"Yes, a tea plantation."

"That does not sound so bad."

"You would have to have seen it to understand. We owned three hills and the valley in between. It would not have been bad if there had been water or soil. Instead we had rock and sand. We tried anyway, but nothing grew."

"Why did you not give up?"

"I did not see that as a choice. Tom wanted to sell the land to some other poor fool. I thought that would make us no better than the man who had sold it to us. I refused."

"And the other man. Robert?"

"Yes, Robert. Robert always did what Tom wanted.

It had been that way since they were boys. We planted another crop. And then the fire struck. Everything was so dry, even the few streambeds. There was nothing we could do to stop it. Everything was gone except the plantation house. I do not know why it was spared—but it was."

"How awful. I am surprised you did not all leave."

"I was stubborn and I still refused to give up—and besides there was Sunita."

"I did not think you were going to talk of her."

His gazed dropped to the plate in front of him. "It does not seem possible to tell the story without her. I found her soon after we arrived. She looked hardly more than a child—skinny and starving and living in corners. Have you heard of the Indian caste system?"

"A little—it seems an odd thing."

"Odd to us, but to them it was simply how life is. Sunita came from nearly the bottom of the system. She would never tell me much beyond the fact that her family had died of illness and left her all alone. Nobody in the village near our plantation would have anything to do with her. I believe they truly were waiting for her to starve."

Anna did not answer, but she knew her face had grown grim.

"Not understanding anything of the realities of life I offered her food and shelter. She began to follow me like a puppy—and as she filled out it became very apparent that she was not a child. Our workers were appalled that I had taken her in—they said it made me as dirty as she. They did not wish to work for me, but in the end they relented—nobody would work in the house while she was there, however. My partners were most displeased and in the end I wrote and asked my uncle for the money to buy them out. They took the money and signed over the plantation to me, only too glad to be gone."

"I can imagine."

Struthers picked up his fork and twirled it about in his food. "And then rubies were discovered."

"A fortune in them."

He laughed ruefully. "No, that is one of the places the facts differ from the rumor. The find was good, but by no means what has been described. It was, however, enough for me to hire enough men to clean the fields and try one more planting."

She reached across the table and stilled his hand with hers, giving it a light squeeze.

"And then Tom and Robert returned. They had lost everything I had given them and wanted more. We argued and they cried foul, claimed I had always known about the rubies and that I had swindled them. I had all the signed papers, but still they insisted I had cheated them."

"It does not sound like anyone would believe them."

"And they might not have if a second fire had not destroyed everything. Many of my men died, as did Tom and Sunita. The fire began in the plantation house. It had clearly been set. I was the obvious suspect. After it was over, I could not bear to be there any longer. I gave half of what I had to Robert—half the proceeds of the mine—and I left."

"Why would you—"

"—give it to him? Because I had not set the fire, but Sunita had. I had told her that I wished to return to London. That I was tired of life in the Tropics. She felt abandoned and—and she set herself ablaze."

"That does not sound like such a simple story."

He raised his face to her and she could see the tears

behind his eyes. "I should have offered to take her with me. I don't know why it never occurred to me. I had enough. I could have given her a life here."

"You loved her."

"Not as you mean, but I did care for her. I had made her my responsibility."

"I still do not see why you gave half the money to Robert."

"Tom had died because of me. Robert had nothing. I guess I wanted to assuage my guilt—and I did feel some responsibility."

"I can see why you understand about Mr. Jackal. What I do not understand is why you are against my helping Maddie."

"Because there are some people who always want more. All the rumors that have swirled about me were started by Robert. Half of all I had was not enough. If even once he had spoken up for me this whole matter would have faded away. But every time the matter is broached he gives a smile that invites people to think the worst of me. I have grown tired of it. Maddie is like Robert. The more you give her, the more she will want. You have done enough. Pay Milson's bills if you must—but do not set yourself up to support her for the rest of her life."

Rising from the table, Anna walked around it. She placed a hand on each of his shoulders and began to massage. "I will think about that—but I will do what I decide is best."

"Of course you will." He leaned back and nestled his head between her breasts. "Now do you think we could turn to something lighter? I know that Cook prepared cream puffs for desert and even the words are filling me with ideas."

She leaned forward, pressed a soft kiss upon his chin. "Cream puffs. I do love cream puffs. And I think we have covered everything."

"I cannot think what else there could be to discuss." He turned his head sideways, trailed his lips over the upper swell of her breasts, caught her pendant between his teeth.

Breath and thought were both leaving her.

There was only one thing—the single thought suddenly filled her mind. "Except my cousins and the robbery. We have not discussed that."

Struthers rolled over in his bed, sighed, reached for Anna—she was not there. He lifted his head from the pillows and stared at her spot. Her side of the bed was smoothed and neat. He hadn't noticed the last time that she did that—although given that they'd been rushing down to meet Maddie, perhaps she hadn't.

There was a folded sheet of paper on her fluffed pillow. He picked it up and smiled. So the game was not yet over. *Tattersall's—12:00. You still owe me one. Can you be gracious?*

Of course he could be gracious—and what did she mean by that? He was always gracious. Why would she think differently?

And Tattersall's? What part of his lessons—because he was very aware that was what they were—could take place there?

Glancing at the clock, he scooted out of bed. It was almost ten, barely time to dress and be ready. He rang for his valet.

Only then stopping to wonder where his wife was. They had shared more than he would have ever believed last night. His gut clenched when he thought of the tale she had told—a knife against that slender throat.

If her cousins had been present he would have killed them in an instant.

He was glad he had the tools at his disposal to remove the threat of her cousins once and for all.

If only he could find a little patience. He would call on Timms again to see if any more information had been gathered. Timms was having them followed. It should be possible to determine if they had met with anyone who could have arranged the robbery.

They would probably be at the Gadsworths' tonight. He could take care of them while Anna met with Maddie. He would have liked to be there with her for the meeting, but sensed there were some things his wife needed to do on her own.

He began to whistle as his valet entered and shaved him. It was going to be a good night.

Anna was whistling herself as her coach pulled away from Tattersall's. She resented having to send an agent in to deal with her request, but Tattersall's refused to admit women, and for once she was not in the mood to fight.

After last night, she felt relaxed—and cleansed. It was good to have no more secrets between Struthers and herself.

For the first time in weeks she felt truly hopeful.

She'd decided how to deal with her cousins in the wee hours of the morning when she'd lain awake, snugly tucked against Struthers. She would proceed with her plan. It was such a simple solution. It would not make them happy, but neither would it leave them with any reason to pursue her.

Off to the bank now to talk with Lady Brattle and collect funds, and then home to await Maddie. Her gut told her that her sister would appear well before the start of tonight's entertainment.

Matched bays. The prettiest pair he'd ever seen—if you could call such magnificent creatures pretty. The damn woman had bought him a pair of horses, a pair that would suit his curricle perfectly. They were even finer than her grays.

She shouldn't have. She knew how he felt about extravagance. He would never have bought them for himself—no matter how he coveted them. Now he would have to pay her for them. He could never accept such a gift from a woman—not even his wife. A handkerchief that she'd embroidered would have been an appropriate gift, or even a new watch fob. She could have bought him a new pin for his cravat to replace the ruby one she'd borrowed.

No, he could never accept such a gift.

Can you be gracious?

Understanding descended. This was another lesson. A lesson he'd come close to failing. Yes, he could be gracious. He'd just have to find a way to show her exactly how gracious.

Struthers had always thought women took too long to dress and Anna was proving no exception. At least he imagined she was dressing, or primping, or some such feminine nonsense. Her maid was probably curling her hair, which was a complete waste of time as he intended to have it back down around her shoulders within the next couple of hours.

He stared up at the Gadsworths' house. Anna had sent him a message, insisting that she would meet him at the ball after she returned home to dress from her day of errands. There was definite merit to the idea of living together. He'd never understood why married couples did, unless children were involved. It had always seemed so much more sensible to keep one's own space. Now he understood fully. He couldn't wait to have the blasted woman under his roof—unless he ended up under hers.

They still had a lot more to talk about and he was rather looking forward to the discussion—and to thanking her for her gift, thanking her properly. Now that he knew how to get her to talk he planned on making the most of it. His nether regions tightened at the very thought.

Although there were other less pleasant matters that demanded his attention. He had not seen the Townsends enter, but surely they would appear—and then he would deal with them.

He should have questioned Anna more last night—found out more of what she planned. She was not a woman to proceed without a plan. But they hadn't finished their discussion—he could not be too upset given the why—and now she would just have to accept that there were some things a man needed to do. When his wife was threatened he had no choice but to act.

And then—when he had dealt with her cousins and she with Maddie—they would celebrate. He had great plans for the celebration. He'd spent most of the afternoon preparing for it—making Timms crazy trying to arrange the one gift he knew she could not refuse.

He shifted, letting the drape of his coat fall forward, concealing his arousal. There were some things a man didn't reveal in public and this was certainly one of them. He moved again, hoping he looked decent. He should probably go in. Anna might not be appearing any time soon and it might be best if he took care of the Townsends before she arrived. Anna was bound to meddle if he let her.

Marching up the stairs with a sense of purpose, he made the appropriate greetings to the Gadsworths. He entered the ballroom and let his eyes skim over the crowd, seeking his target. He could not find them.

And Lady Milson—where was Maddie? It would not be a bad idea to scout out that territory before Anna arrived either.

He stopped, speechless. Of course he could not find her—Lady Milson was a new widow. There was no way she would be at a ball.

Chapter 28

Anna sat in her parlor and waited. She'd been dressed for forty minutes. If Maddie didn't show up soon she would have to leave. She wasn't sure when she'd realized that Maddie's plan was not as straightforward as it appeared. She should have known the minute Maddie mentioned the ball. Her sister would not have forgotten propriety and shown up at the ball in a fit of anger. Nobody had ever been able to control Maddie when she was angry, but she had not seemed furious yesterday. Piqued, perhaps, but not yet in full-blown rage.

Her slippers tapped restlessly on the floor. Where was Maddie?

Was she attempting to deal with Struthers instead?

That would be a mistake for one and all. Maddie did not understand how stubborn Struthers could be and Struthers would not realize how prone to sudden mood changes Maddie had become. She was rarely quite this unreasonable, but if pushed too far she could become even more so.

It would explain her behavior yesterday. Maddie was feeling desperate, and a desperate Maddie might bring a storm down upon them all.

* * *

Should he leave? Struthers glanced around the glittering spectacle of the ball. Couples floated by him and only by careful maneuvering did he avoid conversation. If Maddie could not appear because of her bereavement and Anna did not appear to be arriving any time soon, what did he gain by staying?

The Townsends were showing no sign of making an appearance and he was ready to hunt them down if they had not been lured here.

But what if Anna did arrive and found him gone? Perhaps Maddie had contacted her and Anna would soon be here seeking his help.

Damnation. He saw one friend start toward him and then turn away. He must have a scowl that would sink a thousand ships upon his face.

"Excuse me, sir." A voice spoke from behind.

Struthers turned and found a well-liveried footman looking at him with some trepidation. "Yes?" he answered.

"You are Mr. Struthers, are you not?" the footman asked.

"Yes."

"There is a lady waiting for you in the upstairs library. She requested that you come immediately."

"A lady? Who is she?"

The footman glanced at the ground. "She did not give a name. Just told me to find you."

"And you do not care to speculate?"

"No, sir." The footman stepped back, anxious to leave.

Struthers nodded his dismissal.

Anna or Maddie? He could not think why Anna would call for him to leave the ballroom. It was possible she might have something she wished to discuss in private, but why not fetch him herself or at least give the footman a name? It could have been an oversight, but Anna did not tend to overlook details. He had rarely known her to be impulsive—with that one notable exception at Lady Smythe-Burke's.

Maddie? It seemed much more within her range of actions, but how would she have gotten in? A hat and veil? That would draw more attention than anything. He might arrive upstairs and find the hall full of onlookers waiting to see who the mysterious lady was. No, that was just fanciful.

He sped up the stairs with as much decorum as possible.

There was no one in the hall.

He took a deep breath as he placed his hand on the library doorknob and turned it.

"I spoke with your man Timms a short while ago."

Struthers turned and faced Maddie, who sat in the far corner of the room. Her dress was simple, unremarkable—she looked more a seamstress than a lady. Perhaps that was her secret to gaining entry.

He glanced about the room, as if considering before answering her question. "Why would you talk to Timms?"

"I had not intended to, but when you were not at home I asked to speak to your man. He is most discreet, but probably not quite as much so as you would desire."

He walked forward and stood before her. "Why don't you just say what you mean?"

"He had never heard of me. His expression made it clear my name was completely unfamiliar to him."

"I would imagine that is true."

Maddie sat up straighter in her chair. Her face grew very pale, even her lips lacked color. "If you were planning to release a large number of funds to me I do believe he would have heard my name."

"That is probably true too, although you did not leave me much time to consult with him."

"Don't take me for a fool. I know how these things work for men like you. If you had wanted, it would not have taken much time."

Struthers did not answer.

Maddie rose and walked slowly toward him. Her hips moved in a seductive pattern, but it left him untouched. His thoughts revolved around Anna. If Anna was not with Maddie, where was she?

Could that be why the Townsends were not here? He had always thought the expression *blood running cold* an exaggeration. He did not any longer.

Stopping directly before him, Maddie smiled up at him. It did not reach her eyes. "Do you intend to meet my demands?"

He wanted to turn and leave now—but first he must deal with this. "I understand my wife's feeling that she owes you and wants to help you, but nothing I have seen warrants more than she already pays for your father's care. However, as of yesterday I released Anna's money. It is up to her to make decisions. Timms knows nothing because I have no voice in what you will receive beyond advising my wife not to be overly generous." He should have been more tactful, but he could only worry about Anna.

"That would not be wise." Maddie's smile showed her teeth.

"I am not afraid of you. I find you more of a nuisance than a threat. If it were up to me I would send you away empty-handed. But I will let my wife do what she wishes—she would anyway."

Maddie narrowed her face at his last comment. He could feel the waves of her anger like a physical thing.

Her shoulders heaved and she pulled in deep, gulping breaths. When she had gained some control she walked slowly toward the door. She paused there and turned back to look at him over her shoulder. The gesture was reminiscent of Anna, but the comparison ended there. With Anna, he always felt she was imparting some mischievous secret. With Maddie, he just wished she was gone already.

He was not so lucky.

She still had one last comment to impart. "Don't say I didn't warn you. I will make you very sorry. I have weapons you know nothing about."

And then, finally, she was gone.

Where was Anna?

Where were the Townsends?

Where was Struthers? She would have thought he'd be pacing the Gadsworths' ballroom looking for her, given how late she was, but he was nowhere to be seen. Were they going to spend their lives searching for each other at balls? Prayers that he had not been delayed by Maddie filled her. She should have warned him. Maddie must be handled with care. No matter how much they chose to give Maddie they must make it appear that it was more than they could afford. Maddie would only be happy if she thought they suffered. Little would she know how painless it was to pay her off and be done with it.

Anna's stomach twisted with the thought. What had happened to her sister? She had never been easy company, but when had this bitter edge appeared?

Where was the blasted man? He had to be here.

She spotted Violet across the floor. Violet might

know. Surely she would have noticed if Struthers was here. Anna headed over with steady intent, but before she could reach Violet, Violet slipped through the doors to the terrace. Surely it was too cold for a stroll—perhaps she was meeting her fiancé. Ah yes, Lord Peter was following her out. It was probably not the best moment to interrupt.

Anna turned, looking for someone else who might help her.

Lady Burham? No. Anna was not sure that she knew Struthers and she looked much too intent on the young buck who stood next to her.

If only Struthers were better known in society this would be easier. He was far from unknown, but he'd spent far too many hours hiding in the card room for most of her acquaintances to know him by sight.

The card room. He might be there. She'd have to give him a show of displeasure if he was. He should have been waiting for her, waiting to comment on his gift—and Maddie—and her cousins. She could only breathe a sigh of relief that they were not here.

She turned to cross the room and saw her friend Clara, Lady Westington, ascending the stairs. She considered following her for a moment, but then stopped. She must be heading for the retiring room and nobody wanted to be bothered there. Besides, it was much more important to find Struthers. She would talk to Clara later.

A quick glance confirmed that Struthers was not gambling away the evening. She turned back to the ballroom and saw Violet leading a young blonde in from the terrace—Thomas, Thompson, Timmons—the girl's name didn't matter. And from the way Violet was holding her arm they'd been together for quite a while. A moment later Violet's brother and fiancé also entered.

There was temptation to follow Violet and to ask her advice—Violet always had good advice. But Anna didn't want to share her secrets in front of the girl.

"My dear Mrs. Struthers, it has been much too long since we've had a chance to speak." Lord Tenley stepped out of nowhere and planted himself firmly in front of Anna. "How have you been and how is your new husband? I'm surprised not to see him here with you."

He reached out and placed a hand on her arm. What could the man possibly want?

She turned her head and looked up at him. "Lord Tenley, yes, it has been a long time." She deliberately did not say "too long." "And as for Struthers, I expect he is about here somewhere. I was just looking for him."

"Well, if he can't be bothered to keep track of his wife, perhaps I can be of some help with your needs." He stepped closer and stared straight down into her bodice.

So that was what he wanted. She felt a fool for not realizing. Men did seem to be very singular creatures, wanting only a couple of things in life—money, breasts, and all that went with them. She supposed she should add in drink, gambling, and horses, but that all seemed to go without saying.

"I am sorry, but you must excuse me. I think I see Lady Carrington and I have promised to share some dressmaking secrets with her." She sidestepped into the crowd, doing her best to simply disappear.

Violet was no longer visible and there was still no sign of Struthers. Blast it all. She'd been tense before being waylaid by Lord Tenley. Now her nerves were positively screaming. If she had to be polite to one more bore she'd grind her heels into his toes.

A cool breeze from the terrace wafted against her. The door had been left open a crack. The cold might clear her head. She needed to move with deliberation. It would not do to falter now.

Struthers strode down the stairs with purpose. He would find out if Anna was here. He would tell her about the conversation with Maddie. He would tell her she could do as she wished, but that he would counsel against generosity.

But first he needed to find her. He could not shake the feeling that something was not right.

Stomping onto the main floor, he tried to maintain his calm, tried to pretend nothing was wrong. He scanned the crowd anxiously.

He was so busy looking for Anna that he didn't see Lord Tenley until he'd run smack into him.

He started to apologize, but Tenley cut him off. "Oh, you are here. I was rather hoping your wife was lying. I have always wanted a piece of that woman."

Anna stared up at the night sky. It was dark, other than the soft orange haze that always colored the London sky at night. A few brave stars peered through, but even they seemed muted.

Pulling in a lungful of crisp air, she turned to leave the terrace. The cold might clear her head, but it was still cold and she was not dressed for it. Plus if Struthers was here he would never think to look for her shivering outside.

She took a step forward and stopped.

There stood the answer to one of her questions.

"You always were a sly one. I should have known you made it all look too easy—and instead all you've done is make it easy for me." Maddie stepped away from the glass door to the ballroom and toward Anna. Even with the light glowing from behind, her eyes had developed an eerie glow.

"I don't know what you mean. And why didn't you come by earlier? I waited for you."

"Did you?" Maddie's voice did not sound normal.

"Yes, I have the— What are you wearing? You look more like you're ready to supervise a closet cleaning than to attend a ball."

Maddie held her skirts wide. "You don't like the latest of my looks? I rather think it cries poor widow sneaking into a ball."

That did explain it. "I would comment more, but it would serve little purpose. Why are you here?"

"How else were we going to meet?"

There was something just not right. Maddie looked tired and yet strangely exalted at the same time.

"I rather thought you were going to come to my home so that we could be cordial about this."

Maddie stepped closer. "Did you? How strange, although I admit I had thought to start out with civility. I went back to Struthers's house with just that intention. I see that you wonder why I didn't just come to you. Well, I know well that it is the man who controls the money—no, don't interrupt. I've been interrupted enough. I planned to make it clear to Struthers how much he had to lose. I can be very persuasive with men."

"And what did my husband have to say?" That would explain his lateness.

"He wasn't there. His man Timms was, however. Imagine my shock to learn that the man had never even heard of me. The two of you had all day to plan and the man had never heard of me."

Struthers had not been there. That would mean he must have left, which meant he had to be here somewhere.

"Why would he have? I went directly to the bank myself. I would not involve somebody else in this mess."

That caught Maddie's attention. "You went to the bank—about me?"

Anna resisted the urge to rub her temple. "Yes, it is not all set up yet, but I have begun the process of arranging a steady income for you and the child—and more than enough set aside to pay Milson's debts immediately."

Maddie smiled and her lips trembled slightly. "It's a pity I didn't come to you first. Your husband was not as cooperative and I fear he may have caused me to react impulsively when I was a handed a gift."

Fighting to keep focused on the point, Anna asked, "Struthers? I thought he was not home."

"No, he was not. But I did find him here. He was even more pleased to see me than you."

"I take it he was not helpful?"

"No, not at all." Maddie turned away and walked to the low wall overlooking the gardens. "You have not asked about my gift. Father gave it to me." She held out a few sheets of paper.

Anna recognized them immediately and her stomach twisted into a ball smaller than a pigeon's egg. "What exactly have you done, sister?"

"Exactly what you think—started a rumor, only a small one, but it will spread all the same. There is so little excitement this early in the year and a bigamous marriage—even if only rumor—is still quite a story. It's not like anything else is likely to happen this early in the season to overshadow it."

She couldn't breathe. Anna opened her mouth, but her lungs refused to fill. She tried to speak but no sound came.

"Speechless, sister. I rather thought you might be. It is

a pity I didn't know earlier that it was you I should have addressed. Still, this plan will suit me as well."

Anna finally managed to pull the air into her lungs. "Why? Why would you do such a thing?"

"Because I could. And because Struthers refused to believe I could do anything." Maddie kept her gaze focused out into the darkness, refusing to turn and meet Anna's eyes. "I wanted to punish you for having everything. You should have seen how eagerly the older ladies devoured the contracts with their eyes. I am sure the story will have spread to every corner of the ballroom by now—a secret marriage, a consummated promise—that you then denied."

"I just don't understand why you want to do this. It does not help either of us." Anna truly didn't understand the whole matter.

"You always speak of how a woman should control her own life. This is my way of ensuring that. This is my power. I was so desperate when the creditors were pounding on my door. This made me feel that I was in control." Maddie spoke firmly as if trying to convince herself.

Her mind spinning, Anna tried to make sense of all that her half sister said. Did Maddie really think it was as simple as that? She probably did. Anna had never known her to think twice before taking any action. Sinking down to sit on the low wall, Anna considered all the ways it could go wrong—for both of them.

She really wished Struthers was here, holding her, telling her everything would be all right—as he had last night.

She'd already put aside the money for Maddie. How could this be happening now?

Even if she walked out to the ballroom this moment

and told the whole story there would always be rumors, and if she was honest she'd had enough of rumor even before this happened. Being scandalous, even slightly so, was so very tiring. All she dreamed of these days was a normal life. She'd even have considered giving up Mr. Jackal for one.

She turned to Maddie, her voice weary. "Who did you tell? Maybe we can still stop them from spreading the rumor. You can tell them you were mistaken—or overcome by grief. Why else would a new widow be wandering around a ball in her maid's dress?"

Maddie pulled her spine straight, fighting to stand firm. "I am happy with my plan. Besides, they saw the betrothal contact—and everyone is still talking about how you kissed Lord Adam on the terrace."

"Are you really happy with it? It doesn't sound like a plan to me. Struthers could decide to forbid me to give you anything. This sounds as if he angered you and you hit out as hard as you could without thinking. I do understand that feeling."

"How could you?" Maddie's voice shook a little. "You get everything you want."

"Do I? Did I want Christian to die? Did I want to be left so alone? Did I want our father to be a drunkard? One who couldn't care less about me? Did I want my mother to die?" Anna had not even realized the extent of her pain until the words flew from her tongue. Alone. Was that really how she had felt?

She did not feel alone with Struthers. Was that why she loved him? He somehow saw her as she was and did not turn away. He was always there for her.

Except now, where was he now?

"I am sorry." Maddie's voice sounded sincere—and broken. Her eyes were still wild, but less angry now.

Anna put her own thoughts away and laid her hand across her sister's. "You do see that this will not turn out well for you either, don't you?"

A tear ran down Maddie's cheek, a genuine tear. "Yes, I know." Another tear followed. She looked ready to collapse. "I just don't know what to do. I know I am not rational, but there seems no answer to my problems. I hate depending on others. You may say you're alone, but you always seem to know what to do. I thought I did and I married Milson—and we both know that did not go well. I found out that it was Milson who told his brother about the house party—all I did to get you to marry Struthers and my husband still didn't believe me. And now I am having his baby, and he's dead, and there is no money, and the bill collectors are horrible, and Michael's gone—I always knew he didn't really care about me, and I just can't face it anymore." Maddie's face dissolved in tears and she buried it in her hands. "I just don't know what to do. I never know what to do."

"Shhh." Anna wrapped her arms about her sister and pulled her tight, letting Maddie shed all the tears she had never been able to. "I will take care of you. I should have done a better job of it earlier. You are my family—perhaps my only family since my mother's death." And as she spoke the words she realized they were true.

"But I've ruined everything," Maddie sobbed.

Anna considered, letting her own plan form. "I don't know yet that you have. We'll have to do what we can to clean things up, but let's not worry until we really know. And whatever happens I will care for you and your child. Even if Struthers should forbid it"—*which he'd better well not*—"I have just enough money that he cannot touch. I'll make sure everything's fine. Now just tell me who exactly you told."

Chapter 29

Still sighing with relief that Anna was there, Struthers turned and saw Mrs. Thompson staring at him, her eyes bulging in their sockets. What had prompted that look? Even as he watched, her petite blond daughter wandered up to her and Mrs. Thompson turned and whispered in her ear. The daughter turned and stared at him too, then shrugged, turning back to her mother and beginning to speak with some vehemence.

A hardy hand slapped him on the back. "Well, is it true?" Lord Wilcox, one of society's greatest gossips, smiled up at him.

"Is what true?" He modulated his voice carefully.

"That your wife is actually married to Lord Adam? What a way to get the cake and eat it too."

Struthers felt like he had to command each individual muscle of his face not to react. "What nonsense. Where on earth did you hear such a thing?"

"Why, from Mrs. Thompson. She said she had it straight from Lady Milson, who heard it from your wife's father."

Struthers forced a laugh from his lips. "Somebody is having a laugh."

"I don't know, it sounded real to me." Lord Wilcox leaned in. "I heard there are witnesses."

"Witnesses who said nothing for years. And Lord Adam? Tell me, do you really think he'd sit idly by and let my wife manage her own money while he got none of it?" Struthers forced the corners of his mouth to stay uptilted.

That had Lord Wilcox frowning. "Now I must admit that doesn't sound like the man. I've never known Lord Adam to leave a penny lying on the street, much less ignore a wealthy wife. Perhaps he didn't know."

Struthers raised a brow. "Not know that he was wed? And how likely does that sound? I've been married but a few weeks and I can say I am very aware of the situation."

Wilcox slapped him on the back again. "Must say you do make it sound unlikely. And I do know what you mean about being wed. I'd best go find my own wife or she'll have something to say."

Struthers started to turn away when he saw Anna marching into the room, a much less eager Lady Milson trailing behind her. He'd have something to say to that woman. Anna turned, saw him, flashed a nervous smile, and then turned away, heading straight for Mrs. Thompson.

He grabbed Lord Wilcox by the sleeve and pulled him over to intercept Anna. "Anna, my dear, you simply must dance with Lord Wilcox. I do believe he has a story to tell you." For himself, he grabbed Lady Milson's arm. "And I think we must share a dance also."

He could only stand shocked as Lady Milson dissolved into tears and fled back toward the terrace.

Anna nodded her polite farewell to Lord Wilcox and turned to head toward her original prey. Mrs. Thompson still stood at the edge of the room, her head bent to her daughter—that was who had been on the balcony earlier with Violet and her brother. Well, it didn't matter now. Anna had matters to settle and she would not be put off.

Mrs. Thompson had never liked her and it was urgent that the woman spoke to no one else of what Maddie had told her. Struthers had done a masterful job with Lord Wilcox, but he was only one small fish in a very large pool. If Mrs. Thompson began to spread the rumor further there might be no stopping it, no matter how ridiculous it sounded.

As she moved within a few feet of Mrs. Thompson, the lady turned from her daughter with a look that could only be called victorious. "I rather thought you'd be coming to find me. I can't wait to—"

Her words were cut off as a group came scrambling down the stairs. Lord Wainscott led the group and immediately went into caucus with his wife. That lady's face paled and then grew rosy as they spoke. She turned with great animation to the woman next to her.

"You'll never believe what I just saw," Belinda Thwaite said, in a stage whisper designed to be heard by half the room. "Masters is upstairs in the library and he—he's—" The poor girl's face turned a ghastly shade of fuchsia. "He's having intimate relations with someone."

Miss Thompson turned an identical shade of pink and then quickly fled the room. Her mother turned to Miss Thwaite and asked, "With whom?"

"I couldn't see beyond that I think it was a brunette. It may have been Lady Westington. Lord Wainscott was in front of me. He must have gotten a better view."

Mrs. Thompson gritted her teeth. "It better not have been that Westington woman. I always knew she wasn't out to help." She turned to Miss Thwaite, ignoring Anna. "Are you sure it wasn't a blonde? I think if you think again you'll remember it was a blonde." She turned and headed after daughter. "I'd better find my dear Kathryn. She's been missing for such a long time." She shot Miss Thwaite one more look. "A blonde."

Anna could not even begin to guess what that was about. A buzz had begun to fill the room and as she turned from Miss Thwaite a number of words began to surface—Lady Westington—Masters—sex—brunette—library—fucking—and a number of other terms that weren't even that polite.

Anna cursed under her breath. She had been saved. Nobody was going to talk about her when something as luscious as a couple being caught having sex in the library was out there.

But damn. Did it have to be Clara? Hurriedly she rushed to the stairs and climbed quickly. Just as she reached the top she saw Clara slip out of the library.

"Don't go down there," she exclaimed.

"What? Why?" Clara took a step back.

Anna wished there were more time, time to explain how sorry she was, time to help Clara with what was to come. All she could think to say was "Rumors are flying. They think it was you, but nobody is sure. The room was dark, and they could only see Masters clearly. If you come down these stairs there will be no question."

Clara's face paled, but she pulled back her shoulders. "I don't know what you are talking about."

There was no time for games now. "You know exactly what I mean. I've been told by three different people in the last two minutes that Mr. Masters was caught at a most intimate moment in the upstairs library—although not all of them put it quite so delicately. Miss Thwaite informed me it was you. Someone else informed me it was Miss Thompson—although how the two of you could be mistaken, I am unsure. The third did not know who Masters was with." This whole thing was absurd. Anna knew damn well it had been Clara and not Miss Thompson in the library. She had only to look at her friend's swollen lips. Besides, Miss Thompson had been right in front of her when the news came. Not that she would ever admit to that. She would do what she could to protect her friend.

Clara stepped backed again. A hand rose to her swollen lips. "Oh."

Anna thought quickly, letting the plan form. "So if you sneak down the servants' stairs and enter through another door, it will seem less likely it was you. I would claim you were with me, but I was dancing with Lord Wilcox, and you know what a gossip he is."

"Yes, I do. Thank you for your help," Clara answered. "I don't know—"

"Nobody should be forced to choose marriage or disgrace." Anna wasn't sure she'd ever spoken truer words. Even if her own situation had not been what it was, Anna would have done what she could to help her friend.

There was the sound of somebody else coming up the stairs and Anna quickly nodded a farewell and a warning, and went to head them off. Clara turned and fled back down the hallway.

Anna squared her own shoulders, already plotting what she would say. This new scandal would make her own seem small and irrelevant. No one would care now about the vague rumor of a marriage years ago—not when they could be talking about sex happening at this very party. She was saved.

* * *

Why had his wife gone upstairs? Everybody else in the ballroom was waiting eagerly to see who came down and Anna rushed right up. Did his wife really think before every action as she claimed? It certainly did not seem like it.

Struthers sighed softly to himself and headed up the stairs after her. It seemed like every time they headed off one catastrophe another appeared. He was just preparing himself for what he would find when Anna reappeared. She had her chin up and her shoulders back, but she licked her lips. She was nervous. Her shoulders softened and he knew she had seen him.

"Hello, wife," he said softly.

"Hello, husband," she answered. He could still hear the tension in her voice.

"You know this new scandal will drown out whatever is said about you and Lord Adam. Nobody will be interested in something with so little proof when there are eyewitnesses to this."

She nodded. "Yes, I know."

"You do not seem happy." He held out his arm and turned to lead her back down the stairs. It was an odd feeling to have so many faces turned up toward one and yet have none of them look at you. He was very glad he was not Jonathan Masters or Lady Westington.

"It is hard to be happy when somebody else will face such pain."

"I had forgotten. You are good friends with Lady Westington."

"Since we were girls."

"Ah, I begin to understand."

She stopped just below the bottom step and turned to face him. "To understand what?"

"To understand you. You may think carefully before doing anything for yourself, but let a friend be threatened and you rush right in."

"How could I do anything else?"

"How indeed." He was coming to understand his wife very well, and to like her all the more for it. "I suppose we'll be taking care of Maddie and her child, and doing it in the style she desires."

Anna nodded. "Yes, I suppose we will."

"Despite all she has done? Despite how she tried to hurt you?" He would respect her wishes, love her for her kind heart, but he did not need to like it.

"Yes." She lifted his hand to her lips. "And now, husband, will you take me home?"

"I was going to ask you that." He grinned for the first time in what felt like hours. "I actually have my valet waiting in the carriage with a bag. I rather fancy both your bed and a clean shirt in the morning."

"Well, husband, it appears I am not the only one who can plan."

Anna watched as her husband turned to call for the carriage. He really was a magnificent man with those broad shoulders and tight— No, she was a respectable married woman. Her mind should not be wandering in such directions.

And why not? After the events of the evening and the past few days, why shouldn't she enjoy herself an ogle?

She pulled in a deep breath. Could it really be mostly over?

She'd taken steps to control her cousins before the ball and while there would be details to take care of with Maddie, Anna was sure that her sister would calm down once she realized that she was not going to be tossed out of her home. It probably would not be long after the baby was born before Maddie was out looking for another husband—hopefully she'd have better luck than she had with Milson.

The mess with Clara disturbed her. It was hard to be happy at someone else's cost. Still, there was nothing she could do now. She'd seen Clara heading for Brisbane. If anybody could help Clara he could. She still didn't understand what Clara and Violet's brother had been doing together—well, from the conversation she'd gathered the what—it was the why that escaped her. She could only hope that her friend knew what she was doing and was prepared for whatever came next.

What came next—Anna didn't know if she was prepared for that herself.

It seemed so strange that it might be time to actually move on to the next part of her life.

Even as she thought this she pictured her cousins—Nathanial and Ernest. She'd already dismissed them, but still there was some lingering doubt flavoring her mood. There was nothing they could do—but would they accept that?

Struthers strolled over to her and held out his hand. She placed her own in his, feeling protected as he wrapped his much larger fingers about hers. If only life were always so simple.

He helped her into the carriage and they sat side by side, quiet.

She would have guessed there'd be a ready flow of conversation, but instead there was comfortable silence. Struthers still held her hand tight, letting it rest upon his hard thigh. The tingle of desire flitted about them, but did not settle. She could hear the depth of his breath, feel the warm heat of his body, smell the musk of his cologne—and of him. All these sensations filled her with want, but there was time, the wonderful luxury of time. There was no need for frantic grappling on the bench of a carriage when they would soon be home, tucked warmly in her bed with all the hours until morning ahead of them. Not that she intended to give up carriages. There was something wonderful about hurry, about the feeling that one could not wait another moment. But now, just now, there was wonder in the wait.

The carriage slowed before she was ready. Struthers lifted her hand to his lips and laid a kiss across the knuckles, a promise of things to come. Then the door swung open and he helped her to the ground, her body sliding down against his. There was so much more foreplay in the simplest of movements than she had ever felt in the deepest of kisses—or at least it felt that way now, in this moment.

Even the tread of his feet on the paving stones leading to the door made her belly quiver. His steps were so firm, so heavy, so masculine. My God, she was far gone. She was thinking his footsteps were seductive.

"What's the smile for?" Struthers asked.

"A woman's got to have some secrets."

"Does she now? I rather thought you had more than enough already." His tone was light, but she noted the serious undertone.

"I don't know what you're talking about." She batted her lashes at him. "I thought we settled all of that last night—at least now that Maddie is out of the way."

"We can talk about her later. I don't think she has any part in the rest of this evening."

"I should certainly hope not."

He stopped and turned to face her. "I was rather thinking of those few remaining details from last night."

Did he know about the contract she had signed? Know that she had given away her remaining interest in the shipping firm to assure their safety? "I don't know what you are talking about."

He kept staring. "I think you do. In fact, I am sure you do. My only question is, are you going to tell me now or are you waiting for further persuasion?" His voice dropped low as he said the last.

A shiver ran up from her toes. She knew just what that tone meant. There was great temptation to take the second option. It was so much easier to share her confidences in the dark of night, in the midst of spent passion. It was only then that she felt so open with him, so able to say anything, to tell him anything.

That was a coward's way, however, and she would be no coward. It was important that they be able to talk face to face at any time. "Ask me and I will tell you."

"You will?" He sounded surprised and slightly disappointed.

"I am sure you can think of other things to ask me later." She ran a finger across his chest, letting it slip between the buttons of his shirt to stroke his skin.

"Now you're just trying to distract me. Let us go in and sit—across the room from each other—and discuss what we are going to do about your cousins—and if there aren't better ways to spend your money than buying me horses. There must be more hungry widows and orphans somewhere."

She laughed, deep in her chest. "Do you really think that I can't seduce you from across the room? It is amazing what one can say with one's eyes, suggest with one's glance."

He sighed. "I know you can—and I am not at all resistant. It all depends on how you want to do this."

Maybe she would start with serious discussion and then continue with innuendo and eye contact. "Come, then. Should I ring for refreshment?"

The door swung open as she spoke and she stepped forward, feeling more at home than ever before.

"What on earth is this?" Nathanial's shout could probably be heard on the street. A sheaf of papers fluttered to the ground before her.

Chapter 30

Struthers stared at the two men who stood in his hall, wishing he could pick them up and toss them out the door like the refuse he knew them to be. If Anna were not here he'd take great joy in beating them to a pulp. What on earth were they doing here in his home?

His home? Did he really think of it as his?

He leaned over and picked up the papers, ready to hand them to Anna. His eyes scanned them and he stopped, looked closer, leafed through them quickly. "Why?"

She paled at his simple word. "Because it was the simplest way?"

Could she not have trusted him with this?

He waited. Luckily her cousins held silent.

She smiled bitterly. "I thought of it yesterday. I know I should have said something last night—but I was not decided and I wanted to be sure before I said anything. I do trust you, but I wanted it to be my decision."

"Are you just going to ignore us? I assure you that would not be wise." Nathanial spoke again, his glance focused on Anna.

Struthers stepped forward, coming between them. He held out an arm, gesturing to the parlor. "Let us go and do this in as civilized a fashion as possible." He refrained from adding that his current idea of civility barely included leaving their heads attached to their bodies.

Ernest moved into the room with Nathanial following. Anna stared at Struthers a moment before following. Words whispered in the shape of her lips but did not take substance.

He held out his hand to her. "We will talk about this later—when they are gone. For the moment, trust me."

Her eyes blinked with confusion. He could read the message in her face—how was she supposed to trust him to solve a problem he didn't know the details of?

He glanced to the parlor. Nathanial and Ernest stood just inside the door, their impatience clear.

He mouthed the phrase again. "Trust me. You claim you do—now demonstrate."

She nodded, but did not look convinced.

Trust me. Struthers made it sound so easy, so simple. She did trust him, more than she had ever thought possible. But even after their conversation last night he didn't know the entire situation, didn't know her cousins, didn't know what she had done. He could guess the details from looking at that blasted contract—know what she had willingly given away—but he could not understand the extent of the threat or the solution that she had found.

Even she did not want to fully consider it, consider what these two might be willing to do, might already have tried to do.

Fear could not be shown, however. Pulling her shoulders back, she strode into her parlor and chose a high-backed chair facing the rest of the room. "What do you have to say that needs to be said now?"

"I think you know." Nathanial came and sat across from her.

Ernest followed his brother into the room.

Struthers came into the room last. His glance fell on each empty chair, but he walked over to her, choosing to stand just behind her left shoulder.

"Actually," she said. "I don't. I would have thought the papers self-explanatory. I gave over my remaining interests in the shipping firm. What more could you want?"

"You gave them to Claire, to our sister. That is definitely not what we asked for. You did not see fit to gift us with it."

"Gift?" Struthers's voice was low, but it seemed to echo about the room.

"Yes. Gift." Ernest said each word individually and kept his eyes focused on her.

He thought she was the weak link. He would learn just how wrong he was.

Leaning forward, she smiled. Struthers would have known just how much trouble was in that smile. "I am done playing. I do not respond well to threat—either to myself or to those I love. I do not know the truth of the accidents and violence that has plagued my family—and at this moment I no longer care. It is over. I am done. I gave away my remaining interest in the firm as a gift, even if not to you directly. I do not know what Claire will do with the shares, but then I am tired of trying to decide what is right and wrong for others. If Claire can handle the two of you, that will be wonderful. If she cannot, well then, it will still not be my problem. I have never wanted anything to do with the business. I find the whole matter distasteful."

"You are such a woman." Nathanial did not mean it as a compliment.

"I have always been glad of that." She spoke firmly.

"As have I." Struthers's whisper was meant for her alone.

Ernest coughed and lifted his head to meet her gaze. "If you find it so distasteful why have you held on to the shares for so long?" He sounded genuinely curious.

Drawing in a deep breath she considered what to say. "I suppose because I wanted to find a way to make all the wrongs our family has done right. I thought that if I stayed firm the two of you would come around. I realize now that I was wrong and that we must each make our own mistakes."

"Mistakes." Nathanial spoke with disdain. "There has been no mistake. It was a legitimate and legal business."

"And speaking of legal," she added, "I should tell the two of you that I have already filed the paperwork on my gift. I could not change it even if I wanted to. I am done with this business—legal or otherwise, moral or otherwise."

"And it's not legal anymore, is it?" Struthers spoke to her cousins for the first time. "The slave trade has been illegal for years. And it has never been moral."

Nathanial snorted. "Morals have no place in business. Profit must come first. Don't tell me that you never did anything questionable in India. I will not believe it. I have heard the rumors—and where there is rumor there is often fact."

Struthers took a step forward. "It would be silly to protest, then. You have already made up your mind." He glanced at Anna and she was so glad he had told her the whole story. "However, I learned from my mistakes and learned quickly. I had no desire to participate in events that would leave my soul stained."

A stained soul. Anna had never thought about it, but it was how she had felt since she had first heard true accountings of what happened to slaves on the journey across the ocean. What she'd heard had left her sick for days, and that was before she'd inherited and received her uncle's logs—logs that reflected how much cargo was taken in West Africa and how much was let off in the Caribbean or somewhere in the southern United States. It had taken her days to understand what those numbers meant—to admit to herself what that cargo was and just how great the loss had been. Her soul had been stained and she had promised to do all she could to cleanse it—to give recompense.

She turned her face and saw Struthers watching her, his face filled with compassion. How could he understand when no words had been said? She held his gaze for only an instant and then turned back to her cousins. "I gave your sister my interests—as a gift. Now go. I do not believe the need will ever arise for us to be in the same company again."

Nathanial stood and took a step toward her. "Do not be so hasty, cousin. I believe you have forgotten the rest of our gift. If we do not get the firm, at least we want some money."

She stood herself, refusing to be intimidated. The warmth of Struthers's body moved with her. "No, I did not forget. I have given all I intend to give."

Nathanial puffed his chest out. "That would not be wise."

She felt Struthers start to step forward and put a hand back, stopping him. "I do not care about being wise. I am done—and should something happen to me, I do believe you would have a hard time proving where the remaining pieces of my fortune came from. The funds would stay with my husband."

"Do you really think we will stop because you tell us to?" Ernest spoke from the comfort of his chair.

"I don't know and I don't really care. I have plans for the rest of my funds and you have no part in them. Do your worst." She wished she felt as positive as she sounded. She still could not put out of her mind that in their anger they might harm Struthers.

"Plans—like giving it all away." Nathanial turned to Struthers. "Do you know that's what she plans—to give her fortune to the poor, the orphans, the dirt of our society?"

Struthers's chest expanded and then fell again. "It is her money. I have accepted from the beginning that it is hers to do with what she wishes—even to waste on buying horses."

"Yes, it is my money," Anna added. "I will spend it how I see fit. If it makes me feel better to try and perform acts of charity with it, then who is there to bespeak me?"

"It is crazy. Insane." Ernest spoke from his chair.

"So you tried to prove—and failed," she said.

This time it was Nathanial who spoke. "We did not fail. We merely were prevented by other factors." His glance fell on Struthers and stuck. "It is insane to give away hundreds of thousands of pounds. Nobody in their right mind would do such a thing."

Struthers stepped forward and this time her hand could not restrain him. "Do not—I repeat—do not speak to my wife in such a fashion or you will be very, very sorry. You are very lucky that the investigators I set after you could find no evidence that you were actually involved in any of the misfortunes that have beset us. If I ever do find proof that you tried to harm Anna, that you set the robber upon her, I will make you sorry for the rest of your days."

"What could you possibly do?" Nathanial stepped closer to Struthers.

If the situation had not been so serious Anna would have compared them to two little boys daring each other—each bluffing the other on.

"I don't think you want to know—but I can see you will not leave us alone until I tell you." Struthers spoke calmly, but his voice was filled with ice. "Have you paid attention to the new laws on slavery your country has enacted?"

Nathanial paled and did not answer.

"I see that you have," Struthers continued. "Death is now the penalty for those who engage in the trade." He let the words hang.

Both of her cousins shifted uncomfortably. Ernest finally spoke. "What does that have to do with us? Our ships now carry other cargoes."

"Are you sure?" Struthers placed his body between them and Anna. "I have not had long to investigate and the distances are too great to get fast response. But my man Timms, he can be a miracle worker. He tracked down every man within a day's ride of London who ever crewed a Townsend ship. The stories they have told me would make one wonder just what cargo you now carry. The logs may say one thing, but the truth may be another."

"That's a lie." Nathanial's voice rang shrill.

"Is it? One thing about being in shipping myself is that I have developed contacts all over the world. I suspect that once I receive reports I will find that not all is as it appears. Do you truly wish me to inform your government of what I find? I have a feeling they are looking for an example of how they plan to enforce their laws. Do you wish to try and set it?"

Struthers grew with each word he spoke and her cousins seemed to shrink. Anna had never seen them look afraid before.

"And," Struthers added after a pause, "should that not work you can be assured that I would find another way to make you pay. Many men have disappeared while crossing the sea. I do not think that any would notice if another one—or two—did not return home."

Anna stepped to the side and around Struthers. "Go now." She took the contract from the table where Struthers had laid it and handed it to them. "You can see if your sister is more accommodating than I. I will pray that my husband is wrong in what he suggests, but if he is not I have a feeling your sins will come back to haunt you soon enough."

Ernest rose to his feet in a rush. He had developed a distinct pallor.

His brother did not look convinced. "I still think it's all idle threat."

Struthers reached out and grabbed Nathanial by his neck cloth, physically lifting him from the floor. "As idle as yours were? Do not make me prove my intent. I will and more, besides. You said I had done things in India that lacked moral backbone. I did not deny it and I will not deny it now. However, I do not believe you wish a demonstration. Take what Anna offers and go. I am finding that my wife is generous to the extreme. Be glad that I respect her." He opened his palm, dropping Nathanial.

Her cousin only barely managed to settle on his feet.

He grabbed the contract from Ernest and headed for the door. He did not make any farewell. Ernest followed him out, continually glancing backward as if he expected to be followed.

"Do you think we are actually done?" Anna asked her husband, her heart still beating fast within her chest.

"Not quite," Struthers answered.

"What could possibly be left?"

He reached into his jacket and pulled out a thin sheaf of papers. "I hope these are more pleasant than all the other papers that have been thrust at you this evening. I was going to set you a task in order to receive them—but this moment feels right."

He watched as with some nervousness, she reached out and took the packet from him. Her hands shook slightly as she unfolded them. She gasped.

"It's not as beautiful as the horses you bought me. I accept them as your wedding gift and offer you this in exchange." He gestured to the papers.

"Sherberry? You bought me Sherberry? I never even thought of that. Oh, thank you." Tears trickled from the corners of her eyes.

"Only you would consider a madhouse an appropriate wedding gift. And you will need to thank Timms as well. The poor man went crazy himself trying to get everything accomplished in a day. There are apparently still more signings and filings before it is all settled, but I wanted to be able to hand you the deed."

"Thank you," she said again.

"It was the only thing I could think to do. There is no way to get those poor patients released, but this way you can guarantee them a decent life. You can even get Mrs. Jones her books—a whole library of them."

"I can never say thank you enough times." She threw herself into his arms.

"Stop that or you'll have me crying like a baby."

"I've always avoided crying babies." She gazed straight into his eyes and he wondered if she could read his thoughts. He was almost certain she could when she added, "Although I must confess to looking at babies recently and wondering what it would feel like to cradle my own in my arms, to feel that soft fuzz of hair beneath my chin. I have never thought I was the maternal type, but recently . . ."

"Recently?"

"I keep imagining what our child would look like."

"And if I confess to the same thoughts—unmanly though they be?"

She moved closer, stood so that her breasts brushed his chest. "Somehow I've never had a problem with you being unmanly. Rather the opposite in fact."

"I do believe you are trying to distract me. Weren't you the one who thought we needed to talk?" She started to step away, but he pulled her back. "On the other hand we do have some of our best conversations when we let our guard down. Perhaps we should give that a try?"

Anna pulled the sheet up over her breasts and turned on her side. Struthers lay sprawled next to her, taking up a good deal more than half the bed. Even asleep he took up more space than the average man. The worry lines had relaxed on his forehead and she had never seen him look so peaceful. She snuggled down beside him, laying her head upon his chest.

The strong beat of his heart filled her with reassurance. The world really was at rights.

Oh, there were still problems to be solved.

Maddie and the baby would need to be cared for. Where did one find a good nurse?

And Sherberry. She could not even begin to think of all the changes she would make there, all the reforms she would institute. She smiled just thinking of it.

She would have to talk to Lady Brattle about her funds and then to Mr. Jackal about how much he would need in the near future. How much could she persuade Struthers to give of his own money? He had mentioned that he didn't feel good about where all his fortune had come from.

And Nathanial and Ernest—somebody would have to make sure they were on a ship bound back to Rhode Island. She still couldn't believe that Struthers had collected proof of their continued ill deeds—and his knowledge of the new law. She didn't know that it would keep her cousins under control forever, but threat of death—and more—did seem to have them scurrying for cover. Struthers was an amazing man, finding the solution to problems he didn't even know she had.

And that brought her to her last problem. She pushed herself up and stared down at her sleeping husband. They'd shared passion and secrets throughout the night. It was no wonder he was exhausted. There was only one thing left she still needed to know.

His nose twitched. The devil. He wasn't asleep. He was probably enjoying her adoring looks.

Well, she could fix that.

She swung a leg over him and settled herself comfortably. He was hard beneath her. She did love a man in the morning. Well, truth be told, she loved this man at just about any hour. She began to rock herself back and forth, feeling him grow and swell. Adding a slight hip rotation to the mix, she smiled as she saw his eyelids flicker. Faking sleep would only take him so far.

She centered herself above him, teasing him, sliding back and forth, but never quite taking him in.

She waited.

Another hip rotation. She ground herself against him, finding her own pleasure.

She waited again, leaned forward so her breasts tickled across his chest.

Oh, that was the spot. She rubbed hard, feeling the pull of inner tension.

His hands landed on either side of her hips, pushing her back until he could settle just where he wanted to be. He thrust up into her in a single stroke. She tensed her thighs on either side of him, pushing down against his upward move.

And the ride began.

His hands rose, played with her breasts, trailed along her hips, grabbed and pulled—set the rhythm.

She moaned, let her head fell back—and waited—waited.

She felt him tense, the muscles all along his belly tightening, waiting for that final thrust.

Leaning forward, she planted a hand on either side of his head, met his gaze head-on; her inner muscles tightened about him, pushing them both to the edge—it was time.

The final question.

She felt the loss of control, knew it was almost too late, forced out the words—"Do you love me?"

His bellow filled the room, filled her—a name, her name, a word—a word she would have waited a lifetime to hear.

Her body could wait no longer. She jerked, her eyes closed, the world spun in a multitude of colors.

She collapsed across him, her whole being replete.

And then in a single movement she was underneath. He towered above her, leaning on his elbows. He rubbed the stubble of his chin across her cheek. "Oh no, Mrs. Struthers, don't think we are done. I believe it's my turn to ask the questions."

His lips found the tip of her chin, the hollow of her neck, the curve of a breast, the tip of one—she cried out as his tongue circled her nipple, then the curve of a rib, the flat of her belly—and lower—

Her smile formed as she waited for his question.